Sophie Schiller

Transfer Day

"It's a Long Way to Tipperary" by Jack Judge and Harry Williams. Public Domain.
"Pretty Baby" by Tony Jackson, Gus Kahn, and Egbert Van Alstyne. Public Domain.

Girl in Straw Hat © 2021 by Katerinatodorchyk
Used under license from Dreamstime
Front Cover: Edward Fraas, Public Domain
Back Cover: "Parti af St. Thomas" from a daguerreotype by H. Hanson, 1850

The painting *Salute for King Christian IX on his birthday in 1905* (1946) by Hugo Larsen. Pastel on paper, 54 x 75 cm.

The painting *King's Wharf, St. Thomas* (1907) by Hugo Larsen. Oil on canvas.

ISBN 978-0615653433
ASIN B0089GVINA

Transfer Day is dedicated to the people of the Virgin Islands on the occasion of the Centennial Anniversary of Transfer Day (1917-2017) and especially to Mrs. Louise Brady, St. Thomas educator extraordinaire to generations of children, whose love and enthusiasm for the islands infused all her lectures and students.

Acknowledgements:

I wish to acknowledge the superb counsel of military historian and author Robert Derenčin, not only for his outstanding military expertise, but also for his unfailing encouragement and supportive friendship during the development and writing phases of this book. Robert is an internationally-recognized expert on U-boats, and his unwavering enthusiasm for Erich Seibold's journey kept the fires burning during many lonely years of writing.

And to Professor Halvor Jochimsen, thank you for sharing your family's unique history in the Danish West Indies. I am forever in your debt.

Thank you to Senior Chief Robert F. Marble, USN (Retired) for sharing his submarine expertise and some personal experiences in the region.

Thank you to Elizabeth Gray of the National Archives II in College Park, Maryland, for her invaluable research assistance, enthusiasm and kind words.

A tremendous thank you to three wonderful Danish ladies from the University of Copenhagen: Camilla Grausen, Marie Skovgaard and Anja Bohn Berthelsen, who so generously shared their vast knowledge and love of Danish culture, customs and idioms that helped to create believable characters and situations. Their invaluable comments and suggestions were tremendously helpful and encouraging.

Likewise, I owe a debt of gratitude to Professor and Mrs. John Robert Christianson of Luther College, Decorah, Iowa, who read early drafts of the manuscript and shared some very helpful suggestions as well as their enthusiastic support.

And thank you to Danish journalist Marianne Lentz for her invaluable suggestions and comments.

Thank you to St. Croix historian William Cissel for sharing his encyclopedic knowledge of life under the Danish Colonial Administration.

And a special thank you to historian and writer Jamie Bisher, whose incredible manuscript, "World War I Intelligence in Latin America" proved to be an invaluable research tool that added a whole new dimension to my story. Jamie was always available to answer any of my questions and provided an enthusiastic sounding board.

Transfer Day Sonnet
By J. Antonio Jarvis

Written in 1942 by the late J. Antonio Jarvis to commemorate the Twenty-fifth Anniversary of the transfer of the Danish West Indies to the United States.

There was much grieving when the Flag went down.
Its limp and quiet folds clung to the mast
As though the colors said, "Farewell, at last!"
The cannon's echoes could not quickly drown
Low murmurs running through the saddened town;
Many remembered glamorous years that passed,
Sometimes with lagging feet, sometimes with fast,
While Denmark's regents paused to smile or frown,
The white cross on its crimson field was dear;
Bright symbol of the Motherland and King;
Few saw that Flag descend without a tear,
Rich tribute that great movements always wring.
Some dared to look across emotions felt
And visualize the brave new world to come.

"If Germany wins this war, it means the triumph of the autocratic system. It means the triumph of those who believe not only in war as a national industry, not only in war for itself but also in war as a high and noble occupation. Unless Germany is beaten, the whole world will be compelled to turn itself into an armed camp, until the German autocracy either brings every nation under its dominion or is forever wiped out as a form of government."

- James W. Gerard, 1917, Late Ambassador to the German Imperial Court.

PROLOGUE

Somewhere over the Atlantic
March, 2001

By the time the Boeing 757 had reached cruising altitude over a field of ghost-white clouds, Søren Jensen had the strangest hunch this trip was going to be different. His life was about to change in some monumental way and sometimes the best option was to surrender yourself to the vast unknown. He pushed his seat back, closed his eyes, and took a deep breath. *At the very least I can drown my sorrows in a case of duty-free rum,* he thought. *Didn't Jimmy Buffett once say 'Where I go I hope there's rum?'*

But there was that *other* matter to consider. This trip was the fulfillment of a lifelong dream for Søren. He was hoping that by pursuing a human interest story he would be able to reconnect with his past and learn more about his family's history, and most important of all, to find a reason to go on living. Considering what he'd been through during the past year, it couldn't have come at a better time.

The middle-aged woman sitting next to him stopped leafing through her duty-free magazine long enough to glance out the window. She was occupying the middle seat, wedged in between Søren, a journalist in his late thirties with a scholar's face, light brown hair and inquisitive eyes, and a Rastafarian in the aisle seat sporting a psychedelic Bob Marley tee shirt and a bad case of restless leg syndrome. The lady shifted forward, craning her neck to catch a glimpse of the world at thirty-thousand feet.

"What a sight," she said, interrupting Søren from his reverie. "Simply amazing."

"Makes you realize how insignificant we are," said Søren keeping his eyes fixed on a point far off in the distance. "Like tiny specks in a huge galaxy."

"Oh, I don't think so," she said. "The world only matters because we can see it and appreciate it. When I see all that beauty and splendor laid out before me, I want to drink it all in with my eyes. That's why I keep coming back. Is this your first trip down to the Virgin Islands?"

Søren turned to face her. She was one of those women who would look at home in a quilting club, or maybe in one of those ladies' investment clubs that consistently beat the market. With her short, sandy blond hair, pale green eyes and owlish glasses, there was something homey about her. Something cozy, like warm apple cider on a cold wintry day. Like Lina.

"Yes, although I've wanted to go for years. Just never seemed to find the time..." Søren's voice trailed off when he realized that a cramped cabin at 30,000 feet was an unsuitable place to bring up the past. He glanced out the window again, hoping the conversation would taper off.

"Excuse me if I sound nosy," she said, using that characteristic American straightforwardness that his journalistic side respected, but made his Danish side wary. "But I detect an accent. Are you by any chance Swedish?"

"I'm from Denmark," said Søren, smiling. "Actually, the Virgin Islands used to be a Danish colony until the First World War."

"Yes, I remember reading that somewhere. Do you have family down there?"

"No, not any more. I'm going down for business." Søren turned to watch the cloud-filled sky over the swirling dark ocean, adding, "But it's also to fulfill a lifelong dream."

"Really? That sounds fascinating." The woman's eyes were too wide to ignore.

Søren sighed. "I just hope I'm not disappointed."

And as is often the case during those interminable overseas trips, the lady whipped out a photo from her purse and handed it to Søren with practiced ceremony.

"Actually, I have a sister down there," she said. "Absolutely loves it. Lives on a 47-foot Cheoy Lee sailboat with her boyfriend and swears she'll never go back to living on land again."

Søren studied the photograph of a happy middle-aged couple on the deck of an impressive sailboat that was obviously the culmination of somebody else's lifelong dream. The realization that such dreams were attainable gave him a glimmer of hope.

"Nice," he said. "That's what I call getting away from it all."

The lady wrinkled her forehead. "With the life she's led, she needs it."

Søren nodded. He understood very well about the need to get away from it all. During the past year, his life had spiraled out of control, fizzling into a cloud of despair and crushed dreams. He had faced obstacles so daunting, so dispiriting, they threatened to derail both his life and his career. He wasn't eating right or sleeping right, and relied on alcohol to smooth out the rough edges of his existence. And when drink was unavailable, he was plagued by debilitating anxiety attacks, the kind that could paralyze a person. Some days were so bad he could barely lift himself out of bed.

Søren's wife, Lina, had died of breast cancer the year before and the resulting grief and depression were taking a tremendous toll on his health. His editor at *Denmark Today* knew that if Søren didn't find a way to climb out of his dark hole, alcohol would become his new life-long mistress. For now at least, Søren hoped that covering this human interest story would divert his attention and help him forget about his problems. What he really needed was a miracle.

Søren had dreamt about traveling to St. Thomas for as long as he could remember. The island's history was entwined with his own family's roots and was an inextricable part of his identity. According to family lore, his great-grandfather had been an important official on the island during the days of Danish rule. He had lived in a splendid villa overlooking the harbor of Charlotte Amalie, and all three of his children were born there, including Louise, Søren's grandmother.

From photographs, Søren knew his grandmother had been a small, delicate child with petal-like wisps of blond hair and eyes as clear and blue as the sea. Louise's privileged childhood in the West Indies had given her luxuries that few children could ever dream of, such as her own pony and a donkey cart to haul her and her two brothers around. Louise even had her own nanny, Frederica, a spirited native woman named for one of the Danish queens who instilled in Louise a lifelong love of the people and culture of the Danish West Indies.

Louise and Frederica had shared a special bond. In fact, Frederica had adored Louise, and never tired of regaling her with stories and legends brought over from Africa, including tales about the magical spider, Anansi, and those mischievous spirits the natives called *jumbis*. Frederica had also taught Louise her vast repertoire of

9

herbal remedies, most notably the soothing qualities of lemongrass tea, and the healing properties of aloe vera. And when Louise grew tired of all that nonsense, she would run out to the garden and lose herself for hours amidst the flaming flamboyant trees, the swaying palms, the fragrant jasmine, and the soft, gentle hibiscus. Years later, when Louise was old and bent, her blue eyes faded, her blond hair the color of snow, she would reflect on her childhood in the West Indies. She confessed to Søren that it was those moments spent in quiet solitude amidst the glorious tropical flora that had been the most precious of her life.

While Søren was growing up in Denmark, Louise had entertained him with vivid stories about her father, a larger-than-life figure who would prop Louise up on his lap while he smoked his pipe, recounting stories and legends about the old days of Charlotte Amalie, when tall-masted sailing ships had sailed into the harbor, and swashbuckling adventurers like Sir Francis Drake, Blackbeard the pirate, and the exiled Mexican General Santa Anna would roam the alleyways with wheelbarrows full of silver searching for adventure.

Despite the troubles Søren had experienced during the past year, this trip presented an amazing opportunity. And it had come about almost by chance. His editor had discovered a curious human interest story dating back to 1917, when the Danish West Indies was officially transferred to the United States. He read the story on a Virgin Islands news website and passed it along to Søren during an early morning coffee session. The unusual nature of the story had piqued Søren's interest, and for a hard-nosed journalist like him, chasing intriguing stories and writing award-winning articles was what gave his life meaning and purpose.

Back during the Great War, the Danish West Indies was teetering on the brink of financial ruin, but the islands possessed one asset that was so valuable, it managed to catch the eye of the German Emperor Kaiser Wilhelm II: strategically-located, deepwater ports. As it turned out, the Kaiser wasn't coy about making his desire to possess the Danish islands known. Some historians even speculate that the Danes had sold their colony to the United States to avoid a nasty fight with Germany over control of the Danish West Indies. But that was always mere speculation. Until now.

The story he was investigating concerned a woman from St. Thomas named Abigail Maduro who had died recently at the age of

101 claiming to have personally thwarted a German invasion of the Danish West Indies. This absurd revelation was allegedly supported by documents that Ms. Maduro's surviving granddaughter, Claire Lehman, had offered to share with *Denmark Today* on an exclusive basis. It was the story Søren had been waiting for all his life, and the precise reason he was completing the final leg of his 4,700-mile journey from Copenhagen. But there was a lot more at stake for Søren than just covering this human interest story. This time, his whole life was at stake.

Søren's right shoulder ached from a pinched nerve that had plagued him ever since he left Copenhagen early that morning. Ignoring the pain, he reached for his planner and pulled out the bizarre obituary that had been the catalyst for this bizarre, trans-Atlantic odyssey:

Obituary

Abigail Maduro, 101, of St. Thomas died peacefully at home on February 14th. Born in 1899 in Colón, Panama to Isaac and Rebecca Maduro, formerly of Charlotte Amalie, after the untimely deaths of her parents in 1916, she was raised by her aunt Esther Maduro of Synagogue Hill and graduated Teacher's College, Columbia University in 1920. Taught school for forty years, then retired to write for the Virgin Islands Daily News. Ms. Maduro witnessed the Transfer ceremony in 1917 and later claimed via lectures and articles that she was instrumental in averting a German takeover of the Danish West Indies. She is survived by two children and three grandchildren.

A few hours later, the plane hit the over-the-water runway with a jolt, jerking Søren out of his slumber. He opened his eyes and recalibrated his watch for local time: 4:19 p.m. A perfect on-time landing, he thought. The punctual arrival did wonders to calm his growing anxiety, as did the sight of quaint villas dotting the lush green mountainsides, but on the inside, he was a bundle of nerves.

St. Thomas was the quintessential exotic tropical island. Verdant, hilly, and covered in dense tropical foliage, it rose from the sea like the undulating back of a large green dragon, punctuated every now and then by sandy white beaches, rocky shorelines against a shimmering blue sea that stretched as far as the eye can see. A surge of excitement welled up inside of Søren, quietly displacing the constant tension and anxiety that had overtaken him during his waking hours. He released his grip on the armrest, and waited for the plane to come to a stop.

They halted at the foot of a low hill, then all at once, a ground crew came rushing across the tarmac pushing two large, rolling gangplanks, one of which they affixed to the plane's forward hatch, the other to the rear. Søren raced to the lavatory, splashed some cold water on his face, and combed his hair in preparation for meeting Ms. Lehman, the source who had promised to pick him up at the terminal and drive him to his hotel.

By the time Søren made it back to his seat, the plane's rear hatch was opened, sending a burst of hot, furnace-like air blasting through the cabin, making him feel as if he'd just stuck his head inside an oven. Beads of sweat trickled down his face and perspiration soaked his shirt, undoing all his preparations. Mopping his forehead with a handkerchief, Søren grabbed his bag and followed the long line of passengers down the aisle, resigned to the fact there was no beating the oppressive, tropical heat.

A voice behind him called out, "Good luck fulfilling your dream. Call me if you need any help."

Søren spun around. The voice belonged to his seat-mate, the middle-aged lady with the owl-like glasses. "Thanks! And how will I know when I've succeeded?"

She smiled. "*You* won't know it, but everyone else will. They'll tell you you're *glowing*."

Søren nodded thoughtfully. When he stepped onto the gangplank and caught his first panoramic glimpse of Denmark's former colony, his heart swelled with pride. He felt as if he was completing an unfinished mission that his ancestors had begun more than a century before. It was a feeling that started back in Copenhagen when he was first put on assignment that grew with each passing mile until it had became a veritable obsession. He patted his shirt pocket, making sure the obituary was safely tucked inside, then attacked the gangplank.

A ground crewman greeted Søren with a thick, Calypso accent.

"Welcome to de Virgin Islands," he said, with a broad smile. Søren returned the greeting, but in his zeal to reach the ground, he misjudged the final step and teetered on the edge. Luckily, the quick-thinking crewman grabbed Søren's arm and steadied him.

"A little too much rum punch, eh?" he said, winking mischievously at the dazed Danish tourist. Søren laughed good-naturedly but knew inside the man was right about why he'd almost hit the tarmac on his knees. Along the way, he'd indulged in one too many cocktails.

Following the long line of straggling passengers across the sweltering tarmac, Søren entered the terminal of the Cyril E. King Airport. Inside it was bedlam, with throngs of tourists shouting, haggling, and fighting over the prices of rental cars, hotel rooms, cases of Canadian scotch, cigarettes, and last minute duty-free Swiss watches. Almost without exception they were wearing the standard dress uniform of the Caribbean tourist: Bermuda shorts, sleeveless t-shirts, cotton muumuus, leather sandals, and skin so burned, it made Søren wince. As he scanned the crowd, a handsome island woman with ebony skin and lips the color of a ripe tropical fruit waylaid him. She dangled a tantalizing rum and coke decorated with one of those colorful paper umbrellas in front of his eyes. For just a second, Søren hesitated before accepting the libation.

"Courtesy of our local rum distillery," she said, smiling in a way that made Søren's brain go fuzzy. He downed the drink, grateful for the gift, but realizing only afterwards that the drink was spiked off the charts.

"You can buy a case of rum right ovah dere for your convenience," she said, pointing to a nearby airport store stocked floor to ceiling with every conceivable spirit, and staffed with an army of lithe, gold-decked island women. "*And* we can ship it to your hotel room." Søren nodded, too dizzy to make an on-the-spot decision, but he thanked the woman and made a mental note to surprise all of his friends at the office with a bottle of authentic Virgin Islands rum. Dodging aggressive taxi drivers and tour hustlers, he fought his way to the baggage carousel and caught sight of a beautiful young woman holding a sign that read:

SØREN JENSEN
DENMARK TODAY

Thank Heavens, my source! Søren grabbed his bag from the carousel, swung it over his one good shoulder, and raced through the crowd to greet the young woman.

"Hello, I'm Søren Jensen," he said, offering his hand. "Thank you for offering to pick me up."

The lady returned the greeting. "Welcome to the Virgin Islands. It's a pleasure to meet you, Mr. Jensen. I'm Claire Lehman. My jeep is parked outside. We can chat on the way to the hotel."

Claire Lehman was Abigail Maduro's granddaughter and, in a word, she was stunning. Tall, bronzed, and with reams of luxurious dark hair that cascaded over her shoulders in glistening waves, Claire was striking to look at, but there was something else about her that made Søren take notice. Her eyes had an inner fire, a boldness that resonated deep within him. It was not something Søren could put a finger on, but Claire's fiery inner quality inspired him, stirred him, like finding a cherished book in an old library.

During the drive to town, Claire took a few cell phone calls as she pointed out various sights: the old red Danish fort, the green Legislature Building that had once served as the barracks for the Danish Gendarmes, and at the top of a low-lying hill, Bluebeard's castle, the infamous watchtower of the swashbuckling brigand that had fueled so many of his grandmother's stories and legends.

They drove around the perimeter of the harbor until they were directly opposite the town, then they began to ascend a hill, the base of which served as a cruise ship dock. After a few minutes of winding roads that cut through dense, tropical foliage, they arrived at a luxury hotel built dramatically over a cliff jutting out over the mouth of the harbor. The view of the town across the bay was breathtaking. The glamour, mystery, and excitement of his new surroundings slowly worked their magic on Søren, and his anxiety gave way to a feeling of exhilaration, a feeling he hadn't experienced in years.

"I'll pick you up for dinner at seven o'clock," said Claire, dropping him off at the hotel's front desk. "Does that work for you?"

"Perfect."

She winked at Søren. "And I promise to turn off my cellphone for the duration of our meeting. I told everyone I would be incommunicado for the evening. I just need to finish up a few things in the office first."

"Don't worry, Miss Lehman..."

"Call me Claire," she said, replacing her sunglasses. "Miss Lehman makes me sound like an old spinster. I'll see you at seven."

After an hour in the pool, Søren showered and by 6:30 pm had changed into his white polo shirt and khaki trousers. He added a dash of cologne and checked and rechecked his watch a dozen times before Claire made her second appearance of the day. At 7:13 pm, she glided through the lobby in a silky blue cocktail dress and gold slippers; her lips shimmered with rose-colored lipstick and her hair glistened in an elaborate Grecian updo. For the first time in his entire career, Søren almost relinquished his plans to cover the story so he could concentrate solely on his source.

They drove to a restaurant nestled high in a rain forest that flanked the island's highest peak. While dining on Caribbean red snapper and honey-roasted plantains, they shared stories about their respective childhoods, education, families, and careers. Søren felt the pace of his heart start to slow, and his breathing adjust to island rhythms. He couldn't remember the last time he had felt so peaceful, so natural.

"Is this your first visit in the Virgin Islands?" said Claire, sipping her rum punch.

"Yes, although I grew up hearing stories about the *Dansk Vestindien*. You could say these islands are in my blood. And you? Have you lived here all your life?"

"Just about, until I went to college," she said. "After I graduated, instead of coming home right away, I decided to stay in Boston to pursue a job opportunity. A few years later, I got married and soon thereafter—divorced. I came back only after Grandma had her stroke. But to tell you the truth, I needed a change. And now that Grandma's gone, I have no desire to return to the rat race. So, I took a job in real estate, mostly selling condos to retired couples from the States while I figure out what I'm going to do for the rest of my life. You think life is taking you one way and then it goes in another direction. It's hard to explain."

"I understand perfectly," said Søren, with a wry smile. "I didn't realize you were divorced. Please don't think me nosy."

"No, it's fine," she said. "Mark and I had compatibility issues that therapy couldn't resolve, so we just drifted apart. After a while, divorce seemed like the only reasonable solution. But we're still good friends. I know this may sound crazy, but while I was married, I felt like I was living a lie, like I was living someone else's life. I guess that's why I came back here to where it all began. I needed to put my life back on track and this seemed like the logical place to do it. So far I have no complaints. And you? Do you have a family?"

"I was married for fifteen years," he said, his clear blue eyes looking beyond Claire, as if seeing an image from the past. "I have a ten-year-old son, Henrik. I lost Lina to breast cancer about a year ago."

"Oh, I'm so sorry," she said, drawing her napkin up to her mouth. "I had no idea. I never know what to say at times like that. Abigail used to say, *Let a fool hold his tongue and he will pass for a sage.*"

"*Who* said that?"

Claire smiled. "Abigail, my grandmother. You know, the lady whose life story brought you all the way from Denmark." Her eyes twinkled, causing Søren to blush.

"Yes, forgive me," he said. "I must have drifted off for a minute. My body still thinks I'm on Copenhagen time—"

"Here we call it jet lag," said Claire, cradling her face in her hands. The glow of the candle lent a warm, golden hue to her skin, causing her rose-colored lips to sparkle like wine. "Do you want to hear something funny? The minute I saw you I had the strangest feeling we had met before. Isn't that weird?"

Søren nodded. "I guess you are referring to déjà vu. I've often felt that way myself. It's one of life's inexplicable mysteries."

"Tell me about your work. What inspired you to become a journalist? Was it so you could travel to exotic places like the Virgin Islands?"

"Not exactly," said Søren, his expression now serious. "Actually I took a big risk when I decided to become a journalist. You see, I come from an educated family of lawyers and judges. I was sort of the black sheep of the family. When I told my father my intentions of becoming a journalist, he raised one of his shaggy eyebrows and said, '*The road to hell is paved with good intentions.'* I knew what he meant, but nothing could extinguish my unquenchable desire for the truth. You see, behind every story, every conflict, every clash, every tragedy lays some undeniable truth. When you write the story, the truth will seep out between the lines. The trick is to let the reader discover it for himself. A skillful journalist presents the facts that lead his readers to a truth that is far bigger and far more powerful than the actual headline that draws you in. I guess it started when I was a boy. I got a yearning for an insider's view of the world, the kind you only get by being at the center of things. I knew that in order for my stories to be accurate I had to *get in the trenches*, as they say. You spend time walking in other people's shoes, living their day-to-day life, witnessing their struggles, feeling their hardships. Usually these are people who are caught up in some life-shattering event like an earthquake, a famine, or a civil war. I spent months in Yugoslavia covering the US-NATO bombing campaign, and the humanitarian crisis in Kosovo. My greatest challenge was in documenting the daily lives of the victims and presenting it objectively to the rest of the world for their interpretation. I put the sound of their voices on paper, the smell of their village, the tears of their women. In this way, I put a human face on suffering. On a personal level, it hasn't been easy; some days you just don't have the strength to do it. But if you want to know why I took this particular assignment, it was for a completely different reason. You see, my family has deep roots in the West Indies. I didn't just come here solely to report your grandmother's story. I also came to discover my own past. Ever since Lina died, I've been plagued by restlessness, the need to research my family's history and discover who I am. I've always believed that our ancestors speak to us through the clues they left behind: letters, diaries, photos, and stories. If we're lucky enough to uncover them, hopefully we can learn more about ourselves."

"That's fascinating," said Claire. "I never thought about that before. You sound very passionate about your work, just like my grandmother. She was a passionate woman. And please forgive me if I trivialized your work in any way. I didn't realize you were a war correspondent. Life in these islands must seem like a walk in the park compared to what you saw in the Balkans."

"Not exactly," said Søren, stirring his drink thoughtfully. "I try not to judge people or places by their surface appearance. Many beautiful and serene places have tremendous undercurrents of tension. No matter how tranquil a place may be, there are often opposing forces that try to force their will upon the other. Not too long ago, the Europeans here imposed slavery upon the majority of the people. Human lives were bought and sold for greed and profit. Even after they achieved their freedom, the blacks lacked basic rights such as freedom of the press, the right to vote, or even access to basic education. I believe that by studying the past, you have a better appreciation of the present and will fight harder to preserve the freedom we hold so dear. And that's where your grandmother comes in. My readers want to know how a young girl could stand up to enormous odds and help change the lives of everyone around her. That's why I need you, Claire, to help me uncover the past. I want to go back to Abigail's time and relive her struggles. Can you help me? Can you take me back to nineteen-sixteen?"

With her eyes fixed on Søren, Claire reached into her pocketbook and fished out a stack of papers which she set down on the table in front of him.

"I can do better than that," she said. "I'll let Abigail tell her own story. Here is a copy of her diary; the original is in the safe. I'm pretty sure all your answers are right here."

Søren's eyebrows shot up as he reached for the stack. In the glow of the candlelight, he flipped through the priceless treasure in which Abigail recorded her legacy for posterity.

"Where did you find this?"

"She gave it to me just before she died," said Claire. "I guess she decided the time had finally come. The thing you said about our ancestors speaking to us resonated with me because when I read her diary, I hear her voice speaking directly to me. It's almost like opening a door to the past. By the time I finished reading it and needed to ask her some questions, she was gone. Now she's down in the old cemetery in Altona next to her ancestors, and anything she didn't write down will stay buried forever. To tell you the truth, I didn't know what I was going to do with the diary until you contacted me. That's the reason I agreed to speak with you. If Grandma had had the foresight to record her extraordinary life on paper, maybe we can use the diary to inspire others with her courage and determination. I'm sure Abigail would approve that you've decided to tell her story to the world."

For the first time in a year, Søren had every reason to smile.

The next week was a whirlwind. After conducting interviews with government officials and business leaders about the state of the local economy for obligatory news articles, Søren was treated to an intimate tour of the island by Claire. They visited all the major tourist sites: Fort Christian, Drake's Seat, Bluebeard's Castle, the 99 Steps, the Camille Pissarro House, swimming in the turquoise water of Magens Bay and Morningstar Beach, then dining together almost every night. During this time of discovery, Søren felt himself growing closer to Claire in ways he never thought possible since the death of Lina. He laughed at her jokes and listened with delight as she recounted tales and legends about the old days of Charlotte Amalie. He wanted this trip to never end. Late one afternoon after an especially exhilarating day, Claire announced that if Søren were to properly capture Abigail's story on paper, there was one important place he had to see.

She drove down the waterfront, past the native sloops and the old men playing dominoes on the waterfront, then turned up by Emancipation Garden and left down Main Street, past throngs of street vendors, tourists, schoolchildren in crisp uniforms, and shop clerks in colorful clothing and ornate gold jewelry. She turned up Raadets Gade and ascended a steep hill that offered a breathtaking, panoramic view of the harbor. After making a quick left, she parked the jeep by the side of the road in front of an imposing old house with a sloping white roof, large picture windows, and a wide, canopied balcony. "Well, here we are," she said with an enigmatic grin, then led him up the stairs to the main entrance. Søren snapped a few photos and jotted down some notes, wondering what surprise Claire had in store for him.

"This charming, yet lamentable piece of real estate is known as the old Maduro House," she said. "It's been in my family for five generations. But I must warn you, it's in desperate need of renovations, though I still rent it out on occasion. For some reason, I can't seem to part with it. The house is a clue to unraveling the events leading up to Transfer Day, and a vital link in solving Abigail's mysterious claim."

She turned the key in the lock and opened the front door. When they entered the foyer, it was like stepping back in time. The house was a time capsule of the era of tall-masted schooners and sugar mills, when life moved at the pace of a donkey cart. The furniture was all hand-carved mahogany, prized in the tropics for its durability, and the walls were a patchwork of island history, with faded pictures and paintings depicting the house's inhabitants in old-fashioned clothing that must have dated back over a hundred and fifty years. There were oil paintings of ship's captains, faded photographs of stern-faced matrons with large broods, and yellowed news clippings in picture frames, each item recounting a different episode in the history of the Maduro family and the island of St. Thomas. There were women in high-necked, turn-of-the-century dresses, men in WWII soldier uniforms, and an impish baby in the arms of an elderly black nanny. One particular photo caught Søren's eye. It was studio portrait dating from around the First World War of a dark-haired young woman with almond-shaped eyes and full lips in a day suit with large buttons and a stylish black hat.

"Is this Abigail?" said Søren, pointing at the photograph.

"Yes, it is," said Claire, holding it closer. "Do you see any family resemblance?"

"Oh, yes, she has that same forceful look in her eyes that you have."

Claire looked stunned, and then quickly replaced the photograph, saying, "We'd better get down to business or you'll never get that story written. I have to show you something out back."

Heading outside, Claire led Søren to the back of the house, through a poorly maintained garden with tall grasses, and over to the foundation where a nondescript door peeked out from behind an overgrowth of bushes. After a bit of exertion, and with mosquitoes buzzing around their heads, they managed to pry open the weather-beaten door.

All at once, a stale, musty odor emanated from the room. When Søren's eyes adjusted to the darkness, he saw the room was piled high with crates, old furniture, paintings, and boxes of household items. It was a storage room. Søren noted the existence of an old mahogany bed frame that appeared to be at least a hundred years old, some fine old Danish porcelain, and cartons of fragile, dusty books, all first editions. The room was a treasure trove of island history. Søren felt his pulse quicken.

"This is where it all began," said Claire.

"Where what began?"

"Abigail's story," she said. "You see, after her parents died in 1916, she was sent to St. Thomas to live with her aunt, who by all accounts was a miserable old spinster. As you can probably guess, it wasn't a happy situation for Abigail. In fact, her life was miserable. But one day, something changed. A stranger washed up on these shores that needed her help. And for the first time in Abigail's life, she found purpose and meaning: someone to live for. Risking her own safety, she took the stranger in and also gave *him* a reason to go on living. After a while, things get a bit more complicated and a lot more dangerous, but you'll read about that in the diary."

"Intriguing," said Søren. "Shall we begin then?"

They headed upstairs, prepared some drinks, and sat down by the dining room table to start the task of unraveling Abigail's life. The sun was beginning to set; the humming of the insects had reached a crescendo. Somewhere outside a dog barked, while down in the harbor, a cruise ship was gliding out to sea, leaving a gentle wake in its path. Over on Denmark Hill by the Danish Consulate, someone was pulling the *Dannebrog* down as the lights started flickering all over Charlotte Amalie. Once again, peace and calm descended over the island. Claire took out the diary and Søren switched on his mini voice recorder.

"Ready when you are, Claire."

"Are you sure you want to do this?" she said, taking a deep breath. Søren felt Claire's dark eyes penetrating his—the feeling unnerved him, but it also motivated him. A smile crept up the corners of his mouth.

"I've never been more certain of anything in my life," he said. "I think Abigail has waited long enough."

Part One

CHAPTER 1

Colón, Panama
May, 1916

They caught a whole nest of German spies today. It's the most exciting thing that's happened in Panama since the canal was built. There were three suspects this time, shadowy men with names like Gunter, Klaus, and Bruno, men who would lure unsuspecting canal workers into darkened saloons, ply them with booze, and then squeeze out every ounce of information they could get about the running of the canal. They did it for purposes not fit to print said the American officers in charge. In other words, the *Panama Star* was not keen on printing words like *bomb*, *explode*, and *sabotage* in a family newspaper.

Josefina is yelling at me to come in from the balcony and wash up for dinner, but if I cover my head with a pillow I can savor a few more precious minutes of peace. She always complains that I spend too much time daydreaming about international intrigues, and not enough time doing my chores or practicing the piano.

Mostly I think she's annoyed because I wasted the whole day frolicking outdoors with my best friend, Begoña, instead of polishing the silver like I promised. But that was before all this excitement with the German spies. It's not every day you get to see an angry mob taunting and jeering a bunch of shackled prisoners as they're led to a police wagon. It was so terrifying, Begoña almost fainted. But for some reason, I found myself intrigued by the excitement of it all.

I set down the newspaper and settle back on the wicker sofa to savor the cool afternoon air fragrant with jasmine and rose from Mami's garden. There's no greater pleasure than lying here watching the hummingbirds flitting from flower to flower while Celestina, my parakeet, serenades me from her metal cage. Dear, sweet Celestina.

Caramba! Josefina's footsteps get louder as she storms out to the balcony where she stands over me like an angry rooster. In one hand she holds a bottle of cleaning solution, in the other, a broom, which she waves menacingly for dramatic effect. When she sees I make no effort to move, she wags an indignant finger in my face.

"You're not fooling me, Abigail Maduro. I know where you were the whole day. When your mother comes home she's gonna get a full report. And just look at the state of your hair. Your parents are due home any minute and you still haven't—"

"But there was all this excitement!"

"—cleaned your room, taken a bath, changed your dress. You look like a half-rotten mango."

"But…"

"No buts. Go inside and take a bath."

I don't mean to grate on Josefina's nerves—honest! But sometimes I can't help myself. How can I stay cooped up inside while the world outside beckons? To her credit, Josefina always forgives me, that's because she loves me. She's always been more than a housekeeper to me; Josefina is my *yaya*, my nanny, the woman who practically raised me since Mami started helping Papi in the store. She also cooks, bakes, and does all the laundry, but her primary job is keeping me out of trouble. Josefina's biggest headache is making sure I maintain the proper image of a respectable young lady, the sixteen-year-old daughter of Isaac Maduro, a respected dry-goods merchant. And *not* as I look now, with my long brown hair in tangles and my navy blue sailor dress looking like it was caught under the wheels of a donkey cart. Not to mention my disastrous complexion, which is a little *too* tan after spending hours cavorting in the tropical sun. Josefina says I'm hopeless. The truth is, when adventure calls, I race out to greet her. Can I help it if I always forget to bring along my parasol?

Sliding off the couch, I trudge inside to collect my filthy shoes, torn stockings, and neglected schoolbooks. About halfway to the sofa, I hear a knock. Thinking quickly, I duck behind the cabinet, hoping to keep my bedraggled appearance out of sight.

Thankfully, Josefina sails past me to answer the door.

When she opens it, we're surprised to see Señor Cardozo, my father's lawyer. He stands there clutching his fedora hat as he shifts his weight from side to side. Josefina and I give each other a quizzical look. The rules of Panamanian society are clear on unexpected visits: they are to be avoided at all costs. Fortunately, Señor Cardozo clears his throat, breaking the silence.

"Excuse me for barging in like this unannounced," he says. "But something urgent has come up. May I please come in?"

Josefina nods and Señor Cardozo lumbers in, dragging the stench of sweat and cigars in with each heavy footstep.

"I came as soon as I could," he says, dabbing his sweaty brow with a handkerchief. "It's been a helluva day. Men from the railroad company tracked me down from a business card they found in your father's wallet. Naturally, the wallet was emptied of its contents."

"Did Papi lose his wallet?" I ask.

"Not exactly, Miss Maduro," he says, his face darkening. "I'm afraid I have some bad news for you. You see, there was a train accident near the Culebra Cut today. A tractor rolled onto the rails and collided with one of the carriages, causing it to derail and slide down an embankment. Half a dozen people died. I regret to say that your parents were among the dead."

At that moment my world turns black. I feel the blood rush from my head, as if my life is ebbing way.

"What? That's impossible! There must be some mistake. They're due home any minute..."

"There's no mistake, Miss Maduro. I'm terribly sorry."

I turn to Josefina in desperation, but she looks equally stunned. At first, she merely shakes her head back and forth, and then tears start flowing in rivulets down her caramel-colored face. Finally, she crumples in a mass of tears like a flower wilting from a sudden downpour. I fix my gaze on Señor Cardozo, but his grim demeanor tells me all I need to know. I feel my chest tightening as I struggle to breathe. This can't be happening. Not to me.

"It can't be. I must go down to the railroad office to find out what happened."

Señor Cardozo locks eyes with me. "You don't understand, I've already been to the railroad office. I've been to the hospital. I've seen the bodies with my own eyes. Your parents are dead. I'm truly sorry, Miss Maduro."

"No, no, no I don't believe you."

He shakes his head with pity. "I would never lie about such matters. I hate to be the bearer of bad news, but that's what lawyers are paid to do. I've already arranged for their funeral tomorrow. But there's also the matter of settling your parents' debts and finding you a new home—"

"A new home?" I say, my voice quivering. "Why do I need a new home? This is my home."

"This *was* your home. Unfortunately, I've been looking into your father's finances and I'm afraid you can't afford to keep it."

"What? That's impossible."

I turn to Josefina, but she's already in another world. Her face is awash in sadness. Josefina, my tower of strength, has crumpled right in front of my eyes. Then all at once I burst into tears. My body shakes with uncontrollable grief as my heart breaks into a thousand pieces, the pain carrying me away with each undulating sob. I bury my face in Josefina's chest so tormented with anguish I don't even hear when Señor Cardozo scurries out of the house.

The funeral on Mount Hope is a somber affair. Mami and Papi's coffins are wheeled up in a horse carriage and laid to rest under the watchful gaze of a flock of doves and the rustling coconut trees. The crowd is dressed in black mourning attire and they try their best to comfort me, but my face is like a stone. For the next several days, Josefina and I sit huddled on the sofa, clinging to each other for support as friends and neighbors stop by during the *Shiva* to deliver fresh food and consoling words. But nothing they say can erase the pain and sorrow from my heart.

Meanwhile, Señor Cardozo goes about settling my parents' debts and cabling my relatives, asking them to take me in. He pats me on the head and assures me that no matter how bad things seem, everything will work out in the end. But through the haze, I hear whispers that give me cause for concern. So far, none of my relatives have agreed to take me in, not even my cousin in Curaçao. I soon realize that I have nowhere to go. My grief is replaced with shame as I'm forced to admit that my situation is far more tenuous than I ever imagined.

It's not surprising. Since my parents moved to Panama some twenty years ago, they lost contact with most of my relatives. The only close relation I have is my Aunt Esther, my father's older sister, but I would never want to live with her. She's a hot-headed spinster who spends all her time bossing around her servants and writing poisonous letters to the few remaining relatives who still speak to her. And worse, Aunt Esther is as crazy as a loon.

For as long as I can remember, Aunt Esther has been the black sheep of the Maduro family. My mother used to say that Aunt Esther's greatest pleasure was in ruining the reputations of perfectly fine people since no man had ever done her the honor. The few times Aunt Esther wrote to us, it was to berate my father for leaving her all alone on a declining island with no family for support. After pages filled with colorful rebukes in language dripping with sarcasm, Aunt Esther always finished off by demanding money, which Papi sent, every single time.

While it's true that Aunt Esther's life has been mostly a joyless, unremitting melodrama, it's mostly by her own design. She lives a reclusive life in my grandfather's old mansion in Charlotte Amalie, and survives on a meager inheritance that allows for few conveniences and no luxuries. Her only company is a small staff of eccentric, elderly servants who wait on her hand and foot while surviving on a diet of okra, salt fish, and gossip. Life on a small island can be tedious and dull, and definitely not for me.

My only option is to stay here in Colón and finish my education. If I study hard, I can earn my teacher's certificate and apply for a position in one of the American schools in the Canal Zone where I can make a decent salary. After several weeks with no news from any of my relatives, I feel confident that Cardozo will agree to my plan. But Josefina has her doubts.

For one thing, Cardozo's behavior is starting to look suspicious. Every day he sends wagons with workers who slowly empty the house of its contents on the pretext of paying off my father's debts. Josefina and I stand by helplessly wringing our hands, wondering how all this will end. Right before our eyes the house becomes a

27

barren, empty shell. A sad end to my childhood. At least I still have Celestina, whose singing grows feebler with each passing day.

Today Josefina decides to take matters into her own hands. She puts on her Sunday best and marches me down Central Street, right up to the front door of the bank. We enter on pins and needles, searching for a kind face in a sea of surly typists and clerks. Although outwardly polite, we sense their eyes watching our every move. Finally, a junior clerk approaches us and offers to fetch the manager.

To my alarm, when the manager finally appears, he seems well acquainted with my situation, but instead of offering to help, he delivers the final, shocking blow. He explains in legalistic jargon that Señor Cardozo has secured the legal right to withdraw all the money from my father's account to settle his debts. He shows us a document proving that Señor Cardozo has already withdrawn more than one thousand dollars, leaving only a paltry sum of one hundred dollars. The shock overwhelms me. I feel light-headed and dizzy as the reality of my situation sinks in, that in addition to being alone in the world, I am also penniless.

Later, Señor Cardozo stops by to inform me that the house has been sold and a new family will be moving in shortly. He orders me to pack my belongings and prepare to be sent away, but he neglects to mention where he's sending me as none of my relatives has agreed to take me in yet. I cannot live with this uncertainty. Mustering up my courage, I inform Cardozo that I know he has squandered all the money from my father's bank account. I hotly announce that I intend to file a complaint against him in court.

All at once, Cardozo's face hardens like a crocodile. He stares at me with cold, expressionless eyes, but says nothing. Finally, he turns to leave, but before exiting, he calls over his shoulder, "Good luck, Miss Maduro. You'll need it." The unspoken threat sends chills up my spine.

With the house no longer mine, I have no choice but to move in with Josefina even though she lives in a cramped apartment over a Chinese knick-knack shop. When I broach the subject, she hugs me so hard my heart soars. Josefina is all the family I have left, and I resolve to stay by her side forever. I return to my room to finish packing. As I slam the trunk shut, a telltale lump forms in the back of my throat. There is still one final task I must carry out before I leave for good: I must give Celestina her freedom.

On the balcony I open the door to Celestina's cage. She hops around a little, fluttering her green wings and looking at me with big, curious eyes, but she makes no attempt to leave. I try coaxing her out. "Go Celestina," I urge. "You are free now." But Celestina turns her head sideways and offers only a feeble chirp, unable to comprehend freedom any more than I can comprehend flying. I move back a little, giving her plenty of room to stretch her wings. "Fly away Celestina!"

She steadies her tiny, downy body with her beak, and hops through the open door. She flutters her wings, and without a second glance, takes off in flight. I watch as she sails over the garden and lands on a branch of a nearby tree, calling out in a loud, triumphant chirp. Then I watch as she soars through the air above the treetops, a golden streak across the brilliant sky. "Goodbye Celestina!" I call out. But it's too late, Celestina is gone.

Just then, a noise echoes from the street sounding like tin cans rattling inside a fifty gallon drum. Peering outside, I see a familiar black motorcar pulling up, clattering and sputtering before coming to an abrupt stop. A shadowy figure thrusts open the door and a familiar pair of black wingtip shoes hits the pavement. Señor Cardozo is back! My heart races when I realize he has come to take me away for good.

How foolish and naïve I've been! The money, the house, the furniture, my father's motorcar, he has taken everything for himself, leaving me penniless. And now he wants to dispose of me. A black rage overtakes me as I snatch my purse off the table and race out the back door as Josefina's cries echo in my ears.

I sail through the garden, my eyes filled with tears. To my horror, I stumble and fall in a ditch. My misery increases when I see dirt stains all over my dress, but I refuse to give in to despair. Ignoring the pain, I pick myself up, dust myself off, and continue running, fueled by the determination to save myself from Cardozo's betrayal.

I head in the direction of Begoña's house, hoping her parents will help me. Darting through the crowds, I make sure Cardozo isn't following me, but I know the odds are against me. Señor Cardozo is a powerful lawyer. Fighting him in a court will be very hard, but I refuse to give up without a fight.

Luckily, the streets of Colón are crowded. The steamy air is bursting with a rich cacophony of foreign tongues, each one as indecipherable as the dirty faces on the street urchins who prowl the streets for billfolds. Colón is by no means a rich city. It's not famous either. And it doesn't have much to be proud of given its reputation for being the *pest hole of the universe* and the *wickedest city of the Americas* with all the gambling, drinking and carousing that goes on around here. In fact, Colón's only source of pride is that it serves as the Atlantic entrance of the Panama Canal. Every day, dozens of ships from all over the world line up to make the miraculous crossing over to the Pacific Ocean, a distance of only fifty miles.

I glance over my shoulder. *Caramba!* Cardozo is heading toward me. He swerves around a line of slow-moving donkey carts as he honks his horn like a mad goose. Quickening my pace, I dash across the wide, palm tree-lined boulevard and continue north along the Avenida Bolívar. With a little luck, I can disappear into the crowd before he catches me.

Cardozo speeds us, causing a small commotion with his heavy-handed driving. Before I know it, he's right at my side, beating his steering wheel, yelling at me, and shaking his fist. I try to make a last dash for freedom, but I'm not fast enough. He swerves in front of me and cuts me off, cornering me like a trapped animal. He sticks his head out the window and orders me to get in. Traffic comes to a grinding halt as everyone stops to gape at the odd spectacle. "No!" I scream at the top of my lungs, making sure everyone can hear me. "Stay away from me you dirty old man! Leave me alone!"

The crowd gasps. Cardozo's face turns purple. He throws open the door and marches across the pavement as the crowd stares open-mouthed. I break into a run, but he sprints after me, grabbing me so hard my whole body jerks backward. With his iron grip on my shoulders, he shakes me so hard I fear I will pass out. I struggle to free myself, but he shoves me into his motorcar with such force, he knocks the wind out of me, then he slams the door shut and takes off like a mad dog, cursing and screaming the whole way.

I scream at Cardozo with all my might, striking the dashboard in fury as I demand my freedom, but he just speeds up, his eyes glued to the road as he blurts out that my antics may have caused me to miss the sailing. He weaves down a side street, swerving past a flock of chickens, until the wharf suddenly appears in front of us. My heart sinks. My fate has already been sealed in the form of a transatlantic steamer named *Guiana*.

Based on the flurry of activity, the ship appears ready to sail. Sweaty dock workers hurl cartons of fruit, vegetables, eggs, and fish into the hold as sailors rush around making final preparations. On the wharf, family members hug and kiss departing loved ones, while vendors hawk last-minute panama hats, postcards, and trinkets from rickety pushcarts.

Cardozo grinds to a halt and hands me a crumpled envelope. Inside I discover the remaining hundred dollars from my father's bank account, the money the banker warned me about.

"What's this?" I say with disgust. "Where's the rest?"

"What are you talking about?"

"The money you stole. My parents' life savings. Give it back!"

"That's impossible, Miss Maduro," he scoffs. "The money wasn't yours to begin with. Your father left this world with enormous debts."

"I don't believe you."

"He owed money all over town, not to mention the cost of the steamship ticket. Well, that's all over now. Get on board. Your Auntie's waiting for you."

My face flushes and my muscles tense. I grip the seat with my nails, refusing to leave. Cardozo storms out of the car, marches over to my side and yanks me out so hard, I feel the seams of my dress ripping.

"Good luck with that Auntie of yours," he sneers. "They say she's as crazy as a loon."

He drags me kicking and screaming across the wharf and tosses me into the arms of a bewildered sailor. Though I protest loudly at first, when I see the puzzled stares of the other passengers, I clam up. From his jacket pocket, Cardozo produces a steamship ticket which he tosses at the sailor, saying, "She's your headache now." He turns to me and adds, "You have no say in your life anymore Miss Maduro. Get used to it."

I attempt to slap his bloated, arrogant face, but the sailor holds me back, then he drags me up the gangway under the scrutiny of everyone's eyes. I see the pity and scorn in everyone's faces which increases my misery a thousand-fold. Halfway up, I yell down at Cardozo, "You won't get away with this. I'll get you back!"

Without turning around, Cardozo just offers a deep, guttural laugh, slams his door shut, and speeds off in a cloud of dust.

CHAPTER 2

By the time I reach the deck, I'm disoriented and out of breath. I scramble to get my bearings, but all around me the sailors are snickering behind my back. To my dismay, I have become a crude source of entertainment, like a gypsy's dancing monkey. To my horror, I feel tears welling up in my eyes.

Determined that no one will see me cry, I brush aside the tears, straighten out the creases in my dress, and push the hair out of my face. My only chance is to convince the captain that I was kidnapped, robbed, and forced to board this ship against my will. I approach two sailors and demand to speak to the captain. Stifling a giggle, they point in the direction of the purser's office, but mention he's in no mood for mutineers. Ignoring the joke, I march off, but when I reach his door, my heart sinks.

At first glance, I can see the purser is no pushover. He's a seasoned mariner with a stern, weather-beaten face, a bulbous nose, and hands so large they look like they could tear the jaws out of a shark. He'll never buy my story about being kidnapped, even if it is true. Those German spies back in Colón would have had an easier time convincing the soldiers they were the Crown Princes of Bavaria.

I decide to skip to Plan B, where I tell the purser that my ticket is incorrect, that my final destination is Curaçao and not St. Thomas. This is the only way I can outsmart Cardozo and bypass my aunt's clutches. When my cousin in Curaçao sees me standing on his doorstep like an unwanted bottle of milk, he'll have no choice but to take me in. Thinking how my life hangs in the balance leaves me dizzy, but there's no time for self-pity.

I decide to use the soft approach. Assuming my best Molly Pickford, damsel-in-distress look, I slip into the purser's office, pushing my way through the crowd of passengers. When I approach his desk, I relate my dilemma in the most dramatic terms as the other passengers stare in disbelief. To his credit, the purser listens without flinching. He nods his head, grunts from time to time, and folds his arms over his massive chest.

When I finish my speech, he affixes a pair of horn-rimmed spectacles and leans down to peer at me. Luckily, he can't see my quivering knees.

"Repeat your name please," he says. My mouth is so dry I barely manage to squeak out my name.

He turns to a large manifest that takes up a large portion of his desk and scans the tiny columns with the precision of a seasoned accountant. About halfway down, he places a large finger over an entry, and then turns to a stack of papers on his desk and rifles through them. When he spots a certain telegram, he pulls it out and reads it carefully, scratching his beard like a magistrate about to render a verdict.

"Hmm," he says. "We have a passenger registered under the name Abigail Maduro, aged sixteen years—that would be you I suppose—with passage to St. Thomas where we are ordered to deliver her to a Miss Esther Maduro or her representative. Since the telegram originated in the Home Office, we are obligated to comply fully. As it makes no mention of Curaçao anywhere, I regret to inform you that you cannot disembark in Curaçao. Next!"

"But, sir, that's impossible. There must be some mistake."

"You can read the telegram for yourself," he says. "There's no mistake."

Just then, an idea flashes through my mind. Call it Plan C—for *contagious*. Steamship companies are known for being cautious about taking passengers with contagious diseases from port to port out of fear of spreading disease. If I can convince the purser that I'm too sick to travel, he'll have no choice but to kick me off. If my plan works, I'll soon be lying on a gurney in the Ancón Hospital with a team of sympathetic nurses plying me with bowls of chocolate ice cream and mango pudding. There's no time to lose.

Without missing a beat, I clutch my sides and start moaning in pain. Just as I expected, deep furrows sprout on the purser's craggy forehead. He caught the bait. To heighten the drama, I start rocking back and forth, groaning as if overcome by a serious illness. "Help me! Help me! Something's wrong…" I moan in feigned agony as the passengers look on in horror. Dare I mention that even the great Theda Bara would be impressed?

As expected, the purser dives for the nearest telephone. He grabs the receiver and barks into it, "Send Ian McShane up on the double!" Then the purser turns to me and says, "There now, Miss Maduro. The medic will be up any minute. He'll have a look at you and everything's going to be fine." Luckily, the thick-headed purser doesn't realize that on the inside I'm laughing so hard, tears are almost rolling down.

A minute later in walks Ian McShane. One look at him and I instantly regret my plan. He's a dashing Allan Quatermain in nautical whites and a sea cap, a rugged, quick-witted Irishman with dancing eyes, a shock of red hair, and a smart-alecky grin that lights up a room. In short, Ian McShane is my ideal man.

"Let's have a look at you, Miss," he says, with a Gaelic cadence that sounds like music to my Panamanian ears. He points a flashlight in my eyes and peers down my throat, his body so close I can smell his musky aftershave. He places two fingers under my jaw and applies just the right amount of pressure that causes me to swoon with pleasure. After a few thoughtful minutes, he shakes his head. Never was I more fearful of parting from a handsome stranger's company.

"No fever, no pus," he reports to the purser, who looks at him with utmost gravity. "She looks like a healthy specimen, despite her dramatic and rather excitable nature."

"You sure it's nothing serious?" says the purser, winking at McShane. "If her condition worsens, we may need to employ an old sea cure: tie her up with some ballast and let her sink to the bottom without a trace. It's the only remedy for these exotic Panamanian diseases." My eyes go wide as saucers as I look from one to the other.

"I don't think that extreme sort of cure will be necessary this time around," says Ian, winking back at the purser. "I think our young lady will be a pussycat from now on. I wager a pint of

Guinness her condition improves the minute the dinner gong rings. Back in Ireland, we call it a classic case of cold feet. Don't you agree, little lady?"

I glare with indignation at the two seamen who have made me the brunt of a sailor's joke. Soon I discover that I'll be seeing a lot more of Ian McShane on this voyage. He's been assigned as both my room steward and chaperon, so even if I harbored any ideas about escaping, with Ian McShane dogging me around, I'm a sitting duck.

"That settles it," says Ian, hoisting me to my feet. "I'll take care of the little lass, Wilkins. She's in good hands now."

"See to it she doesn't have a relapse," winks the purser. "Or it's the sea cure for her."

Ian drags me kicking and screaming out of the purser's office and leads me across the crowded deck, cutting a path through the crowd of passengers, harried stewards, ladies in afternoon dresses and their soft-spoken South American maids, men in linen suits and boater hats, potted palms, piles of luggage, wicker baskets, and a small flotilla of baby carriages and their miniature charges. When we're safely out of earshot, I yank myself free.

"Thanks a lot for ruining my only chance of getting off this blasted ship," I say, crossing my arms defiantly.

The seasoned Irishman cocks his head to the side and, to my horror, pats me on the behind. "Bollocks! Get a move on."

He grabs my hand and off we go down a flight of stairs. To my chagrin, I discover that Ian McShane has a tendency for showing up at the worst possible moment and when you least expect him. But I took an instant liking to him.

"Nice trick you pulled back there," he says, flashing his Cheshire cat grin. "But I'm warnin' you, once we're at sea, no more stunts like that. From now on you're going to be a good lass and cooperate with Mr. McShane or I'll put you on galley duty."

"I'm not scared of you," I say. "I'll find a way off this ship. Just try and stop me."

"For your information, I see through yer brave act. You're as scared as a mouse in a chamber-pot. What are you running away from anyway?"

"I'm in a bit of trouble, but I can't explain it just yet. I have to get back to Colón to claim what's rightfully mine. Can you please help me? I'll pay you whatever I can."

"You're not going anywhere. They're paying me to keep an eye on you. But don't worry, once you get the wind in your sails, you'll never go back. And if you stick close to me, I'll learn you all you need to know about navigation. I'll make a sailor out of you in no time. You look like a smart lass. Have you ever used a sextant before?"

"No, why would I use a sextant?"

"There you go, talking like a *land* person again. A sextant, my darling sweet gal, is a most excellent device that can help you find your position at sea with amazing accuracy. Oh, I can see you've got a lot to learn. But I'll take you under my wing and learn you all about sailing at no additional cost. But only on condition you forget about jumping ship."

"No promises."

Ian shakes his head. "You're a doozy, but I've been around the block a few times. I can handle you."

We arrive at my cabin. By some miracle, my steamer trunk is waiting for me, all that's left of my former life.

Ian presses the key into the lock and opens the door, releasing the smell of seaweed and dried fish, but when he turns on the electric lights and fluffs up the pillows, the cabin appears quite cozy. Ian drags my steamer trunk in and plops it down near the berth.

"From the feel of this monster, I'd say you're going on a long trip," he says. "When are you going back to Panama?"

"I'm never going back. This is a one-way trip for me."

Ian scratches his head. "What about your family?"

"My parents are down in South America. They're world-famous archeologists exploring a lost city in the Andes. That's why they're sending me to St. Thomas to live with my Aunt Esther, a reclusive old spinster with a bad case of distemper and a penchant for bossing everyone around her. Not exactly my cup of tea."

"Nor mine," he answers grimly. "Sounds like you're in one helluva mess. Heaven protect you! Well, take heart that while you're onboard the *Guiana* you'll be treated like royalty, even if you didn't have the luck to be born Irish. You have an outside cabin and your own private head with a sea bath. I'll bring you your breakfast at seven sharp tomorrow, but for now, make yourself at home and ring me if you need anything."

Ian holds out his hand for a tip.

"Did I mention I don't tip kids? How old are you anyway?" I say, feeling instantly foolish for saying it.

"Testy, testy…. well, let me explain something to you, 'little Miss Rich Kid.' It don't matter to me if your parents are famous archeologists or even the old Kaiser himself, I'm plenty old enough to keep an eye on you. So don't give me any reason to go reporting you to the captain."

"—but I'll make an exception in your case," I say, stuffing a coin in his grubby palm.

"Much obliged," he says, heading for the door. But before he leaves, he turns to me and says, "Just remember one thing, I've spent most of my life at sea, and if there's one thing I've learned, it's that a bad attitude can sink your ship faster than a German torpedo. I'm willing to give you a wide berth because your parents ditched you for some ancient ruin down in South America, but on this ship, the Captain makes the rules. So think twice before doing anything stupid. And if you give me any trouble, *any trouble at all*, I'll have you down in the galley peeling potatoes. Understand? You rich kids are all the same—nothing but trouble."

"And I don't need a chaperone!" I say as the door slams shut. But it's too late. Ian McShane is gone.

***

My first night at sea is restless, like every night since the death of my parents. I lie on the berth trying to remember the sound of my mother's voice, the smell of my father's aftershave, the feel of his arms hugging me. Sometime during the night, I fall asleep and am overtaken by vivid, frightening dreams.

I see Mami, Papi and me sitting around the dining room table dressed in our best Sabbath clothes, eating Mami's delicious *sancocho* and rice and beans. But despite the warm, delicious food, something is troubling me. I sense disaster looming on the horizon. I walk over to my parents and try to warn them by shaking their shoulders, pulling their hands, screaming in their ears, but they don't hear me. They just stare off in the distance, like zombies. Horrified, I back away. I start running, but a black car chases me down the Avenida Bolívar, catching up to me. I scream and the next thing I know, I'm falling into an endless black pit.

When I open my eyes, the feeling of terror overwhelms me. I lay awake, paralyzed, until it fades away and all that remains is the fear that the dream will return, and I will once again sink into that dark, endless pit. That's why I dread nighttime so much. Not long ago my nights were pleasant with my mother's sweet singing echoing down the hallway; now it's just a black hole of loneliness and misery. And the sad thing is our lives once held so much promise.

My parents, Isaac and Rebecca Maduro, were born in the 1860's to prominent Sephardic Jewish merchant families in St. Thomas, an island in the Danish West Indies. Under the Danes, the Sephardic Jews flourished in the mercantile and shipping trades and the town of Charlotte Amalie grew and prospered as an important trading center. They built a beautiful synagogue on Synagogue Hill in the Queen's Quarter of Charlotte Amalie and lived in beautiful villas with gardens and spacious balconies. But they weren't always so prosperous. Many years before, the Sephardim, as they are called, were exiled from Spain and ended up in Holland because it was more tolerant. Later, seeking a better life, they set sail for the New World. As Dutch citizens, they settled in Suriname, Recife, and in the islands of St. Eustacius and Curaçao, where they flourished. Years later, upon the invitation of a Danish king, the Sephardic Jews moved to St. Thomas to colonize the island and bring business. In those days, Charlotte Amalie was known for being a prosperous port, with silver and gold flowing almost as plentifully as the rum. To the old-timers, those were known as the good old days of Charlotte Amalie, but they didn't last forever.

The Maduro family worked hard and became prominent citizens in St. Thomas society. They established a shipping business a Dry Goods store on Main Street, and built a beautiful villa on a hill overlooking town. My mother always told me how the Maduro women used to ride around town in fine carriages wearing the latest fashions from Paris, employed a houseful of servants and nannies to care for their children, and busied themselves with communal affairs. The center of Jewish life was the beautiful synagogue in Queen's Quarter which they called *Beracha Veshalom Vegmiluth Hasidim,* Blessing and Peace and Good Deeds, and for many years they kept their distinct way of life, but in 1867 their idyllic existence came to an end when a powerful hurricane ravaged the island, destroyed homes and businesses, uprooted trees and crops, and killed hundreds of people. As a result, hundreds of people fled the island in search of a better life on distant shores, including many Jews. Some say St.

Thomas never fully recuperated from this devastating blow, and in many ways, they were correct.

With the building of the Panama Canal in the 1890's, many people began to see Panama as the new hope for the future, this included my parents. And so, Isaac and Rebecca Maduro bid a sad farewell to their families and set sail for Panama, hoping to start a new life. They settled in Colón, an English-speaking enclave on the Caribbean coast, where they established a successful dry goods store. After years of hard work, life once again began to flourish. As I look back on my family history, I see how ironic it is that after years of wandering from shore to shore, I'm the first person in my family to return to a land they had once abandoned. It's almost as if by returning to St. Thomas, I am altering my family's history, and I don't know if this portends good or bad.

The next morning, I awake as sunlight streams through the porthole, tickling my face. Peering outside, I am relieved to see the ocean is calm and the sky is bright and full of promise. Still, I'm worn out from a restless night of tossing and turning, and I fall back on the berth, exhausted.

Minutes later, I'm jolted awake by a forceful knock on the door. Ian breezes in sporting a wide grin and trailing the scent of fresh-baked bread. He rolls in a cart with a steaming hot breakfast tray of tea, toast, oatmeal, and fresh fruit, which he places on my side table with nary a mention of my rude behavior from the day before. Truth be told, I still feel ashamed.

When Ian sees that I make no move to approach the food, he tosses a silky teabag into the pot of hot water and glances over his shoulder to size me up. "Looks like our brave Miss Abigail had a rough night last night. Perhaps you weren't meant for a sailor's life."

"I'm perfectly fine. I slept like a baby."

"Well, those bags under your eyes are telling a different story. Yesterday when you pulled that pathetic stunt in the purser's office, your eyes were all afire and your cheeks had a rosy glow. Today, you look as sallow as a drunken sailor on shore leave. It's probably just a touch of seasickness, and there's only one remedy for that."

"What's that? The sea cure?"

Ian grins like a mischievous schoolboy. "The big bottle from the ship's infirmary."

I open my mouth to protest, but Ian flies out the door. Within minutes, he reappears holding an ominous-looking brown bottle in one hand, and a mercury thermometer in the other.

"*Caramba!* Don't you dare give me that poison," I say, pulling the sheet over my head. "You're no doctor."

"For your information I happen to be the Assistant Medical Officer," he says, shaking the thermometer. "Which is three grades below Captain, so no back talk. Open wide—"

I glower as he shoves the thermometer into my mouth.

"Perfectly normal, for someone looking as sorry as you," he says, yanking it out a moment later. "But if experience is my guide, you'll need a dose of this medicine just to keep the wind in your sails." He doles out a heaping teaspoonful of the putrid concoction and then shoves it in my mouth.

"Tell me the truth," I say, clutching my stomach. "Does anyone else feel as bad as I do?"

"Have no fear. You'll be back to your trouble-making self once you get some fresh air in your lungs," he says. "After breakfast, go up to the library and get yourself a good book, then go out on deck and settle into a nice deck chair where you can catch a bit o' sun and watch the day's activities. You'll be back to breaking hearts in no time. Oh, but watch yourself. We've got a large number of unsavory characters on board. A fine, gentle lass like yourself could get in a heap of trouble with these disagreeable scoundrels."

"What do you mean?"

"Just what I said, there's a rogue's gallery of suspicious types roaming on board the ship and they'd love to get their filthy paws on you. Some of these villains are what you call war profiteers, others are soldiers of fortune. And I heard from a good source there may be a saboteur or two on board."

"A what?"

"You've never heard of saboteurs? Well, if you prefer you can call them what they really are: spies. German spies."

My eyes widen like saucers. "Are you serious?"

"Of course, I'm serious. We're in the middle of a war, aren't we? I hope you're aware of that."

"Of course, I'm aware of it," I say. "Back home in Panama they caught a whole ring of German spies who were plotting to blow up the Panama Canal. But that was different; Panama has strategic importance. Why would the Germans send spies and saboteurs out here in the middle of nowhere?"

"You sheltered little lamb," he says, placing one foot on a chair and leaning in closer. "Let me explain it to you for your edification. For starters, it's all part of Germany's grand plan. Their leader, the Kaiser, is an explosive, hot-tempered brute of a man who can't reconcile his hatred for his British cousins with his love for his British grandmother. You remember old Queen Vicky now, don't you? Well, Kaiser Wilhelm (Some people call him Willy) blames his British cousins for stealing his rightful place in his grandmother's heart, so he went to war to settle that old score. Part of his strategy seems to be dispatching an army of spies and saboteurs to wreak havoc all over the world. Some of them demolish bridges, others blow up ammunition depots, and still others print poisonous articles in foreign newspapers. They also try to sink every Allied ship they can find, even ordinary passenger ships like this one. Do you get it now?"

"If you're trying to scare the dickens out of me, it's working," I say. "Are you telling me this ship is full of spies, saboteurs and *murderers?*"

"Pardon me, but in their line of work it's called *assassination*, and they rarely get caught. For instance, down the corridor is a passenger with a German-sounding name who sleeps with a revolver under his pillow. Another one hides secret messages inside his shoe heels and hat bands, and still another one walks around with a valise chained to his wrist. God only knows what's inside of it. Care for me to go on?"

"You're making this up."

"You can believe what you want," he says, shrugging his shoulders. "But let me give you a little tip. The *really dangerous* ones smuggle suitcases laden with high-powered explosives on board ships just like this one."

"Will you please stop! Now you're scaring me."

"Forewarned is forearmed," he says, wagging his finger. "When they told me I had to keep an eye on you, they didn't tell me I had to learn you yer ABCs."

"Mr. McShane, are you telling me there are German saboteurs on board this ship with bombs?"

"I'm just saying it's always a possibility."

"Then will you please do something before it's too late?"

"I did enough by telling you," he says. "It's time you grew up and realized that if you want to save your own neck you have to outsmart the enemy. The sooner you learn to watch out for yerself the better off you'll be. More than a thousand innocent souls perished on the *Lusitania*, some younger than you. The world's full of danger. The important thing to remember is to trust nobody. A German saboteur won't think twice before slitting the throat of some poor devil that gets in his way."

"You must be joking."

Ian locks eyes with me. "I've never been more serious in my life, Miss Abigail. But keep this strictly between you and me. Scuttlebutt spreads fast on a ship. Don't want to cause a panic."

"I think I've heard enough. I'm going to lock myself in my stateroom and not come out until the war is over."

Ian laughs good-naturedly. "And keep that beautiful face from the world. Forget about it for now. Just go up to the Promenade Deck and have yourself a good time. There's a string quartet after lunch, tug-o-war, and a wooden horse race later on. But one final word of caution: stay away from the stout looking gentleman in cabin forty-four. He's a cold-blooded mercenary."

"What's his name?"

"Calls himself Fritz Dreyer, at least that's what his papers say. He pretends to be a Swiss botanist, but if he's a botanist, I'm Queen Mary. He's a heavy-set chap with a German accent, a bulldog jaw, hair cut like a hedgehog, and a militaristic moustache that puts the Kaiser's to shame. Oh, he's a society gentleman all right, with a proper waistcoat and a gold watch chain, but those steely blue eyes could set your teeth on edge. Also claims that a jagged scar on the left side of his face came from a dueling accident, but that was no accident. Someone tried to kill him and now that poor devil's gone to Davy Jones' locker."

My hand trembles so hard the tea splashes. "Now look and see what you've done. You've got me all agitated."

"What happened to the brave girl from yesterday who tried to outsmart the purser? You might as well know the truth. Now get dressed and go up to the Promenade Deck. Find a nice girl your age to talk to and forget about all this German spy business. And by the way, now that we're better acquainted, you can call me Ian."

"And you can call me Abby."

Ian flashes me his grin and my heart swoons. "That's better. I think you and me are gonna be good friends. I may even practice my Spanish on you."

"A Spanish-speaking Irishman? I don't think the world is ready for that yet."

We laugh at my little joke, and then Ian leaves. After breakfast, I take my straw hat and head to the Promenade deck for some fresh air and also to write in my diary. Thankfully, the day is glorious. The sun shines brightly over the sea, turning it into a field of glistening sapphires. In the distance, white sails gleam on the horizon, a welcome sight in an endless blue horizon.

Finding an unoccupied deckchair, I sat down to watch the ocean and the fluffy white clouds overhead. I write this little poem:

> *Through jungle, swamp, and wretched place,*
> *I seek to find familiar face.*
> *Be it stony mountain that I climb,*
> *Or temperate floral field sublime;*
> *Battling fevers, pirates, or brigands vile;*
> *For there are hidden dangers on any tropic isle!*
> *Whether howling night or fearsome morn...*
> *(Tempests abound where the latitude is warm.)*
> *Ever onward go I, o'er stormy seas I roam,*
> *Wandering forever 'til I find my rightful home.*

I sigh, wondering if I will ever find my "rightful home."

But something else bothers me. Despite the dangers lurking about, the other passengers walk around blissfully unaware, as if all they care about is their own pleasure and enjoyment, as if the world was not at war and people's lives were not at stake. They pose for photographs, lounge on deck chairs drinking rum punch and munching on popcorn and peanuts as they discuss the day's activities. Some even brought their poodles on board. Watching all this frivolity while Ian's warnings swirl through my head makes me anxious. But more than that, I find myself becoming downright suspicious. I start to see things I never noticed before.

For instance, everywhere I go I see suspicious characters lurking in the shadows, creeping around, casting furtive glances, or pretending to be asleep in a deck chair when I know they're keeping a lookout with a spyglass. Other times I catch some men writing secret messages in notebooks, whispering to each other in darkened corners, or drinking in the saloon. Any one of these suspicious types could be a German saboteur preparing to strike. I find it exciting and dreadful at the same time. But it gets worse.

Today while I was making the rounds in the First Class Lounge, I spied a passenger with a pointy moustache who could be a dead ringer for the Kaiser. Another one had a long, forked beard and an overhanging brow just like von Tirpitz, the head of the Imperial German Navy. Later, when I retreat to the library, I spy two mercenary types with close-cropped hair, brooding eyes, and menacing scowls that send shivers up you through clouds of smoke. I sense these two ruffians are not ordinary passengers, but have been sent for some nefarious purpose.

While they read the newspaper, I observe them while pretending to be waiting for someone. When I get close enough, I catch sight of the ominous headline that makes my heart skip a beat: GERMAN U-BOAT SINKS ENEMY SHIP. Suddenly one of them blurts out something in rapid-fire German that causes the two of them to erupt in obnoxious guffaws that sends chills down my spine. I turn and flee in a state of panic, almost knocking down a steward with a tray of coffee mugs.

When I reach the deck, I pause to catch my breath and stare at the endless, rolling waves. I realize that Ian is right. Danger is lurking everywhere. It seems the war is right here in our backyard. But maybe all is not lost. If I can devote my life to hunting down spies and saboteurs, perhaps I can make a valuable contribution to the war effort. Feeling a surge of pride welling up inside of me, I resolve to do my own part to fight the war. And I shall start with Fritz Dreyer, the man in cabin forty-four.

CHAPTER 3

The next morning when Ian comes to deliver my breakfast tray, he does something totally unexpected. He hands me a beautiful bouquet of flowers. "These are for you," he says, blushing. "To apologize for scaring you half to death with all that prattle about German spies."

"Actually, I owe you a debt of gratitude," I say inhaling the delicate fragrance of the gardenias.

"For what?"

"For opening my eyes. For giving my life new purpose. I've come to the conclusion that I can serve my fellow man by hunting down German spies and saboteurs."

Ian buries his face in his hands. "Oh, sweet mother of God, what have I created? I knew you were gonna be trouble. Don't let it get to your head. I only told you to warn you. Hunting spies is a dangerous game. Girls like you should be serving coffee in the canteens and knitting socks for the soldiers in the trenches."

"I can't knit and I always burn the coffee. Besides, I love adventure and intrigue. Maybe this is what I was meant to do. But before I start, I need you to do something very important for me."

"What's that?"

"Learn me—I mean *teach* me everything you know about German spies. I want to be able to read them like an open book. I want to know them better than they know themselves."

Ian bursts out laughing.

"Jaysus, Mary and Joseph! Somebody's imagination is all fired up," he teases, pouring some hot water into the teacup. "As if yours needed any firing up. Miss Abigail, I could tell you were different the moment I laid eyes on you. But I have to warn you, these scoundrels are not amateurs. You can get yourself in a whole mess of trouble if you don't take care. If I've learned anything in life, it's that you can never read another man's heart. The kindest looking man can have the blackest of hearts. But there is one thing I can learn you, and that's how to spot suspicious behavior. Normally spies try to blend in with their environment. They avoid standing out because it draws unnecessary attention. So if a man looks normal in one part of the ship, but he stands out in another part, that's called a *hunch*. A hunch is an odd feeling. Never ignore your hunches.

"Take for example that Fritz Dreyer character. I took one look at him while he was boarding back in Panama and my blood ran cold. I recognized him from a picture I saw in the newspapers about a year ago. He's a dead ringer for the guy who sank a Brazilian ship, but there's no way to prove it. And Dreyer's no fool. He got himself a new set of identity papers saying he's a Swiss Botanist, that's the only reason they allowed him to board."

"What else should I know?"

Ian counts on his fingers. "Look for any kind of strange behavior. Like picking locks, climbing through windows, passing notes, strange sounds like gunfire, maps, dressing in an odd manner, not answering questions. The list goes on and on."

"So, are you keeping an eye on this Fritz Dreyer character?"

"I follow him around. I watch him. I even went down to the baggage compartment to search his bags."

"And what did you find?"

"I gave up after my mates accused me of hitting the bottle down there. If I'd told those clowns I suspected Dreyer of being a saboteur, they'd laugh me back to Belfast. Dreyer's got a sterling reputation. He's part of the privileged set, what we call a real upper-cruster. Or what they call in diplomatic circles, a real bon vivant, a connoisseur of the finer things in life. He also knows how to bribe himself out of a difficult situation."

"So, this Dreyer character is so rich he can afford to ply us with champagne before he blows us to smithereens?"

"May the Lord keep you in his hand and never close his fist too tight," he says, patting my head. "Tell me this, if Dreyer were intent on blowing up this ship, why would he still be on it?"

"He could jump off before the explosives go off."

"Ah, so there *is* a brain inside that cunning little head of yours. But don't worry. I keep my eyes on Dreyer. The two of us have got a little game of cat and mouse going on. For instance, last night while I was pouring him his coffee, I casually mentioned that the Captain of the *Tennyson*—another ship he's supposed to have sunk—was looking to return some of his missing luggage. You should have seen the look on Dreyer's face. His body stiffened and the muscles in his face stretched so hard, I thought they would snap. Then he fixed his cold, penetrating eyes on me and gave me such a start, I needed a swig of whiskey just to keep my wits about me."

"You're crazy! Why did you risk your life like that? It seems you're worse than me. Now tell me something Mr. McShane, how do you know *I'm* not a German saboteur?"

"Well, you've got an Irish sense of humor, all right," he says, his eyes sparkling with wit. "That alone disqualifies you. But if you are a German spy and I didn't see it, then blame me 'cause I'm Irish. Back home, we have a saying that there are only three kinds of Irish men who can't understand women: young men, old men and men of middle age. And when it comes to the likes of a girl like you, I'm all three."

***

After dinner, peels of laughter, the popping of champagne and the tinny sound of a gramophone draw me to the First Class Lounge. I peer inside. The room is dimly-lit and filled with ladies and gentlemen dressed in evening attire chatting amiably over drinks and cigarettes. Clouds of smoke waft through the room, obscuring the faces of the people, while lending an aura of mystery and excitement to the evening.

I circle the room and settle into a cozy corner seat near three military types, a Canadian and two Americans. I order a Pepsi-Cola, and pick up a game of dominoes, but my ears are tuned to the conversations swirling around me.

"Roosevelt's aggressive tone sure has captured the public's imagination," says one of the American soldiers, the one I'll call Soldier A. "Especially when he says things like, '*We are asked to *kiss the bloody hands of the murderers of our women and children,'* but it's only a question of time before Germany steps over Wilson's line in the sand and forces him to revoke this policy of neutrality. Too many lives have been lost."

"Precisely," replies the Canadian, as he inadvertently blows smoke in my face. "But I would have thought that the sight of your Canadian brothers being butchered in France would have been enough incentive to push Wilson to revoke his high-minded policy of neutrality. Even after the Huns torpedoed the *Lusitania,* killing all those innocent women and children, he stuck to his guns. Back in the old days, an unsporting display of cowardice like that would have been enough provocation to call the Germans' bluff. But no, the old college professor played it cool and aloof. A disgrace, if you ask me."

"He's always muttering something about the Hague Convention," says Soldier B. "But the Hague Convention can't help poor King Albert protect his people from the Huns now, can it? The situation over there is a tragedy and a disaster."

"It's a bloody shame what the Kaiser is doing to Belgium," says the Canadian. "But at least the Allies had some measure of revenge when they sank that 700-foot monster they call the *Lutzow.* Over a thousand German and Prussian sailors went down with that hulk."

Soldier B downs the last of his beer. "That humiliating setback must have rankled the Kaiser's nerves even more than that hilarious *Daily Telegraph* affair," he chuckles.

"They say the Kaiser's so high-strung he's liable to snap like a twig," adds the Canadian, snapping a pencil in two, at which point the three men burst into laughter and order another round.

Just then, a man enters the room and all eyes turn to watch him. He strides in like a leopard circling his prey with long, even steps while keeping his lynx-like eyes smoldering on the others. He has a thick, bull-dog jaw, a Kaiser-like moustache and hair clipped so short, it resembles a hedgehog. He wears a dark suit with a waistcoat, and a conspicuous gold watch chain. But what catches my eye is the unusual leather valise that he clutches like plundered treasure.

He strides up to the bar and orders a cognac. When the drink is produced, he tosses down a silver coin and raises the glass to the light to admire its rich amber color. He swirls the elixir around with long, luxurious strokes, inhales its fragrance, then takes a long, satisfying swig.

Just then, light from the chandelier catches the left side of his face, revealing a cruel, jagged scar that runs down the side of his face and disappears beneath his collar. When I see that unmistakable wound, I almost drop my glass. There is no doubt in my mind that the man is none other than Fritz Dreyer, the man from cabin forty-four.

From his pocket, Dreyer produces a silver cigar-case. He opens it and selects a skinny black cigar, which he sniffs and lights with great ceremony. As he puffs the cigar with obvious pleasure, he keeps his grip firmly around the valise. And then, to my utter surprise, the American soldiers greet Dreyer like an old school chum.

"Well, if it isn't old Fritzie," says Soldier A, slapping him on the back. "Haven't seen you since nineteen-fifteen. Do you remember us from that fancy dress ball at the Ambassador's residence in Managua?"

Dreyer looks shocked, but soon recovers.

"How could I forget?" says Dreyer, hiding his surprise. "What a pleasure to see you Captain Simpson. What a pleasure to see you. I didn't expect to run into you out here. What brings two of America's finest war minds to the backwaters of the West Indies? Are you following in the footsteps of your illustrious former president?"

The Americans grin and take another swig of their beers.

"Actually no," says Soldier B. "We're not on a hunting expedition, at least, *not yet*. We're just out here enjoying a bit of fresh air and sunshine. And you, Fritzie, what brings *you* out here? I expected you to race back to Europe to join the war effort. Wasn't it you who wore a German artillery officer's uniform to the Ambassador's ball?"

"Ha-ha! Good memory, Captain Reeves," chuckles Dreyer. "You always had the makings of a superb intelligence officer. Actually, that getup was a gift from my wife's uncle, an avid collector of military memorabilia. I only wore it to please the old codger. As a Swiss citizen, I prefer to remain neutral in these nasty disputes. My personal life is in fact quite dull. To be frank, I don't know where my wife finds the patience to put up with me."

"You could say she married beneath her station," says Captain Reeves.

"Nevertheless," says Dreyer. "I did notice you two avoided answering my question. So, tell me, what brings you out here to these parts? Is your illustrious president seeking to expand his growing empire?"

"You could say that," says Captain Simpson. "We're out here to take a look at some military installations for the War Department. Got to keep one step ahead of the Huns."

All of a sudden Dreyer perks up.

"Military installations?" he says. "Sounds interesting."

"It's an old deal that was first proposed during the Lincoln administration. The Danish islands have enormous strategic value."

"You don't say," says Dreyer. "Of what possible strategic value could a washed-up old Danish sugar colony have for the United States?"

"Call it an insurance policy," says Captain Reeves. "To keep the Huns out of our backyard. We don't want old Tirpitz harboring any false hopes of establishing a submarine base on our side of the Atlantic."

Dreyer erupts in laughter. "Typical American cowboy talk. The Kaiser has plenty of admirers in South America, any one of which would gladly give his ships docking privileges at their ports. The Kaiser has no interest in those rundown Danish islands."

The three soldiers exchange a brief glance.

"So, Dreyer," begins Captain Reeves, changing the subject. "What's in the funny bag?"

"Specimens," says Dreyer, patting the valise. "Valuable seeds of a rare Haitian plant said to have unusual medicinal properties. It's very experimental in nature."

"You know what they say," says Captain Simpson. "All work and no play make Jack a dull boy."

"Guilty as charged," says Dreyer. "But who knows, maybe someday the German flag will fly over the beautiful harbor of St. Thomas. In that case, I would love to receive you gentlemen in my beautiful villa overlooking the harbor."

Dreyer snuffs out his cigar and bids his erstwhile companions goodnight as I realize the implications of his words. As Dreyer leaves, I decide to follow him. I keep to the shadows as he makes his way over to the wireless room where he spends a few minutes harassing the clerk over some missing cables. The clerk sorts through a large stack of messages, selects three, and tosses them to Dreyer, who stuffs them in his pocket and heads for the door. As he breezes past, the wireless operator takes notice of me.

"Up a little late, aren't you, Miss?" he says. "Best get yourself off to bed."

Without a word, I slither out the door, keeping Dreyer in sight while maintaining a safe distance.

He descends an iron staircase until he is far below the decks. All of a sudden, I found myself in a world of gears, cranks, pistons, pumps, shafts, valves, wheels, and boilers, which I take to be the engine room of the ship. The noise is deafening as the boilers churn out clouds of steam, hungering to be fed with more coal, and the pistons move with rapid strokes, like the innards of a gigantic whale. The noise is so terrifying, the air so stifling, that I fear I may never escape this nether world of belching smoke and frenzied machinery.

As I make my way around, I'm surprised to see how oblivious the engine crew appears in their harsh environment. They're hard at work, shoveling coal into the boilers, turning cranks and wheels, studying dials, and occasionally calling out to each other. Overhead, I'm shocked to see an iron grate over which pass the soles of sailors' shoes. Then it dawns on me, I've been led inside the bowels of the ship with no idea how to escape.

Just then, I catch sight of Dreyer heading through the shadows in the direction of some controls. Right before my eyes, Ian's warning about finding suspicious people in the wrong place is coming true, and my heart starts pounding.

All at once a sweaty worker with a coal-stained shirt notices Dreyer in his conspicuous evening suit and top hat, and races over to prevent him from harming himself.

"Excuse me, sir," he says, inserting himself between Dreyer and the controls. "But what the dickens are you doing down here? All passengers must get above decks."

Dreyer protests hotly as he attempts to push the man aside, claiming he just came down to study the equipment. The engine room worker grows testy and a short tussle ensues, ending only when the exasperated man grabs Dreyer by his shirtsleeves and escorts him unceremoniously over to a landing. "This area's off limits to passengers. Please get back upstairs for your own safety."

Breathing heavily, Dreyer stares at the worker with murderous intent. For an instant, I fear that Dreyer will spring on him and do something dreadful. A second later, Dreyer's hand brushes aside his evening jacket and I catch sight of a gleaming pistol lodged underneath. I gasp and muffle my outcry, but before anything happens, other engine workers join the commotion and Dreyer wisely retreats up the stairs.

During the tussle, I notice that one of Dreyer's cable messages flew out of his pocket and landed several feet away. Petrified, I stare at it for a moment, waiting for the moment to pounce. As soon as the coast is clear, I make a dash for it.

"Hold it right there!" growls a voice behind me. "What in the blazes are you doing here? Look fellows, there's another one!"

Caught! Before they can grab me, I dash to the staircase and start climbing as fast as I can until their voice vanish amid the clanking and hammering of the engine room. When I reach the next deck, I race down a corridor in a panic after I realize I'm trapped in the ship's laundry with no hope of escape. With my heart racing out of control, I pass the sick bay, a small surgery, and finally the crew's quarters. Dashing down the passageway, I pass a sleepy sailor clad only in pajamas who stares at me in astonishment. "Sorry to bother you," I yell, as the bewildered sailor scratches his head and shrugs his shoulders.

Thankfully, I reach another staircase which I ascend two steps at a time, hoping I can find my way out of this labyrinth. I arrive at a door marked NO ADMITTANCE and realize too late that I have unwittingly entered the most forbidden area of the ship: the galley.

Fog and steam fill the air, choking me as I follow the scent of baking bread that guides me to the ovens. Once there I find a team of sweaty cooks tending to huge, steaming pots of boiling water as they yell out orders to each other in rapid-fire Italian. The heat from the ovens and the pots is overpowering as I find myself confronted by a huge, sweaty cook who stares at me with a look of astonishment.

The cook waves his arms as he yells something unintelligible. Terrified, I back away, but when he starts toward me, yielding a huge ladle like a foil, I break into a run, making for the nearest exit. What happens next is hard to describe. It's something that only happens in your worst nightmare. As soon as I swing open the door, I crash headfirst into a wine steward carrying a tray of champagne glasses.

The impact causes us to lose our balance, sending us reeling backwards while the glasses continue their forward flight only to meet the wall with a symphonic shattering that results in a thousand tiny shards that crash to the floor like an angry avalanche.

I land with a thud. When I regain my senses, I see the both of us are soaked with champagne (a Bollinger Brut Special Cuvée 1911, and by the taste of it, a splendid year) and the steward's demeanor changes from stunned to enraged.

He picks himself up and starts yelling something I dare not repeat. Wasting no time, I jump to my feet and dash down the corridor. After hurling myself through several nondescript doors, at last I reach the Promenade Deck where I collapse into the nearest deck chair gasping for breath as I pull a blanket over my guilty face.

Despite the catastrophe, I have one small reason to rejoice: I managed to pilfer a German spy's secret cable. Visions of the Victoria Cross and a hero's welcome replace the previous humiliating encounter with the wine steward. I have no doubt that when I present this message to Captain Carey, he'll be so impressed that he will arrange a special awards ceremony in my honor in which he will give a rousing speech praising my self-sacrifice on behalf of the Allies. Naturally, I'll curtsey and explain in my modest manner that I hope my sacrifice will serve as an inspiration to others to help bring an end to the war, and for the rest of the cruise I am wined and dined by the richest passengers. With this pleasant though racing through my mind, I pull out the cable and start reading:

VALUABLE SAMPLES OF PIMENTA RACEMOSA AT TAIL OF BIG DOG 18 28 64 27 CONFIRM URGENT

I feel my brow wrinkling. *Pimenta Racemosa?* Isn't that a Latin word for a plant? Maybe Ian was wrong. Maybe this Dreyer guy really is a Swiss Botanist. Perhaps this has all been a big mistake and Dreyer had good reason for spying down in the Engine Room. I crumple up the worthless message and shove it back inside my pocket.

Suddenly, I sense a dark shadow looming overhead.

"Will you tell me what in Hades is going on?"

Standing over me is Ian McShane, his eyes ablaze.

"What are you talking about?"

"Don't try to fool me," he says, wagging his finger at me. "You smell like a lush. And look at your dress! You're soaked in champagne. Do you have any idea how expensive those bottles were?"

"It wasn't my fault," I protest. "The wine steward bumped into *me* and the rest is history."

Ian's face reddens. "So it was you! I knew it all along, and after you promised to stay out of trouble. Now everyone's saying I'm responsible for that mess."

I slide deeper into my chair, hoping I can disappear. It seems that spy hunting comes with some serious repercussions. I see my Victoria Cross going up in a cloud of smoke.

"Don't be mad at me, I was only trying to help," I say. "Someone has to keep an eye on those dangerous saboteurs."

"The only danger right now is from *you*," he says with a scowl. "Phillips caught you spying on Dreyer in the wireless room, even after I warned you to keep away from him. And Smith says he saw you down in the Engine Room. Says he had to chase you out like a stray cat. Abigail, you're going to get in serious trouble. If Dreyer catches you spying on him, he'll slit your throat like a watermelon. Look what I found in Dreyer's stateroom." He hands me a picture of Dreyer shaking hands with a mustachioed military man sporting a tunic filled with rows and rows of medals and ribbons. "Do you know who this is?"

"I haven't the foggiest idea."

"That's Prince Rupprecht, the Crown Prince of Bavaria. He's the son of King Ludwig, but he's as cunning a military man as you'll ever meet. He's a master of the surprise attack, and from what I hear, Dreyer's no slouch either. Do you see what you're up against?"

"Yes, but I've already made up my mind. I'm going to devote my life to hunting spies and I might as well start with Fritz Dreyer."

Ian takes a deep breath. "Oh, you are, are you?"

"Yes, and you can keep your sextant and compass because my weapons are the spyglass and the pistol. I've found my true calling in life."

"Women," he says, shaking his head. "They're all the same— nothing but trouble!"

"Ian, you don't understand, for the first time in my life I have a chance to make a difference. I want to do something to help the

Allies." I pause to let that sink in. "But I apologize for spilling the champagne. That was foolish of me."

Ian slumps into a deck chair. He pulls off his cap and starts rubbing his head as he lets out a deep sigh.

"I guess I went too far filling yer head with fanciful stories about spies and saboteurs. I should have known a spirited girl like you would stumble into trouble."

"Actually, you did me a favor. Besides, it wasn't a total loss."

"What do you mean?"

I hand him the crumpled telegram. "I stole this from Dreyer."

Ian grabs the telegram and squints in the dim light to read it. "Well, I'll be damned! Now I know why they say it takes a woman to outwit the devil. But hold on a minute…"

"Why?"

"This confounded message was written in code. It's no good unless we get his code book. It must be in his stateroom somewhere. I'll go back and search it, but how? If the Colonel were here, he'd know what to do."

"What Colonel?"

"The one and only Colonel Theodore Roosevelt," he says, grinning. "He sailed with us only a few months ago. In fact, he sat in that very same deckchair almost every day. He was the smartest man I ever met; you could tell just by looking at him he could solve any problem."

"Is that true, or is this just another one of your silly stories?"

"I kid you not," he says. "And there was something truly special about him. When we arrived in Dominica, the whole island showed up to greet him. The town was decorated with British and American flags and they declared the day a national holiday. The people called out, *The King of America* as they cheered and waved their flags."

"How wonderful! Do you swear it's true?"

"It's as true as my eyes are blue," he says. "But the funny thing was, the prim and proper Dominicans, they're black Englishmen, y'know, were bewildered when Mr. Roosevelt pulled up to shore wearing only a plain brown suit and a black hat. Even in Dominica, a far-flung outpost of the British Empire, they're careful to dress proper for every occasion, so you can understand that quite a few eyebrows were raised when they saw Mr. Roosevelt dressed like any ordinary person. It upset their British sense of propriety."

Ian pushes his cap over his eyes and sticks his nose in the air, like a member of the upper crust, causing me to burst into laughter.

"Local dignitaries met him on the wharf," he continues. "And led him over to a podium where he gave a rousing speech praising the loyalty of the Dominican people towards their mother country during times of war. When they heard the grandiose way he spoke, all their worries about his plain clothing melted away. In the end, the people of Dominica gave Colonel Roosevelt such a rousing cheer you'd have thought that King George himself had just spoken to them. And if you don't believe me, you can ask any one of my mates. They were all there."

"Of course, I believe you," I say. "But why are you telling me this story about President Roosevelt?"

"For a good reason," he says. "You see, while Mr. Roosevelt was standing on the podium, a local schoolgirl presented him with a small, wooden cage that held the most charming little parrot you've ever seen. Of course, Mr. Roosevelt graciously accepted the bird, but later, back at the ship, he pulled me aside and asked if I would take the bird off his hands. He explained that he didn't have the proper means to care for it. Naturally I agreed."

"But I don't under—"

"Let me finish the story. The bird and me get along just fine, but since the life of a sailor isn't particularly suited to having pets, I decided that Teddy, that's his name, would be better off with you."

"With me? But you told me you were going to be captain of your own vessel some day. Surely, you'll want Teddy then."

"What's a man without dreams?" he replies. "I started out as a humble boy from Belfast. When I turned fourteen, I ran away from home to escape a bad situation. My father died when I was just a lad and my mother married a brute, a drunk who used to beat me ferociously. I knew that if I didn't run away, he'd kill me. So, I ran down to the docks and talked my way aboard a ship as a cook's assistant. I started at the bottom and worked my way up peeling potatoes, stirring pots, and cleaning out the head. Over time, I learned everything there is to know about sailing and how to defend myself with me fists. But life is no picnic. So, if I can give you just one word of advice, have pity on a man who's down on his luck. Kindness goes a long way in this world. Do it for your old friend Ian."

"Ian, I have my own confession to make. Do you remember when I told you my parents were down in South America?"

"Yes, I sure do."

"I lied. My parents aren't in South America, they're dead. They were killed in a train accident in Panama. That's why they're sending me to St. Thomas to live with my Aunt Esther. I have nowhere else to go. Nobody wanted me."

Ian appears shocked. "Jaysus, Mary, and Joseph! Well, that explains a lot of things. You're all alone in the world. Now it all makes sense. Maybe you and Teddy were meant for each other. And if you give ole Ian McShane a chance, maybe someday I'll take you out on my boat and show you the world. With me at your side you'll never feel alone. I promise you that. Be brave girl! Well, I must be off. I've got watch duty. But I'll swing by tomorrow and bring you the parrot. You, me, and the bird—this could be the start of something beautiful."

Ian's hand brushes my cheek and I feel warm all over as Ian races across the deck, a renewed vigor in his step.

CHAPTER 4

The next evening, the ship is a flurry with excitement. The crew spent the entire day preparing an elaborate masquerade ball with a banquet and a champagne toast. The stewards bring out the best linen, and top each table with a bouquet of tropical flowers, and then adorn the dining room with carnival-like decorations and Chinese lanterns, creating an exciting, festive atmosphere. They place a glittery placard outside the dining room announcing and elaborate dinner to be served of Lobster Thermidor and asparagus tips. One look at that menu and I decide to dine alone in my cabin on the tuna sandwiches and Melba toast.

An hour before dinner, ladies in harem costumes, wigs, and masks, and gentlemen in top hats and frock coats start drifting out of their cabins and head up to the First Class Lounge to partake of the splendid buffet of hors d'oeuvres and cocktails. Soon, the pleasing strains of music float down to my cabin, beckoning me to join the others, but since I'm still in mourning, I decide to refrain. Instead, I read a book from the library as I watch the clock, waiting for Ian. Just as I'm getting ready for bed, I hear a soft knock on my door.

Ian stands there sporting a wide Cheshire cat grin and he reeks of Lobster Thermidor and cigarettes. He pushes a room-service cart topped with a mysterious package draped in sailcloth into my stateroom.

"What in Heaven's name is that?" I say, staring at the wobbly package. "And where were you all night? You smell like a tobacco shop and I was just about to go to bed—"

"Absence makes the heart grow fonder," he says, wheeling the cart as gently as possible. As soon as he shuts the door, he pulls out a flask and takes a long, satisfying swig.

"Are you drunk, Ian McShane?"

"As drunk as a skunk, my lovely lady, but I've never felt better in my life. And now, allow me to present—Teddy."

Ian whisks away the sailcloth to reveal a wicker cage holding the strangest-looking parrot I've ever seen. The bird is bright green, with tufts of red feathers on his chest and the funniest purple splotch on his face that gives him a clownish appearance. I fall instantly in love with this zany bird.

But Teddy is not so sure about me. He cocks his head from side to side, studying me with an inquisitive orange eye. And when Ian gives him a cue, he opens his beak and starts singing, "It's a long w-a-a-y to Tipper-a-a-r-e-e! It's a l-o-o-ng w-a-a-y to go!"

I burst out laughing. "Who taught this bird to sing?"

"Yours truly," he says, with obvious pride. "But Teddy is limited to a strictly Irish repertoire. Later on, you can learn him some Spanish songs. He's got a good ear for dialect."

Ian coaxes the bird on his arm and does a little jig as the bird opens his beak and squawks out, "It's a long w-a-a-a-y-y to Tipper-a-a-a-r-e-e-e! To the sw-e-e-e-test girl I kn-o-o-o-w."

I laugh with delight, but when I reach out to stroke his feathers, Teddy takes a nip at me.

"Not so fast, Queen of the Jungle," says Ian. "Give old Teddy a little time to get to know you. First bring him some seeds, nuts and fruit, and when he gets more comfortable, you can try putting him on yer arm. But don't let him get carried away or he'll be singing to you all night. You don't want to end up bleary-eyed like yours truly. Truth is, I think my mates will be happy when he leaves."

"Are you sure you want to give me Teddy?"

Ian touches my cheek. "I've never been more certain of anything in my life. And this ain't Arthur Guinness talking. The life of a sailor is fraught with hardship. Mates come and go. But once in a while you meet someone you know you were meant to meet. The minute I saw you, I got that feeling. And later, when you told me about your

60

parents, it brought back a lot of painful memories. I wanted to make it up to you." Ian turns to stroke Teddy. "Besides, a smelly, damp ship isn't the proper place for an exotic bird like Teddy, or a delicate lass like you. Take Teddy to your new home on St. Thomas and always keep the wind at your back. And try to remember your old friend Ian. Someday, when I have me own vessel, I'll take you on a tour of the world."

I dive into Ian's arms and hug him with all my might. "Did anyone ever tell you you've got a heart of gold?" I say, staring deeply into his eyes.

"If you found it, you must have the luck of the Irish because no other woman did. Well, I must be off now Abigail. But before I go, allow me to let you in on a little secret."

From his jacket pocket he plucks out some folded papers which he spreads on the desk. They look like crude, technical designs, like something a mechanic or an engineer would draw.

"What is this?"

"Very accurate drawings of the ship's interior," he says, pointing out the different sections. "The parts that most people never see. They show the exact location of the magazines and the engines. I'll wager you a pint of Guinness the writing is German."

"Where did you find them?"

"Where do you think? In Fritz Dreyer's cabin. This proves he came here to do sabotage and if I can just catch him in the act, I'll hand him over to the captain."

"Are you certain?"

"Dead certain. One of our watches claims he saw Dreyer roaming around the powder magazines acting suspicious. That's evidence enough to hand him over to the British for interrogation."

"Powder magazines? Isn't that another word for ammunition?"

"Let me put it to you like this," says Ian, his eyes flaring. "There's enough ammo on this ship to outfit an entire British regiment. Listen to my plan," he says, drawing me so close I can smell the whisky on his breath. "There's a big price on Dreyer's head. If you help me catch him I'll go fifty-fifty in the reward. Are you in?"

"I know I told you I wanted to be a spy hunter but I don't think I'm ready for this."

"Nonsense, you're a natural. Dreyer would never suspect a beautiful girl like you. And there's no better time like the present…"

"I have one condition."

"What's that?"

"I must get off in Curaçao. I can't bear the thought of living with my Aunt Esther. If I help you, do you promise to take me there? Is it a deal?"

Ian shakes his head. "Nothing but trouble. Alright, deal." He grabs me by my arm. "Let's go!" He pulls me out the door and we race down the hall, up a flight of stairs, past a group of masked revelers waltzing in the corridor with champagne glasses.

We reach the dining room and peek in through the etched glass doors. The room is full of diners feasting on chicken consommé, Lobster Thermidor, and potatoes au gratin as they laugh and tell stories about their travels. Harried stewards navigate around the room, presenting course after course as a string band plays a delightful tune to the accompaniment of a singer in a black morning coat and tails. Just then, through billowing clouds of smoke, we catch a glimpse of our prey. Dreyer sits at the center of a table full of rich society types who he regales with tales of his daring exploits hunting botanical specimens in the jungles of Costa Rica and Guatemala as his fork swings wildly in the air.

"Do you see it?" whispers Ian.

"See what?"

"The valise. Look under the table. There's something suspicious about it. It's not a normal looking valise."

I gaze under the table. Sure enough, there it is, wedged in between Dreyer's feet: an ominous-looking black bag about two and a half feet square with silver handles and a brass clasp. It looks far too bulky to be carrying only botanical samples.

"You're right. It's too big to be a valise. Do you think we can grab it?"

"Not while Dreyer's alive," he says, biting his lip. "That crooked devil won't move two inches without it. I'd give my eyeteeth to find out what's inside."

Minutes later, Dreyer rises to leave. He kisses the ladies' hands and bows to the gentlemen, then bends down to retrieve his precious valise.

Ian hisses. "Get ready. Now's our chance."

"For what?"

Ian grins. "To start your career."

I open my mouth to speak, but Ian puts his hand over it.

Dreyer shoots across the room like a bullet, heading straight toward us. My heart races as I look for a place to take cover, but it's too late to hide. Thinking quickly, Ian shoves me behind a potted plant, but I lose my balance and topple over backwards, landing on my backside just as the plant crashes to the floor. Meanwhile, Ian bends down and pretends to be polishing a handrail, careful to keep his face hidden. But nothing in the world can hide his flaming red hair.

Peeking through the branches, I hold my breath, expecting an altercation. Luckily, Dreyer sails past us, never noting the two amateur spy hunters who managed to destroy a fine Chinese porcelain vase in the name of helping the Allies. All the while, the mysterious German keeps an iron grip on the valise like a soldier gripping his rifle for dear life.

Ian jumps to his feet and trails Dreyer down the hall. A minute later he hurries back, motioning for me to follow him.

"He's headed for the boat deck," Ian hisses. "Hurry up. Don't let him escape."

"But he's got a gun."

"I'll have to make sure he never uses it."

"Good luck!"

Together we dash over to the landing and start ascending a narrow staircase, mindful of the frightful yellow moon above us, the churning ocean below us. A blast of wind whips through my hair and pushes me closer to the edge of the railing, forcing me to look below to the inky blackness of the raging swells. The ship rocks to and fro, as if we are battling an impending storm; without warning the night has turned ferocious, the ocean a dangerous abyss, the wind a howling menace. How I wish I could be in my old bed back home. How I wish I had never entered this terrifying world of sabotage.

As we continue our upwards advance, I send up a silent prayer that Dreyer won't turn his angry revolver on his pursuers. Ian, on the other hand, is as calm as a rock, oblivious to the mortal danger we're facing. When Dreyer reaches the Boat Deck, he stops short. A sudden noise has caused his whole body to freeze before he regains his senses and scoots into a quiet corner.

Dreyer cautiously turns his head to the side as if he suspects somebody has been following him. My heart thumps wildly as Ian tightens his grip on my hand. Together, we slide silently behind a bulkhead and take cover behind the nearest lifeboat. From the safety of our concealed position, we follow Dreyer's every move. At the right moment we climb into the lifeboat and pull the canvas over our heads.

Ian takes out his trusty flask and downs a large swig of whiskey, and then offers the rest to me. I look at it cross-eyed, then take it, hold my breath and swallow a large gulp. The fiery liquid burns down my throat and settles somewhere in the vicinity of my knees. But the whiskey does its job; it has taken the edge off my fear. Ian lifts the canvas of the lifeboat ever so slightly, his elbow lodged in my ear, and peeks outside.

He says Dreyer is pacing back and forth like a guard on watch. He waits for the other passengers to clear the deck by pretending to be inspecting the lifeboats and life preservers. Once Dreyer is alone, he crouches down behind a lifeboat and pops open the lid of his valise. In the glow of a deck light, we are amazed to see that the inside of the valise is an intricate system of coils, tubes, and a tiny dynamo, all of which resembles a portable wireless telegraph device. Once Dreyer sets the batteries in motion, we're startled by the hissing sounds, sputtering, and the flashing of sparks that accompany a wireless radio. He pulls out a sheet of paper from his waistcoat and taps out a message with expert precision. Fortunately, the clacking of the keys drowns out the chattering of my teeth. Even Ian is fascinated by Dreyer's fearless demeanor. We are watching a spy in motion and I've never been more fascinated in my life.

"Well, I'll be damned," whispers Ian. "It's a portable wireless radio. Crafty little device! But in order for him to send messages, there must be a radio station somewhere in the vicinity, or at the very least a German ship prowling these waters. There's no way to know for sure. I'd love to know what secrets Dreyer is telling them."

"Do you know Morse code?" I say.

"Yes, but that won't help. Everything he taps out is in code. The filthy scoundrel!"

The wind picks up and lightning strikes in the distance, lighting the sky with ghostly apparitions of purple, mauve, and grey tinged with violent streaks of silver. A sudden clap of thunder startles

Dreyer, causing him to cease tapping and slam the valise shut. He locks it and places the key in his waistcoat, picks himself up, and scurries off through the shadows. When Ian gives the all clear, we tumble out of the lifeboat.

"Abby, go back to your cabin," he says, sweat pouring down his face. "I'm going to arrest Dreyer. This part of the operation is too dangerous for you."

"Ian, *please* get help. Dreyer's armed."

"I can handle the bastard meself, but I can't guarantee *your* safety. Now get moving."

"Alright, but please be careful."

Fighting the wind, and with thunder booming in my ears, I head to the landing. After descending to the Main Deck, I hear the unmistakable sound of a scuffle against the backdrop of roaring thunder and furious lightning: punches, kicks, grunts, the clang of metal, a wooden deck chair crashing to the ground, and a roaring clap of thunder that clashes with a blood-curdling scream that sends shock waves coursing down my spine. Ian is in trouble!

And then I see him. A shadowy figure hastens across the boat deck like a ghostly streak. He descends the steps two at a time, shielding his face with his jacket to conceal his identity. Though his features are obscured, I'm almost certain it's Dreyer. Ignoring my instinct for self-preservation, I race toward him, attempting to prevent his escape. To my horror, I collide head on him, causing both of us lose our balance. Dreyer curses loudly and with his powerful arm, sends me hurtling backwards against the deck.

I hit the ground and see stars all around. Pain shoots up my back. When I'm finally able to focus, I catch sight of an eerie blotch on Dreyer's shirt. Is it blood? Momentarily out of breath, I catch the glint of a knife in the glow of a deck light. He points it at me, his eyes gleaming like a lynx as a vicious sneer forms at the corners of his mouth. I feel a cold fear as I inch backwards, attempting to put some distance between me and that menacing glimmer of steel in his hand, but Dreyer inches closer.

He raises the knife, preparing to strike, and before I know it, I let out a blood-curdling scream from the depths of my throat. I kick my legs and flail my arms in a vain attempt to save my own life, and then everything goes black.

The next thing I know, someone is shaking me awake.

"Miss, are you alright?"

I open my eyes and feel my heart racing. When my eyes focus, I see that the man attempting to revive me is an ordinary deckhand. He must have heard my scream and rushed over.

"Please help," I say. "A man tried to kill me!"

Just then, a whistle blast pierces the night air. Sailors rush around in a panic, shouting out commands as they wave their flashlights in a thousand directions. Captain Carey races from the bridge and heads up to the Boat Deck, his face drawn, followed by a group of officers, some of which are brandishing pistols.

A sailor yells down from the Boat Deck and the men race up the stairs. My heart sinks when I realize that something terrible must have happened to Ian. By now, panic has erupted throughout the ship as passengers stream from every nook and cranny with worried looks on their faces. I assure the sailor I am well enough to return to my cabin, and he hurries off to join the others. But I have other plans. Against my better judgment, I head back up to the Boat Deck hoping and praying that by some miracle Ian is still alive.

My hopes are immediately dashed. A group of sailors huddles against the night sky iridescent with thunder and lightning, bracing themselves against the raging winds, their voices murmuring in hushed, frightened tones. I force my way through them, expecting to see the worst. What I find is a sight that horrifies me. Lying on the deck amidst shards of broken glass and battered deck chairs is an ominous pool of blood. About a foot away, an abandoned sailor's cap braces against the wind, the last remnants of Ian McShane.

"Seaman, retrieve that cap," says Captain Carey, grim-faced.

"Aye, Captain," replies the seaman, bending down to retrieve the forlorn object.

The sailor trains his flashlight on the inside of the cap and reads the name aloud. "Captain, this hat belongs to Ian McShane."

"Sweet Mother of Pearl!" says the captain with a worried look. "Find McShane. Search the entire ship if you have to. I want to know what happened here. There's going to be a thorough investigation."

The sailors fan out, searching every inch of the decks with their flashlights then proceed to carry out a full inspection of all the lounges, eating quarters, the exercise room, library, and all the crew's quarters. But Ian is nowhere to be found. He simply vanished.

Next, the crew turns on the searchlights and they conduct a full sweep of the surrounding waters. My heart sinks when the search turns up nothing. Ian has vanished and is in all likelihood dead, murdered at the hands of Fritz Dreyer.

And then I realize something terrible. I'm the only person on the ship that knows Ian McShane was going to arrest Fritz Dreyer just before he disappeared. And worse than that, Fritz Dreyer has seen my face.

CHAPTER 5

In the wake of Ian's disappearance and presumed death, the captain questions a few passengers, but no one reports seeing anything suspicious. I stay in the background lest I also become one of Dreyer's victims down in Davy Jones' locker.

Mostly I sit alone in my cabin, teary-eyed and full of regret. I have started keeping a diary which helps me to organize my thoughts and become more observant. Teddy observes me with one apprehensive orange eye, occasionally ruffling his feathers and casting suspicious glances in my direction. It will take a while before we get used to each other.

I can't stop blaming myself for what happened to Ian. I should have realized it would end in disaster and stopped him from chasing after Dreyer. How can I ever forgive myself?

The scuttlebutt among the crew is that Ian had accumulated large gambling debts and the fight was over money. While no one can say with certainty that Ian had been gambling that night, there's no other explanation for such a violent altercation. Since Ian's disappearance, the crew's spirits are noticeably damp; they go about their business with more caution and refrain from mingling with the passengers. The entire ship is gloomy.

I'm counting the hours until we reach St. Thomas. Curaçao is now a distant, unattainable dream. To my eternal relief, two days later we finally arrive. A wave of relief washes over me to think I will soon be safe from Dreyer's clutches.

Through the porthole, a charming sight greets me. After we sail through two jagged cliffs, we enter into the most splendid natural harbor I've ever seen. The water is an incandescent turquoise blue that sparkles under the hot tropical sun. Schooners and sloops bob gently in the harbor as pelicans and petrels soar overhead, greeting us with hungry cries before crashing into the water. We pass several ships whose passengers wave at us. There's a Danish cargo ship, a Russian frigate, and a Venezuelan cruiser, all bearing their native flags and colors, looking resplendent in the picturesque harbor.

Charlotte Amalie is more beautiful than anything I could have imagined. The little town sits at the base of several tall green mountains covered with dense tropical foliage while the harbor bustles with activity. Along the waterfront sits a line of stone warehouses with massive black doors through which swarthy men load cargo brought in from the ships. Further back, charming Danish colonial buildings in pastel colors bask under the shade of enormous mahogany trees, while dotting the hillsides are the famous red-roofed houses of Charlotte Amalie. They are connected to the town via a series of steep stairways built into the sides of the hills with ballast brought over during the age of tall ships. Adding to the charm are a variety of tropical gardens bursting with purple bougainvillea, red hibiscus, frangipani, roses, and white gardenias. But everything pales under the towering coconut palms that line the streets and alleyways, swaying gracefully like fans in the cool ocean breeze. The beauty of the town takes my breath away.

My eyes settle on Fort Christian, the majestic red Danish fort with a clock tower built in 1671 to protect the harbor from pirates and invading armies, while just in front sits the charming green Barracks, the home of the Danish Gendarmes, who I spot riding through the town in their tall blue caps and blue coats.

Even more charming than the scenery are the delightful residents of Charlotte Amalie. Ladies in fine muslin dresses and parasols sashaying graciously along King's Wharf, while their counterparts, the market women, move with slow, sensuous strides, bearing their burdens on sturdy, turbaned heads. Everywhere you look, barefoot children scamper about, diving into the water to search for coins or offering flowers to visitors with delightful smiles and squeals of delight when they are offered a prize in return. Along the shore, able-bodied fishermen with sinewy muscles tend to rickety schooners overflowing with bananas, papayas, sapodillas, coconuts, tamarinds, and guava, while sure-footed farmers in straw hats lead donkey carts down to market. It is evident to me that the lifeblood of Charlotte Amalie is her residents and their timeless way of life.

As soon as the *Guiana* is secured to the dock, a team of dockworkers springs into action. From tin-roofed storage sheds, they haul burlap bags filled with cotton, yams, bananas, calabash, mangoes, barrels of rum, molasses and sugar, and store them in the ship's hold. Meanwhile, gaggles of children appear on the scene, offering to dive into the crystalline water to retrieve coins the passengers toss in for their amusement.

The *Guiana's* sudden appearance seems to have caused a small commotion as enterprising boatmen have decided to seize the opportunity for profit. Soon, a small flotilla of boats is paddling furiously to our side, their sailors, Natives in straw hats, shouting to get our attention. They call to us in their sing-song Calypso dialect, coaxing us to buy their trinkets that they toss into the air with zeal. They show us an entire assortment of straw hats, baskets, coral jewelry, and conch shells, the prices of which are subject to constant bargaining and haggling. Other boatmen offer to ferry the passengers into town for a small fee. The excitement in the air is palpable; I can hardly wait to get my feet on dry land again.

And then another curious sight catches my eye. Sitting on the wharf is an enormous mountain of black coal that is baking under the broiling hot sun. Surrounding it is an army of women wearing turbans, straw hats, and sooty, shapeless dresses. Each woman carries a large straw basket which they fill with the dirty lumps of coal. Once full, the women heave the baskets over their heads and haul them up the ship's gangway with slow, plodding footsteps. When they reach the hot deck, they dump the contents into the blackened coal chute, and then offer their hand to a waiting quartermaster, who pays them with three blackened pennies. Once paid, the women turn and descend the gangway back to the wharf where they repeat the process all over again. I find myself moved by this poignant scene.

Suddenly, a gruff voice behind me speaks.

"Those my dear are the coal carriers."

I spin around to find the purser, the one I tried to deceive when I first boarded the ship. As I recall my shameful behavior, I start to blush. To my relief, he pats my head and takes his place at the railing beside me. When I peek over at him, his blue eyes are gazing down at the coal carriers in a kind, sympathetic manner, which puts me at ease. I find myself edging closer to his side.

"Each woman is capable of delivering around two hundred baskets of coal to each ship that arrives for coaling," he says, turning to face me. "Did you know that, Miss Maduro?" I shake my head. "Most people have no idea how much coal it takes to move one of these large steamers, many tons. These poor women work every day, rain or shine, with almost no time for rest. And in return for their hard work, they receive just a pittance."

"How cruel," I say. "To work so hard for so little pay."

"Oh, it's no different anywhere else, but these women are a different breed. They're fighters. About twenty years ago they banded together under their chosen leader and organized a strike, demanding higher wages. They caused the shipping lines sit up and take notice, but the matter is not as simple as you think. Because of the war and the danger posed by the German U-boats, the steamship companies are suffering terrible losses. They can't afford to pay these women more than a dollar or two per day without cutting into their profits. As it is, there isn't enough business going around for every steamship company to make a living."

"How awful to have to lift such heavy baskets, it seems they live a very hard life."

"Indeed they do," he says. "But these women are a hardy lot. As long as the ships keep coming to coal here, they'll have bread on the table, but if the war drives the steamship lines out of business, their life will get even harder. Let's hope that day never happens. Well Miss Maduro, I hope you enjoy your visit to St. Thomas, and I apologize for any inconvenience you may have suffered."

The purser doffs his hat and turns to leave.

"One question, sir," I say. "What about Ian McShane? What's to be done about him?"

He shakes his head. "The poor devil's been listed lost at sea. He'd been drinking heavily and gambling on the night he disappeared, and it appears that he paid for his folly with his life. Never caught the bugger that did it."

The purser holds out his hand and I shake it.

"Good luck to you, Miss Maduro."

"Thank you, sir."

As I watch the purser make his way across the deck, I pity the task he has ahead of him informing Ian's mother about his death. The war, it seems, has claimed another nameless victim.

As soon as I'm packed and ready to go, I grab Teddy's cage and wave goodbye as I descend the *Guiana's* gangplank for the last time. The sailors tip their caps at me and wish me luck as I smile back at them and thank them. Never could I have dreamed that after such an awkward entrance our parting would be so bittersweet.

When I alight on shore, I realize that I have a whole new set of problems. There's no one to greet me. It's as if my Aunt Esther has forgotten about me. While I watch the other passengers crowding into waiting horse carriages and motor cars for the drive into town, Teddy and I remain conspicuously alone. I search in all directions for someone to help as the sun burns my head and mosquitoes buzz in my ears. And then my heart stops when I realize that Teddy and I are not alone.

A short distance away the hulking figure of a man sits and watches our every move. He stares at me with piercing yellow eyes, and when he jumps to his feet and starts toward us, my stomach lurches to my throat as I search frantically for help, but there's nowhere to go, nowhere to hide.

CHAPTER 6

Suddenly, I have an idea, a brilliant plan that may save my life. Not far away, a dilapidated, two-seater carriage sits under the shade of a leafy tree. Its driver, an elderly West Indian man, appears to be fast asleep in the driver's seat. With each snore his body rises and falls like a ship bobbing on the ocean. Not wasting a second, I hitch up my skirt and race to his side, praying that he will be able to take me to my Aunt Esther's house. This old man and his broken-down carriage may be my last chance to get out of here.

As I approach, I see that the driver is even older than I suspected. He must be over ninety years old. His hair is like pure white cotton, growing in sparse tufts on his wrinkled, ebony-colored head. His bony arms are cloaked in leathery skin and protrude from under a threadbare shirt with numerous holes and missing buttons. On his face is a look of angelic contentment.

Gingerly, I tug at the old man's sleeve, urging him to wake up. To my relief, the old man lifts his scrawny arm to rub his eyes, and when his cloudy eyes finally open, he focuses them on me. All at once he breaks into a wide, partial-toothed grin.

"Well, good marning to you, little lady," he says in a sing-song Calypso accent, just as the workers from St. Lucia, Jamaica, and Barbados used to speak back in Panama. I used to love listening to their good-natured banter and their easy laughter as I traipsed through town on my way to and from school. "I've been waiting all day for a Miss Abigail Maduro who was supposed to arrive by steamship from Panama. Do you happen to know her?"

My mouth drops open. "That's me! I'm Abigail Maduro. And who are you?"

"Thank you, Lord Jesus!" he says, slapping his knee. "I was so scared I had missed you. Don't want to vex Miss Nana Jane."

"Who's Miss Nana Jane?"

"She de caretaker of de old Maduro house," he says. "She sent me down to de docks to fetch you. My name is Mr. Isaiah. For ovah fifty years I was Mr. Maduro's personal driver, but now I just tinker around de house and take care of old Clara here. Once or twice a year I take Miss Esther Maduro out for a ride, but I can't remember de last time she went out. I think it was back in nineteen-ten. Well, get in, get in. De whole house waiting on you most anxious ever since we received dat humbug telegram with de awful news about your mother and father, God rest their souls. De old man would have keeled ovah with a heart attack had he been alive."

Mr. Isaiah hobbles down and opens the door for me. Old Clara turns her head to size me up, and then goes back to pulling weeds from the ground. Taking Teddy's cage in hand, I climb into the passenger's seat directly behind Mr. Isaiah. He whistles to a dockworker, who rushes over to help load my trunk. When I glance over at the menacing dark man, I find him sitting down in his favorite spot, sulking and scowling as he swats at mosquitoes buzzing around his head. And then, straining every muscle in his body, Mr. Isaiah heaves himself into the driver's seat, clicks his tongue, and Old Clara starts off down a dirt road that wends around the harbor and back toward town.

We arrive in Charlotte Amalie to a lively procession of horse carriages, donkey carts, and gendarmes patrolling on horseback. As we pass the Fish Market and King's Wharf, I delight in studying the colorful inhabitants of Charlotte Amalie: turbaned ladies in colorful dresses stroll along the wharf while longshoremen heave crates into the many warehouses that line the harbor. Children run barefoot on the cobblestones, and chickens and dogs add to the liveliness of the scene.

Just off the wharf we pass a park and a large hotel, and across the street we see the post office and a custom-house. Tall mahogany trees lord over the town, and frangipani trees and hibiscus bushes add

74

color and beauty. We head down Dronningens Gade, which the natives call Main Street, the commercial center of town, and turn up a side street that is lined with small wooden shacks topped with tin roofs that leads us toward the back of town. The road ascends a steep hill then turns sharply left and keeps climbing until we are about halfway up the hill.

"This is Synagogue Hill," explains Mr. Isaiah. "Part of Queen's Quarter, where your grandfather's house is located."

By now my heart swells with happy memories. All the stories my mother told me about Charlotte Amalie suddenly spring to life. Are these the alleyways where Blackbeard the pirate and the Mexican General Santa Anna roamed back in their day? Are the drunks that stumble out of bars really pirates in disguise? Is there buried treasure hidden on the cays and sandbanks of the Danish West Indies?

We halt in front of a fine villa with a sloping white roof, a covered balcony and large picture windows that I recognize at once as my father's boyhood home. As we approach, I see that the house is very old and poorly maintained as evident by its sagging balcony, missing steps, and fading and chipped paint. But this house has been in my family for a century, and now it's my new home—I must make the best of things. Taking a deep breath, I cover Teddy's cage with a shawl, and follow Mr. Isaiah up the creaky staircase, careful to avoid tripping on the broken steps.

Glancing at the houses at the bottom of the hill, a memory comes flooding back. Another story my mother told me was how back in the old days there were many Maduro families, some rich and some poor. The rich families always lived at the top of Synagogue Hill, where the breezes blew and the air was cooler, while the poor families could only afford living in tin-roofed shacks down at the bottom. Now that I see the forlorn state of Aunt Esther's house, I realize that while it sits close to the top of Synagogue Hill, it more closely resembles the ramshackle cottages down at the bottom.

Mr. Isaiah leads me inside and to my surprise the house is dimly-lit and quiet. There are no pleasing smells coming from the kitchen, no echoes of a woman's voice, no sounds of piano playing, and no whirring of a sewing machine. The only faces that greet me are those that stare out from the faded photographs that line the walls, faces that gaze with silent, lonely resignation.

So much of the house's décor evokes the past. The furniture is all hand-carved mahogany, and everywhere I look there are pictures of distant relatives in old-fashioned clothes. The sofas are sagging and faded, the china cabinet with its blue Danish porcelain is dusty, and hanging askew is a painting of a three-masted schooner that once belonged to my great-grandfather, the *Bathsheba*. All at once I feel as if I'm surrounded by pieces of the island's history that are intertwined with my own family's history. The feeling is overwhelming.

Just then, an elderly West Indian woman with a beautiful face and large child-like eyes appears from a side door. Her face is the color of nutmeg, and it glows with warmth that radiates from within. Basking in her presence, I feel instantly at home. Mr. Isaiah introduces her as Nana Jane, the caretaker of the Maduro house.

Nana Jane carries herself with an unmistakable air of dignity, as if she were the queen of the house and not the mere caretaker. She wears a high-necked dress of blue muslin that is decked with a white apron, and on her head she wears a white turban that frames her face elegantly. She approaches me and studies me with great interest.

"Why, it is Abigail! You have your father's eyes, but your face belongs to your mother," she says, grasping me by the shoulders and hugging me so tight I can smell the scent of cinnamon and cloves radiating from her dress. "Just look at her, Mr. Isaiah! Can you believe Isaac's baby has finally come home?"

"Praise the Lord," says Mr. Isaiah. "I remember the day Isaac and Rebecca left like it was yesterday."

"Abigail, did your parents ever tell you about ole Nana Jane?" she says, her eyes twinkling with delight.

"My father told me you were his *yaya*, his nanny," I say. "He said you taught him to blow a conch shell and dance the quadrille. He always laughed when he remembered how you made him put on a suit and tie and taught him to behave like a proper gentleman. He said you had eyes in the back of your head."

Nana Jane laughed with delight. "How I miss Isaac! What a mischievous boy he was. He was the light of my life." Nana Jane dries her eyes with her apron as she smiled wistfully. "Mr. Isaiah, do you remember how we used to chase little Isaac all ovah de place like a silly mongoose?"

"Oh yes," says the old man through hearty chuckles. "Nevah could sit still that boy. Hard to believe he's already basking in de Lord's presence."

"Amen, well at least now we have Isaac's baby to comfort us in our old age. She'll be safe and sound here with us. No trouble will vex her as long as Nana Jane is alive. I'll make sure of dat."

"Yes, indeed," repeats Mr. Isaiah. "Safe and sound."

Nana Jane fixes her eyes on Teddy's cage. "And what is dis?" she says, peeling off the cover, causing Teddy to squawk in surprise. Startled, Nana Jane jumps backwards and wrinkles her nose. "Your Aunt Esther is not gonna like dis bird one bit. You best get rid of him right now."

"Get rid of Teddy? Never! He's special. He once belonged to President Theodore Roosevelt."

"To *who*?"

"Theodore Roosevelt," I repeat just in case she didn't hear me correctly. "You know, *the president of the United States of America.*"

All at once the two old-timers burst out laughing as if that was the funniest thing they ever heard.

"Some child," says Nana Jane, wiping her eyes. "I ain't nevah heard such a cockamamie story. Next you gonna tell me the captain of your ship was King George de Fifth? Or maybe it was de Kaiser himself?" More house-shaking laughter follows. I shift my weight uncomfortably, starting to feel a little foolish. Nana Jane wipes tears from her eyes and slaps Mr. Isaiah on the back, and then she pulls me into the dining room and tells me to sit down while she fetches Aunt Esther. As soon as she leaves, I turn my attention to admire the once-exquisite room.

I slide my hand across the dining room table, admiring the intricate carvings and inlaid marble patterns. Yellow stuffing peaks out from the fancy embroidered mahogany chairs, and antique Chinese porcelain vases now hold only desiccated flowers that seem to have collapsed from heat exhaustion. In spite of the forlorn state of the house, it still has a certain spark. I'm fairly certain that with a little cleaning and polishing, the crystal chandelier will once again sparkle like diamonds, and the oriental carpet will glimmer like gold. Although Aunt Esther's house is old, it's not beyond hope.

Once you wipe away the layers of dust and cobwebs, the paintings on the wall still look magnificent, and the fancy silver and crystal in the china closet hearken back to better days, when fancy dinner parties would enliven the evenings with song and dance.

Those days are gone now. When the beautiful town of Charlotte Amalie began her long, sad decline, so did my grandfather's old mansion on Synagogue Hill. I close my eyes and imagine being at one of my grandfather's fancy dinner parties dressed in an exquisite satin gown. To my delight a dashing young gentleman in a dark jacket, waistcoat, and white tie approaches me, bows, and invites me to dance. As he leads me to the floor, I catch my reflection in a mirror, amazed that I have grown to be so refined and elegant for my age. To the melody of an imaginary string quartet, my partner and I wrap ourselves in each other's arms and spin in time to the music. As we twirl across the floor, my arms move faster and faster, spinning and circling until—thwack! My arm grazes one of the chandelier's low-hanging crystals, sending it hurtling across the room where it lands at the center of an antique brass mirror, causing an unsightly jagged crack. I freeze and stare at the damaged mirror in horror. Suddenly a gruff voice behind me blurts out, "What do you think you're doing?"

Gingerly I turn around to find none other than Aunt Esther staring at me, her face a terrifying scowl.

CHAPTER 7

After an interminable number of minutes, I attempt to conjure up a reasonable explanation for my outburst. My mind goes blank.

"Well? Don't keep me waiting all day."

Clearly Aunt Esther is not one to suffer fools gladly. Sweat trickles down my forehead while I glance at the broken mirror in distress. Apparently, my aim was impeccable. The force of the crystal gave it a permanent crack down the middle, but the damage to the mirror is minor considering the damage I caused to my first impression with Aunt Esther.

"I—I'm terribly sorry, Aunt Esther. It was an accident."

"Sorry?" She marches over to the mirror to survey the damage while I stand there feeling miserable and stupid. Aunt Esther is every bit as spiteful as her letters suggest. Her delight in belittling others glaringly apparent.

From her present state, you would never know that at one time Miss Esther Maduro was considered one of the great beauties of Charlotte Amalie. But that was many years ago. Time has not been kind to her. Now she's tired and faded, like a withered rose shrouded in black, with a suffocating neckline and a faded pearl necklace that dangles precipitously from her shriveled neck, her sole allowance for glamour. Her coarse, graying hair is pulled back severely and brought to rest atop her head in a disordered bun. Her eyes glare at me with menace and spite.

She plants her hands on her hips. "Well? What do you have to say for yourself?"

"I'm very sorry, Aunt Esther. It was an accident."

"Accidents are what happen during earthquakes, hurricanes, and tidal waves," she snaps. "This damage was deliberate."

"No, no," I protest. "I was only dancing—"

"You mean, you were prancing around like a fool. That mirror has been in the family for generations, but I see it was doomed the minute you arrived."

I look down at my feet, praying for salvation. Thankfully, Nana Jane enters the room and approaches Aunt Esther with one of her eyebrows conspicuously raised.

"Now Miss Esther is that any way to greet your niece?" she says in a cool, even tone. "She's been traveling more than a week now. Mr. Isaiah went to fetch her down at de dock. She must be hungry and tired. We must make Abigail feel welcome."

"I suppose we must," says Aunt Esther, twirling her pearls absent-mindedly. "Well, we knew this day was coming sooner or later. Nana Jane, I seem to have misplaced my spectacles, will you please fetch them for me?"

Nana Jane retreats in search of the missing glasses, leaving me alone with my accuser. Remembering my mother's advice, I try to charm her with a little old-fashioned courtesy.

"It's not nice the way you order Nana Jane around," I say.

Aunt Esther's face blanches. "*What* did you say?"

"She's older than you and deserves more respect."

"Now you listen to me," says Aunt Esther, her face an unremitting scowl. "I won't stand for any back talk. I may as well say up front I'm a little too old to start mothering. I run my house like a tight ship. I have strict rules and I expect you to follow them. There will be no parties, no teas, and no ladies' card games. I frown on all forms of socializing. Lights out at nine o'clock and I expect you to show up for meals on time. You're here only because it's my duty as your closest relative to provide a home for you, but I still expect you to contribute to the household expenses. I've arranged for you to take in a little sewing. I trust your mother taught you how to sew a buttonhole and mend a hem?"

"Yes," I say, alarmed by the threatening tone in her voice.

"Good," she says, crossing her arms. "Then we should get along fine. Put down your things over there and go wash up for supper. Cooky Betty will bring you food from the kitchen."

I wash my hands at the spigot and take my assigned place at the table. Aunt Esther nervously taps her fingers as she waits for the food to appear. After a few minutes of uncomfortable silence, she screams out, "Cooky Betty! Get in here now!"

The sound of broken glass rings out followed by the banging of pots and pans, after which a chubby West Indian woman waddles into the dining room bearing a meager tray of food as she makes a crude sucking noise by pressing her tongue against her teeth.

"Stop howling like a hound dog! I'm coming as fast as I can," says the cook, dumping the tray in front of me so that the food splashes on my dress. "All de time she be harassing me with her outrageous loud demands. Always wanting something; always needing something. I can't get no peace inside dis crazy house!"

I pick up a discarded fork and toy with the food, which looks like nothing I've ever seen before. It's a stew of sorts, with peppers, onions, and pungent meat alongside a mushy mound of cornmeal. When I look at Aunt Esther, she raises an eyebrow and glares back at me.

"Well?" she says with mounting impatience. "Are you going to eat it or stare at it all day?"

"Aunt Esther, what is this food? I've never seen it before."

"It's called *fish and fungi*, and you better get used to it. It's a staple dish around here, along with peas and rice, although we're a little short of rice as of late."

"There's not much on my plate, *whatever* it is."

"In this house we don't waste food."

Nana Jane reappears and hands Aunt Esther her spectacles, which she affixes over her nose and uses them to study me, as if I were a bug under a magnifying glass.

"Extraordinary," she says, touching my cheek with her cold, clammy hands. I stiffen at her touch. "An exact replica of your mother. But you've got your father's clumsiness. What a mistake it was for your parents to run away to Panama. I warned them that nothing good would come of it, and now they've paid the ultimate price leaving me to raise their luckless daughter."

Nana Jane appears shocked. "For shame, Miss Esther! You can't talk like that. Miss Abigail is your niece. She's your flesh and blood."

"It wasn't a mistake," I say. "We were happy in Panama. Papi was very successful and he had lots of friends. Everybody loved him. Papi said he begged you to come live with us but you refused. If you didn't want me to come live with you, then why did you send for me? Maybe I should go back home."

"There's no home for you to go back to," she says, cleaning her spectacles. "You're an orphan now. Just remember that in spite of everything I took you in. The least you can do is show me a little respect and courtesy."

"That's not what I meant—"

"I know what you meant. You're just like all the others, haughty and ungrateful. There was no reason for your parents to run away to Panama leaving me to hold the bag. We had a perfectly good business right here. It was all I could do to pay the bills once your grandfather got sick. And now I'm left with even *more* responsibilities. Did I ask for this trouble?"

"No, Aunt Esther, and neither did I. We're both in this mess together."

Aunt Esther's eyes flared. "You're just like all the rest. I've written to Cousin Pauline a thousand times complaining about the way her family has neglected me. But do you think she cares? Do you think she feels the least bit sorry about my plight? And your Uncle David continues to ignore my letters. And your father, my dear youngest brother, not once did he ask for my forgiveness."

My mouth goes dry. "What did my father do that he needed your forgiveness?"

"It's none of your business. It's between him and me. Now finish your meal while I contemplate your future."

As I watch in astonishment, Aunt Esther heads over to the wash basin and starts scrubbing her hands with a coarse brush. My astonishment turns to shock and consternation as she scrubs them so hard, I fear they will bleed. And all the while she starts mumbling something under her breath that sounds quite upsetting. My heart sinks with the thought that my life will never be the same. The day my parents died was the day my childhood crumbled to dust. Whenever Aunt Esther looks at me, she will always remember how my parents abandoned her and left her to her fate. I will become the repository of all her anguish and feelings of failure. My future feels like a heavy stone on my chest slowly suffocating me.

After dinner Nana Jane shows me to my room. Immediately I'm certain the room belonged to my grandmother because all her things are still here: her antique silver brush set, her vanity table, a handmade crochet bedspread, and silk slippers. All the furniture is made from fine, carved mahogany and the room has an extraordinary view of the harbor through wooden jalousies.

Nana Jane hangs up Teddy's cage and coos to him, then goes to work unpacking my trunk. I notice that Nana Jane seems unfazed by my Aunt Esther's bitter tirades. She watches, listens with mute ears, and keeps a good watch over Aunt Esther. I am drawn to Nana Jane's gentle demeanor and quiet strength; I hope she will be a much-needed ally during this trying time.

"You know your Auntie's not going to like dis crazy parrot one bit," says Nana Jane, sticking a finger in Teddy's cage. "You're just lucky she didn't catch him. So what do you call dis outrageous bird anyway?"

"His name is Teddy, after his former owner."

"You still believe that harebrained story?" she says, giving me an I-know-better-than-you look. "Don't you know dey was making *pappyshow* of you, silly girl?"

"Pappyshow?"

"It means dey was making *fun* of you," she explains. "Who told you dis most outrageous story anyhow?"

"One of the sailors on the ship," I say. "He said President Roosevelt sailed on the same ship not more than three months ago."

"Seerious?" she says, considering the plausibility of that statement. "That may veree well be true. President Roosevelt came to this islan' not too long ago. Miss Lucy said he came here to inspect de harbor facilities. There was a big dinner for him ovah at de Grand Hotel with the Governor's Secretary and a delegation of veree important members of high society."

"President Roosevelt came here to inspect the harbor?"

"Nobody ever told you?" says Nana Jane, raising her eyebrows. "The island of St. Thomas is becoming veree important. The Americans wanting to buy these very islands from Denmark, but Miss Lucy says that Governor Helweg-Larsen refuses to talk about it.

He told King Christian that the islands must always remain a part of Denmark. He said, 'It's a matter of national pride.'"

"How would Miss Lucy know?"

"She knows everything dat goes on inside de governor's mansion," explains Nana Jane. "She is the Governor's cook."

I look at Nana Jane's childlike eyes and her deep-brown, regal features and say, "So tell me Nana Jane, would you like to become an American?"

"True, I never thought about it before," she says, scratching her head. "For as long as anyone can remember, these islands have been a part of Denmark. The pictures of de King and Queen hang in every schoolhouse, post office, and down at the customs house, and de Danish flag always be flying down by de Barracks and at de fort. Can a King sell a part of his kingdom like you sell a piece of fish in the marketplace?"

"I suppose it's possible," I say. "Panama used to be a part of Colombia until the Americans came with their gunboats and snatched it away. Think of all the advantages of becoming a part of the United States. America is a rich country. They can bring many good things to these islands, improve the life for everyone. When the Americans came to Panama, they drained the swamps, fought the mosquitoes, and brought indoor plumbing, schools, hospitals, roads, and bridges. And when they were finished, there was this huge canal that linked the Atlantic Ocean with the Pacific Ocean. Old timers say that before the Americans came, society was in disorder. Bandits roamed freely in the hills and they were always plotting revolutions, but all that stopped when the Americans came and brought law and order."

"*Seerious?*" says Nana Jane with wide-eyed fascination.

"Of course it wasn't perfect," I continue. "The Americans also brought some bad laws, like the Jim Crow laws that forced children into separate schools and workers to ride in separate cars, silver and gold. These laws are very bad, but bad laws can change over time. Consider how much good the Panama Canal has brought to the entire world."

"Abigail," she declares with pride. "You're just as smart as your grandfather. He would be so proud of you."

Nana Jane spies my mother's photograph in the trunk and she cradles it in her arms. "Your mother was the most beautiful woman on the whole island. Every boy wanted her, but she chose Isaac. You remind me so much of her it makes me cry."

I place the picture in a drawer and shut it.

"I don't want to think about Mami now. I refuse to let Aunt Esther see me cry." I turn to Nana Jane and ask her the question that has been eating me up. "Nana Jane, what if Aunt Esther never learns to like me?"

"Dat be outrageous not true," says Nana Jane, horrified. "True, Esther has a funny way of acting, but that doesn't mean she don't like you. You shouldn't bother yourself about Aunt Esther when you have Nana Jane. When I saw you for the first time, I realized why I never left this ole house after so many years."

"Why is that?"

"Because I still have lots of unfinished business to attend."

**

The next morning at five o'clock, a cannon's boom jolts me out of bed. I come to my senses and race to the window, expecting to see a German dreadnought crossing swords with an angry British cruiser, but all I see are a trio of Danish gendarmes down by the saluting battery firing a black cannon. From out its mouth, a cloud of black smoke ascends skyward. Another gendarme stands at the flagpole raising the Dannebrog in the cool morning air.

Even Teddy gets excited by all the noise. He jumps up and down in his cage, squawking and screeching, expecting to be fed. I coo to him and stroke his feathers, realizing that this little morning ritual is just one of many new routines we'll both have to get used to. As I look around, admiring the room again, there's no denying that I feel my mother's presence everywhere watching over me. I take her picture out and set it on the desk.

"Why did you leave me, Mami?" I say to her silent image. "Can you hear me from Heaven?" She stares at me with kind, brown eyes that radiate love and warmth, but they are silent and motionless and will remain so forever.

I peer out into the hall just as Aunt Esther passes by wearing a tattered robe and slippers. She heads over to the washbasin and washes her hands in the prescribed manner, then splashes cold water on her face. After drying herself with a threadbare towel, I can hear her calling out to Nana Jane, "Is he coming back today, Nana Jane?"

Nana Jane's plaintive reply carries down the hall, "No, Miss Esther, his ship not coming back today. Maybe he'll come back next week."

Over a meager breakfast of oatmeal and bush tea, Aunt Esther keeps her eyes glued to the *St. Thomas Tidende,* the local English-language Danish newspaper, as she grumbles about the sorry state of the economy and the scarcity of decent food. I innocently ask Cooky Betty if there's any bread left in the kitchen, and to my surprise she rolls her eyes and says, "No silver in the coffee can, no bread in the cupboard," then she waddles back to the kitchen, shaking her head.

Nana Jane looks up from her tea. "Food, money, and good humor are all scarce on account of the war, but you can pick all the fruit from the trees you want: genips, mangoes, and papayas. Monkeys and children never have to pay for fruit."

After breakfast, Aunt Esther announces that a huge pile of clothes waiting to be mended in the sitting room. My visions of running down to explore the town vanish as I'm confronted by the mountainous task ahead of me. I wonder if I'll ever be allowed to return to school.

Aunt Esther leads me to the sewing room, shows me my seat, and explains what's expected of me. There's clearly enough work to last for weeks and months, from sewing buttonholes and darning socks, to mending hems and patching holes. She hands me a dress and tells me to let down the hem without ruining the fine fabric. I sigh, take up a needle, and put my rudimentary sewing skills to the test. All the while I'm pulling out the stitches Aunt Esther stands over me examining my work, smelling of old wool and mothballs.

"Nice, even stitches," she says after I show her my finished work. "Looks like that mother of yours taught you something useful. Now let's see if you can tackle this buttonhole."

Little by little I make slow, steady progress as I work through the pile of clothing. By dinner time, my fingers are raw and my back is aching. After a meager dinner of yam and bean stew, I collapse into bed like a rag doll, dreaming of better days.

***

Several days later, when Aunt Esther is satisfied that my sewing skills are adequate, she announces that it's time I learned embroidery. The minute I hear that, my throat tightens. If there's one thing I refuse to learn it is embroidery. I realize the time has come to put my foot down. I decide to broach the subject of school.

"Aunt Esther, what about school? When does it start? I can't sit here mending clothes for the rest of my life."

"School?" she says, taken aback. "Who said anything about school? There's no school here beyond the sixth grade, and I certainly don't have the money to ship you off to some fancy school in New York. I'm sorry, Abigail, but there's no school for you."

"What?" I say, shocked. "But that's impossible! I *have* to finish school if I'm going to become a teacher. It's my dream."

She shakes her head. "Forget about your dreams. Unmarried girls in your situation are expected to work to contribute to the household. Once you start earning some real money, then maybe I can get you a job in a dress shop downtown. But until then—"

"A *dress* shop?"

"What were you expecting, Oxford University? Take a look around, the island is in a state of decline. Most of the people are illiterate and exist on a diet of sugar three times a day. No, my dear, you will not be attending any school in the foreseeable future. I hope I've made that clear."

Reality hits me like a cold slap on the face. All of a sudden, I feel weak and dizzy, as though I'm slowly suffocating. I stand up, aware that my knees are shaking and my legs are too wobbly to be of much use. I head to the washroom and grope for the spigot as tears fill my eyes. When at last the water trickles out, I splash some on my face as I break down from the strain. Unable to restrain my anguish, I collapse to the floor in grief, my silent tears streaking my face and dress. When I hear Aunt Esther calling out to me, I wipe my face with a dish towel and reply that I need to lie down for a little while.

Alarmed, Nana Jane rushes to my side. She pumps out a glass of water and urges me to drink it. She brushes the hair away from my reddened eyes and tells me to go outside into the fresh air and sunshine. I nod, grateful to have someone who understands my pain and grief.

As I meander through the garden, I marvel at Nana Jane's wisdom. The fresh air and the sunshine do wonders to revive my flagging spirits. I savor the abundance of fragrant flowers like the cheerful frangipani, the delicate pink hibiscus, and the purple bougainvillea. I marvel at the lush fruit trees such as the mango, the papaya, tamarind, and guava, savoring their rich flavors and luscious scents. The tall grasses tickle my face and insects buzz in my ears.

The birds chirp in the uppermost branches of the trees, filling the air with their songs. I'm so engrossed exploring my new world that I soon forget my troubles.

Suddenly, I look up and notice something unusual. Peeking through the tall grass I spy a non-descript door built into the foundation of the house. Does it lead to a long-forgotten room? In desperate need of a mystery, I wade through the bushes until I reach the door and when I try to open it, I discover that the knob refuses to budge. I try pulling and turning with all my might but it holds fast. Time, humidity, and neglect have sealed the door shut. I run my hands along the frame wondering how I'll manage to coax it open without the proper tools. But the idea of a hidden room in Aunt Esther's house intrigues me, and I vow that one day I'll discover its secrets.

Later, when Nana Jane comes outside to hang up the wash, I grab the wringer, wondering how I can broach the subject of the secret room. Nana Jane sticks a few clothespins in her mouth and starts hanging up the clothes as a breeze blows her apron to her face.

"Nana Jane, how come Aunt Esther never got married?"

Nana Jane makes a face. "Oh, she had a suitor once about thirty years ago," she says, turning her attention back to the clothes. "A fine-looking young man named Jacob Curiel from a rich and prominent family. Back in those days, Esther was a good-looking girl. She had dark hair and eyes and a complexion the color of almond shells. But Jacob was very ambitious, too ambitious if you ask me. He wanted to make a fortune in Panama before they got married, so one day he packed his bags and took the next steamer to Colón. He never even told Esther he was leaving. All he left her was a short note saying he would return one day to claim her. Only that day never came. No one ever heard from Mr. Jacob Curiel again. Some people say he died all alone in Panama. They say he got yellow fever."

"No wonder Aunt Esther hates Panama so much."

"She took it veree hard. She got sick from grief. After a while she started acting funny, washing she hands all de time and rearranging de shelves. She still believes Jacob Curiel gonna come back for her one day, but I don't have the heart to tell her he is never coming back."

"How sad."

"After a while, her friends stopped calling on her and people started gossiping about her, saying she had a nervous breakdown and was going crazy. Your grandparents got sick with worry and hid her in the house, never letting her out of their sight. After a while, people forgot about Esther Maduro and the party invitations stopped coming. Now, she only leaves the house to go to the synagogue once a week. My heart broke for her a long time ago." Nana Jane wipes her brow with a handkerchief, then she rubs her back and groans, "Now Nana Jane must lie down. My rheumatism is speaking to me."

***

For the next several days, I work hard at my sewing, and when I have some free time, I help Nana Jane with her chores as well so she doesn't have to work so hard. Although I do it to ease her discomfort, I also find that I enjoy being around Nana Jane. She teaches me her island songs and I teach her some of mine. Nana Jane also teaches me about the islands, their history, and their folklore, and how the islanders rose up against slavery years ago, when her mother was a little girl. I notice that the closer I get to Nana Jane, the more bitter Aunt Esther becomes. No matter how hard I try to please her, Aunt Esther always seems to hate me.

For instance, yesterday when I was untangling the knots in my hair, she grabbed the brush out of my hand and offered to help. I went along, thinking she was trying to butter me up, but then she started pulling and tugging my hair with such force, it made me cry out in pain. I tried to grab the brush out of Aunt Esther's hand, but that only made her more furious. She tugged even harder, pulling with such force that the brush snapped in two! Aunt Esther's face contorted with rage as she held up the broken pieces, glaring at me as she spat out, "Devil's hair!" then she flung the pieces over the balcony.

Shocked and hurt, I said, "You tugged too hard! You did it on purpose!" The next thing I know, Aunt Esther slapped me so hard, it stung. I stood up in shock, ran from the room, and flung myself on my bed as the tears began to flow. I fear I won't be able to cope much longer with this deplorable situation.

Today, as I help Nana Jane iron the linens, Aunt Esther struts over to criticize how I hold the iron, how I fold the napkins, even how much starch I use. I listen quietly, keeping my anger contained, but my sangfroid seems to irritate Aunt Esther all the more. The next thing I know, she flies into a bitter rage, screaming and yelling. I begin to notice a predictable pattern, no matter how hard I try to please her, all I hear are complaints. I don't set the table right, I don't make my bed right, I leave the kerosene lamp burning in my room, I don't wash the dishes right. Today over dinner, she complained about my table manners. Not wanting to get dragged into a fight, I calmly ignored her and continued eating.

"Did your parents teach you any manners?" she says, seething with rage. "Do you think you can just come here and take over my house?"

"But Aunt Esther," I say, trying to remain calm. "If I stay silent, you get angry, and if I say the wrong thing, you get even angrier. According to you, nothing I do is right."

Aunt Esther's face turns beet red. "You spoiled, ungrateful brat. You've been plotting against me since the day you arrived. And after all the good I did for you."

"What?"

"You heard me," she retorts. "I've seen you talking behind my back. I know what you're trying to do. I won't stand for it. I'd sooner throw you out before I let you steal my house from me."

"Steal from you?" I say, shocked. "What are you talking about? I'm not a thief. You're acting like a lunatic."

Aunt Esther raises her hand, but a quick-thinking Nana Jane pulls me out of reach.

"Good Lord, Miss Esther," scolds Nana Jane, wrapping her arms around me. "How can you say such things? This child never hurt nobody. Hush your mouth!"

"Did you see the way that monster tried to attack me? I'm sure she was just as incorrigible with her own parents. If they were alive today, I'm sure they'd be happy to be rid of her."

My mouth drops open. This was the last straw. I tear myself out of Nana Jane's arms and run to my room, broken in spirit. I fling myself on the bed and sob like a baby. I don't remember ever feeling so alone, so miserable. Being stuck with Aunt Esther in this wretched house is worst than being dead. I realize now that my parents must have fled to Panama just to get far away from Aunt Esther's vicious tirades. I don't know how long I'll be able to survive living with such a malicious woman.

I pick up my mother's picture. "Mami, how could you leave me all alone? Why must I live with this horrible woman? Please send someone to help me. I must get out of here."

My mother smiles silently at me, her kind eyes radiating a look of distress but her lips unable to move. Tears stream down my face as I place her picture back in the desk and collapse on the bed in a fit of sobs.

Later, Nana Jane comes to my room and sits beside me, curling my long, brown hair between her fingers. She places a hot Johnny Cake in my hands and tells me to eat. I can't. I have no more desire for food. I turn my head away and close my eyes. Nana Jane takes my hand in hers as she hums one of her comforting spirituals.

"Abigail," she says at last, pulling my chin up so that our eyes meet. "Never forget what I'm about to tell you. You are a blessing and never a burden. We don't know why de Lord called up your parents to His Heavenly Kingdom, but we have to accept the good with the bad. Your Auntie is a bitter, lonely woman who never had a nice thing to say about anybody. When your grandmother and grandfather died, she started to lose her mind. She don't know right from wrong. Can you at least try to forgive her in your heart?"

"Never."

"Abigail, did they teach you any Bible stories in Panama?"

"Some."

"Did they teach you about King David?"

"A little."

"Well, Nana Jane is gonna teach you about King David. He was the greatest king in all of Israel, but he wasn't born a king. No Siree. He was born a simple shepherd. Some people were bitter that de Lord made him king ovah dem, and while he sat on de throne, King David made many outrageous enemies who made his life hard and bitter. And King David's enemies were a lot worse than your Aunt Esther. But King David was also one of the most righteous men in all of Israel. He wrote Psalm 27 that says, '*The Lord is my life's strength, whom shall I fear? When evildoers approach me to devour my flesh; my tormentors and my foes against me, it is they who stumble and fall.*' Never forget these words, my dear Abby. The Lord will make your enemies fall and not you. The Lord never forgets those who cry out to him, especially orphans. King David also said, '*Though my father and my mother have forsaken me, the Lord will gather me in.*' I promise that the Lord will watch over you and will keep you from harm. Never forget that."

"Do you really mean that, Nana Jane?"

"Of course I do."

I wrap my arms around Nana Jane and hug her so tight I fear we both will burst. That night, as I lay in bed looking up at the stars, I make myself two promises. The first is that I will never allow Aunt Esther to speak like that to me again. And the second is that I will make my own way in the world, no matter what the cost.

CHAPTER 8

When I wake up on Saturday morning, I hurry to wash and get dressed. It is the Sabbath. I greet Aunt Esther in as cheerful a manner as possible, hoping to make peace between us, but she's just as cold and formal as on the weekdays, and doesn't even bother to return my greeting. She places her lace mantilla on her head and silently leads me out the door and down Crystal Gade. I can imagine what the neighbors think of us: two brooding figures who march to the synagogue in stony silence. Family yet not family.

As we enter the synagogue's cool interior, everyone turns in our direction. We make our way through the assembly, aware that sixty pairs of eyes of varying ages watch our every move. What was once a large and proud Sephardic Jewish congregation has been reduced to a collection of grey-haired spinsters, bent, elderly men, widows, a few married couples, some businessmen in dark suits and their richly-attired wives, government clerks and consular officials, and a scattering of children too restless to stay seated. There are no girls my age, no one to befriend.

A few of the old-timers nod in my direction. Perhaps they notice my resemblance to my mother. I offer a shy smile in return and follow Aunt Esther to our seats in the back.

For most of the service I sit admiring the synagogue's interior. The domed roof is supported by four Greek columns, each one representing one of the matriarchs: Sarah, Rebecca, Rachel and Leah, while hanging from the dome is a chandelier that spreads warm light over the congregation. The benches are of solid mahogany forming neat rows around the platform from which the weekly Torah portion is read. And most wonderful of all is the floor, which is covered with sand, an ancient tradition that is found only in synagogues in the West Indies, the exact meaning of which has been lost over time. Sitting in this hallowed atmosphere I feel an overwhelming sense of warmth and peace, like I'm at home.

Wrapped in white prayer shawls, the men chant the prayers in Portuguese, a tradition that our ancestors brought over from Holland centuries before. I glance over at Aunt Esther. Her nose is thrust in her prayer book as she recites the prayers with a dispassionate frown. Likewise, I pick up a frayed prayer book and open it to the prayers I remember from back home. When no one is looking, I peer over it to size up the people around me, wondering if there's at least one person I can befriend.

Out of a crowd of women and children, one young woman in particular stands out for her youth and her beauty. She appears to be in her early twenties, well-groomed, and fashionably dressed. When she looks away, I seize the opportunity to study her in detail. She is indeed beautiful, with an olive complexion, a long, straight nose, and dark hair that she wears piled on top of her head, like the ladies in the *Woman's Home Companion*. In fact, she fits my ideal image of a schoolteacher, especially with her regal bearing and perfect posture. I make a mental to find out more about her from Nana Jane.

When services are over, we file out into the bright sunshine. I watch the young lady escorting her parents and younger brother as they descend the steps and head up to the more fashionable section of Crystal Gade, where large villas with gardens sit overlooking the harbor. I tag along behind Aunt Esther, who barely says hello to anyone and I come to the conclusion that I must give up the idea of trying to appease her. She is completely shut off from the world.

After lunch, Nana Jane and I sit on the balcony going through some old family photographs. My favorite picture is of a young Nana Jane holding my father as a baby. She was so beautiful back then with smooth skin, high cheekbones, expressive eyes, and lovely arched eyebrows. She had the unmistakable aristocratic bearing of a queen.

Sliding off the couch, I walk over to my grandfather's old brass spyglass. Many years ago, he would use it to observe the ships as they entered and left the harbor. He had a great love of the sea, and couldn't bear the thought of ever leaving his beloved villa on Synagogue Hill. As I gaze through the spy glass, I notice the extraordinary detail it affords me of each ship. I can even make out the faces of each crewmember as they work on deck. I glance over at Nana Jane, but she has her eyes glued to the pictures.

"I saw somebody interesting in the synagogue today," I say nonchalantly, keeping my eyes trained on the ships. "A beautiful young lady dressed in the latest fashion. She looks like that famous Italian opera singer, Lina Cavalieri. Do you know who she might be?"

"That sounds like Miss Deborah De Castro," says Nana Jane. "She is the daughter of Moses De Castro, an important lawyer and the governor's most trusted advisor. They live a short way up Crystal Gade."

"I would like to meet her."

"Oh no, your auntie would never allow that."

"Why? Anyway, she doesn't have to know. Please Nana Jane."

Nana Jane purses her lips and says, "Let me dwell on it."

I grin with the confidence. Ever since I first arrived in St. Thomas, Nana Jane has been the only silver lining in my new life. Her smile lifts my spirits no matter how sad and lonely I feel. She always finds the humorous side to any situation, and lightens everyone's mood with her funny stories. Whenever I tell her a joke she laughs, even if she doesn't quite understand the meaning. She just listens for the cues in my voice, then howls with laughter at the proper time, as if it was the funniest thing she's ever heard.

Once I told her a joke about Kaiser Wilhelm and General von Bulow that had her in peels of laughter. One day, I told her, they were out in a field flying a peace kite. The Kaiser drew his sword, pointed it at the kite and ordered his general to *'Machine-gun the blasted thing; it doesn't seem to rise at all.'* Hearing this, Nana Jane roared with laughter although I'm quite certain she didn't understand the message. That's just her way.

Nana Jane doesn't know her exact age. All she remembers is that she was born in the island of St. Croix shortly after slavery was abolished. Her mother came from a sugar plantation called LaGrange, but continued to work there even after she was emancipated. Although the slaves were free, life never got any easier.

95

They worked long hours for very little wages, and mostly made do with growing their own food. When their situation seemed hopeless, her mother made a hard decision. She gathered up Nana Jane and her little sister Adelaide and made a small satchel out of a worn-out blanket in which she placed all their clothes, a comb, a towel, some soap, and a few pots and pans. She counted out her hard-earned coins and brought her daughters down to the wharf and bought passage for all three on the schooner *Vigilant* that ferries passengers between St. Thomas and St. Croix.

After a rocky ride, they reached St. Thomas and Nana Jane's mother quickly found work as a domestic servant in a fine house, earning more in one week than she did in a month sweating in the cane fields. On holidays, Nana Jane's mother would take her and Adelaide downtown to dance the quadrille to a native scratch band, or join up with carolers as they serenaded the governor under his window. The Danish governor always showered his visitors with coins as he wished them good luck in the coming year.

Whenever Nana Jane mentions Adelaide, her voice cracks and her face looks strained. Adelaide, she says, was the sweetest, most good-natured girl who ever lived. She used to love looking at pictures in magazines, sitting patiently like a good little girl while her mother braided her hair in tiny cornrows. In those days, Adelaide always did as she was told, but when she got to be fourteen, something changed. Her sweet nature became irritable and scornful. She would yell, scream, kick, and throw things to the ground whenever she got upset, and the more people tried to appease her, the more inconsolable she became. When Adelaide became too unruly to be taken out in public anymore, Nana Jane's mother fretted about what to do. There seemed to be no solution.

When her employer started to complain about Adelaide's outbursts, Nana Jane's mother knew she had to do something or they'd all be out on the street. One night some men came by and took Adelaide away. Nana Jane's mother cried for days afterwards and was never quite the same. I notice that whenever Nana Jane mentions Adelaide, she always presses her hand on her heart.

Nana Jane's favorite activity comes twice a week. On market days, she takes a basket down to Market Square where she spends hours laughing and gossiping with the market women. She knows the Bible prohibits idle gossip, but she can't help herself. It's her greatest weakness. When I ask her why she doesn't send Cooky Betty down to Market Square instead, she explains that Market Square is more than just a place to buy fruits and vegetables—it's the center of island life. It's where everyone goes to be seen, and to catch up all the news and hear the latest stories. But back during the days of slavery, Market Square had a more sinister purpose.

Market Square used to be the largest slave market in the Eastern Caribbean. Each year, thousands of men, women, and children were kidnapped from the Guinea coast of Africa and brought over on slave ships. Starved, beaten, and separated from their families, the slaves were forced to stand on the auction blocks where they were sold off to the highest bidder like cattle. After emancipation, Market Square became a fruit and vegetable market, but everyone remembers its true history. It stands as a constant reminder of the evils of slavery.

Today, Nana Jane returned from shopping with a big smile on her face clucking about a juicy piece of gossip she'd heard down at the market. By the time I come to investigate, she's standing with Cooky Betty and Mr. Isaiah, chuckling so hard, I know it had to be something supremely mischievous.

"Nana Jane, it's forbidden to spread gossip," I admonish her, a little too self-righteously. "Don't you know how to keep a secret?"

"Heaven Forbid!" she replies, clutching her Bible to her chest. "Gossip is the Devil's handiwork, but I can't stop my own self ears from listening when other folks be talking. And what good would I be if Miss Lucy can't tell anyone what goes on inside the Governor's mansion? If Miss Lucy can't tell nobody, she gonna bust like a ripe papaya!"

Cooky Betty rolls her eyes. "And with all the gossip you're carrying you are also gonna bust like a ripe papaya."

A few days later, I decide it's time to see Market Square for myself. I wait until Aunt Esther dozes off to the droning of her Victrola, then I lay down my sewing, reset the needle on the record, crank up the gramophone, and tiptoe out to the warbling of Billy Murray. I head down Crystal Gade and Raadets Gade with a noticeable spring in my step, letting the warm sun and gentle breezes caress my face as my heart races with excitement. A whole afternoon with no Aunt Esther is an unexpected gift, a reason to celebrate.

I turn onto Main Street, otherwise known as Dronningens Gade, as horse carriages and donkey carts clip-clop past. As I stroll past the stores I pass ladies in fine dresses and parasols, men pushing wheel barrows, nannies with prams, and merchants in linen suits and boater hats; the street is bustling with activity. I follow a plump cook in a straw hat carrying a large straw basket as she heads down to Market Square, my anticipation growing by the minute.

When I reach Market Square, the crowd becomes much livelier. People stroll around the open air market, which is a raised platform with stalls covered by a wide canopy. Everywhere you look men, women, young and old laugh and chat, trading gossip and stories about the old days as bare-footed children run underfoot. Old men sit under leafy trees playing rousing games of dominoes or checkers, and every once in a while, you hear one shout out in victory. The market is bursting with a wide assortment of bananas, mangoes, sapodillas, guavas, papayas, tamarinds, sugar apples, and passion fruit. I walk around savoring the sounds and the smells, observing the market women and relishing their laughter.

And then I spy an unusual sight. Under the shade of a tree, a crowd has gathered around a wrinkled old native woman, a terrifying creature, who is engaged in a brisk trade selling bottles of pink frothy mauby while she yells like a fishwife in colorful language designed to make your head spin. I inch closer to the crowd to get a better look at this spectacle.

The woman is very old, with skin resembling old leather that has been left out in the sun too long. She wears a long, raggedy dress and a white turban, but her eyes are yellow and fierce, displaying a fire from deep within. When this frightening creature opens her mouth, her voice booms like a cannon; each word is a torpedo that hits its mark and explodes.

I stand among the crowd of onlookers as the old woman launches into a vicious tirade against the Danish government, the *bocras* (the term she uses for white people), and all the injustices of the world. Whenever she makes an especially fiery point, she shakes her knotty fist so hard her whole body convulses with anger. The louder she screams, the more the crowd applauds. Other times, the old woman stomps her withered feet with such force, she kicks up a cloud of dust to the enthusiastic applause of the crowd.

Watching this scene from a street corner is a terrified young Danish gendarme who stands guard in front of the Danish West Indies National Bank. He's young, about eighteen years old, and looks as if he bears the weight of the world on his scrawny shoulders. He's wearing the typical uniform of the gendarmerie corps, a blue jacket, starched white trousers, and a tall blue cap. Every time the crowd erupts in jeers, his knees noticeably tremble and his eyes dart from side to side. And although his posture shows the proper militaristic bearing, every time he hears the old woman cackle or shriek, his fingers twitch nervously on his rifle.

"Remember how Queen Coziah fought de Steamship Companies and all de Danish soldiers single-handed and won," she shouts to the delight of the crowd. "The *bocra* not stronger than Queen Coziah! They brought cannons to kill me and I won 'em! Queen Coziah stood up to de *bocra*, King Christian, and all the Danish toy soldiers! You people are like little sheep, but Queen Coziah demands respect and she gets it. The King of Denmark doesn't dare shackle these tired black limbs of mine."

She shakes a shriveled arm to emphasize her point and the crowd erupts in applause. By now, the poor gendarme is wiping beads of sweat off his forehead. I watch the old woman in fascination, wondering what will happen next.

A barefooted man in a straw hat calls out from the crowd. "Queen Coziah, you too old to fight the militia! Go home and rest."

The old woman ignores him, staring straight ahead as if she had never heard the man's jibe.

"You fought your battles," calls out another. "Go home and retire. Let the young people fight."

"Nevah!" shrieks the old woman, her anger more palpable by the minute. "This world is not for resting. Queen Coziah will never retire. Coziah is a fighter and de best bamboula dancer on de whole island, even better even than the ladies in Antigua and *Bassin*." Her declaration is received with more laughter and applause.

"Coziah, you're too old to dance de bamboula," calls out a plump woman in a turban. "Let the young girls dance now."

"I still better than all de young girls," sniffs Coziah. "They can't compete with the Queen of the Bamboula."

More applause and cheers erupts from the crowd. But the old woman appears to have suffered enough of the people's taunts for one day. She sniffs loudly, sticks out her bottom lip, and returns to selling her bottles of the frothy pink elixir.

"Excuse me," I whisper to a lady in a straw hat to my right. "Who is that woman?"

"That is Queen Coziah," says the woman. "She used to be a coal woman. She stood up to the steamship companies for better wages and got them, but now she's too old to lift de coal baskets."

"But she not afraid of de *bocra*," says a toothless old man. "De *bocra* scared of she. She faced the cannons and won them."

I have a sudden urge to stand up to the old woman and prove that I can be just as brave as she is, but her wild eyes, gnarled arms, and wrinkled face make me think twice. I slowly back away. But before I have a chance to escape, someone behind me pushes me forward until I find myself standing face to face with that fearsome creature. Queen Coziah takes one look at me and says with impatience, "Yes, Miss, what you wanting?"

"I, uh, how much is a bottle of mauby?"

"Five bits," she says, drawing back her bottom lip to reveal pink gums and only two remaining teeth.

"Did you really stand up to the soldiers?" I say, trying to sound brave. Hearing this, the old woman throws her head back and roars with laughter. When they people see her do this, they burst into laughter as well. I feel my face start to turn crimson.

"Queen Coziah not only faced them, she won them," she cackles, spitting brown liquid from the corner of her mouth. "Queen Coziah is a double queen 'cause not only is Queen Coziah de queen of all de bamboula dancers, she also queen of bravery! I stared down the barrel of a gun and I won them! Now girl, where's your money? You want my mauby or not?"

She fixes her two black eyes on me like cannons preparing to shoot. My hand shakes so hard, I almost drop the five bit piece on the dusty ground. Finally, I hand it to her, relieved to be almost gone from that place. And then, as an afterthought, the old woman tosses a bottle of mauby over to me before turning her attention to the next person in line, bellowing out, "Next! Hurry up! Don't waste Queen Coziah's time."

I grab the bottle and run as fast as I can, putting a healthy distance between me and that cackling old crone. I hand the bottle to an old woman and turn to look at Coziah. From a safe distance, she looks smaller and less frightening than up close. I see that Queen Coziah is just a shriveled old woman who lives in fear of losing the respect and awe of her people. She knows her days are coming to an end. Something about her inner fire draws me to her. If I can learn the secret of Queen Coziah's courage, perhaps one day it will prove useful, perhaps even save my life.

CHAPTER 9

Before heading back home, I take a detour through town until I find myself standing in front of the Grand Hotel. Charlotte Amalie is swarming with travelers since two large passenger steamers are docked in the harbor, leaving their passengers to frolic and sightsee all over town. Some of them have ended up here at the hotel, hoping to secure a three dollar guest room with a private shower-bath for the night.

Inside the lobby, the mood is cheerful and light. Music from a quadrille band floats in through the open windows and the enticing smell of food wafts down from the second-story café. I grab a coin from my pocketbook, purchase a copy of the *Tidende* and a bottle of pink lemonade, and then head upstairs to the grand gallery to experience the most popular spot in all of Charlotte Amalie.

The dining room is packed with diners enjoying the local cuisine while drinking copious amounts of St. Croix rum while they puff on Havana cigars. Lively chatter fills the room as clouds of smoke and the smell of fried fish and conch fritters waft through the air. Harried waiters wend their way around the tables, dishing out food from the kitchen and drinks from the bar to the delight of the customers. I grab an empty table near the edge of the balcony where I can enjoy the splendid view of the harbor as I observe the happenings inside the restaurant.

I open the newspaper and lift it up so I can watch the people without being observed. Every now and then, I peer around to put a face with a voice, but after several minutes, I get the strangest sensation that somebody is observing *me*.

I look up to meet the startled gaze of a distinguished-looking gentleman with twinkling blue eyes, a soft white beard, and pince nez spectacles. Given his refined bearing and elegant white linen suit and tropical pith helmet, I'm certain he must be an important Danish official on the island, perhaps even the governor. By the way he peers at me, I get the distinct impression I must have broken some unwritten social code.

When the gentleman sees I make no effort to leave, his expression turns to one of annoyance. He fumbles around for his gold watch, giving the impression that he's scratching himself. Polite as ever, I stifle a giggle, but his mannerisms are so comical and charming, I cannot help myself. When at last he manages to grasp his watch, he holds it up with great pride and loudly clears his throat, as if trying to quiet the entire restaurant.

By now, I'm starting to think that everyone on this island is a little bit crazy, but I decide to play along with his game. Assuming a look of great seriousness, I endeavor to study the watch, but my antics only serve to increase the gentleman's annoyance.

"I beg your pardon," he says in a distinct, clipped Danish accent. "But it is my custom to sit at the same table every day at this precise hour. Except Sundays, of course, when Mrs. Neergaard expects me to pay my respects to the Lord."

A waiter rushes towards us.

"Ah, Judge Neergaard, your Honor," says the waiter. "I apologize for this inexcusable breach of protocol. The young lady must have wandered up here and taken your table by accident. Allow me to shoo her away and free it up for you."

"That won't be necessary, Jeffrey," says the gentleman, holding up his hand. "I'm not such an old codger that I can't find someplace else to sit."

"I beg your pardon, sir," I say, standing up. "The mistake was mine. It's no bother for me to change seats, but seeing as there are several empty chairs at this table, perhaps we could simply *share* the table?"

Two pairs of eyebrows shoot up. I feel my checks coloring as I realize the inadvertent faux pas I must have committed. The elderly gentleman and the waiter exchange a quick glance, as if considering the social repercussions of such an outlandish request.

"Fancy that," says the judge, scratching his beard. "The idea never occurred to me. Perhaps I'm getting too old for polite society. Don't mind if I do."

The waiter pulls out a chair for the judge. "Shall I bring the usual, Judge Neergaard?" he says, placing a linen napkin on the gentleman's lap.

"That would be splendid, Jeffrey," says the judge, loosening his stiff collar. "And see to it that the young lady receives something appropriate for her age, perhaps raspberry lemonade or an apple cider." He winks at me and I grin in return.

The waiter vanishes to the bar and reappears bearing the judge's libation, a cocktail of rum, water, and limes, which he sets down with great ceremony in front of him, while to me he presents a cold glass of lemonade almost as an afterthought.

The judge smiles cordially and takes a sip.

"Now that the proverbial ice is broken," he says. "Allow me to introduce myself. My name is Henrik Neergaard, a judge over at the local police court. I serve my King by presiding over cases at Fort Christian. As you have just witnessed, it is my custom to take my daily rum cocktail at this table at the same time each day as a therapeutic remedy for the daily grind before heading home to face the rigors of domestic life. My cocktail is the only indulgence my wife allows me, she being of a more religious temperament. I tell her, let the fools strut up and down King's Wharf like a bunch of silly peacocks, or play their maddening games of tennis, chasing stupid little balls around a clay court like squirrels after nuts. Or worse, taking one of those tedious carriage rides to nowhere, *just to be seen.* I have no patience for such mindless endeavors and Mrs. Neergaard knows the limits of my endurance, so she wisely limits her demands to suit my temperament. I dare say we get along most splendidly in this regard." The judge offers me a naughty grin. "Now young lady, at this point in the conversation it would be appropriate for you to introduce yourself."

"Pleased to meet you, Judge Neergaard," I say. "My name is Abigail Maduro. But my friends, when I *had* them, used to call me Abby. I'm sixteen years old and I was born in Panama, but due to an unfortunate accident that took the lives of my parents, I now live with my Aunt Esther Maduro up on Synagogue Hill, in case you didn't know."

"Did you say *Maduro*?" says the Judge, adjusting his pince nez. "As a matter of fact, I know the Maduro family very well. And indeed I also know your Aunt Esther, although I haven't seen her in years. What were your parents' names?"

"Isaac and Rebecca Maduro. My grandfather, Samuel Elias Levi Maduro, used to be an important official on the island, but he died several years ago. My Aunt Esther is practically the only relative I have left in the world and she wasn't particularly happy about taking me in. She mostly just tolerates me."

The judge nods. "How tragic! I remember your father when he was a little boy and I also know about your Aunt Esther's situation. A terrible shame, if you ask me. She was quite a beauty in her day. And your grandfather was one of the most noble and selfless men I ever met. In fact, I would even say that Samuel Elias Levi Maduro was the best friend I ever had. We were like brothers. When your parents moved to Panama, he was heartbroken. He left us more than ten years ago now, but not a day goes by that I don't miss Sam. Some days I feel I owe him my life."

The judge takes out a wooden pipe from his coat pocket and lights it with a look of fond remembrance.

"Can you tell me more about my grandfather?" I say. "I never had the chance to meet him."

Judge Neergaard puffs contemplatively. "Your grandfather had an extraordinary presence. When Sam Maduro walked in a room, all eyes turned to him. He was magnetic. We attended law school together in Copenhagen about forty-five years ago and were inseparable. When his son Isaac married your mother, I was standing right there beside him, sharing his joy. I also shared in his sorrows. When your parents moved to Panama, I was right there on the dock supporting him. That was twenty years ago. Sam took it very hard, but I understood why your father had to leave. He had to prove that he could make it on his own without anybody's help. And to his credit, Sam never flinched. He was so well-regarded they made him a Lieutenant Colonel in the Danish Militia and a Knight of the Dannebrog. I'll bet you didn't know that."

"What is that?"

"It's a high honor. It means your grandfather was a great man. Never forget that. During the Hurricane of 1867, he risked his life to save the less fortunate. He lent money to anyone who needed it and never asked to be repaid. Sam Maduro would give a poor man the shirt off his back. God rest his soul."

"I never knew that. My parents never told me."

"Probably because they didn't know it themselves," says the judge, puffing on his pipe. "Above all, your grandfather was a modest man who never boasted about his achievements. He just helped others in his own quiet, unassuming way. These are details of your history that you should know. Your ancestors were important Sephardic Jewish merchants and guildsmen in the Danish West Indies, and the Maduro name will always be associated with these islands. After your father and mother left for Panama, Sam faded from public life. He and your grandmother took care of Esther, who had suffered a bout of depression. It was hard on Sam. He watched his beautiful daughter succumb to a terrible illness. He spent his final days secluded in the house, rarely venturing out in public. The few times he dragged himself down to Apothecary Hall to buy the latest remedies for Esther's condition, he kept a tight-lip about his problems. Whenever I tried to broach the matter, he would simply change the subject or pretend not to hear. A short while later he suffered a massive heart attack and died. It was a sad end for a quiet hero like Sam."

"How sad," I say. "I never knew any of this. When we found out about grandfather's death, we were devastated, but it was too late to attend the funeral. Thank you for telling me about my family. My Aunt Esther is so distant; she's almost like a stranger. The only one who talks to me is Nana Jane. I miss my parents very much."

"Of course, you've suffered a terrible tragedy," says Judge Neergaard with great sympathy. "I assure you that one day you'll have your own family. Until then, you and I shall become good friends. Some of the best friendships in life happen by chance. Now then, tell me something, have you given any thought to your future?"

I let out a deep sigh. "That's my biggest problem. I always dreamt of becoming a teacher, but there's no school on the island for girls my age. I read books to supplement my education, but Aunt Esther says it's a waste of time. She doesn't think girls need an education. She forces me to work as a seamstress, which I can't stand. It makes me miserable."

"Indeed," says the judge, scratching his beard. "They say a person must follow his basic nature. After all, we wouldn't expect a mouse to chase cats now, would we? But if your dream is to become a schoolteacher, then you must pursue that goal with the tenacity of a lion chasing an antelope. If you'll permit me, I would like to offer myself as your tutor. I'm quite knowledgeable on many subjects including history, literature, geography, and political economy. With diligent study, I'm sure you'll become quite adept in these subjects and one day, perhaps the student will even surpass the professor."

I blush in spite of myself. Judge Neergaard pretends not to notice as he takes a few more puffs of his pipe. Then he lays it down gently and folds his arms across his chest. "Shall we begin then?" he says. "For starters, let's consider the current state of war. The way I see it, the economic and military rivalry between Great Britain and Germany has reached a dangerous crescendo. Germany's goal under Tirpitz is to become the world's supreme sea power as Germany believes her future lies on the water. What does this mean? They believe that if they build a huge fleet of German ships and torpedo every other nation's ship, then they will become the shipping masters of the entire world, replacing their arch-enemy Great Britain."

"Why don't they just build *bigger* ships or *faster* ships?"

"The answer to that, my dear, is *power*," he says. "Germany will never be satisfied being number two at anything. To the Germans, commercial activities like banking and shipping, and wartime activities like espionage are all part of the same package. The average German banker or businessman might very well be spying on the side. The Kaiser has an army of these spies planted all over the world, each one doing his part to help Germany win the war."

"What do they do exactly?"

"Usually they collect information, also called *intelligence*, about enemy ship positions or other targets worth sabotaging. They radio this information back to Berlin in secret code. Even a tranquil Caribbean island such as this has its own resident spy. Do you see that stocky gentleman with the waist coat and cigar sitting between those two mustachioed sea captains?"

Judge Neergaard discreetly motions to a man sitting in the corner whose face I recognize in an instant. He has the same shifty eyes, militaristic moustache, and bull-dog jaw of Fritz Dreyer, the man who killed Ian McShane and also tried to dispatch me. The shock causes me choke on my drink; I hide my face behind a menu.

"*Caramba!* I've seen that man before. What's his name?"

"That's Herr Lothar Langsdorff," whispers the judge. "He's the German consul for the Danish West Indies as well as the Director of the local Hamburg-America Line office. He's as cunning and ruthless as he is ambitious. You've probably already seen their rather imposing building across from King's Wharf. He knows exactly which allied ships come and go and radios this information to Berlin. He and Governor Helweg-Larsen have crossed swords many times over the years, but the Danish Government has its hands tied. Since Denmark is not at war with Germany, they can't simply expel him without suffering serious repercussions."

"And who are those two other men?"

"Berger and Schmidt, the captains of the *Wasgenwald* and the *Calabria*, two of his steamers. Like all German merchant sailors, they are reserve officers in the Imperial German Navy, which technically makes them active soldiers."

"The last time I saw him," I whisper from behind my menu. "He was going by the name of Fritz Dreyer, a Swiss botanist."

"A likely story," says Judge Neergaard, narrowing his eyes. "Though it doesn't surprise me one bit. He's a sly operator who moves around in diplomatic social circles with the ease of an eel. His main job is to supply a vast network of German cruisers and U-boats with coal, diesel and provisions far out at sea, which makes him one of the worst abusers of Danish neutrality since the start of the war. Last year, the Governor ordered him to cease all intelligence-gathering activities, but he became so belligerent the Governor had no choice but to cut him off. Now Langsdorff and his wife are mostly shunned around town, though they still go out on occasion. I'm one of the few remaining friends he has on the island."

As I eye Langsdorff and the German captains I feel my palms start to sweat as I recall that terrible night on the *Guiana* when Ian disappeared for good. The similarity between Langsdorff and Dreyer is too close to be mere coincidence. I'm positive they're the same man. How can I uncover the truth?

Just then, an older man with bushy eyebrows, wild eyes, and a tattered grey beard hobbles through the crowd. When he spots Judge

Neergaard, he makes his way over to our table in a huff. He's wearing the same outfit as the judge, a white tropical suit and pith helmet, though his appearance is far more rumpled. Most noticeable about him are his sad eyes, which remind me of a basset hound. Actually, his sad demeanor is what I find most fascinating about him.

"Good day, Henrik," says the man with the bushy beard as he shakes Judge Neergaard's hand.

"To what do I owe this pleasure, Jens?" says Judge Neergaard, winking at me.

The newcomer shifts uncomfortably as he casts a wary eye in my direction.

"I must speak to you about an urgent matter that can't wait," he says, revealing the same clipped Danish accent. Judge Neergaard turns to me and says, "Allow me to introduce my old friend, Jens Jørgensen, a lawyer and a highly respected member of the Colonial Council. Join us, friend Jørgensen."

Jørgensen plops down next to us, but can't seem to bend his left leg, so he compensates by swinging it across the aisle like the boom of a ship. Just then, a waiter passing by with a tray of Viennese pastries trips over Jørgensen's leg, stumbles, and topples forward, sending the tray sailing across the room where it crashes into a sleeping mutt. The dog opens one eyelid, perceives that his tail is slathered in meringue, and proceeds to lick it off with long, languid strokes. The waiter gets up in a huff, brushes himself off, and storms off to the kitchen.

"Damned rascals!" scowls Jørgensen. "They're never where you need them."

Just then something dawns on me.

"Sir, is your leg wooden?" I say with surprise.

"Indeed, it is," he says, patting it with affection. "I take it everywhere I go." He yells to a waiter to bring an empty glass, then unscrews the leg and procures from its hollow a half-empty bottle of rum. In one fluid motion, he pours himself a glass of the spirits, and then offers the rest to Judge Neergaard.

"The reason for my visit," continues Jørgensen, "is because the Governor is pressuring me to cease doing business with Herr Langsdorff. He forbids me from going through with the deal to purchase the Hamburg-America Line property, even though it's mostly on paper. He was so adamant, he almost burst a gasket. I need your advice on how to deal with this matter."

Judge Neergaard frowns. "If I've told you once I've told you a thousand times, you're playing with fire. We're in the middle of a war. I cannot be impartial in this matter. My best advice for you is to listen to the governor. You're a lawyer, not the director of a steamship company. Your involvement with the Germans is bound to raise a few eyebrows once the Americans get in the picture. A fancy contract signed with a gold fountain pen doesn't make it less phony."

"Phony my foot!" says Jørgensen, banging his fist on the table. "There's nothing wrong with it. I will hold legal title to the building on Norre Gade which is worth more than $60,000 on paper, and the business is so efficient, it practically runs itself. This deal will make me a rich man. Don't you see? There's no way I can lose."

"Nothing is as simple as it looks on paper," says the judge, wagging a finger at the ill-tempered Jørgensen. "You can't mask a German company with a Danish name without running afoul of the Allies, not to mention the irreparable harm you're doing to Danish neutrality."

"Why don't the Danes simply kick the Germans off the island?" I say innocently. Speechless, the two elderly Danes turn to look at me with astonishment.

"You mean, just order them to pack up and leave?" says Jørgensen, eyeing me inquisitively from under his shaggy eyebrows.

"Exactly."

Judge Neergaard takes a long puff of his cigar. "I'm afraid that would be like pouring gasoline on a fire, Abigail. You see, Germany and Denmark have fought tooth and nail over territory in the past with the end result being the loss of Danish territory like Schleswig and Holstein. If Denmark were to expel the Germans now, there would be serious repercussions. Any show of hostility on Denmark's part could trigger a German invasion, not only here in the West Indies, but also in Denmark, which Germany could occupy in as little as thirty-six hours. Denmark is walking a tightrope, and maintaining civility is the key to her survival."

"That can't happen," I say, recalling a conversation I once had with my father. "The Americans would never let Germany invade these islands. The Danish West Indies are located strategically close to the Panama Canal, which makes them vitally important."

Judge Neergaard appears astonished. "Abigail, where did you learn that? Somehow, I can't believe it was your Aunt Esther or Nana Jane who taught that to you."

"Actually, it was my father," I say. "He used to read the newspaper to me and discuss matters concerning the war. He was always fascinated by international intrigue which must have rubbed off on me. It's a fascination that has landed me in a bit of hot water on more than one occasion."

"There's no lack of intrigue on this island," says Judge Neergaard. "We're small in size but we make up for it with large and glaring headlines."

"If you two are finished getting acquainted," grumbles Jørgensen. "We may as well get back to the matter at hand. And while it's admirable that this young lady has so much faith in the Americans, I believe Henrik is saying that the situation is far more dangerous and complicated than it appears on the surface. King Christian is walking a tightrope. He can't side too openly with Great Britain without risking exposing Jutland to a third front against Germany, which is why we remain friends. Does that answer your question my dear?" Jørgensen turns to Judge Neergaard. "Who is this young lady anyway?"

Judge Neergaard winks at me. "Can't you tell by her sharp intellect, captivating smile, and exotic good looks? That's Sam Maduro's granddaughter, Abigail. Since her parents died a most unfortunate demise, I've taken her under my wing."

"God rest their souls," says Jørgensen. "I'll drink to old Sam's memory—skaal."

The two Danes raise their glasses and down their drinks.

"Mr. Jørgensen, pardon me for asking, but what happened to your leg?"

"I sacrificed it while serving my country," he states with pride, screwing it back in place. "But please don't call me unlucky. You see, there are many advantages to owning a wooden leg. For one thing, you can store contraband in it and fool those pesky customs officials. On a more practical level, you can use it to store pills, money, and other valuables. If money is tight, you can pawn it to raise capital. And last but not least, its loud squeaking noise warns others of your impending arrival long before you enter a room, resulting in a room cleared of undesirable company when you wish to sit down and read the newspaper in peace."

The three of us chuckle at Jørgensen's little joke.

"However, your squeaking leg could also clear the room of *desired* company," I say. "Which would be most unfortunate."

"Alas!" Jørgensen sighs. "Now you know my sad fate."

Just then a loud clanking, sputtering noise reverberates from the street below, followed by a loud honk. A messenger boy comes bounding up the stairs, races over to the waiter, and whispers something in his ear. The waiter nods and hurries toward our table.

"Judge Neergaard, Police master Fischer just pulled up in his motorcar. He is requesting that you join him to discuss an urgent matter. He would also like Lawyer Jørgensen to join him as well."

"He what?" says the judge with a look of annoyance. "What urgent matter could be more important than my evening cocktail?"

"Something to do with the latest strike organized by Mr. David Hamilton Jackson," says the waiter, gathering their empty glasses. "He says it's urgent. Perhaps you should go and see."

The two men stand up and throw a few coins down on the table. Judge Neergaard turns to me and smiles, his blue eyes twinkling.

"It was a pleasure meeting you, Miss Maduro. I hope we can continue our tutoring sessions. Please consider me your friend as well. And if you should ever need anything, please don't hesitate to ask. It's the least I can do for dear old Sam."

"Thank you, Judge Neergaard."

"And allow me to inform you without the slightest hesitation that your grandfather would have been mighty proud of you," he says. "Just as I would be if you were my granddaughter."

Beaming with pride, I watch as Judge Neergaard doffs the brim of his hat and hurries down the staircase followed by a limping and grumbling Lawyer Jørgensen.

Peels of laughter draw me to the railing. Peering down into the square, I see the police master's car has attracted quite a bit of attention from bystanders. Natives stroll around in bare feet and straw hats, pointing to the wheels and lights with amazement. Children scamper about, shining the car's fenders with their dirty shirts and making faces in its gleaming chrome. Judge Neergaard and Lawyer Jørgensen wade through the crowd without much progress. At first, the wild-eyed Jørgensen tries to shoo the people away, which sends them into fits of laughter. When that fails, he resorts to shaking his angry fist at them, causing even more bouts of guffaws. Finally, an exasperated Jørgensen and Neergaard hop into the back seat of the motorcar which speeds off down Main Street, careening past several donkey carts and a flock of chickens who squawk loudly in protest and scurry off in a thousand directions, leaving behind only a cloud of feathers

CHAPTER 10

That night as I prepare for bed, Nana Jane sits by my side and tells me stories about her family history. Her mother was born a slave on a sugar plantation in St. Croix called La Grange. During the slave revolt, she hid in a cave with a dozen other people, surviving on scraps of food. When it was safe to come out, they emerged from hiding after the governor, Peter von Scholten, proclaimed that from that day forward, all the slaves were free. She tells me about her mother's struggles and hardships, and how she eventually saved enough money to come to St. Thomas on a schooner called *Vigilant* to start a new life for herself and her two daughters. I wonder if Nana Jane knows about the strange old turbaned woman I saw down in Market Square, and I work up the courage to ask her.

"How you know about she?" says Nana Jane, raising a suspicious eyebrow.

"I went down to Market Square today," I confess. "There was a huge crowd watching her. Some of the people teased her in a good-natured way, but I could see they respected her. The way she shook her fist and denounced the Danish government terrified me, but she was mesmerizing. Who is she?"

"The people call her Queen Coziah," says Nana Jane. "Back in the day she was the most famous coal woman in St. Thomas. Everybody respected her, the judges, the police, the militia, even the steamship companies, but nobody knows who she really is. Some people say she came from Antigua, others say from St. Croix. The only thing we know for sure is that she's some poor mother's child. Her life story is a mystery, but she risked her life to stand up against injustice. She fears no man, and that is why everyone respects her."

"What else do you know about her?"

"The only thing we know for certain is that Queen Coziah started working as a coal carrier over sixty years ago, right after she mother passed away. She was about thirteen or fourteen years old. Back then, the life of a coal woman was much harder. They worked from sunrise to sunset for veree little money. But Coziah had no choice in the matter. Like all the other children of freed slaves, she took any job she could get. Money flowed like water in those days, but only to de rich people. Poor people were always scraping by for pennies. Coziah was young and all alone in this world, but she was brave, so she took a basket down to de docks and started hauling coal for de steamships. It was a hard life. Rain or shine, under a broiling sun that baked you like a yam, or under a pounding rain that soaked you to the bone, Coziah became a nameless face in a crowd of coal women. Later, when she grew up, she started dancing de bamboula at night. She had a fine, shapely body and she knew how to dance like oil on a hot skillet. She moved to the beat of the drums, hypnotizing everyone who watched her, with arms that twisted like a flaming fire. She also sang witty songs, the same songs the coal carriers sang while they carried the coal baskets up to the coal chutes. Soon, Coziah became de most famous bamboula dancer on St. Thomas, but every day she still carried the coal baskets and grew to hate the smell of soot like the slaves hated the lash."

"What is the *bamboula*?"

"The bamboula is a type of dance the slaves brought over from Africa. It is a rousing, spirited type of dance the slaves used to perform when crop time was over and there was plenty of rum to drink. Later, the townspeople adopted this dance for social gatherings until the Catholic Church forbade it. In those days, people were veree religious and didn't want to anger the Church fathers, but the coal carriers kept the tradition alive. When she was young, Coziah was the best bamboula dancer in St. Thomas and she still thinks she's the best. To understand Queen Coziah, my dear, sweet Abigail, is to understand the history of the West Indies and her people. Life was hard, but with a mixture of rum and bamboula, it became sweeter.

"And then in 1892 something terrible happened. The Hamburg-America Line decided to cheat the coal carriers by paying them in worthless Mexican silver instead of Danish francs. That made de coal carriers furious. 'This is the last straw,' they said. So, one clear morning in September, after the harbor had filled up with steamships needing coaling, Coziah put her plan in motion. She hit de Steamship Companies in their pockets. She called a meeting of all the coal carriers, over two hundred of them, and organized a strike. They carried sticks and machetes and marched down Main Street, right up to the door of the Steamship office where they demanded a raise. From my safe spot by the Danish Colonial Bank I watched the whole thing. I picked up my market basket and pretended to go shopping, then I followed the coal women as they marched all the way down to Market Square, keeping to the shadows, careful not to get caught mixing in with coal carriers, who could be a rowdy bunch. I heard what all the people said to Queen Coziah. When someone asked her, *'Coziah, how long you going to march?'* She replied, *'Til we get dollar for dollar.'* I couldn't believe how fearless she was.

"Later, the coal carriers marched down to the police station, and then over to the government secretary's office. You never saw so many scared Danes in your whole life! For once de bocras were scared of Coziah, but she told de coal carriers not to fight and not to cause a scuffle. She knew that violence would tarnish the righteousness of their cause. Then the coal carriers marched all the way down Main Street until they reached Market Square. But it was not quiet for long. Soon they heard the terrifying sound of leather boots pounding on the cobblestones. Everyone looked up: the gendarmes were coming, armed and ready. Fear gripped the crowd. The men looked on helplessly as the gendarmes marched two by two, revolvers at their sides, bayonet rifles pointing forward, two small cannons leading the march.

"Now the coal carriers were in fear for their very lives. Sweat trickled down their faces and their hearts pounded like drums. They remembered their hungry children back home and waited as the footsteps came closer and closer..."

"And then what?"

"The gendarmes lined up in front of Coziah, the tips of their bayonets aimed straight at her heart. They ordered the coal carriers to disperse, threatening to fire if they refused while the crowd of onlookers held their breath."

"And then…?"

"Coziah never backed down. She was ready to die for her cause. She mustered all her courage and shouted at de soldiers, '*As the Lord is my witness, no bayonet, no bullet and no cannon can pierce through the armor of justice.*'"

"And then?"

"Then a miracle happened. The skies opened up and it started to rain. There was not a cloud in the sky the entire morning, but when Coziah cried out to the Lord, a dark cloud rolled in and a fierce downpour rained down on everyone. The rain caused the soldiers to disperse and so did the coal carriers. Later, the steamship companies agreed to pay them in proper Danish money instead of worthless tokens. Coziah had won! Everyone knew she was a brave woman. And that's how she got her name 'Queen Coziah' because she was a *queen* in everyone's eyes."

"Nana Jane, how did a simple woman get so much courage to fight? Sometimes I feel so anxious and scared inside."

Nana Jane heaves a deep sigh. "Courage comes from deep within a person. When you need it, the good Lord plants it inside you like He sometimes plants wisdom inside a fool. We have to learn to listen to that voice telling us what to do. That is your conscience speaking, and then all your fear will dissolve because you'll be doing what you know is right."

That night as I drift off to sleep, Nana Jane's words echo inside of me along with frightening images of Queen Coziah, who shakes her knotty fist at me, admonishing me to stand up and face my fears. The last thing I hear before I drift off to sleep is the sound of her horrifying cackle.

CHAPTER 11

The next morning, as I'm about to finish breakfast, Aunt Esther sets her fork down and makes an unusual announcement.

"Before we start the day's sewing," she says, peering at me over the rim of her spectacles. "I need you to run an errand."

My spoonful of oatmeal dangles midair as I wait in anticipation.

"The Sisterhood is having their annual meeting today. Cooky Betty was kind enough to bake a platter of cakes for Mrs. Robles, who chairs the meetings. Would you kindly take the platter over to the synagogue and drop it off in the back room?"

I glance over at Nana Jane, who is busy cutting a papaya and hasn't been listening. *What an odd request,* I think. *Especially since I don't recall hearing anything about a Sisterhood before.* As a rule, Aunt Esther avoids speaking to anyone outside the household and I don't recall her acting friendly with anyone in the synagogue. Not knowing what to think, I gulp down the rest of my coffee and head to my room to finish getting dressed.

Before I leave on the errand, I stop by the outside kitchen to pick up the platter of cakes from Cooky Betty, whose mouth is full of crumbs.

"Cooky Betty, what happened to all the cake? There's so little left."

"A lizard came and stole some," she says. "And then a crazy chicken came and gobbled up de rest with his beak. They are all gone now 'cause I shooed them away with my broom."

I laugh at her childish answer and give her a peck on the cheek. These old-timers really are an eccentric bunch, but I love them with all my heart. Every day I learn more and more about them.

I head out in the bright sunshine and stroll down Crystal Gade, past the sounds of babies crying, tinny gramophones, and sewing machines reverberating through the neighbors' jalousies. The smell of kallaloo wafts through an unseen kitchen door. I look up and catch a pair of inquisitive eyes peering at me through an open window, but by the time I blink, they are gone. But I feel them following me down the street.

In the distance, a cock crows and a dog barks. At this early hour, there are only a few workers heading down the mountain by a network of steep, narrow staircases built into the sides of the hills, while farmers lead donkey carts down the mountain roads. Today will be a busy day, I surmise, as I watch a large steamer gliding into the harbor, sending glistening waves over the smooth, turquoise water. Another steamer chugs steadily to port, no doubt coming to coal or offload some merchandise. Another day has begun, another day with no meaning and no purpose.

"Good morning," I say to a passing market woman whose neck strains under the weight of a fruit basket. She returns my greeting blankly then continues on her way, trailed by two barefoot children in tow.

When I reach the synagogue's gate, I unlatch the lock and push it open, surprised to see the courtyard empty. I climb up the steps to the large arched doorway and realize that the door is closed and is probably locked. *Caramba!* I look around for help, but the streets are empty. The workers are heading down Raadets Gade or Commandant Gade, far out of earshot. Unwilling to give up so easily, I tug at the door again, this time using more force, but it remains firmly closed. I set the tray down and, mustering every last ounce of strength, I pull on the door until my face is red and I break out in a sweat. After more pulling and tugging, the massive door finally heaves open.

Inside the sanctuary is cool and dark. The only light comes from some scattered rays that stream in through the half-open jalousies. I pick up the platter and tiptoe carefully across the sandy floor towards the back, wending my way around the benches and pews in the dim light, wishing the caretaker had left the gas lamps on. I trudge quietly, hoping to finish the errand and be out of there as quickly as possible.

Halfway across the room, I hear a strange noise. I stop short. The thought that someone may be in the building makes the hair on the back of my neck stand up. I feel my heart race as I quicken my pace, but fear overtakes me when I realize that the closer I get to the back room, the louder the noise becomes. By now, my heart is pounding and sweat breaks out on my forehead. I regret not turning around when I had the chance.

To make matters worse, the back room is completely dark. I take a few steps forward and listen. The noise stops. Something is not right. I decide the best course of action is to hurry up and deposit the platter as quickly as possible, then turn and run out the door. I quicken my pace and race through the doorway until—wham! I collide into something hard that knocks the breath out of me and sends me toppling backwards. The tray flies out of my hands and lands with a loud clang as I fall with a thud. Pain shoots up my back and when I try to focus, all I see are stars.

When I finally focus, I see that pieces of cake are scattered everywhere. I groan from pain, but before I have a chance to get up, I hear something moving in the dark, something large. I rub my eyes and peer into the darkness only to realize with horror that I have collided into a man who is just as startled as I am. When our eyes meet, I see a look of raw fear.

The stranger jumps to his feet. Frantic, he looks around, as if expecting more intruders. He looks confused and disoriented; his breathing is loud, coming almost in gasps. From the smell of his dirty, wrinkled clothing and his unwashed body I take him to be a vagrant, possibly a thief. Then the hair on the back of my neck stands up when I realize he has come here to steal, and I may have unwittingly thwarted his chances. I rise to my feet and take a step backwards, preparing to run, but to my horror, the stranger has already started towards me.

Paralyzed with fear, I utter a scream. The stranger's eyes widen with panic as he holds up his hands "Stop! Don't scream!" he cries. When I scream even harder, the stranger's face contorts with horror.

A jolt of electricity soars through my body. Picking myself up I race toward the door, bumping into benches and tripping on the sand floor. Behind me, I hear his footsteps pounding as he catches up with me. Panicking, I stumble over a pew and lose my balance. He cries out something unintelligible, which pushes me to ignore my pain and struggle to save my life. By now, my heart is pounding and I see my life flashing before my eyes. The stranger grabs my shoulder and jerks me backwards with his powerful grip, causing me to fall to the ground in a heap.

"Get away!" I scream.

"Quiet!" he yells. "Don't scream or I'll have to do something drastic. And don't try to run away again."

Jerking myself free, I scramble past a pew, but the man lunges at me, causing us both to crash to the ground. His weight crushes me, suffocating the life out of me. I struggle underneath him, screaming and clawing at him.

The stranger panics. He presses his hands over my mouth and orders me to keep quiet. Meanwhile, I pound him with my fists, and claw at his face, but he holds me firm in his iron-like grip.

"Let me go!" I scream, tearing his hands away from my mouth.

"Quiet!" he hisses. "Someone may hear you. Keep still and no one gets hurt."

"Let me go!" I yell again, wriggling out from under his body.

"Only when you stop screaming."

I scream again, this time louder.

"Shh!" he orders. "Do you want the police to come?"

"Then let me go!"

"I'm terribly sorry but I cannot release you until you agree to keep quiet. You are much too loud and I fear you will alert the police. I promise I won't hurt you."

"If you *don't* release me, then I *will* go to the police."

"That is illogical, unless you are the police."

"If you don't want me to go to the police then let me go right this instant."

The man releases his grip. Seizing the opportunity, I smack him across the face. While he is still dazed, I jump to my feet and race toward the door, but he overtakes me and tackles me to the ground once more. I struggle with all my might, but sand is now in my hair and face, and even my mouth, which makes it harder for me to scream. When I finally look at him, I see an unmistakable look of hurt, which shocks me to my core.

"Why did you slap me?" he says, holding me still. "I told you I wasn't going to hurt you."

"Why should I believe you?" I say with indignation. "You chased me and scared me half to death."

"I apologize for that, but I didn't know who you were. I was afraid you would report me to the police."

"Who are you, some kind of thief?"

The stranger bristles. "Certainly not. I've never stolen anything in my life. I just come here to rest and escape from the heat. I had nowhere else to go. I've got enough trouble and don't need some Good Samaritan reporting me to the police for the crime of needing peace and quiet."

"If you've done nothing wrong, then why are you so afraid of the police?"

"Good question," he says, looking perplexed. "I'm not exactly sure how to answer that right now."

He brushes sand from his arms and legs, and rubs his reddened cheek. By all appearances, he's nothing more than a harmless tramp, but there is something unusual about his look. He has an air of dignity and importance, like a prince who has suddenly become a pauper.

"Who are you anyway?" I say, putting my hands on my hips. "And what are you doing here?"

"As to the *'who are you'* part, I'm a sailor," he says, pointing to a duffel bag sitting on a bench. "And as to the *'what am I doing here'* part, the simple truth is I'm stranded. About two weeks ago, I was separated from my ship, but not out of irresponsibility or drunkenness. I became stranded for an entirely different reason."

"You're stranded? You mean like Robinson Crusoe?"

He grins. "Actually, more like Gulliver. But the minute I came ashore, I felt as though I *belonged* here. It was a very strange feeling, but since I felt safe on the island, I decided to try my luck and stay. But it hasn't been easy. I haven't much money so I eat whatever I can get hold of and sleep wherever I can. Sometimes I hide here during the day just to rest or write letters and to keep away from the watchful glare of the gendarmes. Until now, I've kept out of trouble. I've even made use of those worthless art lesson my mother forced me to take. As a matter of fact, when you stumbled upon me, I was about to climb out the window and go up to the hills to do a bit of sketching. The harbor is beautiful this time of day."

Light from the jalousie illuminates the stranger's face and I realize for the first time how handsome he is. Beneath his shaggy beard and tousled blond hair, he has fine features, clear blue eyes, a handsome nose, and straight, white teeth. He speaks in a deep, pleasant voice with a strong accent that I cannot place. He is clearly a foreigner, from someplace far away from the tropics.

"Show me some of your sketches."

The stranger opens up his duffel bag and takes out a small sketch book with lovely pencil drawings of the buildings, the island people, and some schooners out in the harbor.

"You're very good, but why were you climbing out the window? It gives people the impression that you came here to steal. You should have used the door. Maybe I should report you to the police for suspicious activity."

"Please don't do that, Miss. I'm just an out-of-work sailor, not a thief. Just look at my dark tan, tattered clothing, and tousled hair. Additionally, if I was a thief, I wouldn't be talking to you. I would just take the silver and disappear out the door and you would never see me again. But if you still think I'm a thief, go ahead and search my bag. I'll step back and give you plenty of room."

Keeping my eyes glued on the stranger, I grab his bag and start rifling through it. All I find are a toothbrush, a wrinkled shirt, a bar of soap, a razor, a book, some pictures, a few coins, a comb, and a bundle of soiled underclothes, nothing of any value.

"Alright, so maybe you are a sailor. Explain to me why you're so afraid of being caught by the police?"

"Like I said, I was afraid you'd report me. Nobody knows my name and I haven't any identity papers. I was afraid you or someone else would accuse me of a crime and they'd put me in that rather imposing-looking fort down by the harbor. I apologize for scaring you, Miss, but nowadays you never know whom you can trust."

"Where do you come from?"

"From far away," he says, making a sweeping gesture with his hand. "Back home I used to be important person, but here I'm a nobody, a drifter with no past, no present, and no future. I've been reduced to sleeping on hard benches for lack of money, and eating what people discard. But the worst part about being stranded on an island is having no one to talk to. Right now, what I could use most is a friend."

Suddenly I remember what I've been sent here to do. I return to the fallen cake platter, crestfallen to see all of Cooky Betty's delicious cakes scattered across the dirty floor. Aunt Esther will be livid when she finds out I dropped them. As tears well in my eyes, I bend down to retrieve the forlorn pieces, and to my utter shock and surprise, the stranger bends down and helps me to gather up all the pieces. Through my watery eyes, I see his strong hands gently picking up and shaking the sand off the cake pieces and rearranging them nicely on the platter.

"There you go, Miss, no harm done," he says. "Do you forgive me for scaring you?"

I wipe my eyes with my sleeve and regard the stranger. Perhaps if he took a bath, shaved his beard, and put on some clean clothes, he would look less frightful. Maybe he needs my help.

"I forgive you, but I don't even know your name."

He smacks his forehead with his palm. "How stupid of me! Allow me to make a proper introduction. My name is Erich Seibold, merchant sailor, world traveler, lover of philosophy, seeker of wisdom. And now you may count me as one of your admirers."

"Erich," I say, repeating his name. "That's easy enough."

"And you, Miss? What is your name?"

I shake my head. "I shouldn't tell you my name. It's not proper and I'm not supposed to talk to strangers."

"Then just give me your first name. There's no harm in that."

"Very well, it's Abigail."

"Abigail," he says, pronouncing each syllable distinctly. "That's a fine name for a beautiful young girl. And by the way Miss Abigail, you are indeed correct that it's not fitting to talk to strangers. I myself have an iron-clad policy of never talking to strangers, but if you'll give me a chance, you may discover that I'm not so scary after all. In fact, you may end up enjoying my company. You may discover that I have much to offer. I'm articulate, well-spoken in a number of languages; I've read all the classics: Shakespeare, Milton, Goethe, and Tolstoy. I can quote Molière or Rousseau with my eyes closed: *'Belle marquise, vos beaux yeux me font mourir d'amour...'* Just because you caught me sneaking around a dark building hiding from the police doesn't automatically make me a bad person. It might mean that I'm a good person in a very bad situation. And right now, the one thing I could really use is a friend. So if you'll allow me, I would like to make a prediction that I, Erich Seibold, by virtue of my outstanding qualities, will soon become worthy of your friendship. So, Miss Abigail, do we have a deal? Will you give me a chance?"

"Before I give you my answer, tell me the truth about why you're afraid of the police. Are you a criminal? Have you broken any laws?"

"No laws that I'm aware of. At least not any civilian laws, but I doubt I'll be able to convince you of that. So, for now, let's agree that you don't know if you can trust me, and I don't know if I can trust you. But if you'll give me a chance, I promise to do everything possible to earn your trust. Agreed?"

When I fail to respond, he holds out his hand. "*Agreed*?"

Gingerly, I place my hand in his, surprised at how warm and comforting it feels.

"Agreed," I say.

"Good. Now that you've agreed to give me a chance, please start by telling me your full name."

I look down at my feet.

"There's no harm in that," he says. "It's the first step in getting acquainted with someone. I already trusted you enough to let you go through my duffel bag and I usually don't show my friends my toothbrush and razor until we've known each other at least a few days. So, given that you've already seen my most private possessions, you should consider me an old, dear friend."

I laugh in spite of myself which prompts him to laugh as well.

"Well, if you must know, my full name is Abigail Levy Maduro. There are many Maduros on the island. It's an old island name. But I don't recall you telling me how you got here."

"You are very observant. I arrived here about two weeks ago aboard a tramp steamer, the *Cartagena*. When I first discovered these islands were Danish and therefore neutral, I decided to hop ashore, at least for the duration of the war. And I haven't regretted my decision one bit, even after you slapped me a few minutes ago. That slap reminded me how happy I am to be here. In fact, I'm happier here than I've been in years. Tell me something, Miss Maduro, how old are you?"

"Sixteen."

"And do you have any sisters and brothers?"

"No."

"And what about your mother and father?"

I was silent for a moment. "They died a few months ago back in Panama. That's why I'm here now. I came to live with my Aunt Esther. She's a bad-tempered spinster with a big house just up the road a bit. She lives with a houseful of elderly, eccentric servants."

"I'm sorry to hear about your parents," he says, looking downcast. "It seems as though we have a lot more in common than I first realized. We're two people in need of a family."

I glance at the clock. "Oh no, I must get back home. They're expecting me. I wish I could stay longer, but I've been gone too long as it is. My aunt will get suspicious and start asking questions."

I notice Erich eyeing the cake platter. "How long has it been since you've had something to eat?" I say, eyeing his thin frame.

"Two days according to my calculations, which are a bit fuzzy, unless you consider a half dozen mangoes and a rotten papaya to be an adequate meal? I'm almost out of money."

"Then please help yourself to some cake."

Erich grabs some cake and stuffs it in his mouth as if he were famished. Seeing his hunger so plainly, I can't help but feel pity for this lost vagrant.

"Can you get back to your ship?"

"That would be impossible," he says in between bites. "She's long gone by now—probably in Havana. My only hope is to stay here and make the best of things. Try to get a job, earn some money, and forget about the past."

"Why did you leave your ship if you had no money?"

"It's on account of the war. Things are bad out there right now. The sea is a raging battlefield and no man is safe. I calculated that my odds of surviving on land were far greater than crossing the Atlantic again on a tramp steamer. If only I had a safe place to sleep, that would really alleviate my plight. The last time I checked, the Grand Hotel was charging two dollars a night, which is beyond my means at the present. Would you happen to know of a place I could stay? Nothing fancy, perhaps just a room in a house. The only thing I need is privacy. Because I lack the proper papers, my situation is somewhat tenuous."

My mind is racing. "Did you say a room in a house?"

"Yes, although at this point I would take a barn just to get off these hard benches. Don't worry, my needs are very simple. I won't insist on a feather pillow or lavender-scented sheets, just a quiet place to lay my head at night."

A thought pops in my mind. "Actually, I may know of a place, but I need a little time to work things out."

"Take all the time you need," he says. "The war won't end between today and tomorrow. Is it far from here?"

"Just a little way up the hill, but first I must make sure it's private and safe. You wouldn't want any nosy neighbors snooping around, would you? Can we meet again tomorrow and settle the matter?"

"Only if you promise not to call the police."

"Of course, but could I at least tell Nana Jane?"

"Who is this Nana Jane?"

"She's our housekeeper, but she's more like a friend to me. I couldn't keep such a big secret from her."

"But this Nana Jane could go to the police."

"People here aren't like that," I say. "They don't particularly care for the police. And they don't like the governor either, or the government clerks, or the customs inspectors, or the steamship companies, or the planters. In fact, they hate just about everybody, except for David Hamilton Jackson, of course. He's their hero."

"Who's David Hamilton Jackson?"

"He's their leader," I say. "He owns a newspaper, and even traveled all the way to Denmark to complain to His Majesty about the awful conditions in the islands. He demanded freedom of the press and people say King Christian was so taken with him that he granted his request right away, but I don't suppose King Christian ever read any of Mr. Hamilton Jackson's angry newspaper articles."

"That's all well and good," he says, nervously running his fingers through his hair. "But this Nana Jane might get suspicious and tell someone else who, in turn, might go to the police. Let's agree that for now that you won't tell any adults. Not Nana Jane and not even Mr. Hamilton Jackson. Are we agreed?"

"I suppose so," I say. "I guess I can keep a secret."

"Excellent," he says. "Now remember the first rule of war is trust nobody, except me, of course. Sometimes the person you think is your friend is really your enemy, and the person you think is your enemy is really your friend. That's the nature of war. Got it?"

"I think so."

"Good, you're a brave girl, Abigail. It's not every day you find someone willing to help a total stranger." His hand brushes my cheek. "I just hope I never let you down. Can we meet here again tomorrow?"

"Yes, same time."

I turn and head for the door. The minute I feel the sun burning the top of my head, a feeling of remorse washes over me. Aunt Esther took me into her house and now I'm about to break every rule in the book by taking in a strange man, and a foreigner to boot. But something about Erich appeals to me. He's handsome, smart, educated, and has seen the world. But his accent is worrisome. It sounds suspiciously like German which could spell trouble. Can it be possible this well-mannered stranger is really a spy or a saboteur? How can I know for sure? Should I just blindly trust him or try to discern the truth? And though I don't relish the idea of keeping a secret from Aunt Esther and Nana Jane, I also realize that I may be putting all of our lives in great danger.

Part Two

CHAPTER 12

I hurry home to study the mysterious door in greater detail. This time, I'm determined to find out what lies behind it. I wade through the overgrown grasses until I reach it, annoyed to see it's still in the same decrepit condition as before. Using all my strength, I turn the handle, but years of humidity and disuse have sealed it shut. Next, I peer through the small, dirt-encrusted window built into the foundation, but it's impossible to see through it. My plan is starting to look hopeless, but something inside of me refuses to let that wandering sailor down. I have to help him, no matter what.

Slumping to the ground, I pluck a hibiscus off a bush and study its intricate parts, concentrating on solving this dilemma. But no matter how I look at it, it all boils down to one thing: Nana Jane. I will never be able to help that sailor without Nana Jane's help. My only choice is to tell her and pray she doesn't spill the beans. I'm certain that if Aunt Esther finds out, there will be hell to pay.

I find Nana Jane lying under the shade of the mango tree. For a second, my heart stops. She was supposed to be sweeping the garden path, but must have fallen asleep with her Bible on her chest, leaving the broom strewn in a haphazard fashion on the ground. I hate having to wake her up, but the pleading look on the handsome sailor's face, spurs me to action.

I gently shake her shoulder. "Nana Jane, wake up."

She snores loudly and rolls over on her side. With each snore, her body rises and falls, the only assurance that she's still alive.

"Nana Jane, please wake up. I have to talk to you."

Her nose twitches, her eyelids flutter.

"What happened?" she mutters, rubbing her eyes. "Did that crazy bird of yours get loose?"

"No, it's much more important than that. I need your help."

Nana Jane's eyes shoot open and she bolts upright. "More important than Teddy Roosevelt's crazy bird? More important than Nana Jane's nap?" she says, with just the right amount of wit and irony.

"Nana Jane, something happened today that Aunt Esther must never find out about."

Nana Jane looks faint and places her hand over her heart.

"Tell me the truth, what did you do?" she says, regarding me with suspicious eyes. "Did you smash her good china? Break her gramophone? Tell me now before I box your ears."

"I met someone, a man. He's a sailor, actually. He's lost and needs my help. He got separated from his ship and needs a place to stay."

Nana Jane gives me an admonishing wave of her hand. "For that you had to wake me up? Did he ask you for money? Let him go down to Norre Gade and send a telegram home asking for money. We're not a bank and your Aunt Esther is not running a rooming house."

"It's more serious than that. He said he came here on account of the war. He said, 'The sea is a raging battlefield and no man is safe.'"

"Seerious?" says Nana Jane, furrowing her brow. "And how you know he telling the truth? How did you meet this sailor?"

I explain the whole story about how I went to the synagogue to deliver the cake and stumbled into the sailor with the foreign accent, how he protested that he wasn't a thief by letting me search his bag, and his unusual story about how he became separated from his ship and how he was reduced to sleeping on the hard benches for lack of money. I told her how he begged me for a place to stay, how desperate he looked, and also how handsome, smart, and nice he appeared."

Nana Jane throws her head back and laughs. "In all my years I never heard such a crazy story."

"Please Nana Jane, it's not a joke, I have to help this man. He has no friends and I think he may be in trouble. Or it may be that he's running away from something."

"Most likely he's running away from, an angry wife."

"Very funny, but he didn't seem that type at all. Nana Jane, I want to help this poor sailor, but what if it turns out he's some kind of German spy?"

"A... what?" She bursts out laughing again, the kind that makes her whole body shake. This time, she laughs so hard tears start rolling down her face. By this point, my face is turning red and I'm starting to feel somewhat foolish.

"Nana Jane, please stop laughing. This is serious. I have to help this man, but I'm worried that I may be making a mistake. What should I do?"

"First of all," she says, wiping her eyes with the back of her hand. "Lots of sailors pass by these islands every day minding their own self business. I knew from the first minute I saw you that you had your father's wild imagination. Tell me something. Who would this sailor be spying on, Miss Esther Maduro?" More house-shaking laughter follows. "Lord have mercy, if this young sailor man needs help, then you have an obligation to help him. The Bible teaches us to help the stranger. I do believe it say dat."

"So, you're not mad at me?"

"Why would I be mad at you?"

"Because I offered to help a stranger."

"Child, you offered to help him because you have a heart of gold, just like your grandfather, may he rest in peace. He gave my mother, my sister, and me a home when we had nothing and nowhere to go. You have his same merciful soul and generous heart. I knew it from the moment I laid eyes on you."

I hug Nana Jane. "Thank you, Nana Jane. But how can we help this sailor without Aunt Esther finding out? Do you know what's behind that door over there?"

Nana Jane scratches the back of her head. "Let me study the situation." She picks up the broom and beats a path through the tall guinea grass, knocking away overgrown weeds and bushes until she reaches the door. She grabs the door handle and tries to turn it, but it refuses to budge. Next, she spies a rusty old garden spade lying on the ground. She tells me to retrieve it, and then she inserts it into the crack. Using our combined strength and a lot of pulling and tugging, the two of us manage to pry open the stuck door, and when I see what lies behind the mysterious door, my heart races.

The room is just the right size. It's small, but there's a water pump and a window to let in fresh air. There is a musty smell, as if the room hadn't been aired in years, and piled high from floor to ceiling is a jumble of old furniture, wooden crates, a baby crib, an old bed frame, an armoire, various steamer trunks, and even some oil paintings of three-masted schooners. Spider webs dangle from the ceiling, and I hear a cricket chirping from a hidden corner. Clearly the room is in need of serious cleaning.

I also spot some useful items, such as a porcelain washbasin and a pitcher, a mirror, a bedside table, cartons of old books, and stacks of dishes. Nana Jane starts sweeping the dusty floor, pushing a cloud of dust and debris toward the door. We find an old mattress which she beats several times with the broom, kicking up a cloud of dust that settles at our feet. It fits perfectly inside the bed frame.

"Here is a proper bed for your sailor man," she says, plopping down on the bed. "Tell me, does this lucky sailor have a proper name?"

"He said his name is Erich."

"Er-rich," she says, using a guttural 'r' that resonates deep in her throat. "This Mr. Er-rich should be very cozy for a few days, maybe a week, as long as he doesn't mind crickets and spiders. I'll bring down some bed linens and a pillow, but you must nevah—" She wags an admonishing finger at me. "—nevah tell your Auntie Esther that a man is sleeping down here. Not unless you want to give her a nervous breakdown. She won't have no man sleeping in her house, no matter how nice and handsome he be. Men are trouble. Do you understand, Miss Abigail?"

"Yes, Nana Jane," I say, hugging her. "Thank you so much."

***

Early the next morning, I slip away from the house to meet Erich. As I head down Crystal Gade, my heart sinks at the notion that our meeting was just a dream and I will never see him again. Luckily, when I reach the gate, I see him and a wave of relief washes over me. Erich is sitting patiently on the steps reading the latest copy of the *St. Thomas Tidende*. He looks up and waves.

Erich's appearance is different from yesterday, greatly improved. A recent haircut and a shave make him look even more handsome than before, and he exudes the smell of bay rum and soap, evidence of a recent bath. The raw fear that had previously marred his face is replaced with a newfound calm. Greeting him, I feel like two old friends meeting after an unavoidable separation. At his side is his canvas duffel bag, and on his head a straw hat, similar to the ones the Cha Chas use over in Frenchtown. Aside from that, he has no other discernable possessions. As soon as he sees me, he breaks into a wide grin that assures me he is the same man as yesterday. It was not a dream.

"I was afraid I'd never see you again, Abigail," he says, standing up. "I couldn't sleep the whole night, worried that you were nothing but an apparition, the delusion of a desperate, starving man. But now that I see your lovely face out in the sunshine, I know you're a real person and not some figment of my imagination. I can hardly believe my good fortune."

I feel my cheeks blushing. "Oh, it's nothing really. I worked it all out. You can stay with us as long as you like, but I have to warn you that my Aunt Esther is not fond of strange man. In fact, we must be very careful she never finds out about you or there'll be hell to pay. But don't worry, she spends the whole day sewing and listening to the same gramophone records over and over, so you should be fairly safe."

"I can't thank you enough, Abby," he says. "Now that you've given me this information, I understand your situation a little better. Again, I'm sorry about your parents. I understand a little of what you're going through and I'll do whatever it takes to make sure your auntie doesn't find out about me. I'll take full responsibility for anything that happens to you on account of my intrusion."

When we arrive at the house, I show Erich how to circle around to the back yard where the basement door is located. He marvels at the old mango tree, remarking about its enormous height and the plethora of luscious fruit that dangle seductively from its branches. He admires the enormous papayas growing wild in the bushes, and the juicy limes just begging to be squeezed into a glass of sugared water and rum. When I show him the basement room, I expect him to flinch because of its shabby condition, but he doesn't. In fact, he looks profoundly grateful, as if I'd just given him a suite at the Grand

Hotel. He admires the mahogany bed frame, the soft mattress, and even pulls a few books out of the crates. His face appears softened as he turns to me and says, "Abby, I don't know how to thank you." He throws his duffel bag on the bed and sits down. "This is more than I ever expected, much more."

As luck would have it, Nana Jane remembered to put some fresh linen on the bed, a clean towel near the wash basin, a hurricane lamp on the bedside table, some food, and two bottles of lemonade on a side table. Erich takes the bottles, pries them open, and hands one to me.

"Sit down a minute, Abby, I wish to know you a little better."

He pulls up a chair for me, takes out a cigarette and lights it with a match. He asks about my life back in Panama. I feel myself blushing, not because of embarrassment, but because I'm not used to talking about myself. He urges me to open up, telling me I shouldn't keep everything all bottled up inside. Soon, I find myself telling him about my parents, my friends, my life back in Colón, my old school, how we used to run over to the Gatún locks and watch the huge ships passing through, especially the time we saw the American cruiser *Charleston* heading over to the Pacific Ocean. How thrilling that was! I also describe what it's like to swim in both oceans—the Atlantic and the Pacific—on the very same day, how it makes you feel that the earth is somewhat smaller in Panama. Then I tell him about Aunt Esther and Nana Jane and how my life has changed drastically since I arrived in St. Thomas, and how I've been forced to give up my dream of becoming a teacher, and how Aunt Esther forces me to work as a seamstress just to pay the bills. While I'm speaking, I notice that Erich listens quietly, studying me with his warm blue eyes as he nods his head from time to time as if he's storing all this information inside.

"Tell me more about this Aunt Esther," he says, puffing on his cigarette.

"She's my father's older sister and she never married and has no patience for children. She lost her fiancé years ago when he sailed away to Panama and never returned. After many years of no news from him, she started acting strangely, neglecting her appearance, ranting and raving, washing her hands and rearranging the house obsessively. My grandparents tried to protect her by keeping her secluded in the house, and eventually she lost all her friends. Now she lives like a recluse, just sitting alone in the sewing room listening to the same gramophone records over and over, always muttering under her breath. Her situation is beyond hope. I pray that I don't end up like her."

Erich pats my head. "I promise you that will never happen. You have a fire in your soul. You were meant to go places and do wonderful things, but now is not the time. There is much you must learn before you're ready to conquer the world."

I gaze into his eyes. They radiate warmth and compassion, something I thought I would never see again. I long to tell Erich how lonely I've been here on the island, how miserable my life has become, but something holds me back. I need more time to get to know him a little better.

"Now tell me about you," I say, changing the subject. "How do you know French so well? Are you from France?"

Erich laughs. "No, I'm not from France, but my mother used to be a French teacher and she taught me a few phrases. I come from a very cultured and educated European family. I grew up surrounded by books, music, and art. Back then, I was mostly in love with ships, motorcars, medals, and glory. I lived for the sea."

"How did you find your way here?"

He pauses for a moment. "I was working on a tramp steamer headed to Cuba when I decided to try my luck here. I figured the sea was not a safe place to be during a war. When I first arrived, I was a little disoriented and naturally guarded because of my experiences during the war. I'd never been to such an exotic island before and I didn't know how the locals would treat me. The truth is, I felt like a fish out of water. But after awhile, I became fond of the place. I adjusted to my new environment and loved listening to the musical way the natives speak. I absorbed the distinct rhythm and lilt of their dialect, and the way words roll off their tongues like music. Although it took me a while to get used to their way of speaking, I loved the playful way they tease each other in good fun. I spent days just watching and observing their mannerisms, their gestures, their outward displays of affection, which are so different from back home, how they lead their donkey carts to market how the men play dominoes, how the fishermen furl their sails at dusk. And in all this time, I don't recall ever being bored. Now I am utterly captivated by the island and her people. I feel very much at home." He adds with a chuckle, "I guess you could say I've gone native."

"You are so charming," I say with a blush. "I wish Nana Jane could meet you. I'm sure she would adore you as well, perhaps even adopt you like she has me."

"That's too dangerous, Abby," he says, exhaling a long stream of cigarette smoke. "There are some people who would say I have no right to be here. They would call me a criminal and accuse of me of doing terrible things. Remember, this must be *our* little secret. Someday, I hope to repay you for your kindness."

I leave Erich to get settled while I head back upstairs to tackle my daily sewing. As I sit there darning socks and repairing torn hemlines, my heart is filled with a renewed sense of purpose. Now that I have a special friend, there's so much to look forward to. I peek over at Aunt Esther and am not surprised to see her lips pursed in anger and resentment. There's no use talking to her or trying to make peace with her, she's hopeless. I settle back in my chair listening as the Victrola warbles out her favorite song, *'You ask me why I'm always teasing you-ou-ou. You hate to have me call you pretty baby. I really thought that I was pleasing you. 'Cause you're just a baby to me-e-e...'* and I shudder to think that one day Aunt Esther may find out I have deceived her by harboring a strange man in the basement.

Several days later, Erich tells me he found work on a fishing boat and he'll be gone most days from sunrise to sunset. He assures me that everything will work out fine, but many nights as I lay in bed trying to fall asleep, I worry that I've made a terrible mistake by letting a complete stranger stay in our basement. I imagine all sorts of terrible things that can happen as a result, rumors and gossip spreading like weeds around town. When I wake up in the morning, I go through the motions like a zombie, but inside I'm so nervous that when I try to eat breakfast, nothing stays down.

CHAPTER 13

Several weeks later while I'm dozing in bed, something crashes down on my head. Before I come to my senses, I see stars floating all around and there's a shooting pain in my head. Then the ferocious image of Aunt Esther comes into focus. She stands over me, pointing a broom in my face with eyes that seethe with righteous indignation. I gasp, sit up, and move as far away from that frightful creature as possible while I rub the painful spot on my head where she hit me.

"You scheming little brat!" she screams. "Did you think I was so stupid that I wouldn't find out?"

My thoughts fly to Erich. Aunt Esther must have found out about him which means the gendarmes are probably on their way to arrest him. Or is it already too late? Have they already taken him away in chains? Are they coming for me next?

I glance at the door, expecting to see their tall blue hats and blue coats storming into the room with shackles and pistols at the ready. I edge further away until I'm cowering at the edge of my bed. When she raises the broom again, I hold my hands up to shield myself from further blows, expecting the worst to happen. If this is the end, I'm prepared to go down with the ship.

She smashes the broom down on my head. I cry out in pain.

"How could you?" she screams. "I'm at my wits end with you. You've brought me nothing but trouble!"

"Stop!" I yell. "I'm sorry, Aunt Esther. Please forgive me."

"Sorry my foot, you're not the least bit sorry."

She shoves the broom into my chest, sending me hurtling off the bed.

"You devious little brat. You've been scheming with all my enemies all over town."

"No I haven't!" I cry with indignation, grabbing a pillow to shield myself. "It's not true! What are you talking about?"

"I know you've been talking to that no good Judge Neergaard. Have you no shame? Don't you know what he's done?"

Judge Neergaard? Why does Aunt Esther think that Judge Neergaard is her enemy? What is she talking about?

"Judge Neergaard is my friend. He's tutoring me. He wants to help me become a teacher."

"Tutoring you?" she scoffs. "What a laugh. All he can teach you is how to ruin people's lives and reputations. You know nothing about Judge Neergaard. I order you to stop seeing him immediately if you want remain in my house."

Exasperated, she throws the broom down and stalks off, leaving me in complete bewilderment. If a simple conversation with a respected judge can set her off like a blazing cannon, how will she act when she finds out there's a strange man living in her basement? But more worrisome is how irrational Aunt Esther's behavior is becoming and how it increases with intensity. Every day, something else triggers her explosive temper, making it impossible for me to continue living with her. The situation is so bad, I feel as though I'm living on borrowed time.

***

A few days later while I'm ironing some tablecloths, Nana Jane whispers in my ear that today she has arranged to take me to the home of the pretty young lady from the synagogue. It seems that her mother, Mrs. De Castro, sent word that she has a pile of clothes that need mending and she wants us to pick it up right away. When I hear this new, my heart soars. At last I have a chance to leave this stuffy house for a while. I set down the iron and race to my room to put on a nice dress and brush my hair. Soon, Nana Jane leads me up Crystal Gade to the De Castro residence.

Deborah De Castro's home is one of the finest on Synagogue Hill. It's a two-story villa with a sloping red roof, large picture windows, and a sweeping terrace adorned with flaming red roses, fragrant jasmine, and purple bougainvilleas. A team of gardeners is hard at work cultivating the bushes around the house, while assorted washerwomen and housekeepers peek at us through the bushes and jalousies.

Nana Jane leads me up the steps as she explains that Mr. De Castro is the governor's most trusted advisor, a rich and influential lawyer with all the right connections. We only have to knock once before the door is answered by a turbaned housekeeper with eyes that are both inquisitive and guarded. As soon as she sticks her head out, the pleasing strains of piano music drift out from a hidden corner somewhere in the house.

Nana Jane smiles sweetly. "Good morning, Miss Sarah, is Miss Deborah at home?"

"Who shall I say is calling?" says the housekeeper.

"Tell her it's Miss Abigail Maduro, Miss Esther's niece."

The servant shows us in and tells us to wait in the parlor. I follow Nana Jane into the elegant home, admiring the fine furniture, the expensive carpets, and the crystal chandeliers. A few minutes later, the piano playing stops and Deborah greets us in the parlor looking like an expensive oil painting. Her long black hair is piled high on her head with only a few dainty wisps to frame her perfect oval face. She wears a pale yellow dress with an empire waist and matching sandals, the very picture of loveliness.

"Are you Rebecca Maduro's daughter?" she says, sizing me up through lashes as thick as a mongoose's tail. "I can't believe it. I thought I saw you in the synagogue the other day, but I didn't have a chance to introduce myself. How nice to meet you."

"I noticed you as well," I say, looking around, capturing it all in. It was almost too good to be true. "I wanted to meet you very much. I think we are close in age."

Deborah turns to Nana Jane. "Nana Jane, you can leave Abigail with me for a little while. I promise to return her at a reasonable hour." Nana Jane nods and leaves. "Here, have a seat. First of all, I want to tell you that when we got the awful news about your parents, we were devastated. Your Aunt Esther took the news really bad. Later, when I found out you were coming to live with your aunt, I knew you had a hard road ahead of you. But now that you're here, I see you're making the best of things. Did your mother ever mention that she and my mother were best friends?"

"No, I don't recall her ever saying that."

"That's odd," she says, furrowing her brow. "Perhaps I should have dropped by earlier to introduce myself, but between teaching and practicing the piano, there aren't enough hours in the day."

My ears perk up. "You teach school? My greatest dream is to become a schoolteacher. Do you have a certificate? Aunt Esther says there's no school here for girls past the sixth grade..."

"That is correct," says Deborah. "Only the wealthiest families can afford to send their children to Antigua or America to continue their education. I went to New York City to get my teacher's certificate, but given your aunt's financial situation, I'm sure that's not possible. What a shame since you seem like such an intelligent girl. I adored living in New York City with all the fancy shops, not to mention dining at the Waldorf-Astoria or strolling through Central Park. It was a dream come true. I'm sure you're aware that life on a small island can be tedious and dull. There are no eligible men and no matter where you go, you always run into the same dull faces. On the other hand, New York is always exciting and there's always something new to see. I can't wait to go back."

While Deborah prattles on about New York, I wander over to the bookshelf and scan the titles for any books that might help me pass the teacher's examination. The sheer quantity and variety of books overwhelms me. I have a longing to open up each book and leaf through all the pages.

"So, what do you think of my new dress?" she says, inserting herself between me and the bookshelf.

"It's lovely," I say, daring to touch its satiny fabric.

"Watch it!" she says, snatching it away. "The fabric is delicate. I saw a picture of it in Harper's Bazaar and my mother sent a telegram and ordered it. I read that Madeleine Astor was seen wearing it on holiday in Maine, but don't attempt to find a dress like this in one of the shops downtown. It's hilarious how outdated the local society women look in last year's fashions."

"I should probably be getting back now."

"Why so fast?" she says, pushing me down on the sofa. "You've only just arrived. Let's have some tea." Deborah calls for a servant to bring us some tea and biscuits as she drones on about her exciting life. She pulls me by the collar like a little dog to show me her closet full of clothes, her elegant shoes, her porcelain doll collection, her jewelry, even her piano playing. Although I admit her company is charming, I start to feel drained. When I proffer the excuse that Aunt Esther needs me to help with the sewing and ironing, she pulls me into the garden saying there's so much to catch up on.

"You know, I always wondered why your parents chose to move to Panama while mine didn't," she says wistfully, as she plucks a jasmine blossom off its stem. "It always made me feel like I missed out on a golden opportunity to marry a rich Panamanian or one of those dashing American engineers working on the canal."

"Are there no eligible men here you can marry?"

"Not one," she says. "All the good men left years ago, at least those rich enough or ambitious enough for me."

"Being rich isn't everything..." I say, but stop short when I realize she's staring at some uncertain point on the horizon, her eyes glazed over. "Don't you agree, Deborah, that money isn't everything?"

"What?" she says, almost as if she's in a trance.

"I *said*, don't you agree that money isn't everything?"

"I'm afraid the majority of people don't share your view. Almost everyone in our crowd picked up and left for Panama when there was easy money to be made. And those who stayed gave up bettering their lives. They're just waiting for pearls to drop from the sky. My father's an old stalwart; he refuses to leave his position on the island. So year after year I sit waiting for my ship to come in, but at least I have you as a friend. Tell me, did your mother ever mention Agnes De Castro from St. Thomas? That's my mother."

"Not that I recall."

Deborah wrinkles her nose. "That's strange. I'm surprised she didn't, but that was so long ago. When I was little, I used to tag along whenever they went to parties or sea-bathing over at Magens Bay. They used to laugh and joke the whole day, splashing in the water, and then came that terrible rift."

"Rift? What rift?"

"It had to do with your Aunt Esther's fiancé, a man named Jacob Curiel. Suddenly our mothers stopped speaking to each other. And of course, on a small island, it's very difficult to avoid running into somebody. No matter where you go, you're bound to run into the person you're trying to avoid. A short while later, your parents left the island for good. My mother was heart-broken that your mother never said goodbye. But what's past is past."

"What was it concerning?"

"As always, it was about money. Jacob Curiel was a partner with my father and a Danish man in a business deal that went sour. They were supposed to invest a great deal of money in a lumber yard, but they lost everything. Shortly after that, Jacob Curiel left for Panama under a cloud of suspicion. The next thing we heard he was dead. All these years, your Aunt Esther has been blaming my father for what happened to her fiancé and naturally your mother had to side with Esther. But the end result was that two close families stopped speaking to each other."

"How terrible. I never knew," I say. "Now it starts to make sense why Aunt Esther thinks people are always plotting against her. She even accused me of speaking to her enemies."

"If there's anything I can do for you, don't hesitate to ask."

"Deborah, perhaps there is something you can do. May I borrow some of your books? Actually, they're not just for me; they're also for a friend."

"A *friend*?"

"Oh, it's nobody important. Just a certain someone I met who's very well-educated and loves to read. I'm sure you don't know him."

Her eyes narrow. "A him? Abigail, if I didn't know you better, I'd say you were harboring some deep dark secret."

I give her my Cheshire cat grin and head for the library. I figure the less she knows the better.

***

Later that night, I sneak down to Erich's room and give him Deborah's books. His eyes widen with delight as he leafs through them while I regale him with stories about her wonderful house, her beautiful dress, how expertly she plays the piano. All the while, I watch to see if his expression changes, but if he appears interested, I suspect it's only out of politeness.

"…and she has *real* tubes of lipstick and shoes in every color."

"But does this Deborah lady read all these books?" he says, holding up a volume on Napoleon.

"Maybe not *all* of them, but she's very smart and beautiful and elegant. She's a schoolteacher, you know, but her true love is all the finer things in life like clothes, shoes, art, and jewelry. She says I can borrow all the books I want, which means you'll have more books than you can possibly read in a lifetime. And I will be that much closer to becoming a teacher."

"But you didn't tell her about me, did you?"

"No, of course not," I say. "I'm always very careful. Anyway, she's just an acquaintance of mine, not a real friend."

"Remember what I told you," he says. "Trust nobody. It's the only way to avoid unnecessary unpleasantness."

"She mostly talks about herself anyway. Sometimes when you speak to her, she looks right through you, as if she's in a trance."

"That could be an act to disarm you," he says. "Beware of overconfidence. That's when most people make mistakes."

"Tell me the truth, what would be so horrible if Deborah found out about you? She can't do anything. She's a harmless ninny."

"It's not her I'm worried about, but others she might tell. People love to gossip and spread stories. Word gets around quick on a small island."

"Aren't you being overcautious? I get the distinct impression there's something you're not telling me, as if it's *me* you don't trust."

"If I don't tell you everything it's for your own safety," he says, snapping the book shut. "The less you know about me, the better. Because of the war, my situation is somewhat tenuous. Desperate times require desperate measures."

"What do you mean by, *because of the war?*"

Erich shuffles his feet. "Abby, the truth is I escaped the war. Or if you prefer the military term, it's called *desertion*. And desertion during times of war is a very serious offense. So serious in fact, that if the wrong people find out about me, my life would be in grave danger."

I stare at Erich in cold fright. The sudden awareness that I'm unwittingly harboring a fugitive from the war hits me like a bucket of cold water. My throat tightens and I feel light-headed.

"So, you lied to me. You told me you were a simple sailor."

"If I had told you the truth that I was a deserter, would you have let me stay in your house? Would you have trusted me, or would you have gone to the authorities?"

I shake my head. "I don't know. You told me you were down on your luck; you never said anything about desertion. I know what's going on in Europe; I read the papers. I know what happens to innocent people who get too close to danger. Now I feel as though I've put all of our lives in peril."

Erich takes my hand in his. "Abby, listen to me. It was a question of survival. I was desperate and I didn't know if I could trust you. But let me assure you that I have no ulterior motives. You have no reason to fear me, but if you change your mind and want me to leave, I'll be gone by morning and you'll never see me again. Yes, I admit I'm a deserter, but my reasons were honorable. I refused to continue causing the deaths of more innocent civilians. *Can you at least try to understand that?*"

His clear blue eyes search mine in earnestness. He's searching for the compassion and understanding that exist at the core of every human being, but are so scarce in times of war. He touches my arm, sending shock waves through my body. All of this overwhelms me. I struggle to breathe and take a few steps backwards.

"Please don't touch me," I say, pulling my hand away. "Something doesn't feel right about this. I need some assurance that you weren't sent here for some nefarious purpose."

Erich's blue eyes pierce my own. "Abby, I've already told you, I came here of my own free will. Nobody sent me. Please trust me. If I wanted to harm you, I could have done it by now. All I really want is your friendship and understanding. These are not gifts that one can buy in a store. They must be given freely, but if it's too hard, then you have every right to refuse me and I will leave."

He turns my chin so that our eyes meet. "Remember, in times of war, soldiers who put their lives on the line are sometimes the biggest victims. They order us to shoot and kill when every fiber of our being tells us it's wrong. But that is what we are trained to do. When I deserted, I chose not to follow orders. So please don't look at me as a soldier, but as a survivor."

"How do I know I can trust you?"

"We are not so different you and I," he says. "The day you realize we want the same things out of life, your fear will dissolve. I came to this island to escape the war, but no matter how far I go, it seems to always catch up with me. You came here hoping for a future but find obstacles too great to overcome. Let's agree that we need a little more time for trust to develop between us. Let's not rush things or get carried away by fear and suspicion."

I nod. "Very well, I agree. Perhaps if you told me something about your experiences during the war I could understand you better. Would you tell me what it was like?"

"It was hell, Abby, pure and simple hell. No human being should ever have to go through that. Although I was in the Navy and never fought in the trenches, I saw more death than I ever bargained for. I realized early on that survival was merely a numbers game and sooner or later your number comes up. After some pretty close brushes with death, and a horrible, life-altering experience that haunts me to this day, I decided that my best chance for survival was to desert. I sat up nights planning my escape and when the time came, I left that part of my life behind. When I came to this island, I felt as though I'd found paradise. And later when I met you, I found a reason to go on living. I found goodness in the midst of all that evil."

I stare at him. "Whose side were you fighting on?"

"My own side, Abby," he says. "I've said enough for now. There's no need to rush things. Someday I promise to tell you everything. Then there will be no more secrets between us."

"Just promise me one thing," I say. "Promise me you weren't fighting for Germany. I could never be friends with a Hun."

And then Erich does something completely unexpected. He throws his head back and laughs.

CHAPTER 14

A week later while I'm in my room with Teddy, a terrifying shriek pierces the air. Teddy ruffles his feathers and lets out a frightening caw. In a voice full of panic, Cooky Betty summons me from the outside kitchen: "Abigail, come quick!"

I drop everything and race outside. When I arrive. I see an enraged Aunt Esther standing in the kitchen, glowering as she holds an empty bread box where a fresh loaf of sweet bread had been placed only yesterday. Cooky Betty stands nearby, wringing her hands.

Aunt Esther's expression is cold and suspicious. "Miss Abigail Levy Maduro, where is the loaf of sweet bread that was here only yesterday? And where is the banana bread from this morning? Where did all the food disappear to? I know it's not Cooky Betty's fault."

I'm aware that Aunt Esther isn't a rich woman, but with all this missing food, I see the strain it's causing her. A wave of guilt washes over me, yet what can I say?

"For the past several weeks there hasn't been any food left in the house anymore," she continues, throwing the bread box down in frustration. "Will you please tell me what on earth is going on?"

I struggle to come up with a reasonable explanation.

"I-I must be having a growth spurt," I say. "I'm constantly famished. I think I've grown two inches since I arrived."

Aunt Esther's face turns a frightening shade of purple. I know she's getting close to her breaking point even with all the extra money I've been bringing in with my sewing, but I don't want to be the catalyst for a complete nervous breakdown on her part.

"Nonsense," she retorts. "You're just as skinny as the day you arrived. You haven't gained a pound. Somebody must be stealing our food. That's the only reasonable explanation."

"That's impossible," I say. "Who on earth would do such a thing? Why would anyone steal our food? There's nobody around here but us. Besides, the Robles family down the road has lots more food than us not to mention the Monsantos, the Sassos."

"Well, for Heaven's sake, if it wasn't any of *us* who ate all that food, who did?"

"I think I may have given some food to the little colored boy who lives down the street," I say. "He looked so hungry yesterday..."

"You think or you *know*?" she asks, narrowing her eyes. "What are you hiding from me, or are you just a complete scatterbrain?"

My heart beats furiously and I feel my face sweating.

"Yes, now I remember, I *did* give him food. Yesterday he came by saying his mother just had a baby. I thought it was the least I could do to help them out."

An awkward silence follows during which I silently pray that Aunt Esther will accept that explanation. I glance over at Cooky Betty. Her eyes are as wide as saucers, darting between me and Aunt Esther. She sulks back to the kitchen muttering, "Next she gonna say a *jumbi* took it..."

"Very well, but please let me know the next time," says Aunt Esther. "And there's another thing. Cooky Betty informs me that some of the bed linens are missing and somebody broke the handle of her favorite pot. Do you have anything more to confess?"

"No, I didn't do it."

"Well, somebody did it and I *will* get to the bottom of it."

Aunt Esther turns on her heels and marches off. I realize that I narrowly escaped danger this time, but who knows what will happen the next time? And what calamity will befall me when she discovers a war deserter has been living in her basement?

***

A couple weeks later, I'm cleaning out Teddy's cage when I pull out a yellowed newspaper. By the date, I see that it's been over a month since Erich has come to live here. I marvel that in all this time,

Aunt Esther has never suspected a thing. Erich rises early and leaves for his fishing job before anyone else gets up, and doesn't return until after nightfall. Aside from a little missing food and the missing bed linens, there's no hint of trouble on the horizon. Still, I worry that I may be unwittingly helping the enemy. If Erich were a German spy or saboteur, what better cover is there than living with a well-known Creole Sephardic family? And it doesn't help matters that Erich is still cryptic about his origins, not to mention his accent, which sounds distinctly German.

I often get an uneasy feeling that Erich is here for a specific reason, some unknown purpose. Sometimes late at night while I'm lying in bed, my mind races through all the possibilities. And when I sit in the sewing room, the fear becomes so overwhelming at times I lose my ability to concentrate. The needle slips through my fingers; the pounding of my heart leaves me breathless. And all the while the gramophone plays the same infuriating song over and over, *"Your cunning little dimples and your baby hair, Your baby talk and baby walk and baby hair. Your baby smile makes life worthwhile. You're just as sweet as you can be..."* I feel as though my whole world is caving in. I stand up, mutter some excuse about needing some fresh air, then escape to the privacy of my room where I stroke Teddy's feathers in a feeble attempt to assuage my fears. It all boils down to one thing: if Erich is indeed an enemy soldier, I may be putting all of our lives at risk.

When the strain becomes too great, I decide to take action. I jot down a message telling Erich to meet me in Emancipation Park on Sunday. Slipping outside, I shove it under his door. There, it's done. No matter what happens, I'll get to the bottom of this matter. If Erich confesses to being a German spy, I will muster the courage to ask him to leave, regardless of the consequences.

When I open my eyes on Sunday, my heart is full of dread. Waiting all day for my meeting with Erich will be pure torture. The hours creep by as the humming of the insects fills the air and the hot sun makes venturing outside impossible. I try to get absorbed in a book, but my eyes keep wandering back to the clock. I have no desire to eat, to talk to anyone, and I'm so nervous my stomach feels queasy. Yet I know I must be brave and face the truth.

When the time comes, I wrap some fried Johnny cakes, a hunk of cheese, and two bottles of lemonade in a sack, then sneak out of the house. As I head down Crystal Gade and Raadets Gade, I'm thankful that the streets are relatively quiet, with only an occasional stray dog or barefoot child crossing my path.

When I reach the corner of Nye Gade, a multitude of voices reverberate through the shuttered windows of the Dutch Reformed church. Inside the faithful congregants sit on hard wooden benches fanning themselves in their stiff clothes, thick stockings, jackets, and hats. When the organist stops, the minister launches into a sermon about the evils of war. *"But in the last days it shall come to pass, that the mountain of the house of the Lord shall be established in the top of the mountains, and it shall be exalted above the hills, and He shall judge among many people, and rebuke strong nations afar off; and they shall beat their swords into plowshares, and their spears into pruning hooks: nation shall not lift up a sword against nation, neither shall they learn war anymore."*

The words burn right through me, as if the sermon was written just for me. No matter where I go there's no escaping the messages of war. It seems to be closing in on all sides.

When I reach the park, I'm relieved to see that it's full of spectators. Everyone is dressed in their Sunday best eager to hear the band playing rousing marches in the pavilion. Couples sit on benches, chatting amiably as children amuse themselves playing marbles or jumping rope. Ladies in elegant walking suits and gentlemen in their summer linens and straw hats stroll around taking photographs near the bust of old King Christian IX or writing postal cards. An eager crowd heads over to the Grand Hotel for dinner. The air is full of so much joyful laughter that I find myself slowly relaxing.

And then I spot Erich.

He sits by himself under the shade of a lignum vitae tree, just another face in the crowd. As soon as he spots me, his face brightens. In addition to a new shirt and trousers, his face is shaved and he's sporting a new haircut. His blond hair glistens like gold under the hot sun and his eyes sparkle. More than that, Erich looks content; the perpetual fear and worry that marred his face seem to have dissipated with the ocean tide. He blends in seamlessly with the crowd, and there is no hint of anything menacing or dangerous about him. Perhaps I was too quick to judge him. Perhaps I was too harsh.

I breeze up to Erich and take a seat beside him. He squeezes my shoulder as I hand him some food and a bottle of lemonade. He thanks me profusely and eats as though he's famished.

"So Miss Abigail, what is this urgent matter you wished to discuss?" he says between bites. "Has my opera singing been keeping you up at night? Have you found yourself a better boarder? Are you tired of my company?"

I smile in spite of myself. "I just wanted to talk. I've been a little worried lately. When you've finished eating, let's go for a walk on King's Wharf where we can speak privately. I don't want anyone to eavesdrop on our conversation."

Erich furrows his brow. "This sounds serious."

On the way to the wharf, we pass the Fish Market. Although it's closed, the smell of rotting fish permeates the air. Seagulls swoop down to peck at the remains of dead fish, while clean white bones and shiny scales litter the area, a grim reminder of the serious business I have come to discuss. If only things could be different, if the menace of war hadn't reared its ugly head.

We choose a quiet bench at the edge of the wharf, watching the gendarmes over by the saluting battery lowering the Dannebrog for the evening. "So, what's on Miss Abby's mind today?" he asks.

"If you must know, Aunt Esther is driving me crazy. She's always in a bad mood and always trying to control me. She screams at me, she hits me. She can't figure out where all the missing food has gone, and calls me a scatterbrain when I can't explain what happened to it. She scolded me for breaking the door handle, and even for breaking the front step. She even accused me of breaking the handle of Cooky Betty's favorite pot. No matter how hard I try to please her, it's never enough. Her latest complaint is that people will start gossiping when they see me gallivanting around town in an unladylike fashion, but I can't sit in that stuffy house sewing endless piles of clothes for the rest of my life. There's no end to her explosive tirades."

"Hold on, slow down," he says. "First of all, you're no scatterbrain. I knew that from the moment we first met. You're smart and resourceful. Look how quickly you got me a place to stay. You're also trustworthy and extremely reliable, which is a lot more than you can say about most people. And if she ever raises a hand to you, you must defend yourself. It's your right. It's too dangerous for me to rescue you, so if she tries to slap you, block her hand like this…" Erich holds up his arm in a defensive posture. "Now, with regards to this *unladylike* business, believe me when I tell you that you're extremely ladylike. For now, just ignore her harsh words. She's a sick woman. You're not responsible for everything that breaks in that dilapidated old house. She can't accept that she's getting old and her house is falling apart. Also consider the fact that when you first came into her life, she probably saw a little of herself in you and realized she made a lot of mistakes along the way. It's only natural she feels some measure of regret and resentment. None of this is any reflection on you. Regarding the missing food, I shall do my best to make amends."

"Do you really mean that, what you said about me being *ladylike*?"

"Of course," he says, tousling my hair. "You're a beautiful, smart young woman with a wonderful future ahead of you, but more than that, you're a good friend. Look how you helped me by giving me shelter when most people would have shunned me, or worse, reported me to the police. That took great courage on your part. And look how you bring me books and delicious food. All of that shows a kind heart. Before I met you, I was afraid the war had turned me into a hardened, cynical person, but your kind, trusting nature has restored my faith in humanity. That is a gift I can never repay."

Suddenly, I feel guilty for suspecting the worst of him.

"Erich, do you really mean that?"

"Yes, Abby, I would never lie about something as serious as my faith in humanity. Or my trust in you."

I feel a lump in my throat. "And to think I suspected you of such terrible things—"

"*Terrible things?*" he says, taken aback. "What terrible things? Have I given you some reason to suspect me?"

"No, it's just that my imagination is filled with stories about spies and saboteurs. Ever since the day you told me you deserted the war, I became concerned. There's also the question of your accent. I feel like you're not telling me something. I keep having these vivid dreams that you're a German saboteur."

Erich laughs. "It sounds like you've been reading too many gothic novels. The difference between a deserter and a saboteur is like night and day. When I told you I deserted, I was putting my life in your hands. That's how much I trusted you. I didn't expect complete trust from day one; I just hoped that over time I would be able to earn your trust."

"It's the little things, like your accent, the way you quote Goethe. It's all so *German* sounding. Look me in the eyes and tell me the truth: are you or are you not a German?"

Erich sighs. He pulls a cigarette out of his shirt pocket, cups his hand around it and lights it with intense concentration. He blows a long, thin column of smoke as if taking the time to choose his words carefully.

"My dear Abby," he says, shaking his head. "No one can ever accuse you of giving up too easily. There's so much I can learn from you. I suppose after everything you've done for me, the least you deserve is the truth. So, I shall open up my very soul to you. Yes, my dear girl, I'm a German. To be exact, a German officer of the *Kaiserliche Marine,* the Imperial German Navy, but I assure you, I'm not a spy, and certainly not a saboteur. Since the day I deserted and renounced violence, the only danger I pose is to myself."

I bury my face in my hands. "You've just confirmed my suspicions. How can I know for certain you're telling the truth? How do I know you haven't been sent here to help fight the war?"

"Because I'm a deserter, Abby. I'm not a German soldier anymore. I'm a free man. If I still believed in this damned war, I'd be back on my ship fighting alongside my men, not stuck on a poverty-stricken island filled with gossipy old women and undernourished men. Do you think I enjoy life as a down-and-out drifter? Back in Germany I was a respected, educated man, but when war was declared, everything changed. When I left my post I became a wandering vagabond, afraid even of my own shadow, condemned to spend the rest of my life running from my own personal demons. I had a valid reason for deserting the war, reasons I don't care to divulge at the present. I did what I had to do and I don't regret it for a second. But there is one thing that will never change. When I deserted, I became a criminal. And for this very reason, you must never ever reveal my secret to anyone. If the wrong people were to find out about me, it would mean certain death. They would kill me with no hesitation."

"A German officer? Of course, this changes everything. If my aunt were to find out, she would do something terrible. She would throw me out, turn me in to the authorities. I'd be shunned wherever I go. My life would be ruined."

Erich exhales a long column of smoke. "Then we'll just have to make sure this aunt of yours never finds out."

"Maybe she won't, but others might. I'm doomed."

"What *others* are you referring to?"

"Them." I point to the Hamburg-America Line building in its prominent position across from King's Wharf. The three-story German fortress is where Langsdorff undoubtedly plots his sabotage missions. "The German Community here is very powerful and influential. They make it their business to know everything."

"I see you have acquired an insider's knowledge about the shaky political situation here," he says. "That's pretty astute for a girl your age. Of course, I've known about the Germans here for quite some time. I keep an eye on them and watch their comings and goings. Germans despise wartime deserters—they shoot anyone they can find. But don't worry about me. I keep to the shadows. Yet the fact remains that Germans have an uncanny ability to spot other Germans, and a German soldier out of uniform is considered unfit to wear it."

"What about the Danes? Do they pose any threat to you?"

Erich considers my question. "Since Denmark is officially neutral, they're considered my friends so long as I don't give them any reason to arrest me. Most likely, they'll just leave me alone. As a foreign soldier, regulations dictate that I'm supposed to inform the police of my whereabouts, but knowing how fast gossip spreads on a small island, that procedure could get me into hot water."

"*Caramba!* I can't believe I'm discussing wartime strategy with a German soldier. Yet, you don't look like those Huns I read about in the newspapers. You don't look like you have that killer instinct."

Erich grins and puffs on his cigarette.

"Is killing an instinct or a trained response?" he says. "War is not for the faint of heart, my dear. Too much compassion for the enemy is considered cowardice. We are trained to perform our mission, which is protecting and defending the Fatherland. Asking questions is not only forbidden, it's considered *unGerman*, but all that is in the past now. The moment I deserted my ship, I lost my right to be called a German soldier. Back when I was a cadet, they taught us that it's a great honor to die for the Fatherland. And while that is still true, I no longer believe it's a great honor to kill for the Fatherland. I guess you could say that is the reason why I'm sitting here philosophizing with you rather than sinking more precious Allied ships."

"I don't understand everything about the war, but I suppose you did what you had to do. What would happen if Germany invaded these islands? They say the Kaiser wants to establish naval bases from which he could launch U-boat attacks against ships heading to and from the Panama Canal."

"That's his fantasy," he says, waving his hand dismissively. "The West Indies is right in America's backyard. It's too risky a maneuver even for Tirpitz to consider."

"What about the Americans?" I say. "I've heard that Denmark wants to sell these islands to the United States."

"For you, that would be a good thing. For me, not so good," he says, now serious. "If these islands were suddenly annexed to the United States and America entered the war on the side of the Allies; that would automatically make me a German soldier behind enemy lines. But I'll cross that bridge when I get to it. Right now, we just have to sit tight and learn to trust each other. If the situation becomes too dangerous for either of us, I'll disappear."

"I hope that never happens," I say. "Because I never wanted you to leave, I just needed to know I could trust you."

"Of course you can trust me, Abby, but only up to a certain point. Always remember that unless you have a ring on your finger, you should always be on your guard with a man. Do you understand?"

"Yes."

I grin and we both have a good chuckle at his little joke. Erich snuffs out his cigarette and lays his arm across my shoulders. I rest my head against his chest and he hugs me close. For the first time in months, I feel content. Despite all the chaos and upheavals, I start to feel as though there's hope for my future. I think I'm even starting to understand what the poets meant when they endeavored to describe the word *love*.

CHAPTER 15

Nana Jane and Cooky Betty have been in the kitchen all morning arguing over the proper way to make *kallaloo*. When those two start their bickering, the birds and lizards scatter in search of a quieter place to spend the day. Nana Jane shakes her head, insisting the onions must be diced fine, while Cooky Betty stubbornly maintains the flavor of the onions improves when they are sliced lengthwise. Too much of this, too little of that. *You added too much pepper! Did you remember to peel the stems? Why can't you follow a proper recipe? That's how they make it in Antigua, not ovah here!*

Lately those two old stubborn mules have been bickering and fighting like cats and dogs, and whenever Nana Jane gets the upper hand, Cooky Betty goes berserk. Her body shakes and her voice goes up an octave. She has a temper like a sudden water spout; she flares up and sweeps everything away in her path.

"You're not de boss around here," shouts Cooky Betty over the banging of pots and pans. "I *told* you not to use dat pan. I need the pan with the broken handle...the one over there..."

A moment later, Cooky Betty runs into the house, her eyes as wide as saucers, and her face glowing like the moon on carnival night. She waves her favorite pot with her pudgy hand as if it were a religious relic.

"Look everyone! It's a miracle!" she announces in disbelief, holding the pan up for everyone to see. "The pot is fixed!"

I stare at Cooky Betty in disbelief. Indeed, the pot looks almost brand new. Can it be real? Meanwhile, Aunt Esther comes marching out of the sewing room demanding an explanation.

"What's this racket?"

Cooky Betty hands the pot to Aunt Esther, who turns it this way and that, inspecting every inch of it in amazement. With one hand over her heart, Aunt Esther hands it back to Cooky Betty and then proceeds to inspect the broken door handle. To our astonishment, the handle turns easily, as if it were never broken. Then Mr. Isaiah comes hobbling in through the front door announcing that the front step has been miraculously fixed. As everyone scratches their heads in amazement, a delicious little thought pops into my head. Is Erich the cause of all these miracles?

***

When the Sabbath comes, I decided it's high time for me to prove my independence. During the services, I quietly get up from my seat and move to an empty seat next to Deborah De Castro. All the while, I feel Aunt Esther's eyes burning a hole right through me, but I don't care. I sit up straight and hide my face in my prayer book, suppressing a mischievous grin that creeps up the corners of my mouth. When I glance over at Aunt Esther, she's glaring in my direction, red and fuming like a crab out of water, but she's powerless to stop me. I breathe a sigh of relief at this small victory. It's worth it just knowing that I can make my own decisions in life. This victory, no matter how short-lived, pleases me to the depths of my soul, but the minute we get home, all hell breaks loose.

"You ungrateful brat!" she screams, slamming her fist down on the dining room table. "Don't you realize what you've done to me? Are you trying to make me a laughing stock? Haven't I warned you not to mix with that De Castro girl? Have you no common sense? You're every bit as headstrong as your father."

"Deborah is my friend," I answer hotly.

"Ha! We'll see about that. She's just using you. You'll find out her true nature soon enough. I won't stand for this."

"What are you talking about?"

"It's none of your business. Don't waste your time with that family of back-stabbers."

"I don't plan on spending the rest of my life sitting here, sewing and cleaning, cleaning and sewing. I have bigger plans."

"Plans?" she says with derision. "What sort of plans?"

By now, Cooky Betty and Nana Jane are moving in closer. I sense their shadowy figures hovering protectively in the background. I hear them catch their breath.

"I going to become a schoolteacher," I say. "I want to do something useful with my life, not just sit here and grow old."

"A *schoolteacher*?" Aunt Esther drags out the word, making it sound like *street sweeper* or *washer woman*. Just *where* do you think you'll get the money for teacher's college? Don't you know that when your father died, he left you penniless and your grandfather's money is all but gone? Don't you realize by now that we're paupers?"

"*Paupers?* But Grandfather was one of the wealthiest merchants in St. Thomas," I say. "We used to own ships and a Dry Goods store on Main Street…"

"Not anymore," she says. "And it's time you knew the truth. The store is long gone and there's no money left, at least not enough to pay for teacher's college. You're lucky I was able to take you in. Señor Cardozo sent me two hundred dollars to cover your expenses. If I didn't, he was threatening to stick you in an orphanage."

"A *what*?"

"You heard me," she says. "And it's where you might end up if you continue breaking the rules of this house."

"Now Miss Esther, stop dat crazy talk," scolds Nana Jane, moving in closer. "Miss Abby is not going to no orphanage. Not as long as I'm alive."

"Stay out of this, Nana Jane," says Aunt Esther. "She might as well know the truth. She lives in a fantasy world of her own making."

"Abigail is your niece. You've no call to threaten her like that."

"This is my house and I make the rules. If *you* don't like it you can all jump in the harbor."

"Stop!" I scream at Aunt Esther. "What's wrong with you? When will you start treating me like family?"

I run to my room, slam the door, and then collapse on the bed in tears. These past few months have been devastating. Between losing my parents and my home, Ian's tragic disappearance on the *Guiana,* and being on the constant receiving end of Aunt Esther's vicious tirades, it's too much to bear. At least I still have Teddy. I look up through tear-streaked eyes to see my trusty parrot gaping at me with

158

orange eyes as he ruffles his feathers and paces back and forth. My crying makes him nervous. I wipe my tears with a handkerchief and walk over to his cage.

"You wouldn't put me in an orphanage, would you, Teddy?"

Stroking his feathers, I take him out of his cage and place him on my desk where he savors his freedom by hopping around and spreading his wings wide.

I decide to take out my diary and write down everything that's been troubling me. I find that getting it all off my chest is a great source of comfort. When I finish, I lay down my fountain pen and gaze through the jalousies at the harbor below. This old house is not my home. Without Mami and Papi, it can never be my home. My only option is to run away.

And then, as if reading my thoughts, Nana Jane comes in to check on me.

"Aunt Esther hates me," I say. "She doesn't want me here. I'm going to run away."

"Foolish child," she says, clucking her tongue. "Of course, you're wanted. Nana Jane loves you; Mr. Isaiah loves you, even Cooky Betty loves you and Cooky Betty don't love many people. She thinks the world of you. If you left, she would be heartbroken."

"It's too late. I've already made up my mind."

Nana Jane lifts up my chin and gazes in my eyes. "How could you consider leaving ole Nana Jane? You're all I've got left to live for. Without you, my life will be so empty."

"It's not you I'm leaving, it's *her*. She's hated me since the day I arrived."

Nana Jane shakes her head. "Let me tell you something important. And listen well. Only the Lord knows why your parents had to die and you had to cross the ocean to live in Nana Jane's house. Make no mistake; this is *Nana Jane's* house you're living in. I've been taking care of this house for fifty years. When your auntie lost her wits, your grandfather put me in charge. This much I can tell you, if the Lord brought you here, it was for a reason. So put on a brave face like Queen Coziah and make the best of things. If you leave, you'll break ole Nana Jane's heart, and you must never do that, promise?"

"Of course, I promise. I love you, Nana Jane."

"I love you, too, as if you were my own daughter."

"Nana Jane, can you please tell me something?"

"What is it, child?"

"What happened to your sister?"

"Men came and took she away."

"Where to?"

"Down by the Municipal Hospital," she sighs, rubbing the back of her neck. "When I used to visit her, she acted like she didn't know me. She would just sit there talking to de walls, screaming and carrying on like she had a *jumbi*. I felt so helpless watching her I couldn't stay very long. I prayed for Adelaide, but there was nothing I could do to fix her. Slowly, her life slipped away. From that time on I felt like she was dead, like my sister only lived in my heart. A few years later, she got gangrene on her legs and died. The doctors couldn't save her life."

"I'm so sorry, Nana Jane."

I hug her so tight I thought we both would burst.

***

For the next several weeks, there is no improvement with Aunt Esther. In fact, I think she has gotten worse. When she isn't sewing or listening to her Victrola, she sits and writes angry letters to distant cousins, or rearranges the china closet, or goes to the washbasin and scrubs her hands over and over. All I can do is look on in pity.

At the same time, I notice that our food supply is dwindling. When Cooky Betty serves me a plate of fish and fungi or peas and rice, there's barely enough to feed a mouse. I'm starting to get the impression there's not enough money to feed us. I also notice that Aunt Esther is barely eating. She gets thinner and thinner by the day, which seems to exacerbate her erratic moods. And when I remember all the food I've given to Erich, I feel a wave of remorse. Later, I retreat to the kitchen to speak to Cooky Betty.

"Cooky Betty, why is there so little food in the house?"

"No money in de cupboard," she says, washing a dish.

"What do you mean by *no money*?"

"Just like I told you, there's no money to buy food," she says, growing agitated. "De cupboard is empty!"

Nana Jane limps into the kitchen. "That's not the real reason. We have money, but all the time you eating up all the food until there's nothing left. By the time you serve us it's almost all gone. Girl, you got to control your appetite."

"My eye!" says Cooky Betty with great indignation. "What about all the food that's gone missing around here? Am I responsible for all dat?"

"Look at your fat behind," says Nana Jane, making an exaggerated gesture of Cooky Betty's posterior. "It's almost as big as a sofa."

"Who you calling fat?" says Cooky Betty. "At least I don't get involved in all dat gossip and melee down in Market Square like you. Woman, you can't control your *mouth*!"

Nana Jane's eyebrows shoot up in rage. She wags a finger at the brazen Cooky Betty. "Girl, are you making *pappyshow* of me? You better not vex me up or I'll wash your mouth out with soap and Brillo."

I roll my eyes. This kind of bickering can go on for hours, so I slip out of the kitchen and leave them to their own devices. All I know is, we're desperately short of food and I must bring more food into the house before the squabbling gets any worse.

The rest of the week is a disaster. Nana Jane crawls back into bed moaning about her rheumatism, while Aunt Esther makes me wait on her hand and foot on account of some tropical fever. The minute I finish one task, she orders me to do something else. All day long I serve them tea, take their temperatures, change their bed linens, fetch their slippers, and dole out spoonfuls of medicine. I'm beginning to feel like a mother hen to two old eccentric biddies. I hardly have time for myself let alone Erich.

"Nana Jane, why don't you go sit out on the balcony," I say after massaging her aching leg. "You've been cooped up in this house forever and you're not improving."

"My knees just willfully refuse to lift me up from bed," she moans. I frown, but bring her some fresh sweet bread anyway.

"How did you know Nana Jane needed some sweet bread?" she says, stuffing some in her mouth.

"A little bird named Cooky Betty told me," I say "She misses your nagging, but if your appetite is any indication of the state of your health, I'd say you're as healthy as a horse, or a donkey. Or a goat, or whatever is eating all the fresh grass on the island."

"Are you making *pappyshow* of ole Nana Jane? If I was thirty, no, twenty years younger I'd box your ears. Now go run down to

Market Square and fetch me some of Miss Sandy's mauby. It's the only thing that calms down this humbug rheumatism."

Every time Nana Jane's knees act up, she claims the only thing that works is drinking copious amounts of mauby, a frothy drink made of sugar and boiled tree bark. She tosses me a few francs and tells me to run down before it's too late. I gladly take the money, grateful for any chance to escape that stifling house. I found Miss Sandy's stall and make the purchase, but before heading back home, I decide to check up on Judge Neergaard at the Grand Hotel.

Seeing Judge Neergaard always brightens my day. The elderly gentleman with the soft white beard and twinkling blue eyes is starting to become like an old friend. I find him in his usual place, sipping his rum cocktail and puffing on his pipe, but underneath his stoic demeanor, I can sense he's relieved to have my company.

"Well now, if it isn't my dear friend Abigail Maduro," he says, motioning for me to sit beside him. "Where have you been lately? It's been such a long time since our last meeting that I was starting to get worried. Jeffrey! Bring the young lady your best lemonade with lots of ice."

"I can't stay very long, Judge Neergaard, Aunt Esther has taken to bed, and Nana Jane's rheumatism is acting up again. I've been waiting on them hand and foot."

"Did you say Nana Jane is not feeling well? Then I shall drink to her health—skaal." He takes a large swig of his rum cocktail and smacks his lips. "A finer woman never graced these shores. She was quite a beauty in her day. Women like Nana Jane give this island all its beauty, mystery, and allure. It's a damned shame all of that will soon come to an end. Did you hear the latest news? The Americans are offering an enormous sum to purchase this washed up old sugar colony. Soon it will be ours no longer."

"How much did they offer?"

The judge leans in closer. "The princely sum of twenty-five million dollars in gold. An amount guaranteed to send shivers down the Kaiser's pompous spine. Of course, the Rigsdag is only too happy to accept this generous offer. You see, Denmark held onto these islands as long as she could. This dwindling old sugar colony has been draining the royal treasury for years ever since they introduced that devilish beet sugar. And now, with that scalawag David Hamilton Jackson and his dreadful newspaper riling up all the

162

laborers, the political situation has become untenable. All we hear about is this nonsense about labor unions and government corruption, and they launch strike after strike until nothing works anymore. The whole system is broken and there's no way to fix it. The only honorable way out for Denmark is to sell the whole damn colony. It's a damned shame..." His voice trails off. "Are you aware, Abigail that the citizens are actually starting to *resent* their mother country? Woe is the day that the sun sets on this proud Danish colony. Long live the King."

Judge Neergaard lifts his glass and toasts the portraits of King Christian X and Queen Alexandrine that grace the wall. As soon as he raises his glass, dozens of other patrons do as well until a sea of crystal glasses floats high above our heads, shimmering under the light of the gas lamps. "Long Live the King," murmurs the crowd, as they lower their glasses and take a thoughtful sip before returning to their discussion.

"But Judge Neergaard," I say, perplexed. "All this agitation and strife are not just occurring here. People are demanding more freedom everywhere in the world. The Danish government can't go on censoring the newspapers forever. They have to give the people some freedom of expression. *Somebody* has to tell the truth about what's going on down here: the terrible working conditions, the poor salaries, the lack of education, the malnutrition."

"True," says the judge. "The King is a reasonable man. Mr. Hamilton Jackson took quite a risk traveling all the way to Copenhagen to make his argument about freedom of the press. I watched the planters snicker behind his back as he dragged his dilapidated, moth-eaten suitcase up the gangway to the steamer *St. Thomas.* Then I watched as a broad smile lit up his face as he turned and waved to a ragtag crowd of ne'er-do-wells that had gathered on the wharf to see him off. The planters were smirking among themselves that the Rigsdag would show him the door, but to everyone's amazement, Hamilton Jackson was treated with utmost courtesy and respect, given an honorable reception in Copenhagen, even after the planters sent the government numerous cables denouncing him as an agitator. King Christian was so impressed with Hamilton Jackson's eloquent manner of speaking that he ordered the Rigsdag to acquiesce to his demands."

"What about you, Judge Neergaard," I say. "Do you support Mr. Hamilton Jackson and his policies?"

"Let's just say that the miraculous turn of events was enough to make a believer out of me," he says, winking. "Anyway, after that enormous success, the blacks started calling him the 'Black Moses' because, truth be told, the poor devils were earning only 20 cents a day laboring under the worst conditions. They saw his efforts bear fruit just like when Moses came down from the mountain bearing the tablets of the law. Soon afterwards, change occurred. Their lives started to improve, but by that point it was too late for Denmark to continue holding on. The Rigsdag calculated that if they caved in to the workers' demands, they would buy enough time to sell their beloved islands to the highest bidder. No argument could convince the King to change his mind. When change came, it came fast, with the result being that our cherished and beloved way of life here will soon come to an end."

"What about you?" I say. "What will you do once the Americans take over? Do you plan on staying?"

"I suppose I shall return to Denmark," he sighs. "My daughter Louise has been nagging me for years to come live with her in Copenhagen. She married a university professor and they have three wonderful children. My fondest memories are when I used to sit Louise on my knee and tell her stories about the old days of Charlotte Amalie. Oh the memories! But that was so long ago. Yes, we had a beautiful life here in the *Vestindien*, but once the Dannebrog is lowered for the last time, it will mark the end of my illustrious career. A sad and bittersweet end indeed."

"I'll miss you so much, Judge Neergaard. But what about the rest of us? What will happen to us?"

"You mean, like your Aunt Esther and Nana Jane? I suppose they'll make fine Americans out of you. Are you ready for that? Do you relish the opportunity to become an American?"

"Very much, indeed! I've always dreamt of going to an American school and becoming a teacher."

"And so you shall," he says. "If you want it bad enough, you'll find a way to make it happen. Remember, you're a Maduro. Nothing can hold you back."

"Except that we're in the middle of a war. Something terrible could happen. The Kaiser could decide to invade these islands and claim them for Germany."

"Don't waste your time worrying about such things," says Judge Neergaard. "Invading these islands would take men and resources away from where they're really needed, fighting the land and sea battles in Europe and the North Atlantic. And frankly, I don't think he's up to the challenge anymore. He stands on the precipice of losing face again in front of the entire world."

"Lose face *again*? What do you mean?"

"Back in 1908 he made a mockery of himself that he's never been able to live down," says Judge Neergaard. "The British newspaper, *Daily Telegraph*, humiliated the Kaiser by publishing an unscripted interview in which he made blundering statements like, '*You English are mad, mad, mad as March hares*' which erupted in a firestorm of protest and became a huge embarrassment. People started calling for his abdication which shattered his confidence. The result of this humiliation can be seen in the releasing of waves of Prussian violence against thousands of innocent people all over Europe. No, my dear, the Kaiser's plate is full enough."

Not long after my meeting with Judge Neergaard, a new crisis emerges, one that threatens to bring the war to these very shores.

CHAPTER 16

Some unexpected news has cast a pall over the island. While Deborah and I are visiting in her parlor, her father's carriage pulls up and Mr. De Castro storms into the house in an agitated state. He's gripping a news cable which he reads over and over with worry lines etched over his forehead. Deborah asks what the matter is, but he just shakes his head, saying it's something about the war. I think he said it reached *a frightening new crescendo.*

The news concerns a pack of German saboteurs who managed to blow up a munitions depot in New York harbor. The blast was so devastating it caused tremendous damage to the surrounding area, and was powerful enough to throw a child from his crib, killing him. The newspapers are reporting that President Wilson is furious over the attack, calling it a blatant act of sabotage and threatens to intern all German ships docked at American ports.

Mr. De Castro explains that the German people are starving and desperately need shipments of food and supplies the ships are bringing. If Wilson impounds them, he says, the crisis will reach a new tipping point because the Kaiser will see it as a slap in the face. With all this haranguing, who knows what could happen?

In addition, the Germans are furious when they hear that British steamers are permitted to load up with munitions and the best food from America and steam off to feed and arm the Allied soldiers, while German ships are forbidden from doing the same. Naturally, the Germans protest this double standard in the newspapers, but when no change occurs, they resort to blowing up the ammunition to ensure that *nobody* gets it. Mr. De Castro says it's only a question of time before the Germans launch another attack and America will be dragged into the war.

At the mention of the word *attack*, I'm filled with dread that Erich might somehow be involved with these saboteurs. Maybe I was too quick to trust him. I realize how the situation is far more dangerous than I ever imagined. All of a sudden, I feel dizzy and lightheaded.

"Abigail, are you alright?" says Mr. De Castro, studying me intently. "You're as white as a ghost. Did we scare you with all this talk about German saboteurs?"

My heart now pounding, I reach for a chair.

"I think I'm coming down with something," I say weakly.

"You do look rather pale," says Deborah. "You should take better care of yourself. Should we call the government doctor?"

"No, I'll be fine," I say. "Nana Jane keeps a store of *chibble* for occasions like this."

"That's just Obeah nonsense," says Mr. De Castro, raising a stern eyebrow. "Don't let Nana Jane convince you that by boiling breadfruit tree leaves or muttering strange incantations you'll be cured. That's native mumbo jumbo."

I nod meekly, but my mouth is too dry to speak. A lump forms in my throat that tells me the only solution to cure my anxiety is to confront Erich. I must get the truth out of him no matter what the cost.

Later that night, after Aunt Esther and Nana Jane have gone to sleep and their loud snores echo down the hallway, I climb out of bed and sneak out to the balcony. As quiet as a lizard, I climb over the railing and shinny my way down until it's safe enough to let my body fall into the soft grasses below. The minute I hit the ground, the insects cease their humming, and unseen creatures scurry into the bush. I wade over to Erich's door and tap on it gently.

"Erich," I whisper. "Are you there?"

"The door opens a crack and a pair of cautious eyes peers out. Silently, a strong arm pulls me inside and shuts the door behind me.

Erich's brow is creased with worry. "Are you all right, Abby? Why did you come here?"

"Why do you look so nervous?" I say, squeezing out of his grip. "Unless you have a *reason* to be nervous, such as if you're hiding something from me."

Erich narrows his eyes. "Are you having doubts *again*? I thought I cleared up that matter the other day."

In the glow of the candlelight, Erich's chest rises and falls under his cotton undershirt with each anxious breath. He leans one arm against the stone wall and regards me with a mixture of worry and concern. The croaking of the insects provides a welcome, if somewhat comical, distraction to the uneasy silence that hangs between us. I glance to the side, hoping to hide my growing distress.

On the table sits a cold, half-eaten meal and an open book. The floor has been nicely swept and the bed properly made. A razor, a toothbrush, and a bar of soap are lined up neatly near the washbasin and a towel is folded with military precision nearby. Everything looks so normal, so innocent. Even Erich with his golden hair, intelligent blue eyes, and clean-shaven face is above suspicion. No one in his right mind would suspect Erich of being a German saboteur.

"There was an explosion near the Statue of Liberty," I say. "A pack of German saboteurs blew up a munitions depot. The police are saying that pockets of German saboteurs are hiding all over America, just waiting for the orders to strike. Or maybe that's one little detail you neglected to tell me."

His eyes widen noticeably. "Is that true? Are you sure about that? Who told you?"

"It's in all the news cables from America. Listen, Erich, I took a tremendous risk in bringing you into my home. It's time you told me the truth about why you came to this island. I need to know everything, the whole story. All our lives are at stake now."

Erich appears shocked. "Abby, I've already told you the truth that I deserted. Yes, I admit that I was once a German soldier, but that's in the past. I deserted for personal reasons. Do you think I lied to you?"

I lock eyes with him. "Were you sent here to sabotage the transfer of these islands to America?"

Erich laughs nervously. "Are you crazy? Of course not! Your imagination is running wild. Let's get one thing straight. Nobody sent me here. I escaped and came of my own volition. And second, if headquarters in Berlin ever found out I was still alive, it would mean disaster for my family since it would be tantamount to admitting that I'm a deserter. Right now, the whole world thinks I'm dead, including my parents. If the wrong people were to find out about me, they would kill me without a second thought."

"Your parents think you're dead? I don't understand."

"Because I rigged my own death. I dove off my ship into the ocean, like a dolphin. The hour was late, it was dark, and nobody was around. My crew never found out what happened to me. I'm sure they assumed I drowned. *'Herr and Frau Seibold, we are sorry to report that your son Leutnant zur See Erich Seibold is missing at sea and presumed dead.'*"

"So, you faked your own death? And nobody in the world knows you're here but me?"

"Exactly. Nobody but you, God, and a certain kind-hearted Spanish steamer captain. But if you're still convinced I'm a dangerous German saboteur, I'll pack up my things and leave."

"No!" I say, grabbing his arm. "Don't go. I'm sorry for suspecting you, but I needed to know the truth, not the censored version you keep telling me. So perhaps it's time you told me the entire truth about why you deserted. If we're going to learn to trust each other, we might as well start there. Don't you think I deserve at least that much?"

Erich's face softens.

"Yes my dear, you're right," he says, touching my cheek. "I've been asking of you what I myself was incapable of giving, blind trust. After all you've done for me, you deserve at least that much. I just hope it wasn't a terrible mistake—my deserting, I mean. Perhaps I belong back on my ship fighting alongside my men. I have no business imposing on you, putting you and everyone else at risk. You're a good girl, an innocent girl. It was wrong of me to expose you to such danger. You've already done more than anyone else would in your situation."

He slumps down on the bed and buries his head in his hands, tightening his fists until I thought he would burst. I regret having suspected him. As if sensing my remorse, Erich reaches up and pulls me toward him.

He cups my face in his hands. "Abby, I care for you very much. I don't blame you for being scared. I know what goes on in that house with your aunt. I hear how she screams at you, berates you, abuses you. Sometimes I watch through the windows. I've seen her slapping you. I hate her so much I wanted to punch a hole through the window, grab the old crow by the shoulders, and shake some sense into her head. I know how difficult your situation is. And believe me, if circumstances were different, I would remove you from this house. The fact is, I deserted because I couldn't stand what was happening to me any longer. I couldn't continue to do what they were ordering me to do. Something inside of me changed."

"Erich, I don't regret meeting you. You've changed my life, given me something to live for. Please tell me what happened over there. What made you desert?"

His face loses all expression. "Because I killed a man, an innocent man. A man whose only crime was trying to protect his ship. But the rules of war say you must kill or be killed. So I killed him and now I live with tremendous remorse."

"How did it happen?"

Erich walks over to a corner of the room, kneels down, and pries open a loose floor board. From its hollow he retrieves some objects that he places gently in my lap.

"Take a look at those. Do you know what they are?"

"They look like military insignia of some sort," I say, turning them over in my hands.

"Did you ever suspect your dashing friend of being a U-boat officer?"

I stare at him with incredulity. "A *what?*"

"My dear, what you are holding are my shoulder boards from the Imperial German Navy and my U-boat medallion, the only vestiges of my past life, but don't worry," he waves his hand dismissively. "I'm not considered a dangerous weapon anymore. When I deserted, I became a pussycat."

"Are you saying you were a U-boat officer?"

"That's precisely what I'm saying, little lady. So now you know the whole truth. Your friend, Erich Seibold, was the terror of the seas, a dangerous U-boat officer charged with sinking Allied ships and scaring women and children in the night. Erich Seibold, the great predator of the seas. These objects could be quite valuable to the right people. They're considered precious war booty."

I swallow hard. "And you trust me with this secret? How do you know I won't go to the authorities?"

Erich lets out an ironic laugh and plucks a cigarette from his pack.

"Because you need me as much as I need you. And from the look of your big brown eyes, I can tell you have a love of intrigue and danger. Am I wrong? You remind me of that English expression, is it *curiosity killed the cat*? So then, how shall I start?" He takes a deep puff on his cigarette and exhales a long cloud of smoke. "I guess it's always best to start at the beginning. The gentleman who stands before you looking like a beggar or a tramp actually comes from a distinguished old German family. My full name is Erich Günther Seibold and I was born in the shipbuilding city of Kiel in the year 1890, which officially makes me twenty-six years of age. Until a few months ago, I held the rank of *Leutnant zur See* in the Imperial German Navy and I last saw action in the Azores aboard the U-158. As I mentioned before, there's a price on the head of every German deserter, so what I'm about to tell you would be sufficient to get me shot by a firing squad. Do you understand how serious that is?"

I swallow hard. "Yes."

"Good," he says, taking another drag of his cigarette. Then he locks eyes with me. "And you still wish for me to continue?"

"Yes, I want to know everything."

"Very well Miss Abigail Levy Maduro," he says, with a wry smile. "I shall endeavor not to disappoint you. My father, Klaus Gunter Seibold, was a mechanical engineer who spent his entire life in the Kiel shipyards. My mother, Birgitte Nathansen, was born to a Danish Jewish family from Schleswig, but she moved to Kiel when she married my father. I spent many summers with my Danish cousins, so that's how I picked up a few words of Danish. I didn't know then that those Danish phrases would give me a chance at a new life. My happiest days were when I was a little boy and my father would take me for walks around the harbor and over by the canal. He had this amazing memory, an almost encyclopedic knowledge of all the warships that docked there, and he would thrill me with stories about each ship's history. Don't misunderstand, it's not that he was a militaristic Prussian; it's just that he had his own inner demons to conquer. You see, when he was a young man, he suffered a debilitating injury that rendered him unfit for active duty.

Frustrated over his lack of service, he made me the focus of his unrealized dreams. He wanted to turn me into the war hero he could never be. Of course, I knew all along what his unspoken plan was, but I went along willingly, joining the Navy, pretending that his ambitions were mine. When I got older, I wanted to prove my manhood by earning the medals that he could not, especially the Iron Cross, the greatest honor a German soldier can receive."

Erich pauses to let that sink in, and then he takes another long puff and continues.

"When I graduated from gymnasium, I attended the University of Kiel, studying engineering, philosophy, and English. That's why I can communicate so effectively with my little island comrade. Later on, since military service is compulsory in Germany, I attended the reserve officer's school. They called us young recruits *einjahriger freiwilliger,* which means 'one-year volunteers.' After basic training, I became a *vizesteuerman,* which is a senior non-commissioned naval officer. Abby, I'd be lying if I didn't tell you that those early years were glorious. As long as we weren't at war, we could pretend to be as brave as our favorite war heroes. You see, being trained to kill is fine as long as it's purely theoretical. Once you have to face the enemy and fight, killing becomes another thing entirely. The truth is, I probably would have been happy spending the rest of my life in the Kiel shipyards designing and building ships just like my father did, rather than using the ships for their intended purpose, which is to sink ships and kill men. But it was too late for regrets because by August of 1914, at the ripe old age of twenty-four, Germany entered the war and our Belgian campaign was immediately implemented. All of a sudden, I found myself called up for active duty. The Kaiser was ordering us to serve the Fatherland.

"Now, all of us recruits had heard amazing stories about the exploits of the *unterseeboots,* or U-boats as we called them. In the early days of the war, we heard tales about the adventures and exploits of the U-9, which was under the command of Otto Weddigen. As far as heroism goes, Weddigen was a living legend. In the span of one hour in the North Sea, his ship attacked and surprised three British armored cruisers, sinking them before they could even react. By the time the Commander of the third cruiser, the *Cressy,* had spotted the U-9 periscope, it was too late to outrun the torpedo. The *Cressy* ended up at the bottom of the sea just like the other two.

172

For young naval cadets like us, the propaganda of Weddigen's conquests and heroism was a powerful magnet to attract new recruits. Being no different from the others, I wanted glory at any price. Also, it didn't hurt that the U-boat crews were better treated than the other sailors; they were considered vital to Germany's goal of naval supremacy. Without a second thought, I signed up to be a submarine officer with dreams of glory and success: *Für Kaiser und Reich.*

"After six months of intensive training, I received my first assignment as Second Watch Officer with the title *Leutnant* on the U-158, a Mittel-U type submarine freighter of 70 meters, commissioned into the Imperial Navy and outfitted with 16 torpedoes and one 105mm deck gun with 220 rounds and one 88mm deck gun. On the surface, the U-158 could easily go 16 knots; underwater, we did about 9 knots. We felt invincible, but daily life was difficult. Living inside a stuffy, foul, hot iron canoe meters below the surface took hard work, guts, and determination. At first, we banged our heads on pipes or hand wheels, and our initiation ceremony involved being drenched with sea water that poured through the conning tower, and learning to sleep on shared bunks. Don't even ask about the privy. We were tough and determined, and amidst the stale, nauseating air, with plenty of bruises for our trouble, my crew developed a sense of camaraderie that bordered on true brotherhood. And in spite of the harsh conditions of wartime duty onboard a submarine, sleeping, eating, working, and keeping watch within the cramped confines of a steel hull reeking of diesel oil, cooking smells, urine, and the grime that coated every surface, we thrived. Rubber boots and wool socks could never alleviate the constant dampness of our underwater world.

"Our first campaign was in the North Atlantic, under the command of *Herr Oberleutnant* Heinrich Schultz, a likable fellow of twenty-eight who'd already had a few years of U-boat experience under his belt. I spent those first few months learning everything I could about operating a U-boat. When I wasn't on watch duty, I assisted with the hydroplanes or at the electric helm; other times I calculated our position at sea using maritime charts. Whatever time was left was spent poring over the ship's engineering manuals to learn everything I could before the going got tough. The truth is, I wasn't just learning how to run a ship, I was trying to learn how to survive. Underneath the surface, I was worried that our chances of survival were practically nil.

"Our orders were to sink all enemy ships and any ship—no matter what the flag—suspected of carrying food and supplies to the Allies. Sometimes we would stop an apprehended vessel first by sending a search party onboard to interrogate the captain, after which we would order the crew and passengers to the lifeboats before scuttling the ship. That was how we operated in the beginning, but as the war progressed our tactics changed. We became much more aggressive until it reached a crescendo, in my opinion, with the sinking of a small British liner, the *Essex*, which claimed the lives of eighty civilians. I remember standing in the conning tower watching those poor wretches through my binoculars during their last painful minutes of life. Many of them had suffered terrible burns from the explosions; others were searching for loved ones with frantic, hopeless expressions. Still others were knocked overboard by the falling debris and were flailing helplessly in the water. Their screams haunt me to this day.

"Nothing can prepare you for the horror of witnessing violent, chaotic deaths. But we knew we had a mission to accomplish, and there was no time for philosophical discussions. This was war. We sank beneath the waves and moved on to our next target, hungry for more success.

"During this campaign, the closest we ever came to losing our lives was in the North Sea. As long as I live, I shall never forget the terror I felt the night we were rammed and almost sunk by the British cruiser, *Hawley*. I was on watch with two seamen, the air cold and damp, the kind that wraps around you like a snake, refusing to let go. The surface of the ocean had an eerie stillness, like the no-man's land between enemy trenches in France, a place of cold, black deadly seawater where nothing lives. A fog hung over us like a cloak. We didn't know at the time that the fog would almost become our death shroud.

"All of a sudden, the third mate, Siegmann, broke the silence by whispering, 'Shadow bearing three-oh-oh, looks like a freighter.' I turned in his direction and peered through my binoculars. Five thousand meters ahead, a faint shadow was crossing our path. An enemy freighter: payday.

"'Captain to the bridge,' Siegmann yelled into the tower. We heard the message repeated over and over until the Captain appeared through the hatch. We promptly showed him the target.

"'Good job, men. Now go down and plot out the attack,' Schultz ordered, eyes fixed on the target like a cat on a prized bird. 'On battle stations—right full rudder—both engines full ahead.'

"The torpedo crews rushed to the tubes and everyone manned their battle stations. The fog drifted in even thicker, causing us to temporarily lose sight of the freighter, but we persisted through a few agonizing minutes until the fog lifted and we were treated to the sight of our trophy.

"'Tubes one to four ready for surface attack,' said Schultz. 'Open tube doors. Stand by.'

"'Tubes ready for firing,' shouted the torpedo men from down below.

"'Shoot!" Schultz shouted.

"With a shudder, the torpedo shot out and sped towards the hapless freighter. After a full minute, a furious explosion lit up the night sky, tossing debris into the air, cracking the hull like it was made of balsa wood, creating a scene right of Dante's Inferno. Mortally wounded, the freighter listed to starboard as the crew fought in desperation to lower two lifeboats into the water. The next thing we knew, we were hit by a horrible crash from behind, followed by the terrifying sound of metal smashing into metal. Sparks were flying everywhere. The men screamed and everyone lost their footing. The unthinkable had happened. We'd been rammed.

"'Dive!' yelled Schultz. On instinct, we dove through the conning tower hatch, jumping for our lives before the enemy ship could fire her huge guns at us. We plunged below the furious waves in record time to save our necks. 'Enemy Cruiser!' screamed Schultz. I ran to my battle station, heart beating like a kettle drum.

"Schultz was still tightening the lock on the hatch by the time we had dived down to twenty meters. Thankfully, everyone survived; we had all made it safely back inside. As our ship sank below the murky depths, we remained silent. We were in a world of total darkness and we clung to whatever we could as coffee mugs, tools, and eating utensils crashed around us in the inky blackness.

"When I came to my senses, I realized that my head was throbbing. In my haste to man my battle station, I hit it against a pipe. More than I worried about the gash, I feared the pounding of my own heart, which felt as if it would burst. During the entire course of the war, I can't recall a time when I was more afraid than our attempt to escape that enemy cruiser. Up until that moment, we had been the hunter. Now the tables were turned and we had become the hunted. My limbs were numb; sweat ran in rivulets down the sides of my head. Our worst fears came true when we heard the unmistakable droning of enemy propellers above our heads. The enemy cruiser was lying in wait, biding its time until we would be forced to surface, at which point they would train their guns on us and blow us to smithereens. I prayed that the crew would not turn on the officers out of fear and desperation.

"Perhaps this requires a bit of explanation. You see, Abby, throughout the course of the war, we had been living under the cloud of a terrible rumor that was spreading like wildfire among U-boat crews. The story was that one of our U-boats had shamefully surrendered to a British Patrol Boat after attempting to outrun it. The crew had mutinied and disgracefully murdered all their officers. In a fit of savage brutality, the crew stole the officers' revolvers and shot them one by one in the head or through the heart, leaving their lifeless bodies to be discovered by the horrified British sailors when they boarded the sub to investigate. This was a cautionary tale that we dreaded hearing more than any other, but we knew it could happen to any one of us if the conditions deteriorated to that extent and savage fear was allowed to set in. Every sailor knows that even the steeliest of minds can snap under intense pressure, something we never took for granted. Even the most loyal crews could turn into savages if they lost their sanity. And given our present dire situation, we knew we needed a heaping dose of lady luck to survive this disaster.

"We stayed submerged for ten hours, forced to listen to the incessant droning of that enemy ship hovering above us like the Angel of Death while we remained trapped inside the cold, clammy hull of steel that, at any moment, could become our tomb. We kept as still as mice, only walking when absolutely necessary, and even then, only after tying rags around our feet and using any handy container for our bodily functions. Schultz was worried that the impact of the ramming might have strained the seams of the hull or cracked the plates of the ship. If that were the case, we'd all be in mortal danger if the cracks reached the batteries, releasing a deadly chlorine gas into the ship. The chlorine gas could burn our lungs and eyes, killing us in a slow, excruciating manner.

"After ten hours of hell, our batteries started to drain. The U-158 was barely moving and we had drifted down to about 55 meters, well below the safety level for our class of ship. If the batteries had run down completely and we lost all possible propulsion, then Schultz would have been left with only two choices. Since no submarine can remain suspended in water forever, he could have used our compressed air supply to push the U-158 to the surface where the enemy cruiser would have blown us to bits, or he could have let her settle to the bottom, where she risked being crushed by the tremendous water pressure. It was a choice of death by enemy hand or death by our own hand. Which method would Schultz choose?

"Before that, our most immediate concern was fresh air. Some of the men were gasping for air, a sign that the air had become fouled with carbon dioxide. How long could we play this game of cat-and-mouse and still survive? Eventually the mouse would be forced to exit his hole by starvation, dehydration, or asphyxiation, whereupon the cat would pounce on him. Schultz finally made up his mind. He decided to try a little navigational trick: he planned to elude the enemy by making some sharp turns, first starboard, then port, then starboard again, moving at a slow speed of only 3 knots, never staying in the same place for very long. A groan of relief passed among the men. After a few hours of careful plotting and turning, his scheme worked as the sound of the propellers grew fainter in the distance. For three more excruciating hours, the U-158 remained submerged. Only when Schultz was certain that the cruiser was gone did he decide to take us up to the surface. After what seemed like an eternity below the murky depths, Schultz flung back the hatch, clawed his way up the conning tower, and gasped in the fresh air. Soon the diesel engines came back to life and the fans sucked fresh, cool air into the hull, blowing out the last bit of foul, contaminated air. The rest of the crew clambered to the surface and lay on the deck, gasping for fresh air. We had come terrifyingly close to asphyxiating a hundred feet below the surface, never to see the sun again.

"Soon the Admiralty in Berlin sent us a change of orders. We were ordered to head immediately to latitude 37 degrees 43 minutes 60 north and longitude 25 degrees 40 minutes west, coordinates that every seaman knew belonged to the Azores, lush, temperate Portuguese islands in the Atlantic. The men were overjoyed. At this point, a plan of escape began to form in my head.

"The Azores are the halfway point between Europe and the Americas, and there has always been a constant tug-of-war between the European powers to establish a naval base there. And so, in the early morning hours of June 1st, just before sunrise, we surfaced in the balmy waters off the sleeping town of Ponta Delgada. As the conning tower broke through the surface, I opened the hatch and climbed onto the bridge. There before me lay the breathtaking view of Ponta Delgada, a historic city that hadn't changed in the last hundred years. It was like a scene from old Europe, with red-tiled Spanish-style houses and beautiful gardens, cobblestone squares mingling with Portuguese forts and ancient churches. I inhaled deeply, trying to clear my head from the stale submarine air that we'd been breathing for days, and trained my binoculars on the roads. By the look of things, all was quiet. The only sign of life came from a few fishermen and dockworkers headed to work on foot. The rest of the town was fast asleep; there wasn't an Allied ship in sight. I hated to think what would happen to this peaceful little island if they became another pawn in the game of war. All those beautiful Spanish buildings turned to rubble.

"We spent the next several months patrolling the waters around the Azores, with orders to stop, search and sink any vessel, enemy or neutral that carried cargo intended for the war effort. The U-boat was the perfect medium for war, and the war was the perfect medium for the U-boat. The *Kriegsmarine* knew that they could not deal with the superior British Navy on an even basis, so they relied on the silent, lurking U-boats to turn the tide in favor of Germany. In all that time, we sank five Norwegian steamers, four French sailing vessels, two American and six British steamers, one Greek, one Canadian and one Italian steamer. All in all, we killed over forty innocent civilians. Many nights I lay awake in my bunk thinking about the loss of life, wondering how their widows and orphans would survive without a bread-winner. I wondered if the world would some day call me a murderer.

"A few days later we spotted the *Emilie,* a British cargo steamer heading for Brest in France. Just by the look of her, we knew she was loaded with valuable supplies for the Allies. We ordered her to halt by firing a machine gun warning shot across her bow, but she refused. Left with no choice, we fired a shell at her aft deck, killing one crew member and causing extensive damage. The *Emilie* had no choice but to halt; Schultz put together a six-man search party to go onboard, of which I was one. Our mission was to locate any illegal contraband, anything that would justify sinking her. Each one of us armed with a trusty Luger pistol, my five mates and I boarded the ship.

"Once on board, we demanded to see the manifest, which the Captain dutifully brought for our inspection. I scanned it, but it looked like an ordinary shipment of iron ore. I suspected that down below she was carrying a far more valuable prize. I stayed with the Captain in the bridge as my men fanned out around the ship. A few minutes later, my suspicions proved correct when they came back reporting that the bow section of the ship contained boxes holding at least 50,000 rounds of .303 caliber rifle ammunition. Bingo. We'd hit the jackpot. I eyed the Captain, ordering him and his men to abandon ship as we intended to sink it.

"'Sink my ship if you dare,' said the steely-eyed Captain. 'My crew and I refuse to leave; we will remain onboard.'

"I held my breath. This Captain was no fool. He was pushing us into a stalemate position, but I was in no mood to concede. I shook my head, refusing to back down.

"I have orders to sink your ship,' I said. 'Take the lifeboats and we'll make sure your position reaches the proper authorities.'"

"And then, from the corner of my eye I caught the glimmer of steel. One of the crew lunged at me with a knife aimed straight at my throat. In an instant, I drew my pistol and fired. The seaman reeled backwards, collapsing against a bulkhead and sliding to the floor as blood spurted from a mortal wound in his chest. The other crewmembers watched in horror, then turned their venomous, hate-filled eyes on me, muttering curses and oaths that increased the horror I felt inside. It was one thing to sink a warship at a safe, impersonal distance, but it was another matter entirely to shoot a man at point blank range. I was nauseous with disgust, but there was no time for philosophical discussions. We had a mission to accomplish and all of our lives were in danger.

"'Get out now!" I screamed. All at once, the remainder of the ship's crew scrambled to drop the lifeboat into the water. My men and I also abandoned ship, heading back to the safety of the U-158 where we proceeded to slice the *Emilie's* hull in two with a well-placed torpedo that struck just under the bridge, sending her, the boxes of rifle ammunition, and those ill-fated sailors to the bottom of the sea.

"While my men chalked up another victory, I was reeling with disgust over the terrible deed I had committed. I had killed an innocent man. A son. A father. A brother. A husband. That night, while I lay in my bunk, I was seized with profound remorse. Though the danger was long gone, my heart still pounded from guilt. I was also tormented from the horror of having played executioner to a man who was simply defending his ship. And no matter how hard I tried, I couldn't shake off the guilt of having killed an innocent man. After a few sleepless nights, I decided that I could no longer take up arms against innocent civilians. I now faced a serious dilemma.

"It was not something that you could put a finger on, but the incident of the *Emilie* changed me forever. My years as a naval cadet had not prepared me for the human side of war; that civilians could be blown to bits like pawns in a chess game. The luckier ones who made it to lifeboats had faces of fear and despair, like hunted animals. And as I watched them drifting aimlessly on the cruel sea watching their ship and dead mates disappearing below the waves, I became disgusted. I decided that I could no longer continue serving the Fatherland in this capacity. The war had gone too far. Later, while I lay in my bunk, I plotted my escape.

"Up to that point, I had served my Kaiser and Fatherland wholeheartedly, but I made up my mind to desert no matter what the cost. I knew that my chances of surviving aboard a U-boat were slim, roughly fifty-fifty. At the age of twenty-six, I was considered one of the 'old men' aboard the ship, so I devised a plan to stage my own death.

"After a few days, we returned to prowl the waters off Ponta Delgada. The engine personnel wanted to carry out some routine repairs to the starboard diesel engine and I knew this was the perfect chance to carry out my plan. As the U-158 lay on the calm surface, I waited for the right moment. As I lay in my bunk, I fingered the Kaiser Wilhelm twenty-mark gold coin that I wore around my neck. It was a present from my father, a token of good luck he had given me before I shipped out. All around me, the men were joking and laughing amid the smell of boiling meat and potatoes, the stench of diesel, and the loud snores of the torpedo men in their bunks. At that moment, every memory came into sharp focus, my home back in Kiel, my parents, my school, my boyhood friends (many of whom were already dead), my Commander, my comrades, and my career in the navy. Everything slipped into nothingness until my mind was blank save for my immediate goal of desertion and freedom.

"As Second Watch Officer, I was called up to the conning tower at 0100 hours to perform some routine maintenance near the stern and check for any damage. At the time, I wasn't thinking too far ahead; I was taking everything one step at a time. I zipped my leather jacket over my shirt and dark blue trousers and sat down to buckle my boots. With the thoughts that swirled in my mind, I was aware that my heart was racing with fear and anticipation, pumping adrenaline to every muscle in my body.

"I tried to ignore it as I threw open the hatch and gulped in my first breath of fresh air in more than a day with the iron-clad determination to carry out my plan regardless of the cost. At my side came Becker, a young enlisted man who donned the binoculars and kept watch while I made final preparations to descend down to the danger zone.

"After checking and rechecking my tools and tucking my trousers into the rubber boots, I descended the conning tower and inched my way across the slippery, steel deck of the submarine. Every U-boat sailor had heard horror stories of watchmen being carried out to sea by freak waves, solid walls of green water appearing out of nowhere that swept unsuspecting sailors overboard, never to be seen again. I knew that one wrong move on my part could send me sliding overboard, into oblivion. That was also part of my plan, a plan to stage my own death.

"I glanced over my shoulder in the direction of land and saw a faint, flickering light in the distance—a welcome sign of human life in this endless desert of salt water. Cold breakers splashed around me, soaking my trousers, invading the protective layer of boots with cold, briny water. I steeled myself by gripping the antenna wire for dear life as I continued aft.

"A moment later, Becker called out that he was heading down the hatch for just a minute to retrieve something. I glanced up as he disappeared down the conning tower, realizing that the moment had come. The blood froze in my veins. Here was the perfect chance. There would never be such a perfect opportunity to escape.

"My eyes darted between the ship and the light on shore, calculating the distance, estimating my odds of survival. Drowning is always a distinct possibility, as is shark attack, but my chances of surviving the war aboard a U-boat were even slimmer. And so, the moment of decision had come. It was now or never.

"As my heart pounded in my chest, I filled my lungs with air and dove into the frigid water. The sudden cold sent shockwaves through my body, like a thousand icy knives tearing at my skin, pulling me under the waves. When I finally surfaced, I gasped for air and swam like mad in the direction of shore. Driven by my survival instinct, my arms chopped through the surf like the propellers of an airplane as I headed in the direction of that glowing light, the light that symbolized life.

"My will to live—to reach the light—became my sole reason for not giving up. As my arms pounded the water, I was filled with hope. I don't know where the strength came from, but the flickering light was starting to get closer. And then, somewhere in the distance, I heard Becker shouting my name. I thought about turning back, but the light was pulling me closer. Now was no time for regrets. To my men, I would soon be counted among the dead. That night, I swam fueled by the fear that I would be found out by my own men as a reviled deserter.

"So now you know the whole truth, Abby," Erich concludes grimly. "How *Leutnant zur See* Erich Seibold escaped the hell of war. I hope you realize that a man who risked his life to desert his ship cannot possibly be a spy. Maybe you think me a coward or a traitor, but what I really am is tired and fed up. I promised myself that I would never raise my hand against an innocent man. That, my dear Abby, is why I am here today with you. So, either you can choose to believe me or ask me to leave."

"I don't want you go," I say, taking his hand. "Stay with me forever, Erich. I promise you'll be safe here."

A wry smile curls up the corners of his mouth. Erich tousles my hair, and then places his war mementos back in their hiding place for safekeeping.

"If there's one thing I've learned, it's to never make promises that are impossible to keep."

CHAPTER 17

Two weeks later, a news cable circulates the island like wildfire. It seems that on August 4th, the American Secretary of State Robert Lansing met with Danish Foreign Minister Constantin Brun in New York City to sign the treaty for the sale of the Danish West Indies to the United States. The treaty was sent to the United States Senate for ratification, after which it will be sent to the Rigsdag. Once all the formalities are completed, the Danish West Indies will become a new territory of the United States even as America inches closer to war. When this happens, Erich will find himself behind enemy lines with a whole new set of problems to face. I decide to take matters into my own hands by consulting with Judge Neergaard about how to handle this messy situation.

When Aunt Esther falls asleep to the droning of her gramophone, I set down my darning needle and tiptoe out of the house. As my eyes adjust to the sunshine, I make my way down to the Grand Hotel, where I know the judge will be sipping his daily rum cocktail. As soon as I reach the second floor gallery, I stop short. Sitting beside Judge Neergaard is none other than Lothar Langsdorff, the man I will forever know as Fritz Dreyer.

Since the first time I saw him sitting with his two steamer captains, I've been living under the fear that he would recognize me from that terrible night on the *Guiana,* when Dreyer tried to silence me with his knife.

Before the men have a chance to notice me, I slowly back away, but it's too late. Judge Neergaard has already spotted me and waves me over. Hanging my head and slouching, I slither into the only empty seat as Langsdorff's eyes burn a hole right through me. Mustering up my courage, I raise my face to confront Ian McShane's killer, but his dreadful sneer, militaristic moustache, and bulldog jaw cause my body to quake. I turn away, afraid my flushed face will betray the intense fear that grips me.

"Who is this girl?" says Langsdorff, clipping off the end of his cigar. "I'm sure I've seen her face somewhere before."

"Allow me to present Miss Abigail Maduro," says Judge Neergaard with pride. "She's the granddaughter of a dear old friend of mine. She hails from a distinguished old Creole Sephardic family, but I've come to consider her as one of my own. Abby, I trust you have the patience to join two old windbags as we discuss the most tiresome topic of late, the striking coal carriers. Perhaps you can add your own unique perspective on this exasperating matter. As Director of the Hamburg-America Line, Herr Langsdorff is facing an imminent strike if he doesn't cave in to their incessant demands for more money. And money, as we all know, is appallingly scarce these days."

"As scarce as atheists in the trenches," laughs Langsdorff, expelling foul smoke as he puffs his cigar. The likeness between Langsdorff and Dreyer is unmistakable. I'm certain they are one and the same, and if I was harboring any lingering doubts, I also recognize the silver cigar case from the *Guiana*.

"Back in Germany," continues Langsdorff, "They're spending vast sums of money buying up all the iron and steel the world can produce to build enormous ships for the Fatherland while von Tirpitz gives the orders to sink everyone else's ships. It's conceivable that in a very short span of time, there will be no more non-German ships left to sink, let alone coal. The world's ships are literally disappearing off the face of the earth. Forget about a raise, these women should feel lucky just to have jobs."

"While I abhor the Kaiser's policy of sinking the world's merchant fleet," says Judge Neergaard with a touch of iciness in his voice. "Even *his* fleet requires coaling, which brings us back to the problem of these coal-carriers. We're just skirting the issue. While I sympathize with their plight, their life being the hardest of all those who earn their living off the sea, we must reach a compromise of some sort. Something must be done to improve their situation without breaking the coffers of the steamship companies."

"I met their leader," I say, as both eyes turn to me. "Have you ever heard of a woman called Queen Coziah?"

"Daresay I know her," says Judge Neergaard. "She has a face you can never forget. When she sets those blazing orbs on you, you feel as though you've met a medusa, or the devil. Her voice bellows like a demon, a sound that turns your blood cold. About twenty years ago, the police dragged her into my courtroom for some petty crime. I gave her a light sentence, but you should have seen the outrage she displayed at being found guilty. She was so indignant, she raised the rafters of my courtroom, and it required two burly policemen to hold her down. She was unruly, uncivilized, and behaved as if she was possessed by the devil. But she knew how to work a crowd—she was uncanny that way. She commanded attention from everyone in her midst, like a circus performer, and kept each one hypnotized. Needless to say, the people drank in her words as if she were a prophet.

"The first time I met the devil woman face to face was back in 1892, during the first coal carrier strike she organized. She was so unruly she almost got herself killed during that spectacle. As I recall, she narrowly escaped getting shot, but they managed to put her bony, black legs in irons and drag her into my courtroom. The militia charged her with inciting a riot and as she stood there listening to the charges, I'll be damned if there wasn't smoke coming out of her ears. During my entire career on the bench, I don't recall ever feeling more uncomfortable at a sentencing than on that day."

"A trial is just a formality," interrupts Herr Langsdorff. "You should learn from the French. They ship their criminals off to Devil's Island whether they're guilty or not. Have you forgotten what you Danes did to old General Buddhoe during the 1848 slave revolts? They hauled him off in chains and banished him to Trinidad, warning him that if he ever showed his face again, they'd hang him. That's the only way to deal with these rabble-rousers. You've got to show them who's the boss."

"I don't allow theatrics in my courtroom, Herr Langsdorff," says Judge Neergaard, raising one imperious eyebrow. "I have a reputation to uphold. The evidence against her was very strong but my common sense told me to find some way to reduce the charges and let her off with a warning. The Negroes have an uncanny ability to make martyrs out of their folk heroes and I didn't want to stir up a hornet's nest. So, I reduced the charges to disorderly conduct and told her she was free to go if she paid a small fine. I remember the great feeling of relief that washed over me when I thought that would be the end of it."

"What happened next?" I ask.

"The blasted firebrand wouldn't accept the charge," says Judge Neergaard, chuckling at the memory. "She stomped her foot and even had the audacity to claim that God was on her side. And as to the charge of disorderly conduct, she countered that by claiming that her conduct had never been more orderly and purposeful in her entire life. Needless to say, I was shocked, but I couldn't appear to sympathize with her plight lest I set off a wave of labor unrest all over the West Indies—you know how fast news travels on the grapevine."

"And then?"

"She proclaimed she never touched that *devil rum* all her life, and certainly not on the day in question. She declared that rum made her all *bazudi*."

"So what did you do?" said Langsdorff.

"Following standard procedure, I dictated her testimony to the Clerk in Danish using decidedly less colorful terminology. When I struggled to translate *bazudi* into Danish, the entire court broke out in laughter, including the Negro policeman and the bailiff, who knew enough Danish to find the situation comically absurd. I was burning under my collar—no prisoner had ever humiliated me in public like that before. I pounded my gavel on the desk and read the impertinent woman the wording of the statute, which clearly stated that wielding sticks and batons in public, aside from being a public nuisance, fits the legal definition of disorderly conduct, and according to the court of His Majesty, King Christian IX, I ordered her to pay a fine of one Kroner to the Clerk of the Court."

"Good for you," said Langsdorff, grinning maliciously. "You showed the little troublemaker who's boss. She deserved hard labor where she would learn to respect authority."

"Is that how you would have handled it, Herr Langsdorff?" says Judge Neergaard. "As I recall, it was that simple, illiterate coal woman who had the last laugh."

"How so?"

"On the day of the strike, she was surrounded by over forty armed soldiers and not one of them dared to lay a hand on her. Her fiery rhetoric and Scriptural quotes mesmerized the entire crowd. After that success, the people raised her stature by calling her their Queen—no small honor among a bunch of self-righteous moralists. I would even go so far as to say this simple coal woman triumphed more than all the armies of Europe for single-handedly holding the Steamship Companies, the militia, and the policemen at bay for an entire day, and all without a single shot being fired. In the end, those blasted coal women got their raise. They won, thanks to the bravado of a simple, uneducated peasant woman who made history."

"Those Negroes are an impossible bunch," says Langsdorff. "If it was up to me I'd tell them all to go to the Devil."

"No doubt you would, Herr Langsdorff," says Judge Neergaard, leaning in closer. "But when they start marching down Main Street singing 'Onward Christian Soldiers,' clapping their hands and invoking the name of Heaven, even the Kaiser himself would have a bit of a public relations mess on his hands with society's more religious elements. Queen Coziah took the ruling class by surprise using religion as her shield with her clever plan of non-violence, and in so doing, she proved that the old ways of doing business over the barrel of a gun are over for good. I suppose this means that men like you and von Tirpitz will soon be relics of a bygone age."

"Never," sniffs Langsdorff. "War is a sacred duty, a badge of honor."

"That's all well and good," says Judge Neergaard. "But if German business interests start suffering on St. Thomas once the Americans take over, is your Kaiser prepared to back up those words with action?"

"The Kaiser will do anything necessary to protect German interests anywhere in the world," says Langsdorff. "Of course, the easiest solution would be to simply move our steamship office over to Dutch Curaçao, but I've grown rather fond of this little island. I've invested too much time and money to let all of our property go up in smoke. If the Americans unwisely decide to chase us Germans away, the local economy will be out thousands of dollars in tax revenue, and these coal women you admire so much will be permanently out of jobs. Henrik, you have a responsibility to influence the Governor that local shipping interests are strongly opposed to the transfer. Only he can urge the Rigsdag to put a stop to it once and for all." Langsdorff snuffs out his cigar and rises to his feet. "Now, if you'll excuse me, I have some important business matters to attend. Good day to the both of you."

Langsdorff bows stiffly and marches out of the building. From our seats, we observe him crossing the square and heading down Tolbod Gade in the direction of the Hamburg-America Line building.

"Business matters that probably involve sending coded messages to Berlin," says Judge Neergaard. "Or supplying an armed cruiser with food and ammunition."

"I have a question for you, Judge Neergaard," I say, carefully weighing my words. "It's strictly theoretical, of course. Let's say there was a German soldier who escaped to St. Thomas and was captured by the Americans. What would happen to him?"

"Interesting question," says Judge Neergaard, scratching his beard pensively. "Especially for one so young. Someday I hope to find out what fuels your vast imagination. Let's see, there would only be a problem if the Americans entered the war on the side of the Allies, in which case the German soldier would find himself behind enemy lines. If he committed no act against the Americans, then he would just be rounded up and placed in some sort of internment camp until the end of the war. However, if he was caught participating in some sort of sabotage or espionage activity, then the matter becomes much more serious. Most likely, the soldier would have to face a military tribunal and await the decision of the court. Sometimes, they're just kept in prison. If they're guilty of some terrible crime, they're shot. But these situations are complicated and can drag on for years. There's no easy answer."

"What if the German soldier was really a deserter that was trying to escape the war? What if he's innocent of any crimes?"

"My dear, in war there are no innocent soldiers, only lucky ones and unlucky ones."

CHAPTER 18

A few days later I wake up to the sound of Cooky Betty shouting that a miracle occurred during the night. Aunt Esther, Nana Jane, and I run outside to the kitchen to see what happened. Cooky Betty is jumping with glee as she pulls us in to see for ourselves.

In the kitchen, we get the shock of our lives. The counters are piled high with every conceivable type of food. There are fresh loaves of bread, tins of sardines and herring, Danish butter, English tea, French marmalade, biscuits, crackers, oatmeal, tea, coffee, an assortment of jams and jellies, smoked fish, cheese, sacks of rice, canned salmon, canned beans, Italian spaghetti, even bars of Swiss chocolate. We marvel at the unexpected windfall and everybody grabs a box to sample.

Immediately, Cooky Betty and Nana Jane start fighting over a box of chocolate biscuits like two spoiled children. Aunt Esther grabs the chocolate with her chest puffed up as she takes credit for our good fortune by boasting she must have a secret admirer. Everyone rolls their eyes, but we all agree that no one knows the identity of our secret benefactor. Of course, I have my suspicions, but circumstances dictate that I remain silent.

Two days later, Erich tells me he has a surprise for me. We take old Clara from her pasture and ride down to Frenchtown. Once there, Erich reveals that Mr. Greaux has given us permission to take his fishing sloop out for a day of sailing. When I bring up the subject of the mysterious presents, Erich feigns ignorance. I play along with his little charade knowing full well that his modesty won't allow him to take credit for his acts of kindness, but he was interested in hearing how tickled the old ladies were about the gifts.

Today is a perfect day for sailing. The turquoise water sparkles under the blazing sun as our sloop glides over the waves with ease. Erich shows me how to hold the tiller, and I can't help but imagine that we're pirates or adventurers sailing the Caribbean, living off the land, drinking coconut milk, pulling papayas off the trees, and fishing for our sustenance. We drop anchor in Mosquito Bay and dive into the crystalline water for a refreshing swim. Balancing the food on our heads, we swim ashore to enjoy a picnic lunch on the beach. Later, as we rest under the shade of a palm tree, we talk and laugh and share memories. The day is so perfect I hope it never ends.

"You should have seen the looks on their faces, especially Cooky Betty," I say, chuckling. "They couldn't believe their luck. They were fighting over the biscuits like children. Even Aunt Esther was speechless. She thinks she has a secret admirer out there. As I was leaving the house, I caught her admiring herself in an old dress that she hasn't worn in years. She still believes she's going to get married someday."

"I hope your Aunt Esther doesn't get any ideas," laughs Erich. "It was a simple gift, not a marriage proposal."

"You have a lot to learn," I say. "Three old spinsters living under one roof. If you were to suddenly appear on their doorstep, they would be fighting tooth and nail over you."

"Someday I would like to meet this Cooky Betty and Nana Jane," he says, biting into a ripe mango. "After the war ends, of course. Once they find out I'm a German U-boat officer, I doubt they'll be so welcoming."

"Nonsense, it doesn't matter to them where you come from. All they care about is that you're my best friend. It doesn't hurt that you're very handsome."

"Is that so?" says Erich. "You know, if it wasn't for my parents back in Germany, I could easily spend the rest of my days out here in the tropics, fixing up the house, replacing the old roof, repairing that broken-down old horse carriage. Everything a man could ever want is here except a wife."

"A wife?"

"Naturally," he says matter-of-factly. "No man is an island. Even an old sailor like me needs the love of a good woman."

"What about me?"

Erich bursts out laughing as if that was the funniest thing he had ever heard.

"What's so funny about that?"

"Forgive me for laughing," he says. "But at the age twenty-six, I'm already considered ancient by U-boat standards. By the time you're ready to get married in two or three years, I'll already be an old man of twenty-eight or twenty-nine. One would hardly expect a beautiful young girl of eighteen to want a battered old seadog like me."

"You're not a *battered old seadog*," I say. "On the other hand, I do see lines on your face every time you laugh. And I recall you once mentioning that you were old enough to remember Bismarck, and anyone who can remember that old windbag must be ancient."

Erich pinches my cheek and I throw my head back and laugh, relishing this moment of pure happiness. I remind him that he never finished his story of how he escaped his U-boat by diving into the cold Atlantic.

"You were naughty to leave me hanging on the edge of my seat," I say. "And at the most exciting part, while you were surrounded by sharks and swimming for your life."

He clasps his hands behind his head. "Must you constantly be entertained? Well, if it's stories you want, then its stories you shall get. Let me think. Oh yes, after diving into the cold, clammy Atlantic, I swam for my life. My arms and legs pounded the surf, fighting the treacherous currents with every ounce of strength I could muster. Fighting the cold, I swam until I could swim no more, almost to the point of exhaustion, but something inside of me refused to give up. Some unseen force kept pushing me forward. Blocking all extraneous thoughts, I concentrated on heading for that tiny point of light on the shore, the only sign of humanity in the inky black ocean.

"Soon, a numbing sensation started spreading throughout my body. To my horror, I realized I was freezing to death. Determined not to give in to terror and desperation, I gulped in a breath of fresh air and pushed myself even harder, determined to reach the glowing light before hypothermia took hold and drowned me. Fortunately, the light grew larger, bolstering my hopes for survival. I don't remember how long it took me to reach the beach, but by the time my feet touched the rocky shore, I was completely exhausted. Like a crab in its final throes, I clawed my way up the beach, shivering and disoriented as I dragged my weary body over rocks, shells, and gritty sand. Inside I rejoiced because I knew I had cheated death, but just barely.

"For a long time, I lay on the beach shivering but happy, gazing up at the moon and the stars as if for the first time in my life. The minute I saw a shooting star, I laughed out loud—I knew I was destined to live. During all those months on the submarine, I never had the opportunity to gaze at the sky for pure pleasure. Most of the time, we prowled below the murky depths like a hungry shark. But as I lay on that Azorean beach, I knew my destiny was changed forever. Yet, I also felt strangely insignificant lying on that lonely stretch of beach. I craved human company to share the joy of my newfound freedom. Instead, I staggered to my feet and saluted my ship and my mates, who no doubt were searching for my remains in vain among the black waves. I apologized for deserting them and wished them Godspeed, and then I ripped off the shoulder boards from my leather jacket and stuffed them in my pockets. With this symbolic act, I severed all ties with the *Kaiserliche Marine* and my U-boat forever. Henceforth, I was a deserter.

"Meanwhile, I knew that Germany had recently declared war on Portugal, which meant that I was now on enemy soil. Given the high number of Allied casualties, I knew I would be a target of vengeance if the islanders ever suspected I was a German soldier. I shuddered to think of that possibility, but with my shoulder boards gone, I looked like any ordinary merchant seaman in my dark blue trousers, leather jacket, and shirt.

"I mentally adjusted to my new reality that I was living the life of a runaway German soldier. I would have to learn how to survive like any ordinary civilian, by relying on my wits and cunning to stay one step ahead of danger. I also needed a new identity, one that would be both believable and logical, but whose?

"As I stood there surveying the long stretch of beach, the only sound came from the gentle breaking of the surf on the shore and the occasional cry of a seagull. Left with no choice, I hiked down the beach, keeping to the shadows, hoping I would find adequate shelter for the night.

"As luck would have it, about a mile down the beach I found an abandoned old shack, one that had probably once belonged to a fisherman given the broken nets and useless traps that lay scattered about. I peered inside, cognizant of the pounding of my heart.

"To my great fortune, the hut was deserted and appeared to have been forgotten. There was no hint of food or any sign of life anywhere, just an old cot and a moth-eaten blanket situated against one wall. I peeled off my wet clothes and hung them from a nail, and then I wrapped myself in the blanket and collapsed on the cot in total exhaustion. I fell into a deep sleep from which I thought I would never awaken.

"The next morning, as the sun's rays pierced through the wooden slats, I woke to a banging noise just outside the hut. Fearing an attack, my eyes shot open and my senses switched to full alert. As carefully as possible, I inched my way off the cot and crawled along the floor toward the window. Then, the high-pitched shriek of a child echoed through the open window slats. I froze in shock at the strange sound. I couldn't remember the last time I had heard the voice of a child.

"I rose to my feet and peered through the window slats. No more than twenty feet away I saw a Portuguese boy of about four or five sitting on the sand with his baby goat at his side. The boy was hard at work banging a rock against a pineapple, trying to feed the bleating animal. I scanned the horizon for signs of the U-158, but it was long gone. The only objects that bobbed on the surface were pieces of floating driftwood, buoys, and the occasional small dingy. And then a chill went through my body. I got the strangest sensation that my past life had been wiped away, that I was born anew. I blame this temporary insanity for the following serious lapse in judgment.

"Oblivious to my own nakedness, I stepped outside the hut as if it was the most natural thing in the world to do. Startled, the little boy dropped the rock, stood up in shock, and ran down the beach screaming, 'Soldado Alemão! Soldado Alemão!' as if I were the Kaiser himself. Not wanting to be separated from his master, the baby goat ran after the boy, bleating hysterically.

"I smacked myself on the head, 'Dummkopf!' Here I was a professional soldier trained to survive almost every conceivable situation and this act of stupidity could have cost me my life. I caught my reflection in a pane of glass. My skin was ghostly pale from months underwater, and I had several months' worth of beard, not to mention the fact that I was completely naked. I uttered a loud oath, cursing my own stupidity. *'That boy thinks I'm a German soldier and I haven't uttered a single word of German!'* I knew full well that I could not afford to repeat this mistake. As a German, I was the enemy, and the next mistake could be fatal. I knew that my survival depended on altering my appearance to avoid detection since, in times of war; you can never rely on luck alone to save your life.

"Anxious to avoid a run in with the boy's father, I dressed quickly in my stiff shirt and trousers, grabbed my jacket, and evacuated the area, making sure to clear my footprints with a long, leafy branch. When I reached a dirt road, I hurried towards the nearest town, hoping to blend in with the locals. When I arrived in a sleepy little fishing village, I breathed a sigh of relief. No sign of police anywhere.

"I spied a small, nondescript barber shop whose proprietor had to be at least ninety years old. Gesturing wildly, I described needing a haircut and a shave and offered to sweep the shop and make a few repairs in exchange for his services. My miming attempts must have worked because the Portuguese barber was only too happy to oblige, his poor vision being a factor that worked in my favor. Soon, I looked and smelled like a new man. I picked up the broom and cleared the floor of my incriminating blond hair, and then I set about fixing a broken chair. On the way out, I spied an old Greek fisherman's cap collecting dust in the windowsill. A useful disguise, I thought. After a hearty goodbye, I grabbed the hat and formulated my next plan of escape."

"What happened next?"

"I haven't bored you yet?" he said, exhaling a thin stream of smoke, and then snuffing out the cigarette in the sand. "You still have patience to hear more of my crazy story? If I didn't know better, I'd say you were interrogating me for the authorities."

Erich closes his eyes, lies back on the white sand, and pulls his straw hat over his eyes. "Let me just rest for a minute," he says. "Even deserters are entitled to a little rest and relaxation now and then."

***

That evening as I try to sneak back into the house by climbing over the terrace railing, something smashes down on my head,

194

sending me crashing to the floor. When I look up, I see a horrifying vision: multiple versions of Aunt Esther's enraged face as I cry out in pain and shield myself from further blows.

"Where have you been all day?" she screams, pounding me with her fists. I scream and draw back in terror from her vicious onslaught.

"I've warned you over and over about gallivanting about town with the wrong crowd. You're a disgrace. Just look at you. Your hair's a mess and you've got no stockings on. What will the neighbors say when they see you looking like a tramp? Don't you know everybody's gossiping about you? What excuse can I give them for your behavior? What future will you have if you spend all your time cavorting in the streets with the riffraff?"

My mouth goes dry at this ugly accusation. Her allegations hurt more than the gash on my head. I feel like slapping her face, but I'm grateful when Nana Jane comes rushing to my side.

"Miss Esther!" screams Nana Jane with indignation. "Are you crazy? How dare you hit this poor child? She needs a mother's care. Have you no sympathy? No heart?"

"I'm the one who needs sympathy," says Aunt Esther, her mouth twisting in rage. "Did I ask to have a wild girl on my hands? She's been nothing but trouble since the day she came."

"You must have pity on Abigail," Nana Jane protests. "She's suffered enough already. I'd give my own life to protect this innocent child. Don't go listening to no malicious gossip from no uppity neighbors. They don't know Abigail like I do."

"I'm trying to do what's right by her," retorted Aunt Esther. "But you refuse to see my side. What kind of future can she expect if she earns herself a bad reputation?"

I swallow hard at the bitter truth of that statement. Maybe Aunt Esther is right. Maybe I am throwing my whole life away in the name of a silly and impossible friendship. When the neighbors see me traipsing around town with Erich, they're bound to start talking. On the other hand, knowing that I have no future and no hope of becoming a teacher, what's left to lose? I even feel helpless continuing my mission of becoming a spy hunter. Langsdorff and his men are too powerful, too dangerous. Only one thing is for certain: I will never abandon Erich. No matter what happens, I will never give up the best friend I've ever had. I will protect Erich no matter what the cost.

CHAPTER 19

The next day, Nana Jane returns from Market Square bursting with the latest news. In addition to a basketful of yams and cassavas, she brought back details of an unofficial ballot that has left tongues wagging all over Charlotte Amalie. The ballot was held in St. Croix, with 5,000 citizens voting in favor of joining the United States. Only eleven people (planters and members of the old guard) voted to remain with Denmark. The wheels have now been set in motion. We're on a collision course with the future and not even Lothar Langsdorff and all his money, power, and influence can stop the transfer of the Danish West Indies to America from going through.

Since Sunday is my seventeenth birthday, Erich has promised to take me hiking up Bluebeard's Hill. As soon as we meet down on Raadets Gade, he notices the bruises on my forehead where Aunt Esther hit me. Without my telling him, he knows exactly who's responsible.

"Did that vicious aunt of yours do this to you?" he says, his face reddening. "Tell me the truth."

"Yes," I say. "She called me a disgrace because I go out *gallivanting* in the streets. I don't care about her anymore. She can say whatever she wants."

"That witch," he says. "How dare she lay a finger on you? I have to put a stop to this. I feel responsible for your troubles. I should be protecting you from that spiteful woman."

"I have to learn to protect myself," I say. "I can't expect you to be there every time she goes berserk. And besides, it's much too dangerous. If she found out about you, there'd be hell to pay. She'd call the police for sure."

"I can risk jail but I can't risk her attacking you. If she tries it again, I won't be able to hold myself back from teaching that old crone a little kindness."

"There won't be a next time," I say. "I've got a few tricks up my sleeve. She has a particular weakness that I can use in my favor. Promise me you won't interfere. This is my battle."

"You sound quite sure of yourself," he says. "I shall have to trust you know what you're doing. But if I ever catch her hitting you, she'll have to answer to me."

It turns out to be a spectacular day. Despite the heat, we spend the day hiking and climbing up a steep path that winds up Bluebeard's Hill, a prominent hill on the eastern side of town, then we spend some time exploring the grounds around the old watchtower, which everyone calls Bluebeard's Castle, hitching a ride on a donkey cart, then settling into a shady spot under a tree to eat lunch while enjoying the view of the harbor. While we eat Johnny cakes and mangoes, Erich takes a small package out of his pocket and shyly hands it to me.

"This is for you, Abby. It's for your birthday."

I tear open the package. Inside I find a beautiful cameo pin with the delicate face of a lovely young woman with flowing hair and a long neck carved out of mother-of-pearl. The pin is exquisite and must have cost a small fortune.

"Erich, it's beautiful, but why?"

"I saw it in one of the shops on Main Street and knew it was meant for you," he says. "Her profile reminded me of you."

He pins it on me as I finger its delicate carvings.

"If somebody asks me where I got it, what should I say?"

"Tell them your Guardian Angel gave it to you."

"My *Guardian Angel*?"

"Or you can say the truth, that a runaway German U-boat officer gave it to you as a thank you for hiding him in your aunt's basement. I only hope I can live up to the title of *Guardian Angel*. I may have failed as a soldier, but I won't fail as your protector."

"You're not a failure for refusing to fight an unjust war. Nobody has the right to judge you for what you did. Besides, who knows what would have happened to you if you had stayed on your ship.

198

For all we know, you might have died by now. Instead, you chose life and fate brought you to these shores. Now since it's my birthday, as part of my present, you must finish telling me the story of how you escaped the Azores."

"So, the little cat is still curious?" He grins. "Aren't you tired of this old sailor telling you his fish tales?"

"Never! Your fish tales are better than the Arabian Nights because I know they're true."

"Smart girl," he says. "Well, since you put it that way, I can't afford to let you down. Now where did I leave off? Oh yes—my plan to escape. I found myself alone in the Azores, wandering the cobblestoned streets of San Miguel worrying about my pressing need for money, otherwise known as gainful employment. It's an accepted fact that employed people are never as suspicious as loafers, so I knew it was imperative that I find some job to get me off the streets. My next pressing problem was a new identity, but whose? I figured it would be relatively easy to land a job as a merchant marine, where I could travel around as a civilian, always keeping one step ahead of the Germans and the British while earning a bit of money on the side. I spent some time pondering how to solve this dilemma.

"I knew it would be impossible to procure false identity papers in such a remote corner of the world without paying an exorbitant bribe and drawing unwanted attention on myself, so I decided to flee San Miguel as soon as possible, lest my sudden appearance be linked to any U-boat attacks in the area. Given the strong, anti-German feelings running rampant among these shy and peaceful Portuguese fishermen, I dreaded the idea of being sniffed out as a German and becoming the target for their righteous indignation.

"Keeping my demeanor as cool and steady as possible, I concocted a cover story for my future employer, that while I was on my last assignment, I had lost my papers at sea. Better yet, I decided to tell him that my papers were stolen by one of the crew—a Turk. This excuse is credible given that sailors are notorious drinkers, and the Azoreans produce some of the world's finest wines and liquors in the world. I decided that the safest nationality was Danish given that Denmark is neutral and I already knew a few Danish words from the summers I had spent there as a youth visiting my Danish cousins. I also planned to tell them that I had suffered an attack of appendicitis (I still have an old scar) which required surgery. And now, after a

199

successful recuperation, I was fully recovered and desperately in need of work. Satisfied that my cover story was foolproof, I strode towards the village on a cobblestoned street that wound around pristine hills and emerald-green valleys dotted with flowers and occasional herds of goats.

"After an hour, I came to a quaint little fishing village situated near the coast. To my surprise, the town was quiet. The only sound came from the flapping of sheets on a nearby clothesline or the tossing of garbage out of a window. The few townspeople I saw were wrinkled old women sitting in the square wearing the traditional black scarves of devout Portuguese Catholics. Seeing their taciturn, ancient faces was like stepping back in time to the previous century since so little of their lives had changed since then.

"As I drank in the sights, I got the eeriest sensation that someone was watching me. You know the feeling, it's like a prickly sensation you get on the back of your neck when someone's eyes are following your every move. I started sweating and looking over my shoulder, fearful that some unseen predator was waiting to pounce on me. Tensing my muscles, I jerked my head around, but the only eyes that met mine were the cloudy eyes of a broken-down, old alley cat. The half-blind cat was staring blankly in my direction, and quickly returned to the important task of licking his haunches. I threw my head back and laughed. The feeling of relief was indescribable.

"The harbor was alive with the pastel-colored boats of the local fishermen. Almost the entire male population of the village was out on the water scouring for their sustenance with old-fashioned nets while the women minded the cooking and gardening. In another time and under different circumstances, I would have liked to stay longer in San Miguel, to explore the island's villages, to hike her lush, green hills, and relish her natural wonders. But given the fact that the world was still at war, and I was a German deserter, I had to get out of there as soon as possible.

"I wandered down the narrow streets and alleyways, following the unmistakable scent of fish stew emanating from an unseen window. At last, I found the source: a tavern, the kind that is typical to small, Southern European villages, where weathered old men congregate to tell their fish tales or meditate over a bottle of ouzo. I reckoned that this tavern might be just the answer to my prayers: a sailor's haunt.

"I entered the tavern, aware that my strange appearance and pale face would draw attention. My strategy was to keep my German nationality an absolute secret until I could talk my way into a job on a merchant vessel. Just then, a thought popped in my mind, a saying that my grandfather used to teach me about how to survive in this world: *'Bluff, my boy, is what carries a man through the world. Act as if you are certain you can do a job, and you'll generally convince the other fellow that you can.'* I straightened my back and approached the man who appeared to be the owner of the café, explaining to him in English that I was an out-of-work Danish merchant mariner looking for a job. The man, whose chubby face and a bulbous nose belied his serious bearing, understood me perfectly. He offered me a steaming cup of coffee and told me to sit at a certain table while he went to fetch the right man. A short while later, the chubby-faced man reappeared followed by a tall, dark, bearded man in his fifties who he introduced as Captain Miguel Franco, the captain of the *Cartagena*, a tramp steamer out of Bilbao, Spain on its way to the West Indies. My heart soared. Salvation seemed close at hand.

"Captain Miguel looked me over, assessing my capacity as a sailor, and then he launched into a lengthy interrogation where he tested my knowledge of seamanship and my previous maritime experience. Remembering my grandfather's advice, I mustered up all my confidence and told him my name was 'Knud Hansen' from Svendborg, a Danish fishing village. I then explained that I was an out-of-work merchant mariner who had started out as a cadet and worked his way up to Third Mate, a position I left due to an attack of appendicitis. I assured him I had a clean bill of health and was fit to work as a helmsman. I also mentioned that I knew basic navigation, signaling with flags, and that I spoke several languages. All this seemed to please Captain Miguel, although I couldn't say for certain since he kept his poker face the entire time.

"When I finished my little fairy tale, Captain Miguel pulled out a large Cuban cigar and puffed on it contentedly. I took that as a good sign. After some time, he opened his mouth and said in very good English, 'I lost a good man in Portugal two months ago. It was a terrible experience. He got sick with pneumonia and the doctors tried to save his life. I told them I would pay them anything to save the life of my friend Ricardo Ferreira, but there was nothing they could do.'

(He crossed himself when he said this.) 'So, you see, I need a good man right now.' Captain Miguel leaned back in the chair and folded his arms across his chest.

"'So, Hansen, are you coming to Havana with me, or not?'

"'Yes sir,' I said, bolting upright. 'I need this job and I've always wanted to see the West Indies.'

"A broad smile broke out on Captain Miguel's face.

"'You Danes are some of the best sea dogs around and trustworthy men to boot,' he said. 'I need a man with a good eye that can spot a U-boat periscope at 100 meters. Many good ships have gone down with all hands onboard. Once we reach the Antilles, we'll be home free, but a careless ship is a scuttled ship and I don't have to tell you that one mistake can finish us off out there. The sea takes no prisoners. You look like a nice lad so I'll take you on as a helmsman with Third Officer's watch and pay you five dollars a week to start. We've got a load of Spanish cement and tiles, and we're awaiting an additional load of Azorean wine that my Cuban pals are keen on receiving. I have one scheduled stop in Puerto Rico if they cable me that a shipment of sugar is ready for drop off in New Orleans. That's how I pick up a little extra cash on the side. Other than that, it's just us and the open sea. Are you with me or not?'

"'Count me in, Captain,' I said.

"The gregarious Spaniard extended his plump, weather-beaten hand and shook mine with a powerful grip. After the captain instructed me to report to the ship at seventeen hundred hours, my heart leapt with joy, scarcely believing my good fortune. In a matter of minutes, I had landed my first job as a free man, and nothing in the world could make me go back to the hell of war.

"I left the café and found a dry goods store where I traded my precious Kaiser Wilhelm twenty-mark piece for some new dungarees, a canvas sea bag, a wool sweater, socks, marine soap, a genuine English toothbrush, and a pair of seaworthy leather boots. When it was time to pay, I removed my precious gold piece and handed it to the shopkeeper, a stout Portuguese man who bit it with his two remaining teeth. Satisfied that it was real, he eyed me uneasily when he realized the coin's German origins. Nevertheless, he placed the coin in his cash box and wrapped up my purchases, his silence becoming almost an unspoken pact between us.

"The shopkeeper's total incomprehension of any language other than Portuguese and my ignorance of the same ensured a swift deal with the minimum of formalities, so we resorted to a vigorous handshake to seal the deal. I gathered up my new belongings and headed back to the wharf, eager to leave San Miguel and her suspicious citizens far behind.

"I located the *Cartagena* with ease. A motley crew of Mediterranean-looking sailors was busy loading a large shipment of Azorean wine into her hold. The *Cartagena* was a typical cargo ship about twenty years old, showing her age in a number of places. The lifeboats needed a fresh coat of paint and there were creeping patches of rust all along the hull. She was about 300 feet long and weighed about 3,000 tons, not a huge catch for a U-boat ace like me, but not peanuts either. The way these ships sink after a direct torpedo hit to the hull meant that, had we been hit, not even one cask of that Azorean wine would have made it to Cuba in one piece. She had derrick supports fore and aft and an enclosed bridge. In short, she was a regular tramp steamer and I could have fared a lot worse. The *Cartagena* was my new ticket to freedom and I loved all 300 feet of her glorious steel hull, just as I had fallen in love with the U-158 the minute I saw her back in the Kiel dockyards.

"I requested permission to board and when Captain Miguel saw me alighting from the rope ladder, he clapped me on the back like a long lost cousin.

"'I'm glad you didn't change your mind like all the others,' he said, balancing a cindering cigar between his teeth. 'Not many sailors are interested in navigating the treacherous waters around the Azores if they can avoid it. Those blasted German subs and raiders have turned these waters into a graveyard for ships, a regular Davy Jones Locker. Well, my Viking friend, are you ready to set sail?'

"'Yes, Captain, ready and able,' I said, flashing my most self-assured grin that my growling stomach and lack of sleep could muster. I silently mouthed a thank you to my grandfather for his sage advice and did my best to ignore Captain Miguel's fleeting comment about the *blasted German subs*. Nations sympathetic to the Allied cause usually harbor strong anti-German sentiments and are not shy about voicing them. If only Captain Miguel had known that I was personally responsible for sending many of those merchant ships down to the Atlantic seabed, he would have wasted no time in sending me to swim with the sharks.

"'By the way, Hansen,' said Captain Miguel on his way to the bridge. 'You can berth in the pilot cabin near the bridge. There's room for you there. I'm taking over the Third Mate watch. Join me on the bridge at 2000 hours after you've had a good meal.'

"'Aye, aye, sir,' I said, catching myself before blurting out *'Jawohl,'* the proper German response to a direct order from a commanding officer. I thanked my lucky stars that I managed to catch myself before uttering that near-fatal mishap as I navigated my way across the cluttered deck, dodging barrels, crates, and assorted ropes that were waiting to be stowed below-decks. I found my berth and was grateful to find it empty. At the very least, I had some much-needed privacy.

"We pushed off while it was still daylight and set a course directly for San Juan, Puerto Rico: our first designated landfall. I'll never forget my first night on the *Cartagena*. It was one of the most exciting nights of my life, because, for the first time in years, I was free. I relished the chance to be responsible for my own life and to make my own decisions. Of course, I was also excited to be heading to the Caribbean with its pristine beaches, beautiful women, endless bottles of rum, and succulent *fruits de mer*. After unpacking, I left to join the rest of the crew in the mess, hungry and tired.

"The crew was a hodgepodge of Spaniards, Portuguese, Azorean, and Cuban sailors. They sat around a banged-up wooden table on chairs nailed to the floor, regaling each other with fish tales about extraordinary luck and daring bravado. As soon as they saw me, they greeted me with a rousing chorus of, 'Here comes the extra ballast we picked up in San Miguel,' and 'Hey sailor, hope you have your bottle of quinine handy, those Cuban mosquitoes can't resist fresh Danish blood.' I smiled and took my rightful place among the men as we all dug in.

"I was relieved that the men had taken a liking to me. Overhead, a brass oil lamp swung from a beam, casting a warm glow over their dusky faces and their bowls of lumpy soup. Soon, I learned to call each one by name as they launched into an argument about the possibility of picking up some tropical disease while down in the Caribbean, either malaria or yellow-fever, which is just one of the hazards of venturing into the warmer climes. They were blissfully unaware that just a short while ago, while at the helm of the U-158, I had been an even greater hazard to their health.

"After the meal, I joined Captain Miguel in the bridge and we enjoyed coffee while he regaled me with stories about his youth in Bilbao and how he had come to command the *Cartagena*. As he spoke, we kept our eyes peeled on the surface of the ocean, searching for any sign of trouble. Captain Miguel shared some entertaining stories about his travels in Denmark; nevertheless, he admitted he hadn't been back to Copenhagen since before the war broke out.

"I left the watch at 0000 hours and returned to my berth, exhausted but satisfied. That first night, I slept like a stone and awakened to reveille, a tin whistle, at 0600 the next morning. When I opened my eyes the sun hit my face, an experience I shall never forget. I wasn't used to the novelty of waking up to sunlight and the presence of seagulls swirling overhead. I stuck my face out just to feel the sun's rays against my skin; for a submarine sailor who'd spent countless months onboard a cold, clammy U-boat, it was pure heaven. I had grown accustomed to sleeping and waking in endless darkness. My first morning on the *Cartagena* was splendid; I ate a hot breakfast with my messmates then reported back to the bridge.

"Morning found us in seas brisk and not too choppy. The First Mate, still at his watch, was reporting calm seas ahead with no sign of periscopes or phantom ships lacking identifying marks. At 0800 hours, Captain Miguel joined us on the bridge and showed us our plotted course.

"'So, Hansen, how do you like the *Cartagena*?' said the captain. 'Her beauty won't take your breath away, but she can carry a mountain of cargo on a fairly low registered tonnage, and just listen to those steam engines purring like a kitten. I'll take you on a tour of the engine room later. Weather permitting, we should be making ten and a half knots and burning very little of our precious coal in the process. When heavy fuel consumption eats into my profits, I have to schedule more deliveries that put me into a vicious cycle where I never get ahead. So far, so good. Anyway, I forgot to tell you that a customer of mine in St. Thomas radioed that he finally has the money to pay off an old debt. So, since we're already headed in that direction, I thought we'd make a short stop there before hitting San Juan. I can do some coaling there as well.'

"'St. Thomas?' I said, not realizing I was about to make a big mistake. 'I've never heard of that island. Where is it exactly?'

Captain Miguel locked eyes with me. "'That's one of your Danish islands. You've never heard of your own colony?'

"'Oh, yes…St. Thomas. How stupid of me,' I said. 'When do we arrive?'

"'In about ten days, if the weather holds,' he said. 'I'll schedule a full day of shore leave. That should give you enough time to meet some old friends of mine. Hey, Hansen, I have a feeling that you and I are going to have a beautiful future together roaming around the West Indies.'

"'Thanks, Captain,' I answered, grateful that he had placed so much trust in me, but worried that I would somehow slip up.

"As the day wore on, the skies darkened and the wind picked up until we were inundated by a storm front. The cold, briny water lashed at the ship with foamy white fingers that cut through the decks with razor-sharp precision. The noise of the crew screaming orders at each other coupled with the roar of the wind and sea was ear-splitting. After spending so much time below the surface, I wasn't used to their loud, aggressive banter and the rough ride. Truth be told, I was a bit of a greenhorn, and spent most of my time observing their behavior and trying to emulate their natural ebullience.

"In spite of the stormy weather, my lungs gulped in the fresh air that purified my system after months of choking on the foul stench of the submarine air. The experience was liberating for my body and my soul and I hoped that I didn't appear to be a novice in front of the seasoned crew. If they harbored any questions about my abilities as a sailor, they never mentioned it and, in time, they accepted me as one of their own. I attended to my duties and by dusk the foul weather was right over our starboard beam, with the waves coming in solid. On an upward slope of water, the bow pointed skyward, then fell downward into a white explosion of hissing spray that cut through your clothes and stung your eyes. We had entered a violent, inhospitable maelstrom of endless seawater and salt sprays that was nonetheless exhilarating. We reduced the engines to half speed which slowed our progress, but I was too excited to care. Finally, I was sailing on the waves instead of lurking in the depths.

"After the Third Officer watch, Captain Miguel paid me a visit in my cabin bearing two steaming mugs of coffee and a yellowed, worm-eaten book, which he threw in my direction.

"'You're lucky, Hansen,' he said. 'I found the English copy of my favorite book, *The Cavalryman of Segovia*. Do you know how many times I've read that book? At least fifty, especially on these long runs. I tried lending it to some of those uneducated buffoons, but they prefer to spend their time playing cards, gambling, and looking at dirty pictures. The story is about a man who assumes the identity of his sister's dead husband, a cavalry officer who he resembles, in order to escape an unwanted engagement. But no matter where he goes, he discovers he owes money all over town in addition to finding out there's a price on his head. He also learns he has a secret child with a woman who he never met before who's now demanding support. The poor man learns that by changing his identity to avoid problems, he winds up with even greater problems than he ever bargained for. He gets into a few scrapes and almost loses his head, but the ending is a real kicker.'

"'At least he changed his fate,' I said, trying to sound nonchalant. 'Isn't freedom worth any price? Tell me, how does this comedy of errors end?'

"'If I told you, you wouldn't bother to read it. Besides, you Danes have a soft spot for long, gloomy tales that match your long, gloomy winters while we Spaniards prefer tales of knights and chivalry, like *Don Quixote de la Mancha*. Anyway, if you read it to the end, you might learn something.'

"'Begging the Captain's pardon, but if I wanted to feel like I was back in Denmark, I'd be there now. The last place in the world I want to be is Europe. I'm keen on seeing Havana while the rest of the world goes to hell.'

"'Then let me be your tour guide,' chuckled Don Miguel, procuring a flask of rum from his jacket pocket and pouring some into our coffee mugs. 'I know the Caribbean like the back of my hand. Just keep your eyes peeled and let me know if anything more sinister than a turtle's head pops up over the waves. You can never be too careful and we still have much territory to cover before we're out of the woods. Those dastardly German U-boats can still get the better of us if we're not vigilant.'

"'Don't worry, Captain, I can smell Germans a mile away.' I said, contemplating the irony of being blown up by my own ship. 'The last thing I want to lose is my ticket to Havana because of some blasted U-boat.'

"'Keep in mind, Hansen,' said Captain Miguel. 'The *Cartagena* is seaworthy, but one well-placed torpedo can rip her to shreds. I can't bear the thought of losing my precious lady of the sea. Hey, did you ever hear why they give names to ships?'

"'Not that I recall,' I said. 'But not every ship has a name. Some have numbers, like the U-boats.'

"'Ah, but a ship is a more noble a creature than those floating torpedo carriers,' said Captain Miguel. 'Every ship has her own purpose, her own destiny. Some old sea dogs even claim a ship possesses her own soul. Some even possess their own eccentricities, ones their builders never imagined. When a ship comes off the assembly line, she's more than just the sum of her parts; she's a new creation, like a woman, a temperamental, stubborn, beautiful woman.'

"'What about warships?' I said, downing my coffee. 'Are they also like temperamental women, or just ruthless killers?'

"'My dear friend, ships do not kill, men kill.'

"We sat drinking coffee and rum, this Spanish philosopher and I, discussing our families, our homes, childhood memories, and our favorite books until well past midnight that night and for the next nine consecutive nights, becoming quite close in the process. During that time, I came to the decision that I would not continue to Havana with the *Cartagena*, but would disembark once we reached St. Thomas. I concluded that I would be much safer in a neutral Danish island until the end of the war than in Puerto Rico or Cuba with their hordes of American soldiers. I hated having to part from Captain Miguel after all his kindness, but I dared not forget I was still a deserter of the Imperial German Navy, and my top priority was survival.

"By the time the *Cartagena* pulled into the harbor of St. Thomas, I knew I had made the right decision. The hardest thing I had to do was tell Captain Miguel that I was leaving his employ. He looked shocked and saddened by this unexpected announcement, but he recovered and wished me well. The truth is, he was not any sadder than I was at this parting. He paid me my wages and gave me a goodbye hug, but his sailor's eyes couldn't hide his true feelings. I told him I hoped that one day we would meet again. Captain Miguel had taught me an unforgettable lesson, the meaning of true friendship."

CHAPTER 20

By the end of August 1916, the most unusual thing occurs. While the citizens of Charlotte Amalie snooze peacefully in their beds, a Danish warship called the *Valkyrien* quietly glides into the harbor and settles down near the Danish West India Company dock.

As the townspeople rise from their beds, they stumble over to their jalousies for a peek at the day's commerce. When they rub their eyes and see what's floating in the harbor, they do a collective double-take. Lying at anchor is a sober relic of the Mother Country: a Danish cruiser in all its glory lording over a motley assortment of rickety sloops and rag-tag schooners.

A short while later, a delegation of concerned citizens gathers along the water's edge to gawk at the floating kettle drum. They marvel at her guns and turrets, observe how large her cannons look, how very young and innocent her soldiers appear as they perform routine maintenance on the deck, their blond hair glistening like spun gold under the tropical sun. They assume something important is afoot as it isn't *every* day that a Danish cruiser abandons the Mother Country in the middle of a war to visit her far-flung colony in the West Indies. If the *Valkyrien* saw fit to leave the Danish coast unguarded, something important must be up.

I hurry through breakfast and dress as quickly as possible, and then I head to the balcony to study the *Valkyrien* through the spy glass. There's no mistaking that the guns on deck are real, and the young blond men are not schoolboys but real naval sailors. And though I doubted the *Valkyrien* would last long in a sea battle against a modern German cruiser, there's no doubt her cannons could do a bit of damage before sinking beneath the waves. Without a doubt, the arrival of the *Valkyrien* is the biggest news yet. My instincts tell me some sort of international intrigue is indeed brewing.

Down on King's Wharf, I join the crowd of curious spectators that by now has grown from a mere delegation to a huge throng. Their nervous chatter fills the air as they gape and point at the warship with a mixture of curiosity and wonder. Some of the old-timers scratch their heads under their wide-brimmed straw hats, recalling the old days when a Danish warship would only cross the Atlantic if she was bringing someone important to the islands, such as the Crown Prince, which automatically meant days of feasting and celebration. Now, however, since Denmark lies helpless along Germany's northern border during *dis most terrible war*, any overt display of celebration would be out of the question.

I decide to seek out Judge Neergaard to get to the bottom of this. Luckily I don't have far to look. I find him sitting in Emancipation Garden near the bust of old King Christian IX. The sight of two elderly Danes communing in perfect harmony in this remote park in the Danish West Indies fills me with delight. Sometimes I believe I can even detect a faint smile forming under King Christian's stony green exterior.

"Abigail, how good to see you," says Judge Neergaard when I approach him. "No doubt you've seen all the interesting activity that's taking place out in the harbor, a sign that progress is moving at a very rapid pace."

"Are you referring to the Danish cruiser?"

"Indeed I am," he says. "I've known for quite some time she would be coming."

"Why is she here?"

"She's here on important business. She's carrying an emissary from the Rigsdag. But what most people don't know is that she has another very important purpose, one I shall soon tell you about. But first, let me test your knowledge to see how clever you are. Tell me something do you know what it is a judge does?"

"He decides if a person is guilty or not," I say, with some measure of satisfaction.

"Correct," he says. "A judge weighs the evidence regarding the guilt or innocence of a defendant and reaches a corresponding conclusion. With regard to civil law, the matter becomes more complex. More sticky, as they say. A judge listens to two opposing sides who've sworn to tell the truth, yet proceed to tell completely different stories. From the tangled bits of evidence, a judge must extract the most likely version of the truth. This, my dear girl, has been the basis of my entire career, and I've always believed that I've executed my duties faithfully to His Majesty."

"What does this have to do with the Danish cruiser?"

"Everything, my dear," he says. "You see, the world today is in a similar situation. Think of all the countries together in one gigantic courtroom, each one asserting that his position is the only true and correct one. Is this possible? On one hand, we have America, the world's leader in freedom and democracy. The great German philosopher, Goethe, remarked that, *'Amerika, du hast es besser,'* which means that America has the best system in the world. On the other hand, we have Germany, who believes that they are the rock upon which the world depends for their salvation. To further this aim, the Germans have taken up the sword and the rifle. Now let me ask you this, can both of these opposing forces be correct? Or is there only one truth? And to complicate the matter further, caught in the middle of these two opposing forces is tiny Denmark, a proud, old seafaring nation who tries to conceal her antagonism against Germany for seizing her Duchies of Schleswig and Holstein, yet attempts to not side too openly with Great Britain."

"Denmark is not a military rival on the scale of Great Britain," I say.

"But the wounds over Schleswig and Holstein run deep," states Judge Neergaard. "Once again, Denmark is caught in a vicious tug-of-war, leaving the future of these islands hanging in the balance. If Denmark plays the ostrich and hides her head in the sand, she risks another German invasion. The same could also happen if America forcefully annexes the colony as a ploy to scare off the Germans. Given these options, what choice does Denmark have left?"

I shake my head.

"The honorable one," he says. "The Danes will transfer their old sugar colony to America, and *that* is why the *Valkyrien* is docked in the harbor today. Think of it as an insurance policy against labor strikes, riots, or anything else that could disrupt the smooth transfer of the islands."

"The laborers aren't striking right now, and everything appears to be quiet."

"Outwardly," he says. "But there is a growing unrest among the workers. For political expediency now is the best time to launch a massive wave of riots to force the issue. I also have it on good authority that the *Valkyrien* is here for yet another reason altogether. The Rigsdag is sending a strong message to Berlin to steer clear. Does that rather lengthy explanation answer your question, my dear?"

"Most definitely," I say, winking mischievously. "At the very least the Danish cruiser will rankle Langsdorff's nerves."

"I like the way you think," he says, with a shrewd look. "And I have no doubt Langsdorff will be putting on quite a performance at the Governor's dinner party tonight."

"The Governor invited Langsdorff to a dinner party?" I say. "I thought those two hated each other, especially with all that espionage activity he's been conducting right under the Governor's nose."

"It's a matter of duty," says Judge Neergaard, his eyes twinkling with pleasure. "The governor is throwing a formal dinner party and all the society people are invited, including Langsdorff in his capacity as German Consul. Which leads me to a very important question, would you care to join me as my special guest?"

"I'd be thrilled."

"Splendid, expect my carriage at eight o'clock. Mrs. Neergaard sends her regards and deepest regrets that she's not feeling well enough to attend. As for you, my dear, tonight shall be your formal introduction to society."

***

I spend the entire afternoon preparing for the party. I take a long bath, wash my hair and pin it up so that it frames my face with delicate ringlets. Then I powder my face with rouge while Nana Jane irons my fanciest dress, a long, ivory linen tunic with a belted waist and lace collar, which I top off with Erich's cameo pin. I know my mother would be proud of me. I make do by propping her photograph on the desk and turning around in front of it so she can see me from all angles.

"Do you like it, Mami?" I say. "I'm not that little tomboy anymore jumping into the canal with my dress and stockings on. I'm a proper young lady, and tonight will be my formal introduction to society."

The beaming smile on my mother's face tells me all I need to know.

Just after eight o'clock, Judge Neergaard's carriage pulls up in front of the house. My heart swells with pride as I kiss Nana Jane and Cooky Betty goodbye and stroll out the front door with my head held high.

"Good evening, Abigail," says Judge Neergaard, inviting me into the carriage. "You look splendid. I wish I could be the one to give you away on your wedding day, but since that is doubtful, I will have to make do by escorting you to the Governor's dinner party." He stands up, doffs his top hat and puts on a little show by wriggling around in his formal suit. "How do you like my white tie and tails?" He grins. "Do I look like a penguin?"

"Of course not," I say, matter-of-factly. "Everyone knows penguins don't have whiskers and smoke pipes."

By the time we arrive at the Governor's Mansion, horse-driven carriages are arriving from all over Charlotte Amalie. The men are attired in formal white tie and tails and the ladies in fancy ball gowns and tiaras. There is much hand-shaking and air-kissing as the guests greet each other with, *"Det godt at se dig"* and *"God aften."*

Judge Neergaard takes my hand and helps me alight from the carriage. Together we ascend the red-carpeted staircase to the grand entrance where we are greeted by Governor Helweg-Larsen and the First Lady of the Danish West Indies. We sail through a river of guests and enter the magnificent ballroom.

The room is spacious and ornate. At the center sits a magnificent dining table draped in white damask and set with fine porcelain, silver cutlery, and crystal glasses that sparkle in the light of the chandelier. Everywhere you look, Limoges vases are brimming with roses, jasmine, and gardenias casting a delicious scent over the proceedings, while suspended overhead are the portraits of King Christian X and Queen Alexandrine in whose honor we are about to toast.

Champagne is poured to all the guests as a string quartet launches into a pleasing Viennese Waltz. Judge Neergaard takes me around, introducing me to some of Charlotte Amalie's fine old ladies, who smile with pleasure as they recall stories about my grandfather. Some of them invite me to their house as I offer them a graceful curtsy. Amid all this finery lies the promise of a magical evening indeed.

We take our seats at the far end of the table near some high-ranking members of St. Thomas society. To my right is the wife of a young Danish banker, and directly opposite me is the owner of the Grand Hotel. Judge Neergaard sits to my left.

I catch sight of Jens Jørgensen winking at me from his place further down the table. And to my surprise, not far away from him is Lothar Langsdorff accompanied by his Danish wife. Judge Neergaard whispers to me that Herr Langsdorff was only invited in his capacity as German Consul and not as Director of the Hamburg-America Line. Nevertheless, Langsdorff cannot hide his true feelings; he wears a sullen expression that will soon prove to be anything but diplomatic.

As we wait for the meal to be served, Judge Neergaard launches into an explanation about an old Danish toasting custom. The host always offers the first toast of the evening, which is in honor of his Majesty the King. As I watch the excited faces of the guests, the Governor rises and performs this sacred duty. In turn, the guests do likewise, raising their sparkling champagne glasses in honor of the King.

As if on cue, a team of servants in black tie present us with silver trays laden with rum soufflé, West Indian broiled fish, conch fritters, and yam pudding. The guests are soon feasting and drinking copious amounts of spirits. As I gaze around the room, studying the faces of all the important guests, I am bolstered by the knowledge that Judge Neergaard has chosen me as his special guest. I'm sure that somewhere in heaven, Mami and Papi are proud of me.

After dinner, some of the gentlemen retire to the smoking room for cognac while the younger couples waltz to a string quartet. Judge Neergaard pulls me into the room as he explains another old Danish custom in which host goes around the room greeting each guest in order of importance by holding his glass at chin height, looking his guest in the eye, and then taking a sip. The host finishes by lowering his glass a little and giving a courtly bow, all the while keeping his eye on his guest as the guest mimics the same gesture in return. The host repeats this formality starting with the next most important guest and down the line until he finishes with the least important guest. If the host happens to be angry at somebody, he can always humiliate him by saying, "I cannot recall if I have toasted you yet, Herr...?" as is just what happens on this particular night.

Throughout the evening, the subject of the impending transfer was not mentioned openly, but there was an undeniable tension in the air because of some anti-Danish articles that were published in German newspapers. Judge Neergaard explains that oftentimes the Germans underestimate the extent of Danish pride, and on this particular night, it was glaringly apparent.

While the majority of the Danish citizens of St. Thomas side with Governor Helweg-Larsen in his strong opposition to the transfer, they understand that since he is a servant of the King, he must represent His Majesty's wishes without the slightest hesitation. While the Governor chats with some merchants about the disastrous decline in shipping, he declares to the assemblage, "Ladies and Gentlemen, war is an evil midwife who only delivers misery and death. Peace is the only true path to prosperity, growth, and freedom. Let us all pray for a swift end to this war."

Suddenly a threatening voice booms out above the rest.

"Without war the world makes no progress."

The room falls silent. All eyes turn to Lothar Langsdorff, who is staring directly at the Governor. Judge Neergaard stiffens and the Governor's face loses all expression as he faces his adversary head on. Everyone holds their breath, waiting to see what will happen next.

Langsdorff snuffs out his cigar. "When the world is at peace, it slides into anarchy," he says in a menacing tone. "War is the only true path to greatness. Any nation that does not profit by taking from smaller nations is doomed to perpetual weakness and eventual obscurity."

"Are you suggesting, Herr Langsdorff," says the Governor. "That only war makes nations great? That the strong can take from the weak without fear of repercussions? Do you actually believe that the only way forward is through war and bloodshed? Need I remind you that even precious German blood is being spilled in the trenches—"

"Even the great Bismarck failed to understand that a nation only builds power by seizing colonies," booms Langsdorff. "Colonies are like gold in your pocket. Germany has always suffered from the myopic policy of forcing their ships to beg for coaling rights at European-controlled ports while the British control over a quarter of the world. The war will reverse this intolerable situation and make the world a more even playing field for the Germans."

The Governor's eyes narrow. "Let me see if I understand you correctly, Herr Langsdorff. You justify the mass killing of innocents, plundering other nations, and conquering more territory on the grounds that Germany lacks adequate coaling stations?"

"I have no opinion of my own, Herr Governor," states Langsdorff with cold indifference. "I merely repeat what I'm told. We Germans choose our friends out of political necessity."

"I see," says the Governor, exhibiting a devilish grin. "Then allow me to propose a toast to friendship." He goes around the room, toasting each important guest in the afore-mentioned manner, but when he gets to Herr Langsdorff, he quips, "I cannot recall if I have toasted you yet, Herr Langsdorff..."

Langsdorff's face darkens. His hand clenches his drink so hard the stem breaks. He looks as if he's about to explode as he says in a voice dripping in contempt, "Your Excellency, when I am the Governor of the new *German West Indies*, we can discuss this topic further."

"*In vino veritas*, Herr Langsdorff," says the Governor. "Wine has the amazing ability to loosen tongues, but it can just as easily loosen inhibitions. And we wouldn't want that to happen, would we? Who knows, after a few more drinks, you might start believing that you really are the governor of these islands, in which case you could stumble into my bedroom and greatly upset my wife. Although, if the reverse were to occur, I doubt your wife would be the least bit distressed."

The room bursts into laughter. The irate German grabs his wife by the arm and pulls her out of the party. Still laughing, the guests crane their necks as they watch Langsdorff storm down the hall, demand his hat from the butler, and order his carriage. Visibly shaken, Judge Neergaard bursts out of his chair and dashes after Langsdorff, muttering something about attempting to avoid an international incident. I follow close behind, realizing too late that Langsdorff is at his most dangerous whenever he feels cornered.

"Herr Langsdorff, wait!" calls Judge Neergaard, catching up with him. "Don't leave in such a huff. This was supposed to be a pleasant dinner party. You of all people should know that political discussions are out of place among the weaker sex. When will you realize that the Danes naturally sympathize with the Allies? In the future, it would be more prudent of you to refrain from expressing such strong, pro-German sentiments."

Langsdorff bristles. "Henrik, the Governor and I have had numerous disagreements about Germany's position in the war. He has never held himself back from accusing me of acting with deceit. Let's just say that he has his job to do and I have mine. As long as I'm German Consul of the Danish West Indies, the old rule still stands that states diplomacy is the patriotic art of lying for one's country. As you know, war is a serious matter; I have full faith in my leaders. It's unfortunate that Herr Governor doesn't share my opinion, but what he thinks will soon be of no consequence when we take matters into our own hands."

"Just what are you implying with that statement?"

"I've spent far too many years watching from the sidelines," says Langsdorff. "It's time Germany took over these floundering islands and made them lucrative once again. It takes a strong leader to put these laborers in their place so the planters can turn a profit once and for all. Naturally, when I assume my new position as Governor, I will control the island's only coaling station as well as the wages of all the coal carriers and laborers."

"So that's your plan?" says Judge Neergaard, narrowing his eyes. "Seizing these islands for Germany? You'd better think twice. I have it on good authority that an entire regiment of Marines can be here at a moment's notice to quash any foolhardy invasion attempts. The Yanks don't suffer fools gladly, especially when it comes to empire expansion in their back yard."

"I'm not afraid to call your bluff," says Langsdorff. "The Americans already have Puerto Rico. These Danish islands have no intrinsic value to anyone other than the nation with the fastest-growing navy, the nation that will one day rule the entire ocean. All it requires is one cable for Berlin to send over a König Class battleship to chase away the high-minded Danes and their American doughboy lapdogs. It would be foolish to let such a good resource go to waste."

218

Looking past Judge Neergaard, Langsdorff fixes his blazing orbs on me. "That girl who is always with you, I know her from somewhere. I'm positive I've seen her before. I won't rest until I remember…"

"She's of no importance to you, Herr Langsdorff," says Judge Neergaard, tightening his grip around my wrist. "And if I were you, I'd avoid any more belligerent talk. And no more threats about a German invasion. The Governor can have you expelled and advise the Rigsdag to send a formal letter of protest to Berlin—"

"We'll have to see about that, *Herr Richter*," sneers Langsdorff as he takes his wife out to the waiting carriage. "And I will inform Berlin what they can do with that protest letter as soon as I take my rightful place in the Governor's Mansion."

Langsdorff and his wife storm out in a huff; Judge Neergaard appears visibly shaken as he leads me back to the ballroom. When I pass the governor's wife, fear and worry are etched on her face as she fans herself and remarks to a group of ladies how she fears the war situation will soon spiral out of control.

CHAPTER 21

The next morning, I sleep much later than usual on account of all the champagne I drank at the party. When I wake up, the tinny sounds of Aunt Esther's Victrola reverberate down the hall and everything appears normal, yet I have the strangest feeling that something isn't quite right.

I peer over at Teddy, who's oblivious to everything except a piece of papaya that he's busily breaking apart with his beak and claws. I hop out of bed and stroke his satiny feathers, then peer down at the sleepy town. On account of the oppressive heat, life seems to have come to a virtual standstill. The normally boisterous palm trees hang like wet mops; horses trot listlessly down Main Street, and donkey carts plod with heavy steps towards Market Square, their tails swishing away flies.

Workers pull their straw hats down over their eyes and lounge under the shade of trees or in alleyways. There's not even a stray dog to be seen, and no children playing in the park. The temperature is soaring and not a single leaf moves on any of the trees; the hibiscus flowers sag under their own weight and not a songbird can be heard anywhere. All the while, my uneasy feeling grows, and it has nothing to do with the heat.

I tiptoe down the hall and peer into the sewing room. Aunt Esther is sitting in her usual chair embroidering a flower pattern onto a handkerchief while she repeats over and over, '*Told her so many times, told her so many times.*' Meanwhile, down the hall, Nana Jane warbles out a spiritual about the glories of Kingdom Come, resulting in a disharmonious clash of voices against the tinny tones of the gramophone. To make matters worse, Aunt Esther yells out, "Nana Jane, it's dusty in here. I'm wheezing. Do something urgent." Soon after comes Nana Jane's languid reply, "I'll fetch de feather duster, Miss Esther."

"No, no, that won't work," yells Aunt Esther. "You'll kick up too much dust. Use a wet rag instead."

I crouch down behind a door while Nana Jane runs around trying to solve Aunt Esther's problem. As soon as the coast is clear, I race back to my room, throw on some clothes, and slip outside to check on Erich. For some odd reason, I have a growing hunch that something is wrong with him.

Brushing aside weeds and bushes, and with insects buzzing around my head, I make my way over to the basement door and press my ear against it. Silence. I turn the knob and open it, fearful of what I might find.

Erich's room is dark and still. The open door lets in a dusty stream of light right down the center. Suddenly, I hear a moan echoing from the bed in the far corner. I step inside, shocked to see Erich lying in obvious pain, with one arm dangling over the side of the bed, as if he lacks the strength to lift it.

"Erich!"

I run to his side and press my hand to his forehead. It's burning hot with fever and his lips are murmuring something in German. I'm pretty sure he's delirious. What should I do? I grab a towel, thrust it in the washbasin, wring out the excess water and place it on his forehead, hoping it will give him some relief. I must get his fever down. In my heart, I know the only option is to fetch the Government doctor.

"Erich, hold on. I'm going to bring the doctor."

Erich nods faintly, and then turns to the side and drifts back to sleep. It's obvious from his face he's in pain. I hurry upstairs and pull Nana Jane into a corner.

"Nana Jane," I whisper. "Something's wrong with Erich. He's burning up with fever. I think he has malaria."

Nana Jane wrinkles her brow.

"Seerious?" she says, scratching her chin, as if considering the implications for all of us. "Go fetch de Government Doctor down on

Kongens Gade. Tell him to come quick. I'll bring Erich some lemon grass tea. Go quick!"

I fly down Synagogue Hill as fast as I can. When I get to Main Street, I head up Kongens Gade and start searching for the doctor's house. When I find the right one, I pound on the door, hoping and praying that he's there. After a few minutes, a servant girl opens the door with the doctor's baby perched on her hip.

"Yes...?" she says, regarding me with supreme annoyance.

"I need the doctor. There's a sick man in the old Maduro House on Synagogue Hill."

"What's his problem?" she says, her face expressionless.

"He's burning up with fever," I say. "Either typhoid fever or malaria. I think he's dying."

"I will tell de doctor when he comes back," she says, already closing the door. "He's down in Frenchtown delivering a baby. You best run along now."

Before I can say anything, she slams the door shut.

"Please tell him to come quick," I call out, although inside I feel the situation is hopeless.

I leave the doctor's house in a cloud of despair and take shelter in a shady spot between two wooden shacks that affords me a clear view down Crystal Gade as far as the Dutch Reformed church on the corner of Nye Gade and Crystal Gade, the route I expect the doctor to take. With Nana Jane sitting by Erich's side, I know he's in capable hands. I count the minutes and pray silently.

After waiting for what seems like an eternity, I see a breathless red-faced man in a pith helmet, white tropical suit, clutching a black medical valise struggling up Synagogue Hill. I rush to meet the doctor half way down and escort him the rest of the way up. When we finally reach Aunt Esther's house, the doctor starts mounting the front steps, so I pull him aside and calmly explain that the patient is not in the house, but in the basement.

The doctor looks suspicious at this pronouncement, which grows to worry as I lead him through the dense grass to the nondescript basement door. When I motion that he should enter, the doctor furrows his brow, but I urge him on.

Nana Jane is sitting by Erich's side, holding his hand and dabbing his forehead with a wet cloth. He moans a little and I notice the glass of tea on his bedside table is untouched.

"Well, well. What have we here, Nana Jane?" says the doctor, standing over her to get a better look at the patient. "It looks like we have a sick young man who was lucky enough to come across two dedicated nurses."

Nana Jane blushes and rises from the chair.

Dr. Christensen sits down and takes Erich's arm. "Pulse is racing, but that's to be expected," he announces.

He selects a thermometer and reports that Erich's temperature is high. Next, he takes a stethoscope from his medical bag and listens to Erich's heart. As he concentrates, I study his face. His features are angular, accentuated by a long nose, bushy eyebrows, sad-looking eyes, a hairy moustache, and clipped brown hair. His expression is slightly detached, gravitating between kind and stern.

Dr. Christensen takes out a handkerchief and wipes the sweat that runs down the sides of his face in rivulets. The air in the basement is too hot and stuffy for a sick man, but moving Erich upstairs to the main floor is impossible. If the doctor asks why Erich is forced to sleep in a hot, stuffy basement, I won't have a credible explanation and he will undoubtedly become suspicious.

When he finishes his examination, he replaces his instruments while keeping his eyes on Erich. Behind the doctor's stern brown eyes, I know he's making mental calculations about this unconventional situation that clearly doesn't add up in his mind.

"This case is an otherwise healthy young man who's been having some difficulty adjusting to our tropical climate," says the doctor with a look of concern. "Nana Jane, give the patient an aspirin tablet every four hours until his temperature stabilizes. Keep him hydrated. Make sure there is a water pitcher next to his bed at all times. Report to me immediately if his temperature goes up. Now, will one of you ladies kindly explain to me what in heaven's name is going on here? What is the patient's name? And what the devil is he doing in Esther Maduro's basement?"

"He nevah told us his name," Nana Jane says coyly. "We saw him on de road looking sick, so we brought him inside, told him to rest."

"Is that so?" says the doctor, his moustache twitching.

Nana Jane and I exchange an almost imperceptible glance.

"So, let me see if I've got this right," says the doctor, folding his arms over his chest. "We have a no-name patient who gets sick and stumbles upon two dedicated, full-time nurses solely by chance on a back street of Charlotte Amalie thousands of miles from wherever he comes from. I'd say the odds of that happening are infinitesimal. If that story is indeed true, this young man is extraordinarily lucky. Now young lady, do you wish to add anything to this cock and bull story?"

My heart races; I stare at my feet. On cue, Dr. Christensen dives into Erich's belongings. He searches inside Erich's clothes, starting with his shirt pockets, then his trouser pockets. From a discarded pair of pants on the floor, he pulls out a small billfold that is worn and crumpled. He opens it and extracts a small photograph and a gold pendant of sorts.

"I'll be damned," he says. "This picture shows the patient in a German naval uniform. And the name scrawled on the back says *Erich Seibold*. Furthermore, the medallion is undoubtedly German and depicts a U-boat complete with Prussian crown and cross. If I'm not hallucinating, my best guess is that this young man is actually a German naval officer, probably from a U-boat. But how the devil did he end up here, in Esther Maduro's basement?"

Dr. Christensen bolts to his feet and starts looking around, as if expecting more German soldiers to jump out of the shadows. The greater the worry on Dr. Christensen's face, the harder it is to stifle our giggles. Nana Jane gives me a warning kick when a chuckle escapes my lips which I camouflage by coughing. While Dr. Christensen circles the room looking behind all the crates and furniture, we trade a nervous glance.

"How odd," says Dr. Christensen. "It appears the patient has been here for quite some time based on how organized the room looks. His reading material is quite advanced. Very strange. Anyway, I'm going to take a blood sample, and if the baby I delivered today doesn't develop any complications, I should be able to check it under a microscope tonight. Nana Jane, I'll let you know the results tomorrow if I find any malaria parasites. If that's the case, you can pick up a bottle of quinine at the Apothecary Hall. If the sample just shows fewer white blood cells than normal, we'll call it a routine case of Dengue Fever and you already know the treatment for that. His vital signs are stable, so keep him comfortable and hydrated, and give him aspirin to reduce his fever. In a few days' time, when he can sit up, give him some chicken broth so he regains his strength. When this young man is back on his feet, I'd love to hear about his interesting journey. I'm sure it would make a fascinating tale."

The doctor pricks Erich's finger and smears a drop of blood on a glass slide. Then he packs up his equipment and rises to leave.

"Doctor, if the young man has malaria, what are his chances?" asks Nana Jane.

"Don't worry, Nana Jane," says the doctor. "Malaria rarely attacks healthy people of sturdy constitution who sleep eight hours a night, eat a healthy diet, and moderate their liquor consumption. Malaria attacks the weak, the malnourished, and those with a penchant for overindulging in spirits. I'll wager this young man lives long enough to recount his war stories to quite a few great-grandchildren some day. That is, if he manages to avoid the trenches."

"Dr. Christensen, may I ask you a question?" I say.

"Yes?"

"Actually, it's more of a favor."

He raises his shaggy eyebrows. "A favor?"

"Just between us, please don't mention anything about this patient to anybody. The truth is, he's a friend of ours and he needs his privacy. He wouldn't want people talking about him. He's very shy, you see."

Nana Jane stares straight ahead, keeping a poker face with her lips pressed firmly together.

"I see," says the doctor, glancing between Nana Jane and me. "And does the lady of the house know there's a German soldier living in her basement?"

"No sir, Miss Esther is not aware," says Nana Jane, shifting her weight from leg to leg. "We haven't told her because she don't like strangers. All de time she have nervous attacks and she won't take any more of your ether."

"Is that so?" says the doctor, twitching his moustache. "Alright then, just keep the patient comfortable for now and await my findings."

The next morning, Mr. Isaiah leaves a copy of the *Tidende* lying on the dining room table. When I read it, my heart sinks:

GERMAN U-BOAT SUNK IN NORTH ATLANTIC

London. Sept. 4—Admiralty reports a German U-boat has been rammed and sunk in the North Atlantic after a fierce battle with an armed cruiser. The War Ministry reports that U-158 was sunk at midnight after she was spotted off the Irish coast setting fire to a Norwegian schooner, the Bergen. The crew of the Bergen escaped. Another schooner, the Haugesund, also escaped and does not dare put out to sea again, says a correspondent.

I remember that the U-158 was Erich's ship and now it's gone forever. When he finds out, he'll be so devastated there's no telling what he'll do.

CHAPTER 22

The blood test proves that Erich doesn't have malaria, just a bad case of dengue fever. He's laid up in bed for a week, with me and Nana Jane taking turns keeping him company, giving him aspirin, and feeding him chicken soup and lemon grass tea.

By the following Sunday, Erich looks like a new man. He sits up in bed, his cheeks are flushed, and he plays a rousing game of cards for money with Nana Jane.

"So, you're the famous Nana Jane I've heard so much about," he says, smiling. "I'm pleased to meet you. Abigail thinks the world of you. Thank you for everything; I feel like I owe you my life."

"No need to thank me," she says. "If you pay me what you owe me from your losing streak, we gonna get along just fine."

"You drive a hard bargain," says Erich, reaching for his billfold. "I'll tell you one thing, though. Abby sure is lucky to have you."

"Oh, I could have retired years ago, but every time I tried, something always stopped me. And then when Abby came to live with us, it all made sense. Now get yourself some rest or you won't make it back to your mother and father back in Germany. I'll be back tomorrow if you're in the mood to lose even more money."

Nana Jane throws down her cards and picks up Erich's soiled clothes to wash.

"I'll leave you two alone for a little while, but let Erich rest, Abby."

After Nana Jane leaves, I sit down and unfold the newspaper article.

"Erich, I found this in last week's paper. I think you'd better read it."

"What is it?"

I hand him the article. "It's about your ship, the U-158. She's been reported lost at sea."

As he scans the article, his eyes go wide and then he slumps back in bed, moaning, "Oh, no…oh no…"

I immediately regret showing him the article.

***

The next day, I deliver a batch of mended clothes to the De Castro residence when Deborah pulls me aside, blushing.

"Abigail," she says with a voice that is unnaturally high. "Forgive me for asking, but I heard a strange rumor that I refuse to believe."

"What is it?"

Her painted lips quiver for just an instant.

"A neighbor of mine said she saw you down on King's Wharf walking with a strange man. And another time she saw you riding a horse with the same man down to Frenchtown. Is this true? Or is she just making up stories? Abigail, you know you're my dearest friend but if you have anything to confess…"

"Oh, it's nothing, that's just Knud," I say, using Erich's alias from the *Cartagena*.

"Knud?" she says, furrowing her powdered brow. "Who's Knud? Mrs. Robles also happened to mention that he was rather handsome. Abigail, are you keeping a secret from me?"

"Certainly not," I say with indignation. "Knud is a friend of mine, a poor fisherman who I help out from time to time with food and clothes, like you would feed an alley cat. There's nothing wrong with that, is there? It's called charity. Now don't go mentioning any of this to Aunt Esther. Her money situation gives her heart palpitations, not to mention what it does to her fragile mental state. It would only make everything worse. And certainly don't go mentioning any of this to Mrs. Robles. Knud is a very proud person; he wouldn't like people gossiping about him. Can I trust you to keep this secret?"

"For Heaven's sake, why all the secrecy?" says Deborah, taken aback. "There's no need to be ashamed, although I suspect there's more to the story than you're telling me."

My mind goes blank. If I lived to be a hundred, I could never reveal the truth to Deborah that this poor fellow is really a deserter from a German U-boat. Her carefully coiffed image would recoil at the unvarnished truth.

"Abigail," she says, trying to contain the shrillness in her voice. "*Tell me the truth.* Has this man compromised your integrity? Are you in some sort of trouble? Because if you are, I'll have no choice but to tell—"

"I wouldn't do that if I were you," I say, interrupting. "Nobody has compromised my integrity. Knud is counting on my help. If Aunt Esther finds out, well, you know how jittery she is. She could literally lose her mind. Do you realize how serious that is? Go down to the Municipal Hospital and have a look at the insane wing. The patients there scream and pound the walls day and night. Their eyes glaze over and their limbs drop off. Is that what you want to happen to Aunt Esther? Are you that heartless?"

"Oh dear," she says, wringing her hands. "I had no idea the situation was so serious. I thought everything was going well for you. Imagine, dealing with your Aunt Esther's fragile mental condition in addition to helping the needy and doing all that sewing and mending. Abigail, I've misjudged you. You're a lot more capable than you look. I never thought you had it in you to follow in my footsteps and dedicate your life to helping the less fortunate. I'm truly humbled that you've decided to take me as your role model."

I don't remember ever being left completely speechless.

***

Since Erich's illness I didn't dare bring up the menacing events at the Governor's dinner party. I figured he had enough on his mind without worrying about Langsdorff's ominous plot to invade the Danish West Indies. About a week later, I find out just how delicate the situation is with the Germans when I eavesdrop on a conversation between Judge Neergaard, Governor Helweg-Larsen, Jens Jørgensen, and another Danish official. I should have known something was brewing when the judge was missing from his usual spot at the Grand Hotel. When I questioned the waiter about it, he informed me that the governor had called him over to the Hotel 1829 for an urgent meeting.

"But I wouldn't advise you to go over there," says the waiter, throwing a towel over his shoulder. "It wouldn't be proper. Go and find yourself a ladies' tea party."

"Thank you, but I have no interest in ladies' tea parties. Besides, when you dedicate your life to hunting German spies, there's precious little time left over for *tea parties*."

The waiter huffs and walks off, shaking his head.

The Hotel 1829 sits atop a small hill just behind the Grand Hotel and boasts an impressive view of the harbor and town. It started out as the fancy villa of a French sea captain, but was later converted into a hotel whose entrance is at the top of a grand staircase in the West Indian open-arms style. When I enter the lobby, the hotel is strangely quiet and there is no trace of any government officials.

I search around for someone to ask, but the front desk clerk is busy arguing with someone on the telephone. At the center of the room, a servant mops the floor with tired, languid strokes. When I try to attract the clerk's attention, he turns his back to me, forcing me to tug at the coattails of a passing waiter.

"Excuse me, sir," I say. "I have an important message for the Governor."

"Just give it to me," says the waiter with impatience.

"That's impossible, I must deliver it myself."

He points to the dining room, and then disappears through a kitchen door, leaving me alone again. I tiptoe into the dining room and spot the Governor's party immediately. They're sitting in the far corner. I recognize the governor, Judge Neergaard, and Jens Jørgensen, but the fourth man is someone whose name I can't recall, but who I remember seeing at the governor's dinner party. Later I learn he is Peter Nielsen, the governor's secretary. Luckily, they don't see me. They're enjoying steaming plates of *frikadeller*, a Danish meatball dish, and sampling bottles from the hotel's wine cellar. When the maître d'hôtel asks if I need any help, I put on my most innocent face and tell him I'm waiting for my father. He points to a side table and tells me to sit. As soon as he turns his back, I sneak away and hide behind a potted palm situated right near the Governor's table.

I notice right away that the Governor is dispirited. He sighs and takes a large swig of wine, then loudly clears his throat. "What is that saying the natives have?" says the Governor, pressing his palm into his forehead. "Oh yes, 'Men at the rum shop and women at the church.'"

"Very insightful, Lars," says Judge Neergaard, pensively. "I get that admonishment from Wilhelmina every time I miss Sunday services. Even Lord Byron once wrote there's nothing better to calm the spirit than true religion and a drink of rum, and that's without ever having tasted our superb St. Croix variety. Although it may be blasphemous to admit it, during moments of intense heartache, my greatest sources of comfort come from a tender Schubert melody and a cozy bottle of rum."

"Ever the poet, Henrik," says the Governor. "Your words are like a soothing balm to my soul. These last few years have not been easy, and the events of last week make it glaringly evident that our troubles are far from over. I never thought it would come to this: a desperate fight for survival with our national pride and sovereignty at stake. Since time is growing short, let me explain why I've asked the three of you here today. First of all, as your Governor and as the King's loyal servant, I have voiced my opposition to the transfer in the strongest possible terms, even going so far as to send numerous telegrams to Finance Minister Brandes outlining the precise reasons for my opposition." The Governor pulls out a telegram from his pocket, unfolds it and lays it down for the others to read. "As you can see here, I have outlined every valid reason that Denmark should retain the *Dansk Vestindien*, even if the Royal Treasury incurs a temporary financial loss as a result."

"I don't suppose that was appreciated by Minister Brandes," interrupts Jørgensen. "Especially since the government has already incurred a loss of twelve million dollars by mobilizing the army and the navy."

"That's exactly my point," says the Governor. "And why I feel that my countrymen have turned a deaf ear to me." The governor turns to Judge Neergaard. "Henrik, these past few years have turned us from friends into brothers—"

"And serving with you has been the greatest honor and privilege of my life," says Judge Neergaard.

"—nonetheless, the sun is setting on our beloved colony. Your feelings are no different from mine regarding the transfer, and I've been doing my utmost to dissuade the King from going through with it. Between the falling sugar prices, the strikes, the labor unrest, and the threat of German encroachment, the political situation has spiraled out of control. It looks as though we have no choice. As we speak, the Americans are preparing to hand over twenty-five million dollars in gold bullion for the privilege of adding these islands to their growing empire while our beloved homeland grows ever smaller. It pains me to have to inform you gentlemen that due to my fierce opposition to the transfer, and because he now views me as an impediment to progress, Finance Minister Brandes has demanded my resignation. The King is silent and the Rigsdag is awaiting my formal letter. And so, my dear colleagues, my illustrious career as Governor of the *Dansk Vestindiske Øer* has come to an end."

"Excellency," says Judge Neergaard. "Rest assured that we, your closest allies, know that you have done everything possible to stop this deplorable transfer. The colony's sagging economy has left the Rigsdag with no other choice; the islands are a drain on the royal treasury and desperate times bring desperate measures."

"It should not be a question of money," says the Governor, banging his fist on the table. "Where is our Danish pride? Would England sell Jamaica? Would France cast aside Martinique? Would the Dutch put Curaçao on the auction block? There's no excuse for this disastrous drop in Danish national pride."

"But Lars," says Peter Nielsen. "Don't overlook the fact that Denmark has spent vast sums of money building up the army and navy to fend off a possible German invasion, with no possible way to pay it off but for the sale of these islands. If it wasn't for this blasted war, the Royal Treasury would be enjoying a surplus. The situation has become too big for anyone to control. You can't fight this war by yourself. The only honorable thing to do is return to Copenhagen secure in the knowledge that you served your king until the bitter end. Let the Americans take over and face these problems."

"So, if Peter is correct," says Jørgensen, frowning. "We are to just sit here like a bunch of women waiting for the damned treaty to be ratified so they can throw us out of our homes? Is that what the rest of you intend to do?"

Jørgensen studies the crestfallen faces of his compatriots and then breathes a loud sigh of resignation.

"That's not what I meant to say at all," says Peter Nielsen. "While His Majesty can no longer afford to keep this colony as a part of Denmark, at least the act of selling it allows us to wait out the end of the war in greater comfort and security. Given how serious the situation is especially after considering Herr Langsdorff's threats, it's the most pragmatic approach. Isn't all of Danish history full of pragmatic decision-making?"

The Governor chuckles and takes another sip of wine.

"Well, whether you gentlemen realize it or not," says the gravelly-voiced Jørgensen. "These islands still have tremendous strategic value which I intend to exploit. And no piece of paper called a *treaty* can annul past agreements, especially with regard to our friendly German community. The Hamburg-America Line has invested great sums of money to build up their docks, warehouses, and office buildings, and they employ hundreds of people on St. Thomas alone. Langsdorff made a point when he said that Germany lacked sufficient coaling stations. We have a moral obligation to help them protect their assets during the shaky transfer period. I've offered him expert legal advice on how to shield their assets from any potential government expropriation. Of course, I'm more than willing to help them navigate the legalities of the treaty, which is why I wanted Herr Langsdorff to join this meeting."

"Langsdorff doesn't belong here," says the Governor, stone-faced. "He's a *persona non grata* as far as I'm concerned, especially in light of how he behaved at the dinner party. I regret not expelling him when I had the chance. Need I remind you that Langsdorff is fully aware of my position regarding his unsavory business practices? There will be plenty of time to discuss business under the Americans once I'm gone."

Judge Neergaard turns to Jørgensen. "Jens, we're all cognizant of Langsdorff's real mission here, and if you think you can run his operation under the noses of the Americans, you're not only gravely mistaken but possibly delusional. Since none of this is my affair, I won't attempt to either explain or even understand your actions. I realize that war drives men to desperate acts." Judge Neergaard turns back to the governor and adds, "Lars, you've done an outstanding job under very trying circumstances. You deserve to return to Denmark with your honor and dignity intact. What happens from now on is not of your doing and is no longer under your control. As for the rest of us, we shall remain loyal servants of the King, and when the Dannebrog is lowered for the last time, we'll know that we have served him honorably right up to the end."

"Hear, hear," responds Nielsen.

"Henrik, Henrik, Henrik," says Jørgensen, his wild eyes glowing with zeal. "Everyone has their mission. Lars has his, you have yours and Langsdorff has his. It's not my business to tell Langsdorff how to run his affairs, but if you expect me to bury my head in the sand just because of a change of flags, you're dead wrong. That's not called being *delusional*, but *practical*. The only difference between us is that instead of taking the first steamer back to Copenhagen, my mission here will continue out of respect for past agreements and past friendships. The way I see it, my actions are based solely on Danish national pride."

"Let's not confuse national pride with personal enrichment," counters Judge Neergaard. "There's a war going on and from all reports, it's a veritable bloodbath. During the month of August alone, Germany sank over 120 merchant ships and 35 neutral merchant ships because they were suspected of carrying supplies to the British. The Central Powers also sank close to 200 ships during that time and caused the loss of countless lives. How can you sleep at night knowing you're aiding and abetting Germany in their mission to take over the world's shipping lanes? Langsdorff boasted that Hamburg has plans to build new 8,000-ton freighters after the war. Who do you think is behind this project?"

"Rich industrialist, of course," scowls Jørgensen.

"Wrong!" says Judge Neergaard. "It's your friends at the Hamburg-America Line with Albert Ballin as chairman and chief conspirator. The Kaiser is now boasting that they're turning out ships capable of sailing 10 knots faster and at a cheaper cost than ordinary steamers. Their ships will soon be commanding the oceans. Need I remind you of the enormous implications of a German victory in this war, not just to shipping, but to our entire way of life? While Denmark is neutral in this conflict, we must not supply the ammunition for the gun Germany shoots at the Allies."

Jørgensen's face turns beet red; his wooden leg shoots out from under the table. He unscrews the hapless appendage to the horror of a passing waiter, and pounds it on the table.

"Now you listen to me," yells Jørgensen. "I'm talking about our ancient Danish legal system that no fanciful treaty can undermine."

The waiter takes a few steps back and runs to the kitchen.

"Calm down, Jens," says Governor Helweg-Larsen. "Let's not aggravate an already difficult situation."

"I'm not doing this because I support Germany," Jørgensen shoots back. "I'm trying to uphold our ancient Danish legal system. And I've actively supported the treaty from the beginning. I'm even paying my own way to travel back to Copenhagen to argue in favor of its ratification. I believe more than anyone sitting at this table that we need a strong American presence to keep the Panama Canal safe and secure. Politics is politics and business is business. We must honor our contracts."

"Tell me, Jens," says Judge Neergaard, with just a hint of iciness in his tone. "Does our Danish legal system allow for the sending of coded messages to Berlin from steamers docked in our harbors? And does it allow for the supplying of German cruisers in direct contravention of our sacred neutrality?"

Jørgensen looks as if he's about to explode.

"Gentlemen, we're not going to settle our differences here and now," interrupts the Governor. "Precious time is running out. Let us toast the health of our beloved King and homeland—skaal."

The men raise their glasses and drink.

"And allow me to propose a toast to *you*, our dear Governor," adds Judge Neergaard. "Thank you for your loyal service and I speak for everyone when I see we are saddened to see you go—skaal."

All of us in that room, me included, knew exactly what would happen next. The treaty will be ratified, the transfer will go through, the Americans will take over, the Germans will invade, and then all hell will break loose.

CHAPTER 23

Things are going from bad to worse. Erich has been missing for almost a week. After recuperating from dengue fever, he went back to work on his fishing boat, but never returned. As soon as I realize how serious the situation is, I hurry down to Frenchtown to speak with Mr. Greaux, but all he does is shrug his shoulders and claim he hasn't heard from Erich either. He has simply vanished.

My mind races with all sorts of frightening scenarios. Maybe he was kidnapped. Maybe he's languishing in a hot, stuffy prison cell. Maybe he's lying sick in a hospital bed and can't speak. Maybe he's stuck in Fort Christian, lonely, scared, confused, losing all hope. The uncertainty tortures me, but if I try to talk to Nana Jane, I know she'll just admonish me for letting myself get attached to an itinerant sailor. She'll make jokes that he finally got fed up with Aunt Esther's confounded victrola and left for good. Maybe she's right.

In my heart I know she's not.

The only person who can advise me is Judge Neergaard. But telling him the truth about Erich will only make things worse. I decide to ask him in a general way and keep from revealing anything incriminating, to protect him as well as me.

Judge Neergaard and his wife occupy a fine villa on Government Hill, just a short distance from Kongens Gade. I climb up the ninety-nine steps, wondering which house is theirs, and when I'm about halfway up, I spy a young boy playing marbles in the dirt. I ask him where the judge lives and he points to a white villa with green shutters surrounded by hibiscus and bougainvillea bushes. When I see the judge's black horse grazing nearby, I feel a wave of relief that he's at home.

I knock on the front door and listen for the sound of footsteps. When the door bursts open, I find myself eyeball to eyeball with Wilhelmina, the judge's housekeeper. She's a large, imposing, *take no prisoners* type of woman with a stern face, no discernable neck, and eyes that peer right through you.

She sizes me up. "What you be wanting?"

I clear my throat and explain with utmost gravity that I must speak to Judge Neergaard about an urgent matter that cannot wait. Wilhelmina's eyes roll as she pulls me into the house and points me to the room where the judge is busy entertaining a guest. I knock on the door and wait to be called in. As soon as I enter, I see that the guest is none other than Dr. Christensen. The look of surprise on their faces matches my own, but it's too late for me to turn around and disappear.

"Come in, Abigail," says Judge Neergaard. "What brings you here? Is everything alright with your Aunt Esther? How is Nana Jane faring?"

"They're both well, thank you," I say, glancing at Dr. Christensen. "Actually, I've come about another matter."

"Is there something I can help you with?" says the judge, motioning for me to take a seat beside him. Dr. Christensen sips his cocktail as he eyes me with interest.

"Actually, I'm looking for someone," I say, trying to sound cool and detached. "A missing person."

"A missing person?" Judge Neergaard raises his eyebrows. "That sounds serious. Tell us about this person."

"Well, it's a young man of medium height with blond hair and blue eyes who arrived here several months ago and hasn't been seen in over a week. He left all his personal belongings behind in a strange manner. Is there someone fitting that description over in Fort Christian?"

"No, my dear," replies Judge Neergaard. "The jail has its usual assortment of drunkards, petty thieves, vagrants, smugglers, and those with a propensity for disorderly conduct and public disturbances. Nothing out of the ordinary, such as what you're describing. Perhaps you could be a little more specific."

"Does this have anything to do with that mysterious patient I treated up at the Maduro house?" says Dr. Christensen. "The no-name patient?"

"What patient are you referring to, Viggo?" says Judge Neergaard, eyeing him with curiosity. I feel my cheeks turn red as Doctor Christensen proceeds to spill the beans about the mysterious German patient he treated in Esther Maduro's basement who was suffering from a case dengue fever. Considering the circumstances, I suppose he had no choice. Erich's life could be at stake.

"This young lady summoned me to treat a foreigner who was lodged in the basement of Esther Maduro's house," explains Dr. Christensen. "He looked to be no more than twenty-five or twenty-six, and after perusing through his personal effects, I'm quite certain he was a German and not used to our climate. He exhibited all the classic symptoms of tropical fever, so I took his vital signs and a blood sample to rule out the possibility of malaria, but the test was negative and I haven't heard from him since. He looked young and healthy so naturally I expected he would make a full recovery."

"Did I hear you correctly?" says Judge Neergaard, adjusting his pince nez spectacles. "Did you say there was a *man* lodged in the Maduro house, and a *German* one at that? Are you quite certain? Abigail, can you please explain what is going on here?"

I feel my heart pounding. I swallow hard.

"Dr. Christensen is correct," I say, shifting in my seat. "There *was* a sick man staying at my aunt's house, but he got better and left a while ago. I think he said something about catching a tramp steamer down to South America. This particular man I'm talking about is someone completely different."

"Come now, Abigail," says Judge Neergaard with mounting impatience. "Something's not adding up. Tell us the whole story. Where did you meet this German and how did he end up in your aunt's basement?"

"And not just *any* German," interrupts Dr. Christensen. "From his personal possessions, he appeared to be a German naval officer, from a U-boat, no less."

Judge Neergaard's pince nez drops to his lap.

"Good Heavens," says the judge, blanching. "Are you quite certain about that?"

"I saw it with my own eyes," says Dr. Christensen. "And when I happened to mention this strange discovery to Herr Langsdorff, he gave me the oddest look and became noticeably agitated. When I tried to come up with a plausible scenario about how a German U-boat officer could wind up in the Danish West Indies, Langsdorff's face darkened like an approaching storm. He narrowed his eyes, took his cigar, and smashed it into an ashtray.

"I asked Langsdorff if military protocol required a German soldier out of uniform to report his whereabouts to the nearest police station or German Consulate, and he answered in a threatening manner, saying 'It would be considered suicide for a German soldier out of uniform to advertise his whereabouts to the nearest German Consulate.'"

My stomach jolts. The blood rushes from my head and my heart starts racing. I have to get out of that room. I have to find Erich and warn him that Langsdorff knows about him and his life is in grave danger. Maybe it's already too late and that's why he's been missing. Maybe he's…dead. Muttering something about needing to get back to Aunt Esther, I turn on my heels and race out the door with Judge Neergaard's voice ringing in my ears, "Abigail is something the matter? Are you in trouble? What's going on?"

***

After racing all the way up Crystal Gade I take refuge in Erich's room, but without his presence the room feels empty. His bed is cold and his picture lies forlorn and destitute on the table, like an abandoned relic. I pick it up and gaze at his parents' faces; the look of pride in their eyes is unmistakable. A gnawing pain in the pit of my stomach reminds me about my own parents, and the terrible vacuum in my life their death created, the one I tried to fill with Erich. The longer he's gone, the more my hopes for his safe return are dashed. I fear that wherever Erich may be, something terrible has happened to him. The worst part is not knowing whether he's dead or alive.

Later that night in my room, I stare up at the stars for the longest time, unable to fall asleep. And then, unexpectedly, I hear a strange tapping sound at my window. Thinking it might be a bird or a lizard, I sit up in the dark, unsure of what to do. I hear it again, the same odd sound. I jump out of bed, race over to the window, and peer out into the darkness. By the light of the moon, I study the ground around the house. Above the humming of the insects and the occasional barking of a dog, a suspicious-sounding bird call emanates from somewhere down by the old mango tree. *That was no bird,* I think. And then I see him. Crouching in the bushes near the tree is a shadowy figure that barely moves. A glimmer of moonlight on his face sets my heart racing.

"Erich," I cry with delight. I race outside and fling myself into his waiting arms. "Where have you been? I've been worried sick about you." I run my hands along that familiar cheek that now sports a full beard; his clothes exude the scent of coal dust, sweat, and sea spray.

"Abby, I'm afraid I have bad news for you," he says. "I was dragged back into the service of the Fatherland by none other than Herr Lothar Langsdorff who managed to find out about me. After what I've been through, I'm lucky to be alive."

"I know about Langsdorff," I say. "Something dreadful has happened and I feel responsible."

"Don't blame yourself," says Erich. "Let's go inside. I'll tell you the whole story."

Erich leads me through the tall grasses to the basement door. He jimmies it open and reaches for the kerosene lamp and lights it with a match he produces from his shirt pocket. He slumps down in a chair and motions for me to sit beside him as he pulls off his work boots. In the glow of the lamp, I see weariness in his muscles and resignation etched into his face; his eyes betray a mountain of worry.

"How are you holding up, Abby?" he says. "Is your aunt treating you any better?"

"She's the same," I say. "We mostly ignore each other. Thankfully, Nana Jane watches over me like a hawk."

"I told Nana Jane that I'm counting on her to protect you from your aunt," he says. "Since I'm condemned to live my life in the shadows, she must be ever vigilant. Especially when they send me out to sea—"

"They've sent you out to sea?"

Erich nods with a grim countenance.

"As I told you, Herr Langsdorff caught up with me," he says. "He's been watching me for some time. He used his position to blackmail me into joining his spy ring. He forced me to go on a clandestine mission and the whole time I was gone, the only thing I worried about was you. I dreaded dying out there and you not knowing what became of me. I didn't want you to think I had deserted you. That was the hardest part of the whole thing."

"I would never think you deserted me. But I was going crazy from fear and worry."

"The situation is not good," he says. "Langsdorff did some investigating and found out that I deserted my ship. He's been using that knowledge to blackmail me into committing sabotage."

"Caramba!" I feel the noose tightening around my neck. "How did the fiend manage to blackmail you?"

"It's quite simple," Erich explains. "All he had to do was threaten to ruin my parents' lives by publicizing my desertion. In this manner, he easily took control of my life and got me to do his bidding. So now Langsdorff holds all the cards. All it would take to get my father kicked out of the Kiel shipyards is one little cable from Langsdorff since in the mind of the average German my desertion is tantamount to treason. I'll be regarded forever as a criminal, a traitor. Any good German would be justified in shooting me on the spot. Now you know the ugly truth. This is the bed I have made and I have to lie in it."

"But you're not a traitor. You didn't switch sides or help the enemy."

"Naval Intelligence figured out I staged my death," he says. "Desertion during wartime is a crime punishable by death."

"We can't let this happen. Langsdorff must be stopped."

"Any suggestions?"

"Not at the present, but I'll come up with something. How did this mess get started?"

"About two weeks ago I was coming home from work late one evening when I got the strangest feeling someone was following me. Even after I changed directions several times, the man continued to shadow me. When I caught a glimpse of his reflection in a store window, the hair on the back of my neck stood up. I knew by the sight of him that my pursuer was a German, a German intelligence agent.

"Since I was unarmed, my heart started racing as I wondered what defensive move I could make to save my life if he pulled a gun on me. When I realized all I had to rely on were my wits and brute force, my muscles tensed with worry. Against a bullet, these weapons are useless. The next thing I know, the inevitable happened. I felt the sensation of cold steel pressing against my back and froze in terror. *Is he going to shoot me point blank?* Then the man hissed into my ear in German, 'I know exactly who you are, Seibold. If you don't want to get shot for desertion, you will come with me.'

"When I realized the man knew my identity, the blood ran cold in my veins. Left with no choice, I allowed this predator to lead me down some streets and right up to the front door of the Hamburg-America Line. My heart sank, but I resolved to die with my dignity intact.

"From what I could tell my pursuer was at least ten years older than me with a wide build, a short haircut, a bulldog jaw and a Kaiser-like moustache that could not conceal his contemptible sneer. He leads me through a dark office full of desks with typewriters, telephones and stacks of files and invoices. The office was closed; the clerks had all left for the evening, leaving no witnesses to this blatant kidnapping. He turned on a gas light and led me up a staircase that groaned under the weight of our footsteps. On the second floor, he led me down a darkened hallway, right up to a door marked PRIVATE. With his pistol still pressed against my back, he shoved me into the office and shut the door behind us.

"My abductor illuminated another gaslight and took a seat at the head of a large, mahogany desk. Holding the pistol in a menacing manner, he motioned for me to take the empty seat opposite him. After placing the Luger pistol in a holster under his jacket, he poured two glasses of rum, downing one with poised self-confidence, while handing me the other. Then he lifted his feet on the desk in the manner of petty dictators and leaned back, staring at me with cold, calculating eyes.

"'So, *Lieutenant zur See* Erich Seibold,' he said, his voice dripping with contempt. 'An *officer* of the Imperial German Navy. Quite an impressive curriculum vitae, and what a pity to be lost at sea. What a loss to the Fatherland. No doubt your mother and father cry every night thinking they are the parents of a German soldier who sacrificed his life for the Fatherland. What greater honor can there be for a good German than a son who's a hero in their eyes and everyone else's. Nevertheless, the wheel of fortune is always turning and soon your dear parents may find themselves the parents of a despicable traitor, a deserter. A coward! What a pity that such fine people as your parents could lose everything they worked for. Life would become a misery. Your father would be run out of the Kiel shipyards. Your mother would be shunned around town and taunted. Neighbors would shut their doors in her face. The mailman would throw their letters in the mud. The garbage collectors would spill garbage on their front step. What a shame if that were to happen. Starting over at such an old age is extremely difficult. Most older couples who have lost everything just give up and put a bullet through their brains. What a shame. Tsk. Tsk.'

"'I don't know what the hell you're talking about,' I said. 'I'm no deserter. I have a medical discharge for a ruptured gall bladder and I've got the scars to prove it.'

"The German erupted in loud, derisive laughter. Then he placed his hands behind his head and leaned back in his chair, a sardonic smile plastered on his face that reminded me of a sadistic torturer who enjoys toying with his captive the same way a cat toys with a mouse.

"'Don't play games with me, Seibold,' he said. "I know exactly who you are. I cabled Berlin and got a full report within two days. They are most anxious to find out what became of their brave, self-sacrificing *Lieutenant zur See* Seibold and they're waiting for my answer. It seems that Berlin thinks you may still be of use to the Fatherland.'

"'Who are you?' I said, feeling as if Langsdorff's claws were slowly wrapping around my neck.

"'Forgive me for not introducing myself earlier. I am Herr Lothar Langsdorff, the German Consul for the Danish West Indies and I also happen to run this large and efficient steamship office when not out on the high seas serving the Fatherland.'

"'A diplomat, a spy, and a businessman? Aren't those jobs incompatible?'

"'Quite the contrary, Herr Seibold,' he said, pouring himself another drink. 'I wear many hats and all are quite complementary.'

"'What do you want from me?'

"'It's not what I want from you, Seibold, it's what I can give you: your good name back. It's not too late for you to redeem your worthless hide by serving your Fatherland again.'

"'And if I refuse?'

"'Don't be stupid,' he said, reddening. 'I can fix things for you with Berlin. I'm the only thing standing between life as a decorated soldier or as a hunted fugitive or a cowardly deserter. You need *me* a lot more than I need *you*.'

"'This war is not going to end the way Berlin thinks it will,' I shot back. 'It won't solve Germany's problems and it's only a question of time before the Americans jump in. Then none of us will come home as decorated soldiers, just a bunch of lost causes.'

"'You misguided fool,' shouted Langsdorff. 'The Imperial German Army is far superior to any ragtag army the Americans can patch together. Those disorganized rebels will capitulate along with the British, the French, and the Russians in no time.'

"'Don't put on your victor's crown quite so fast,' I said, keeping my voice as steady as possible. It's a long way to Tipperary.'

"'Swine!' yelled Langsdorff, bolting to his feet. 'You should be jailed for speaking out against the war. The only way *forward* is through war. Make no mistake, the only hope for the world is by conquering the ignorant masses and spreading *Germandom*.'

"'It's easy for you to preach warfare from this cushy office on a far-flung tropical island. You know nothing about war and death. I've fought battles; I've seen innocent civilians murdered in cold blood to teach them how to respect Germany. Is that your idea of respect? There is no glory in war—only death.'

"'Fool!' he screamed. 'I'm offering you the chance to restore your name. You had better do as you're ordered if you care about your parents.'

"'What choice do I have?'

"'The same choice Germany had when England started this bloody war. If you want to blame someone for all this death and destruction, blame the Tommies for trying to prevent us from reclaiming what is rightfully ours. They are responsible for dragging millions of innocent civilians into this conflict.'

"When I realized I couldn't reason with that monster, I had no choice but to capitulate to his outrageous demands," says Erich, running his fingers through his hair as he sighs.

"What happened next?" I say.

"First he made me cut the wires of the telegraph station on Norre Gade to cut off communication between the Governor and the

Rigsdag. Then he ordered me to sabotage the station out on Krum Bay. He's trying to make it look as if anarchy has broken out down here, anything to thwart the transfer of the islands. After that, he ordered me to undertake an even bigger mission, one with more serious implications."

"How serious?"

"Very serious," he says, raising an eyebrow. "Langsdorff ordered me to report aboard the *Manitowoc*, an American-flagged freighter. At first I hesitated, confused as to how I, a German naval officer, could serve my Fatherland on board an American-flagged vessel. With Langsdorff's henchman's gun pressed to my back, I swallowed my fear and climbed the gangplank, doubting I would ever step foot on dry land again. As soon as I reported to the Captain, he gave me my orders and I finally had the answer I was seeking. The purpose of the mission was to transfer several tons of oil and food—smuggled out of New York under several tons of coal—to a U-boat at a predetermined point in the Atlantic. Langsdorff's cohort handed the captain a piece of paper with some fixed coordinates that Berlin had sent by wire, and several days later we made a rendezvous with a U-boat in open water about three hundred miles south of Bermuda. The entire operation lasted just over a week, and with a great deal of secrecy. While I was in charge of the crew, nobody asked me any questions and I realized they were just as much in the dark as I was. By chance I overheard them discussing a rumor that buried underneath that mound of coal was an iron chest filled with a quarter million dollars' worth of pure gold. Although I can't say for certain, I'm fairly certain the gold was also transshipped to that U-boat out at sea."

"Did anyone from the U-boat recognize you?"

"I highly doubt it," he says, winking at me. "I suppose I've put on quite a few pounds from your island food, not to mention how tan I've gotten these past few months. I pulled up my collar and kept a low-key presence. The crew went about their business like toy soldiers and I offered them no information. I can assure you that if the Americans ever found out that the Germans were using the *Manitowoc* to aid the Kaiser's war effort, there would be hell to pay. The entire crew and the captain would be arrested and shipped to an internment camp for the duration of the war. Abby, the situation has become critical. Langsdorff has me in his grip and I may have to escape the island on some tramp steamer headed down to South America."

"You'll have to go much further than South America. I hate to disappoint you, but South America is crawling with German spies as well. And running away won't stop Langsdorff from carrying out his threat to ruin your parents' lives. If you stay here at least you can fight him. Somebody has to put a stop to Langsdorff."

"Maybe I can fight Langsdorff but I can't fight an entire regiment of American Marines," he says, looking downcast. "It's only a question of time before the Americans arrive to claim their new possession. And when that happens, their stake in this game will increase. When they start rounding up all the German citizens, I'll be arrested and thrown into a prison camp. Once the other German prisoners discover I'm a deserter, I'm as good as dead. And time is running out. Langsdorff just announced that he has one final mission for me, one he claims will earn me the Iron Cross."

"The Iron Cross? What's that?"

"It's the highest honor a German soldier can receive," he says. "But that's not his plan. I have good reason to believe that once I complete this mission, Langsdorff will put a bullet through my head."

Part Three

CHAPTER 24

A few days later, Erich and I hear a chilling prophecy from the lips of Queen Coziah herself. We are standing among the crowd of onlookers down in Market Square as she holds court beneath her favorite flamboyant tree. Her eyes are burning with their usual fiery indignation, and like a madwoman, she clenches her fists, stomps her feet, and screeches out one passionate diatribe after another. Sometimes it's against the Danish Government, other times it's against the steamship companies or the miserable working conditions of the coal carriers. Each tirade is more fearsome and aggressive than the last, building up to a rapid-fire, staccato-like frenzy.

As soon as Erich sees her, he freezes. He is fascinated by her formidable countenance, her fierceness, her savagery. Even I have to admit that Queen Coziah appears to be possessed by a vengeful spirit intent on wreaking havoc on the rigid social order of this fading colonial outpost. In this regard, Queen Coziah is utterly mesmerizing.

"Who is that creature?" he whispers. "Some kind of voodoo lady?"

"That's Queen Coziah," I say, keeping my eyes fixed on her. "She used to be a coal carrier back in the old days. When the steamship companies started paying the workers in worthless Mexican silver, Queen Coziah rose up and become their leader. She used her cunning and daring to organize a strike to demand payment in Danish money and her scheme worked. She made the Policemaster, the steamship companies, and the Governor all sit up and take notice. People say Queen Coziah is a born leader whose iron will keeps the people firmly at her side. She was so powerful, even the steamship companies were forced to cave in to her demands.

"The people rewarded Coziah for her bravery by calling her their queen. And now even though she's old and frail, everyone still looks to her for inspiration and leadership. She stands there selling her mauby, putting on a good show for the crowd, while the nervous depositors of the Danish West Indies National Bank and the gendarmes look on with consternation."

Erich seems impressed. "So for leading a march, the people made her their queen? Well, if she's a queen, then it's only fitting that she be given a proper throne."

Spying a dilapidated wooden chair just outside a rum shop, he hurries over to retrieve it. He dusts it off and presents it to Queen Coziah in a courtly manner, saying, "Madame, a woman as worthy as you deserves a seat of greater importance than the dusty ground." At first Queen Coziah appears startled, but slowly gives Erich her hand and allows the handsome foreigner to guide her to the chair.

"There now," he says. "A woman who made history deserves a proper seat of honor."

Coziah locks eyes with Erich, and then draws back her lips to reveal toothless pink gums.

"Queen Coziah fought de *bocra* but every man must fight he own battle," she cackles. "Any man who can look down de barrel of a gun and laugh is de master of he own fate."

Erich appears startled, and then takes a few steps backwards.

"No use running, Kaiser man," she screeches. "No man can escape his destiny. When de time comes, they will come for you, but this time, you will fight back."

"Erich, she's talking directly to you," I whisper.

"Yes, but what the devil does she mean by 'looking down the barrel of a gun'?"

"I don't know, but I'm not sticking around to find out," I say, pulling his arm. "And if your trembling arm is any indication of your state of mind, you'd better run too. Come on; let's get out of here before people start noticing us."

"And one more thing, Kaiser man," says Queen Coziah, pointing to the Heavens. "De obeah man says de big one is coming. A tempest bigger than '67 is gonna blast through here on account of de war. All de jumbis veree angry. Mark my words, de big one is coming. And as for you girl, take this potion and give it to your enemy. You'll will be good and rid of him."

Into my startled hands, Queen Coziah tosses a tiny bottle about the size of a drumstick that contains a green potion of some sorts. I stare at the menacing liquid with hesitation, then slide it into my pocket for safekeeping. Upon hearing these scary pronouncements, the crowd gasps in fright, then bursts into a fretful chatter. Erich and I push away from the vexed throng and hurry down the nearest alleyway.

"What a relief to be away from that character," says Erich after we'd gone a safe distance. "Explain to me what an *obeah* man is. I have never heard this term before."

"Obeah is another word for voodoo, an African belief in spirits and magic," I say. "An obeah man is like a village priest. Nana Jane says that whatever the obeah man says, everyone believes. According to what Queen Coziah just said, the obeah man is warning people that a hurricane bigger than the one in 1867 will hit this island soon. It seems that the war in Europe is making the voodoo spirits angry and they're sending the hurricane as a punishment."

"That's rubbish," he says, scoffing. "There's nothing scientific behind it. Yet everyone seems to respect her, and she looked at me as if she could read my mind. As if she had special voodoo powers. To tell you the truth, I was a little spooked."

"She spooks everybody and gets away with it," I say. "Don't worry. Nobody has the power to read minds. She can't possibly know you're a sailor from a German U-boat. Besides, dozens of sailors pass through this island every day and you could be any one of them. You don't look unusual or different. I can't think of a single reason why she chose to tell you that strange prophecy, to master your fate by staring down the barrel of a gun, not unless she's been drinking too much rum and went all *bazudi*."

"Even if she drinks," says Erich, "that doesn't make her prophecy any less terrifying. I got that same creepy feeling back in the Azores when I was sure that everyone could read my mind and knew I was an enemy soldier. I was terrified one of them would stick a knife in my back at any moment. That voodoo lady gives me the oddest feeling."

A few days later, a rumor circulates the island that Governor Helweg-Larsen has resigned his post and left the island for good on a steamship bound for Copenhagen. As he sailed away, he was quietly replaced by Commander Henri Konow from the *Valkyrien* with no public ceremony, no speeches, no reception. The only indication there was a change in governor was a small notice placed in the *Tidende* by the Danish Foreign Minister confirming that Konow had been appointed as acting governor until the transfer goes through. It seems that Judge Neergaard was correct. The Danish Government is leaving nothing to chance.

Nana Jane says the people grew tired of Governor Helweg-Larsen and the old ways that he represented. He was roundly viewed as a negro-hater, and they resented his inability to ameliorate the volatile labor situation with their chosen leader, David Hamilton Jackson. Apparently, the people have been clamoring for him to resign for quite some time. Aunt Esther pipes in from the sewing room that all this change has brought nothing but trouble and unnecessary attention to our islands. She says all of this intrigue will only lead to disaster.

Strangely enough, the island's animals seem to have heard the obeah man's prophecy since they have all started acting strange. The normally languid lizards that spend their days sunning themselves on rocks or on walls have disappeared into cracks. Calm and placid dogs have started barking round the clock, or growling ferociously for no discernable reason. Sometimes they even break free from their ropes and run away, as if escaping some invisible menace.

Even Teddy is acting odd. He spends the entire day pacing back and forth, squawking and biting the bars of his cage as if he's trying to escape. I hate to see him in such an agitated state, but if I let him out, he may hurt himself or fly away. No matter what I do, whether it's talking to him calmly or bringing him more food, nothing calms his frazzled nerves.

"What's the matter big guy?" I say, stroking his feathers in an attempt to soothe him. Teddy's response is chilling. For the first time in months, he turns on me, biting me with his beak until the skin breaks and blood runs while his orange eyes show only abject fear. I snatch my finger away, recalling the promise I made to Ian to never let Teddy out of my sight, but Teddy is becoming a stranger, and a resentful one at that.

To take my mind off matters, I head outside to help Nana Jane with the laundry. When I return to my room, something terrible has happened. Teddy is not in his cage.

I search the entire house, frantic with worry, but there's no sign of him anywhere. As my cheeks burn with rage, I march over to Aunt Esther and demand an explanation.

"Where's Teddy?" I say, seething with undisguised hatred.

"Gone," she says, waving her hand dismissively. "It was time for him to go. Between the smell of his cage and his loud screeching, he became a royal nuisance."

"How could you? Teddy was my pet. You had no right to interfere."

"He was *loud* and *dirty*," she says. "And you had him long enough. I should have freed him months ago. Any responsible person would have done the same."

"You had no right you miserable old wretch!"

Aunt Esther's face turns cold. "Watch your impertinence. I don't recall ever giving you permission to keep a parrot in my house. Need I remind you that you are merely a guest in my home?"

By now my face is hot with fury. "You're a bad woman, Esther Maduro. Now I know why your fiancé ran away to Panama. He was running away from you."

Aunt Esther's hand flies up to her throat and she gasps for air. "W-Why you—"

I don't give her the pleasure of finishing. I flee from the house and start searching for Teddy in the garden and all the surrounding areas, in the trees, under bushes, on the rooftops, windowsills, and under terraces, anywhere a Dominican parrot would think to hide. I refuse to let Aunt Esther win this battle, but after more than an hour of frantic searching, I'm forced to give up. There's simply no sign of Teddy anywhere.

Heartbroken, I return to the house, but inside I'm seething with rage at Aunt Esther. Seeing Teddy's empty cage hanging listlessly in my room is a constant reminder that she has stolen the last vestige I have of Ian and the solemn vow I made to him. In a fit of despair, I snatch the cage off its hook and fling it over the balcony where it lands in the dense bushes below. In my heart, I despise Aunt Esther for robbing me of my hope and ambition. The only good that has come out of this is that I finally managed to stand up to her. If I know Aunt Esther, I'm sure she's biding her time until she exacts her revenge. Her wrath is far from over.

For the next several days, I refuse to pick up a needle, refuse to enter the sewing room, refuse even to acknowledge Aunt Esther's presence. Once and for all, I'm determined to teach that bad-tempered shrew a lesson. I think she may have gotten the hint because she retreats to the sewing room where she listens to her gramophone records over and over, stealing everyone's peace of mind, while I retaliate by stuffing cotton in my ears, eating up all the sweet bread in the kitchen, and reading the newspapers cover to cover. I've also started scouring the newspaper for available positions downtown. One way or another, I'm going to improve my lot.

Throughout these long, hot days, I keep my spyglass trained on the German steamers down in the harbor, watching for any suspicious activity. With the governor now safely out of the picture, I have no doubt that Langsdorff will try to launch his coveted German invasion so he can claim these islands in the name of the Kaiser, while securing his own longed-for place in history.

Meanwhile, the noise from the animals has not abated. If anything, it's gotten worse. All day and all night you hear a constant stream of frightful animal noises, including the constant barking of dogs, the whinnying of horses, the fretful braying of donkeys, the screeching of alley cats, and the restless chatter of high-strung birds that sometimes results in ferocious fights with feathers flying in all directions before the agitated creatures give up in despair and retreat further into the bush.

And then everything goes quiet. All the noise is replaced with an uneasy calm that spreads over the entire island. Not a breeze blows, not a leaf quivers, not a palm frond flutters. Not even the dogs bark anymore; they seem to have all run away. The harbor also undergoes a silent transformation; the water turns an eerie shade of green for no apparent reason. We watch and wait with bated breath until the ninth day of October 1916, when all hell breaks loose.

By all reports, a ferocious hurricane is charging toward us. Adding to this complication is the fact that Erich has gone missing again. And now even his knapsack is gone. First Teddy and now Erich; it seems there's no end to this spate of bad luck.

The next morning when I wake up the sky has turned an ominous shade of gray. Soon it starts drizzling which increases in intensity until there's a virtual downpour, blocking all visibility. The wind also intensifies, becoming more frightful as the day wears on. Mr. Isaiah shuffles in looking worse for wear, his shirt soaked and his pants a frightful mess covered with mud and leaves. He announces that the barometer has fallen to 29.70, a sure sign of an impending storm, and then he leads old Clara down to a barn for safekeeping. As I watch those two old-timers disappear down the hill, I hope and pray that Mr. Isaiah will make it back in time.

Soon, the sound of hammering and sawing start to reverberate throughout Queen's Quarter as everyone scrambles to board up their windows and secure their doors before the storm hits. I look to Aunt Esther for direction, but she has made herself busy sorting the family photographs while babbling incomprehensibly to herself. I peer up at the roof, worried about the soundness of this old house and its ability to survive another hurricane; I am aware that any object not nailed down will be blown away forever.

When Mr. Isaiah returns, I urge him to begin boarding up the windows. He picks up the hammer while I stand by holding a jar of nails. He instructs me on how to hold the boards over the windows while he hammers them in place. Later, he reminds me to fill all the tubs, sinks and bottles with fresh water from a nearby cistern while Nana Jane and Cooky Betty retreat to the kitchen to prepare a batch of Johnny cakes and fish patties to keep us fed throughout the storm and for several days afterwards. Their nervous chatter and bickering combined with the sound of banging pots and breaking glass carries throughout the house. Even on a day like this those two can't agree on anything.

By two o'clock in the afternoon, the gendarmes fire a warning shot from a cannon down by the saluting battery to signal the hurricane's imminent approach. As I gaze southward, I spy a black wall of ferocious black water forming on the horizon. My palms sweat and my knees start to quiver when I realize it's heading straight toward us.

Meanwhile, Aunt Esther paces the house like a nervous cat. Her constant fretting and hand-wringing is not helping matters any. She watches the neighbors down the hill through the spy glass and worries that everyone else is better prepared than we are. Where are the hurricane lamps? Do we have enough blankets? Will the water supply hold out? Why isn't there more canned food? In a vain attempt to calm her agitated state, she picks up the broom and starts beating the cobwebs on the ceiling as she mutters, 'Why are we always the least prepared of everyone? Why can't things ever be done on time?' I just look at that miserable woman and shake my head. The only thing that results from Aunt Esther's tantrums is more frazzled nerves for the rest of us.

When her strain reaches the breaking point, Aunt Esther turns to Nana Jane with a panicked look on her face and asks in a childlike manner, "Nana Jane is his ship coming in today? What if he's caught in the storm? What will become of him?" Nana Jane looks at her with tired eyes and shakes her head, "No Miss Esther, his ship not coming back today. Maybe he nevah coming back."

Aunt Esther turns ashen and clutches her throat with the hollow-eyed look of a mad woman and exclaims in a hoarse voice, "Surely you don't mean that! Tell me you don't mean that. *Tell me you don't mean that!*" She bursts into tears, shakes her knobby fists at Nana Jane, then runs to her room and slams the door shut. I turn to Nana Jane for answers, but she also appears to be visibly shaken. I know the time has come for me to take the lead.

Putting a towel over my head, I head out to the balcony to observe the flurry of activity on the decks of the *Wasgenwald* and the *Calabria*. Taking up the spyglass, I observe as the deckhands struggle furiously against the oncoming storm to secure the ships to the wharf with heavy ropes; the ships must be able to withstand the crashing waves and violent winds that they're expecting. Officers haul out boxes that must contain their wireless radio and important documents for safekeeping on shore. I see that Langsdorff, ever the consummate planner, is not taking any unnecessary chances with his prized steamers and the valuable service they provide to the Kaiser's war effort.

I head back inside, bringing in the spyglass and the wicker furniture. Now that the house is prepared, my thoughts turn to Erich. Worried sick about his situation, I take some food from the kitchen and secrete it down to his room, hoping and praying that he'll make it back in time before the storm hits. When I open the creaky door, I feel the emptiness of the room mirroring the emptiness I feel inside. My anguish and turmoil over my own helplessness grows by leaps and bounds. I place the food on his bedside table and scribble out a note telling him how much I've missed him and how worried I've been about him. In my heart, I pray that both he and Teddy have found adequate shelter to ride out the storm, but now I have other important matters to attend. I must keep watch over Nana Jane, Cooky Betty, Mr. Isaiah, and Aunt Esther. Without me, they are utterly alone and forgotten in this world.

By late afternoon, the sky turns an unnatural shade of purple. The wind picks up from the north-northeast and howls like a raging freight train. It is so terrifying; I fear for Erich's life as well as our own. And then the rain starts falling. Buckets fall from the sky, blinding every living thing, drenching every exposed object, blocking all visibility and causing darkness to descend over the entire island. The wind picks up, whipping the palm fronds with blinding ferocity. Coconuts fall, branches crash to the earth, crates, wagons, stray boards, metal roofs, and anything not nailed down is picked up and hurled through the air by the angry wind. Entire trees are uprooted, as well as telegraph wires. Then comes the roar of thunder from the heavens; we feel as though the world is coming to an end.

By six o'clock in the evening, the barometer has fallen to 29.260, an almost unheard of low pressure reading. It seems Queen Coziah's obeah man has predicted correctly. If so, we are at the mercy of nature as she pounds us with a ferocious hurricane. The whole island is now fighting for its life.

When the clock strikes nine, Mr. Isaiah estimates that the wind is blowing anywhere from 130 to 140 miles per hour. He says that anything not nailed down will never be seen again and any ship caught on the sea will be sunk. As the barometer creeps even lower, to 28.10, the surf comes ashore, pounding the buildings and houses along the water's edge with a blinding fury, blowing people into the air as if they are puppets. Our house also trembles and shakes, but doesn't break apart. Peering out through a crack in the door I watch in horror as a piece of galvanized-iron sheeting is blown through the air and crashes into a nearby roof. The screams of the people mingle with the howling of the wind; the devastation is enormous.

Cooky Betty is in a state of panic. She runs under the dining room table, crying for mercy. Attempting to stay calm, Nana Jane opens her Bible and starts reciting, *"For he spoke and raised up a stormy wind, which lifted up the waves of the sea. He caused the storm to be still, so that the waves of the sea were hushed..."* I coax Cooky Betty out of hiding and set her comfortably on the sofa with a warm blanket, and then I dash over to the Victrola and wind it up so the music will drown out the storm, but it's impossible. Nothing can hide the terrifying sounds of shattering glass, tin roofs sailing through the air, donkeys braying in misery, dogs howling in fright, door frames tearing loose, and roofs collapsing like matchsticks. I hold her hand as we listen to the anguished cries of our neighbors, which is more frightening than anything else. Maybe the Obeah man was right. Maybe the war really has angered the *jumbis*.

Luckily, Nana Jane and Cooky Betty have disregarded their differences and cling to each other like frightened children until they're fast asleep on the sofa. But I can't sleep. I stay awake most of the night, keeping watch over the house and my newly adopted family, only stumbling into bed well past midnight after checking that Aunt Esther is safe and sound in bed and Mr. Isaiah is snoring in Grandpa's old planter's chair. The worst part of everything is not knowing if I will ever see Erich again. By the time I fall into an uneasy sleep, the howling wind is still ringing in my ears.

By first light, the worst of the storm is over. Little by little, people emerge from the wreckage to start the laborious process of rebuilding their homes. The once-beautiful town of Charlotte Amalie is a disaster. Quaint wooden homes and shacks have collapsed into useless fragments of wood or have simply blown away. Even the stone warehouses have suffered tremendous damage; they stand like open crates along the waterfront with nothing left of their roofs. There isn't a building on the island that hasn't suffered some type of damage, whether it's shattered windowpanes, missing roofs, or outright collapse. Debris, wreckage and the bodies of dead birds and animals litter the ground, making it impossible to navigate safely through town.

The people are in deep despair. Men, women and children in torn clothing who have lost everything weep openly in the streets. There's no food, no clothes, no shoes, and no basic medical supplies. Some of the people meander like zombies through the wreckage, searching in vain for missing loved ones.

The harbor, the lifeblood of the island, is in a state of turmoil. The ship *St. Hilda* was blown clear onto King's Wharf, a sight that both fascinates and terrifies. Dinghies, masts, sails, ropes, fish,

257

seagulls and assorted flotsam have washed ashore, creating a jumbled mass of foul-smelling wreckage. The Danish bark *Thor* was wrecked by the storm and sank like a toy boat in the harbor, causing the deaths of numerous sailors.

Luckily, the Danish cruiser *Valkyrien* escaped major damage as did its brave sailors, who work night and day to rescue the surviving crew members of the *Thor* with their searchlight. The docks, buildings, and warehouses of the West India Company also suffered severe damage while, across the harbor, the Hamburg-American Lines suffered similar damage to their wharf and buildings on Hassel Island, with the additional complication that their steamers *Calabria* and *Wasgenwald* were blown clear ashore, rendering them practically useless. But there's still no sign of Erich.

To take my mind off my problems, I spend the next several days organizing our supplies, cleaning up the debris around the house, sweeping the paths, doing the laundry, buying supplies from a makeshift grocery set up on Vimmelskaft Gade for those who can't make it down to Market Square, and helping Mr. Isaiah remove the boards from the windows. The natural sunlight that streams into the house seems to lift everyone's spirits, even Aunt Esther's. I'm grateful that everyone is safe and our house is still intact, but with Erich still gone, my heart is heavy. And given Langsdorff's propensity for making people disappear, I fear the worst.

CHAPTER 25

Slowly, the citizens of Charlotte Amalie begin to dig their way out of the hurricane's destruction. Roofs are repaired, homes are rebuilt, and cisterns are cleaned of debris, waiting for the next rain shower to fill them with life-saving water. Ships arrive in port daily bringing much-needed supplies, but they also evacuate people back to their homes in Antigua, Tortola, and Anguilla. Some people are too broken by the devastation and don't have the strength to start all over again. Without me, I doubt Aunt Esther, Nana Jane, and Cooky Betty would have the strength to continue. It is this knowledge that keeps me strong during my weakest moments.

And while the war seems as far away as ever, there are hints of it all around. For one thing, the Danish cruiser still floats in the harbor; her lanky sailors can be often seen marching down Main Street singing patriotic songs to the music of a marching band. We even spot the occasional Allied warship heading to battles in the North Atlantic. They pass by like ghostly shadows on the horizon, while whispers of an imminent German invasion escape the lips of indiscreet foreign elements that refuse to back down. As I have come to discover, rumors on a small island often get blown way out of proportion until they take on a life of their own.

It pleases me that all the hard work of repairing Charlotte Amalie to its former beauty is well underway: a coat of paint here, a new roof there, a fixed shutter here, a new window there. The constant banging and hammering that fills the air drowns out the braying donkeys, barking dogs, and neighing horses. Barefoot children run around the wreckage, fetching water, assisting with repairs, taking care of horses and goats, helping the old timers any way they can. Graceful schooners and sloops that were blown ashore and left in tatters are patched up and made seaworthy again. The less fortunate ones remain at the bottom of the harbor, broken beyond repair.

In the latest issue of the *Tidende* we read that Governor Helweg-Larsen made it safely back to Copenhagen where he declared in an interview that the general opinion in the islands favors the sale to the United States. He reports that the situation in the islands is not good due to a laxity on the part of the laborers that threatens to spoil the sugar harvest. He says that while he personally regrets the sale, if it will help Danish interests, then, *"We must sell them without asking about the Negro laborers' opinion. The Negroes are children, and they will soon find themselves comfortable under changed circumstances."* Something about the Governor's remarks disturbs me. I run outside to show the newspaper to Nana Jane, who is busy hanging up the wash. I ask her why the laborers are refusing to harvest the sugar quicker, why they let the crop go to ruin.

She runs her apron across her forehead. "The reason is because ever since de slaves were freed, their lives have not flourished. They continued working on de same sugar plantations as they had during slavery. And they always suffered terribly. Eventually they got so frustrated they set fire to all de rum distilleries and warehouses. That was called the Fireburn. It was a message to the white people that de working conditions had to improve."

"But why does Governor Helweg-Larsen call the Negroes 'children'?"

"Because like children de black people never had control over their lives," she explains. "All de time they tell us what to do and they order us around. Even after Emancipation our leaders had to stand up for their rights and de struggle was long and hard. But our leaders pulled us up with them. Leaders like General Buddhoe, the Fireburn Queens of St. Croix, Queen Coziah of St. Thomas, and now Mr. David Hamilton Jackson. They are leading the way forward for us. Now it seems the people are tired of Danish rule and want to join America, a rich and prosperous country. Abby dear, it is time for us to truly be free."

"Does this mean you're ready to become an American, Nana Jane?"

"I'm an old woman now," she tells me, lifting up my chin so she can see right in my eyes. "My life is almost over. It makes no difference if Nana Jane is Danish, African, or American. De only thing that matters now my dear, is you."

"Really?"

"Of course. Why else would I let you keep a *German soldier* down in de basement?"

"You did it for me?"

"Yes, and I would gladly do it all over again."

***

A week later, my anguish turns to elation when Erich finally returns. This time Langsdorff forced him on another mission, one even more dangerous than the last. He ordered Erich to board a steamer bound for Venezuela to retrieve a shipment of glass vials containing a dangerous substance called *anthrax*. Erich explains that the Germans shipped the anthrax to Venezuela, hoping to smuggle it to America where they plan on sabotaging American livestock by hiding it in sugar cubes and feeding it to horses, pigs, and cows, killing them.

Erich says he managed to elude detection this time, but can't be certain just how much longer his luck will hold out. "I have to warn you, Abby, it's just a question of time before the authorities arrest me," he says. "And the next time I go missing, it will probably be for good."

CHAPTER 26

Erich's words set me on edge. Most nights I can barely sleep. All I see is trouble ahead with no end in sight. The first chance I get I steal down to the Grand Hotel to consult with Judge Neergaard about the precarious situation with the Germans. But everywhere I go, I get the peculiar sensation that Langsdorff's men are watching my every move.

When I arrive at the hotel, I see it is still being repaired from the hurricane. Work crews are busy slathering on fresh coats of paint, repairing broken window frames, reattaching doors, and cleaning up the mess left by the storm. The lobby is full of stranded travelers whose ships were either damaged by the storm or sunk, and are awaiting telegraph messages from loved ones back home. Luckily there are enough accommodations to feed and house the overflow.

I follow the smell of fried fish up to the second floor where I'm pleased to see that Judge Neergaard has not changed his customary schedule. This time, however, he's joined by the hotheaded Jens Jørgensen, who looks relieved to see me as well. I greet the two old-timers like old friends, wondering how I'll be able to broach the subject of Erich's delicate situation without arousing suspicion.

"Abigail, how good to see you," says Judge Neergaard, his eyes twinkling with pleasure. "Won't you please join us? I trust your Aunt Esther and Nana Jane are faring well and are recuperating from the storm. For my part I have donated more than five hundred kroner towards rebuilding the park. Much more than that, I cannot do. I'm afraid that Jens and I have become like two old donkeys waiting for our master to call us out into the field, even though the both of us are past the age to be of any practical use anymore. Since we both managed to survive this latest disaster, I suppose that's cause enough for celebration. Allow me to propose a toast to our health and to the health of our Majesty, the kindest master anyone could hope for. And to the town of Charlotte Amalie, may she return to her former state of beauty…skaal."

The two gentlemen raise their glasses and down their drinks.

"Words, just words," says the gravel-voiced Jørgensen. "What good is fanciful toasting if Charlotte Amalie is about to be handed over to a strange suitor? By this I'm referring to the upcoming sale and transfer. We have only ourselves to blame for this man-made disaster. We let our beloved colony just slip through our fingers."

"What's done is done," says Judge Neergaard. "Take heart that the two of us are still sitting here like a pair of old planters pining for the days when sugar was king and the rum flowed like liquid gold. As long as the Dannebrog still flutters over Fort Christian, the dream still exists. Look around you, the world is in a state of turmoil on account of the war, and there's no place that hasn't suffered and seen its beautiful days dwindle down to nothing. How could we have maintained this unprofitable old sugar colony while the glint of gold sat grinning at us on the table? Yes, my friend, the good old days are gone forever, but for us, they will never truly disappear. They will live on in our hearts as we move on to the next phase of our lives."

"I can't and I won't," scowls Jørgensen. "I will bring the good old days back if I can manage it. In hindsight, it was a terrible mistake for me to go to Copenhagen to support the transfer. It was short-sighted and foolish. I can no longer tolerate what's going on here. I hate this whole damned business."

Jørgensen bangs his fist on the table as his face turns red and his wild eyes roll back in their sockets. "Denmark is suffering from madness brought on by the shock of losing Norway in 1814 and Schleswig-Holstein in 1864, and I for one have no intention of fading away into the sunset. For this reason, I'm going to increase my financial stakes in the *Dansk Vestindien*. My agreement with Langsdorff to take over the Hamburg-America Line properties seals it."

"Don't you realize what a risk you're taking by investing in a German-owned property during the middle of a war?" says Judge Neergaard soberly. "It's an open secret that Langsdorff is using his steamers to help the Germans track allied ship movements and to supply German warships out at sea. Jens, you're not a young man anymore. You stand to lose a great deal of money."

"Nonsense, this is strictly business," says Jørgensen. "Even the Americans are no strangers to strategic business alliances. Look at all the treaties they made with the Indians. As long as the insurance company recognizes me, Jens Jørgensen, as the rightful owner of the Hamburg-America Line property and assets, which will be renamed the Harbor Accommodating Establishment, there's no risk of loss whatever. I gave Herr Langsdorff a Promissory Note in the amount of $210,000 to cover the cost of the properties, the steamers, the inventory, and all the coal, without the slightest bit of trepidation. I've drawn up contracts that meet every legal requirement, and recorded them in the Official Books at the Police Station and in the Governor's office with terms quite favorable to me. Langsdorff benefits by converting his German business into a Danish one, while I rake in enormous profits by conducting business as usual. All under the noses of the uptight Americans! There's no way I can lose. Nobody in his right mind thinks the Americans will jump into the war this late in the game. The way I see it, in our best case scenario, the war will be over by New Year's Day, which is only two weeks away. In my worst case scenario, I'll run the steamship office while becoming quite chummy with the Americans. I may even decide to pick up baseball or golfing. Mark my words, Henrik. You'll be sorry you didn't invest your own life savings when you still had the chance."

"And if the war isn't over by New Year's?" says Judge Neergaard, furrowing his brow. "I remember a little article I read in the papers stating that German Chancellor Von Bethmann-Hollweg said something to the effect that, '*Any further suggestions of peace by Germany would be futile and evil.*' Not the appropriate words to foster a swift end to the war, are they?"

"Politics, pure and simple politics," says Jørgensen, his clipped accent betraying his growing impatience. "You've been stuck in police court for too many years. All you do is listen to one case after another, sitting there like a weary King Solomon dispensing justice to a bunch of undeserving derelicts. Meanwhile, the clock goes tick-tock, tick-tock, and you wait for the hour when you can cast aside your burdens and take that lighthearted stroll over to the Grand Hotel where you drown your sorrows in your nightly rum cocktail.

"Henrik, you gave your whole life for the idealistic principles of justice and integrity. Men like you are a dying breed. You're a man of honor, but in life and war, eggs and oaths are easily broken, and you can never be certain who is telling the truth. Deep down inside you know that every man when pressed to the wall will say whatever it takes to win. So you resort to relying on your gut. And you pray to God that it never fails you because if it does, this world will be one step closer to anarchy.

"And now, with regard to Germany, I also recall Bethmann-Hollweg saying that Germany was fighting for nothing but her right to life and liberty, and the Allied lust for conquest made peace impossible. When he said that, everybody knew it was absurd, but we didn't stop living or drop our commercial interests over some nonsensical political rhetoric, did we?"

"I only meant that you should think it over…"

"I'm telling you I've thought it over well and good," says Jørgensen. "And I've made up my mind. In the next few days you'll see an advertisement in the *Tidende* announcing the change in ownership of the Hamburg-America Line that will keep the Americans off my back."

"Very well, then," says Judge Neergaard, doffing the brim of his hat. "In accordance with the old saying, '*Wise men do not quarrel with one other,*' we shall leave it at that."

A worrisome thought pops into my mind.

"What if they manage to sabotage the transfer?" I say.

"What if *who* sabotages it?" says Judge Neergaard.

"The Germans, or more specifically, Herr Langsdorff," I say. "Langsdorff's goal was never just to conduct business. He's always wanted full control of these islands. He said so himself."

Judge Neergaard chuckles at this suggestion.

"Abby, you have a penchant for intrigue, but even Herr Langsdorff knows his limits."

***

A few days later, Erich and I are heading down Strand Gade when we notice that someone is shadowing us. Even after we change directions several times, we never manage to lose him. When I stop to gaze in a store window, I catch a glimpse of his reflection. Our pursuer is an ordinary-looking man of average height who wears a brown suit and sports clipped brown hair and a bushy moustache. His disposition seems rather jumpy by the way his hands fumble at his sides and the nervous way he rubs his nose.

"Erich," I whisper. "Someone is following us."

"I've noticed him for quite some time," he says. "Follow me."

He grabs my hand and we race around an assortment of donkey carts, two-seater carriages and gaggles of fish women and market women carrying large straw baskets. We dodge a troop of laborers hauling crates from ships docked in the harbor to the stone warehouses along the shore, but as luck would have it, I trip, lose my balance, stumble into a fragile crate of china, and send it smashing to the ground. The porter yells and screams as shards of porcelain scatter in a thousand directions, causing a small commotion. To the indignant cries of a warehouse manager, Erich pulls me by the arm and we make it halfway down the street before the astonished porter recovers his senses. As we dash for safety, I glance over my shoulder, shocked to see our pursuer following us in hot pursuit.

We quicken our pace and head down another street past warehouses, linen and china shops, a barber shop, a restaurant, and then we turn down a side alley, but only after diving headfirst under a horse carriage. Almost home free, we emerge into a palm-lined alleyway that heads to the back of town, but no matter how cleverly we attempt to dodge our pursuer, he always manages to stay hot on our trail.

All of a sudden, we round a corner thinking we've lost him for good only to find him standing right in front of us, his face a menacing scowl. I gasp as Erich's muscles tense. The stranger takes one step closer, cutting off our escape.

"Why rush away on such a pleasant afternoon?" he says, grabbing Erich's right shoulder and forcing a concealed pistol into his flank. "The boys in the office are anxious to have you over for some tea. Get moving!"

By his accent, I know right away the man is one of the Germans employed by the Hamburg-America Line. He shoves Erich down the alleyway and stuffs the pistol back into its holster. "It's not polite to let your tea get cold." Then he turns to me, glaring, "Get lost, Sweetie. Your friend and I are going to have a chat."

My stomach lurches to my throat. I am powerless to do anything as the man forces Erich down the alleyway, one hand hovering over his pistol.

Determined not to leave Erich alone with these predators I shadow them from a safe distance, keeping my presence concealed behind wooden crates and half-open doors. Soon they arrive at what appears to be a deserted warehouse. The German opens a side door, pushes Erich inside, and then shuts it behind them. I edge my way closer, pressing my hand around the doorknob and squeezing ever so carefully, but the door is locked shut. My worst fear has come true. Erich is trapped.

Valuable minutes tick by as I realize that Erich's life may be in danger at the hands of armed and dangerous men. My heart beats like a drum as I search for a way to free him. Visions of the terrible night on the *Guiana* when Ian disappeared swirl through my mind. I resolve to fight Langsdorff with all my might. My determination grows to do everything possible to thwart his schemes and save Erich's life. I won't let Langsdorff do to Erich what he did to Ian. This time I will make him pay dearly for taking an innocent man's life.

After circling the building, I realize that the small opening at the front of the warehouse meant for the small metal wheelbarrows that bring merchandise from the ships might do the trick. I calculate that I can just manage to fit through the opening if I gather up my skirt and squeeze in head first. As luck would have it, I succeed without an inch to spare.

Once inside, my eyes adjust to the darkness. The air is damp and musty and smells as if the warehouse hadn't been aired in years. It has a spooky ambiance, as if the people who were working there dropped everything and fled in haste. There are broken crates scattered about, nails, screws, glass fragments, and broken furniture dispersed in a haphazard fashion. Faded yellow pieces of paper and telegrams with barely-legible print are strewn among the wreckage, as are crumpled envelopes and ancient ledgers. Eerie cobwebs dangle from the rafters; a broken typewriter lies on its side, gas lights are covered in layers of dust, and lizards scurry up the sides of the stone walls. I worry that rats might be scurrying underfoot, or scorpions. At the center sits a large wooden desk with two chairs at either end, the only useful pieces of furniture. I look around in haste. They will be here any minute and I must find a safe place to hide.

The sound of men's voices signals their approach. Thinking quickly, I dive behind a bookshelf and crouch low to the ground. Pushing aside two books, I make an opening wide enough to peer through. I try to still my pounding heart as I wait in anticipation for the showdown that's about to take place.

Langsdorff walks briskly into the room followed by Erich and the other German with the pistol close on his heels.

"I summoned you here today because you have not yet fully repaid your debt to the Fatherland," says Langsdorff as he takes his place at the head of the desk and motions for Erich to take the chair opposite him. The other German stands to the side, smoking a cigarette. "There's one last task you must accomplish before I can recommend you for the Iron Cross."

"What is that?" says Erich grim-faced.

From his breast pocket, Langsdorff brandishes a gleaming Luger pistol which he places on the desk squarely between him and Erich with that same smug, self-satisfied expression that I saw back on the *Guiana*. Langsdorff enjoys toying with Erich like a puppet, sending him into harm's way for his own aggrandizement, then tossing him aside like a useless piece of rubbish. I must find a way to tip the balance in Erich's favor.

"As you're aware," continues Langsdorff, pulling a cigar from his pocket and lighting it with a match. "The newspapers are full of reports about the upcoming transfer. Berlin has ordered me to put a stop to it. They want me to create a *diversion* that will scare away the Americans for good. They want this accomplished before the Americans transfer the $25 million in gold bullion to the Danes."

"What does this have to do with me?" says Erich, shifting uneasily in his seat.

"You will provide the diversion," says Langsdorff.

"I'm not following you."

"It's all very simple," says Langsdorff. "Next Monday, Governor Konow is scheduled to deliver a speech to the riffraff in the park. He will be standing in the pavilion with other local officials. You will take this pistol and finish him off. One clean shot. No mistakes. Then you will disappear and my men will find a local drunkard to frame for the murder and no one will be the wiser. Fail in your mission, and your father will be dismissed from his job, your mother will be publicly shamed when she goes around town, and the two of them will be forced out of their home. Need I also mention that I can have you arrested and jailed as an enemy agent?"

"You're telling me to assassinate Konow?" says Erich, his voice rising in anger. "That's insane. He's a military commander of a neutral nation. What you're asking me to do is impossible."

"I'm not asking you, Seibold, I'm *ordering* you," says Langsdorff. "You'll be shot if you disobey. This is your only chance to make history and earn some self-respect in the process after the cowardly way you deserted. Don't forget you *betrayed* your Kaiser and your Fatherland and deserve to be shot. Nevertheless, I still believe you're capable of accomplishing great things for the Fatherland, which is why I've decided to give you a second chance. If you're smart, you'll jump at this opportunity to clear your name and prove your worth. For my generosity, I deserve your gratitude and undying obedience."

"And if I should choose not to?"

"Then Seibold, your parents will have the unpleasant task of burying the same son twice."

"Since when has Germany made provisions for the assassination of neutral military leaders?"

"In war, there are only two sides, us and them. Choose your side, Seibold."

"I refuse to kill an innocent man."

"*You are a German soldier*," screams Langsdorff. He stands up and circles the desk to face Erich. Then he presses his finger into Erich's chest, his eyes blazing with fury. "You're not entitled to your own opinion. Your mission is to shoot as ordered."

"You madman!" shouts Erich, pushing Langsdorff's hand away. "You think that shooting the Danish Governor in a cowardly fashion will change anything? It won't because it makes no sense. The Americans will pay anything to take over these islands and keep Germany out."

"Oh, but that's where you're wrong," says Langsdorff with sly conviction. "It makes perfect sense. The Americans will think the natives are staging an uprising and will back out of the deal. It's the only logical outcome when revolutions erupt in volatile parts of the world. That's when the directors of the Hamburg-America Line will approach the Kaiser about the necessity of taking over these floundering islands. A German cruiser will show up in the harbor twenty-four hours later, giving me the proper manpower to take over the entire island without firing a single shot. And you, Herr Seibold, will be rewarded for your valuable contribution. The *Deutsche* West Indies will become a valuable new submarine base and you will be rewarded with a special position, and all because of one well-placed bullet."

Erich's face turns crimson. "You fool. You think one gunman can cause an uprising on the entire island? When the people have no guns and not enough to eat? You're mad and I refuse to have any part in this. I tore off my shoulder boards when I deserted. I can never go back to Germany now."

"You're wrong, Seibold," says Langsdorff, his eyes glowing with lynx-like fury. "You can still be of use to your country. And if serving your Fatherland is not enough incentive, my men can arrange an unfortunate accident to befall the lovely young lady who was so kind to give you shelter. What a shame if something terrible were to happen to her. I happen to know she has some very influential friends on the island, people who are capable of bringing the full weight of the law down on the head of anyone suspected of causing her unfortunate end—"

Erich springs like a leopard and lunges at Langsdorff's throat.

"If you touch her, I'll kill you," screams Erich, squeezing Langsdorff's neck. Turning crimson, Langsdorff kicks like a madman and tried to reach for Erich's throat. When that doesn't help, he claws at Erich's face. The other German springs into action, landing on top of Erich. With all his might he tries to pry Erich's hands loose. He gets Erich into a chokehold and the two wrestle for control. From my hiding place, I watch the entire struggle with my heart pounding, but powerless to stop them from trying to murder Erich. The feeling of helplessness overwhelms me as I myself to keep to the shadows.

Erich gets one foot behind the German's leg, and with his free arm, smashes the man across his chest, forcing him to the ground. Langsdorff watches with disgust as his partner lands on his back, writhing on the floor in a humiliating fashion.

"You worthless coward, I should kill you for that treasonous act!" sputters Langsdorff, rubbing his red neck. "You should be grateful that I offered you this final chance to save your worthless hide."

"I will only say this once," screams Erich. "If you touch one hair on that girl's head, I will make it my life's goal to hunt you down and kill you with my bare hands."

"Watch it, Seibold," says Langsdorff. "I give the orders around here. Now get moving before I change my mind and finish you off myself."

Keeping his eyes on Langsdorff, Erich grabs the gun. The other German scrambles to his feet and throws his leather holster at Erich with a look of contempt.

"I'm not finished with you Langsdorff. I'll deal with you later," says Erich, his face bloated with disgust. In return, Langsdorff laughs at him with disdain.

"Seibold, you're a lousy damn fighter, but I have full confidence in your ability to make history on Monday. And remember don't let the Fatherland down a second time."

Erich storms out of the warehouse, slamming the door shut behind him. Langsdorff and his henchman start arguing with each other in German, then also depart with a loud bang, leaving me alone to contemplate the seriousness of what just occurred. Langsdorff's message is unmistakable: Erich must either shoot the governor or Langsdorff's men will shoot me.

I grope my way out through the opening, dazed with the knowledge that my days are numbered. As I totter through the cobblestoned alleyways, waves of fear and anxiety course through my body. I realize there is no chance for escape: Langsdorff and his men know exactly where I live.

CHAPTER 27

My life is in turmoil. I can't face Erich and I can't reveal what I know to anybody. Not even to Erich. After thinking things through, I decide that it's better not to divulge to Erich that I know about Langsdorff's threats. If Erich finds out how anguished I feel it will only cause more trouble. I worry he may lose control and do something that will get us in even more trouble.

Still, every time I hear a rustling in the bushes, a tap at the window pane or a sudden knock on the door, my heart skips a beat. When I open the door a crack and see it's just the boy from down the hill coming to fetch a cup of sugar or a spool of thread, I breathe a sigh of relief. I don't know how much longer I can take living under the constant threat of danger. Sooner or later, somebody will have to put a stop to Langsdorff.

The day before the governor's speech, Erich warns me to keep away from the park. He says that certain people are planning to cause a disturbance and I would be safer staying at home. He says that if things become dangerous, he won't be around to protect me and he'd feel a lot safer knowing I was here with Nana Jane.

I listen and nod my head, but keep my plans to myself. I am not going to let Erich fall for Langsdorff's blackmail and wind up dead. Somebody has to keep an eye on him lest he do something crazy because of his high-minded principles. I also secretly fear the possibility that Langsdorff's ruthless nature is rubbing off on Erich.

"What kind of disturbance," I say casually. "And how do you know about it?" Erich looks at me with growing impatience, and a side of him emerges that I never thought I'd see. He turns into a cold, calculating soldier, the kind that follows orders without question. The chill in his voice turns my blood to ice water.

"America is not the only ambitious country seeking to build an empire," he says in the vaguest manner possible. "Germany has her own plans for these strategically-located islands. That's the nature of war. That's the nature of life."

"What do you mean by *Germany has her own plans*?"

"*Deutschland* has no intention of standing by and letting Denmark hand over these valuable islands to the Americans, at least not without a fight. In war that's what we call collateral damage."

"And who will be this *collateral damage*?" I say, narrowing my eyes.

Erich stiffens and looks away. I know he intends to sidestep the subject.

"You're a civilian, Abby," he says in a militaristic voice that is so out of character for him. "The less you know the better. The biggest favor you can do for yourself is to stay out of danger. I know your life has been chaotic these past few months, but now is no time for heroism. Make sure all of the women of this house stay inside tomorrow, including you. Bad things can happen."

"Is this you speaking or Langsdorff? Don't you realize that he's just using you? Why do you let him order you around like a puppet? This nightmare will only end when he kills you or you kill him. And God help us if he gets you first." I grasp him by his shoulders and stare into his eyes. "Erich, don't you realize what's happening? He's blackmailing you."

"Don't try to change my mind," he says coldly, removing my hands. "I've made my decision. And there's another thing. I'll be gone for a little while. Whatever happens tomorrow, I don't want either you or your aunt implicated. My problems have nothing to do with you."

"Where are you going? Off to perform another one of Langsdorff's deadly missions?"

Erich shuts his eyes tight.

"Abby, when I deserted, I knew I would have to live with the consequences, but for the life of me, I never imagined that the people

I loved and cared for would come into harm's way. And despite everything, I've come to realize one simple fact. Inside, I'm still a German soldier, and once a soldier, always a soldier. The rules of warfare are eternal; sometimes a soldier has to sacrifice his life for the good of his country. It's a matter of honor."

"Is this terrible deed you're about to perform also a matter of honor? It seems Langsdorff brainwashed you with all his talk of war and duty. You were always a man of conscience and honor; now I feel as though I don't know you anymore."

"I knew I shouldn't have discussed this with you," he yells, kicking a chair. "I stayed here too long and dragged you unwittingly into this mess. I should have left long ago, long before you got attached. Or before I got attached—"

I stare into Erich's eyes, wondering where all this will lead. Inside, I'm a mass of confusion. Erich has voiced the unstated truth that has existed between us: we are in love. Only now, the man in front of me is no longer the Erich I know. Outside he is the same, but inside he has changed. The man before me has a cold, hard, calculating edge to him. I risked everything to save Erich's life because I believed he hated war and would never return to the fight. It seems I was wrong.

"Langsdorff has no intention of giving you the Iron Cross," I say, breaking the silence. "He's going to kill you when he's done with you. He eliminates everyone who gets in his way."

"I know," says Erich, slumping down on the bed. "He keeps me around only so long as I suit his purpose, but it's not just my life on the line now. They've upped the ante and are threatening *your* life as well. They're exploiting me in the lowest possible manner, by threatening to kill the very person I've pledged to protect."

All of a sudden, a vision of Queen Coziah flashes in my mind. I recall her strange prophecy down in Market Square.

"Erich," I say, sitting next to him. "Do you remember that old voodoo lady we saw down in Market Square? The one they call Queen Coziah?"

"The scary-looking one?" he asks. "How could I forget her? Right now, I'd rather concentrate on more pleasant thoughts."

"She said something important. *'Any man who can look down the barrel of a gun and laugh is the master of his fate.'* Don't you realize what that means?"

Erich eyes me with cynicism, and then shakes his head. "It means the old lady has a helluva sense of humor. I've never met a man who could look down the barrel of a gun and laugh. And based on my experience, sometimes it's worse for the man who pulls the trigger. He's haunted by visions of his victim's agonized face every night of his life until he goes insane."

"That's what I'm trying to prevent. What Coziah meant is that the only way to stop Langsdorff is to look him in the face and laugh. Show him you're not afraid. Break that powerful grip he has over you."

"I wish it were that simple," he states grimly. "It's not just my life he's threatening. He can still do tremendous damage to my parents' lives, but it gets much worse. Now Langsdorff is threatening to harm you. Maybe I have the power to throw my own life away, but I have no right to throw yours away. I promised to protect you at all costs. My only option is to either obey Langsdorff or kill myself."

"You're wrong," I say. "There's still another way. You can destroy Langsdorff by refusing to do his bidding and crushing his empire. Then you can learn to love life again and maybe even forgive yourself for that terrible tragedy on the *Emilie*."

Erich breaks into a small smile. He kisses my forehead.

"I will Abby, if you promise to show me the way."

***

The next morning, when the gendarmes fire the five o'clock morning salute, I wake up in a cold sweat, my heart racing with terror. Thankfully, the sound of Cooky Betty calling me for breakfast knocks me back to my senses as I hurry to get dressed and wash my face. When I reach the dining room, I try to avoid Aunt Esther's rancor on this fateful day, but as soon as I see her drinking her coffee with an unpleasant frown on her face, I know that trouble is brewing.

Aunt Esther slams down the *Tidende* with its news about the Governor's speech saying all this upheaval and change is making life unbearable.

"I'm going to write a *scathing* letter protesting this wretched transfer," she says, her normally ashen face now beet red. "By the time I'm finished, they'll know exactly what Miss Esther Maduro thinks about selling these islands to the Americans."

Cooky Betty's eyes go wide as saucers. She flees to the outside kitchen. I look at Aunt Esther's scowling face but say nothing.

Nana Jane waddles into the dining room to announce that she will be heading over to the Governor's mansion to help Miss Lucy in the kitchen. She says with all the extra dignitaries to feed over dinner, they're short of hands. I wait until she heads to the outside kitchen before inquiring if they might need my help at the Governor's mansion as well.

Nana Jane fixes her indomitable gaze on me.

"Help?" she says. "Aren't you in enough hot water as it is?"

"What are you talking about?" I say, keeping my veneer of innocence intact despite the fact that Nana Jane can read my thoughts.

"You know very well what I'm talking about," she says, pursing her lips. "You still have that German soldier hidden down in the basement in case you think I forgot. The two of you had better be careful when the American soldiers come. They won't like it one bit that one of the Kaiser's boys is living under their noses, making *pappyshow* of them."

Nana Jane shoos me back into the house with a warning to keep out of trouble.

***

For the next several hours, I keep my eye glued to the clock as I work my way through a mountain of sewing. When it's almost time for the speech, I bring Aunt Esther a cup of tea with lavender and honey, a mixture that's sure to put her to sleep. I wait until her head nods, and then I wind up the Victrola and start the record from the beginning. Once the song is playing, I lace up my shoes and tiptoe towards the door.

All of a sudden, a booming voice screeches behind me. "Just where do you think you're going?" I freeze in terror. When I turn around, my face turns ghost-white as Aunt Esther narrows her eyes to a suspicious squint.

"I'm going to hear the Governor's speech."

"You'll do no such thing," she says, getting up from her chair and placing her hands on her hips. "You'll stay put and attend to your sewing. The last thing I need is for you to go gallivanting around town, being seen with the wrong element."

"I promised to meet Deborah De Castro."

"How many times do I have to warn you to keep away from that family? They lied, cheated, and stole all my fiancé's money."

"They *what*?"

"You heard me," she says, her chest heaving. "The De Castros ruined my life!"

"That's impossible. They're good, honest people."

"That's what you think," she says, eyes blazing. "Moses De Castro is not the man he pretends to be. He was the mastermind behind a fraudulent business deal that swindled all of my fiancé's hard-earned savings. He had no choice but to flee to Panama to earn every penny back. He promised to send for me, but he never did and I've been sitting here wasting my life year after year, watching myself grow old, and knowing that all my best years are gone. *Gone!* And all because of those crooks. Even if Jacob were to come back today, it's too late. My life is ruined."

"But your fiancé died," I say, shocked that she still hasn't faced the truth after all these years. "He can't come back, just like Mami and Papi can't come back—"

"Liar!" she shouts, her face contorting with rage. "He *will* come back. He's *not* dead."

In a fit of anger, she grips the collar of her dress, pulling and twisting the threadbare fabric until the buttons pop off. It seems as though Aunt Esther is trying to choke herself. I gasp when I realize the worst has finally happened: Aunt Esther has gone stark raving mad.

I try to stop her from harming herself, but she flails her arms in my direction and breaks free, screaming like a banshee as she rips and tears at her dress, contorting her collar with more fury than ever. When she catches her reflection in the mirror and sees all the damage she's done, she bursts into tears and collapses in a heap on the floor. When I try to comfort her, she recoils and runs to her room, slamming the door behind her.

Distraught and close to tears myself, I flee the house to escape Aunt Esther's mental breakdown. If she doesn't improve soon, there's no telling what may happen. She may even end up like Nana Jane's sister, frightened, alone, unwashed, and dying in an isolated mental ward with no hope of a cure. And knowing what terrible fate Langsdorff has in store for the Governor, and the danger it poses to Erich's life, I see only darkness at the end of the tunnel.

By the time I reach downtown, half the island is already there. In honor of the speech, everyone has put on their Sunday best as they parade down to the park in family or church groups. People wave as they greet each other, the young, the old, men and women, and always with a slap on the back or a peck on the cheek, trading stories or catching up on the latest gossip. All around, peels of laughter and the high-pitched cries of babies fill the air; excited chatter drowns out the noisy chirping of the birds. It seems as if the entire island has only one goal, to catch a glimpse of the new governor and to hear a message about the transfer of their islands directly from the representative of His Majesty King Christian X.

Out in the harbor, the sailors of the *Valkyrien* have donned their prim white uniforms in honor of the occasion, and are completing their final maneuvers on deck. The Dannebrog is hoisted up to rousing salutes and cheers, and the full attention of a regiment of sailors that appear no larger than toy soldiers, each one holding his rifle that glistens like hot tar under the burning tropical sun.

When the clock on Fort Christian strikes two, a delegation of officers headed by Governor Konow leaves the *Valkyrien* on a small boat that motors over towards King's Wharf. Upon landing, they are met by a delegation of local officials who escort them to a horse carriage that will drive them the short distance to the park.

Just as Governor Konow steps foot on land, a brass band begins playing a rousing march that stirs the people's hearts to a patriotic fervor that results in an outpouring of love for their King and motherland. During the ride, Konow is followed by a regiment of Danish gendarmes who march boldly in their crisp, blue uniforms, tall blue caps, and starched white trousers. They, in turn, are followed by a ragtag procession of native women in turbans and long dresses dancing, twisting, and swaying to the music, while barefoot children laugh and shake frangipani pods, *shuk shuk*, with great merriment.

People cheer the amusing spectacle as they wave their miniature Danish flags not knowing that hidden among them is a reluctant assassin who is waiting for the perfect moment to strike.

As Governor Konow and his men alight from the carriage, the crowd rushes up to greet him as he climbs the stairs of the pavilion. When he reaches the stage, he is met by local dignitaries dressed in formal suits and top hats that reflect the proper solemnity of the occasion. At the signal, one of the men steps forward to address the expectant crowd.

"Ladies and Gentlemen," he says, surveying the vast audience which has taken over the park and stretches all the back to Tolbod and Kongens Gade. "I am honored to present His Excellency, Commodore Konow of the *Valkyrien*, His Majesty's Governor of the Danish West Indies."

The people clap and cheer as Governor Konow takes center stage. In his eyes is a look of resignation and on his face a taut expression that belies the happiness of the occasion. Forcing a smile, Governor Konow pulls a sheet of paper out of his pocket. After clearing his throat he opens his mouth to speak, but his voice does not resemble that of a naval commander, but more like a parent preparing to say farewell to his children. Children he knows he will never see again.

"Ladies and Gentlemen," he says. "Dear loyal citizens of the Danish West Indies, I bring a message from Christian the Tenth. By the grace of God, King of Denmark, the Vandals and the Goths of the Royal House of Glücksberg and Schleswig, Holstein and Sonderburg, we send to our beloved and faithful subjects in the islands of St. Thomas, St. Jan and St. Croix our royal greeting and we wish to convey to you that we are standing on the precipice of a new era. We have resolved to cede these Islands to the United States of America. The Rigsdag in Copenhagen has voted in favor of the treaty transferring the Danish West Indies to the United States and President Wilson has signed the treaty. We have done our utmost to secure you protection in your liberty, your religion, your property, and private rights, and you shall be free to remain where you now reside or to remove at any time, retaining the property that you possess in the said Islands, or disposing thereof and removing the proceeds wherever you please.

"And so, the Islands of St. Thomas, St. Jan and St. Croix, which have always been a part of Denmark, will be annexed to the United States of America and your destiny will be linked to that great nation. King Christian asks that each and every one of you not feel betrayed by this cession. With careful consideration for the best interests of his subjects, King Christian has arranged to deliver you to a good nation, a kind nation, a nation both governed by laws and comprised of lawful men. With sincere sorrow do we look to the severing of those ties that for years have united you to us and the mother country, and never forgetting the many demonstrations of loyalty and affection we have received from you, we trust that nothing has been neglected on our side to secure the future welfare of our beloved and faithful subjects, and—"

All of sudden, a shot rings out! The blast pierces the air, causing panic to erupt instantly in the crowd. People scream in terror, horses whinny and rear, and pandemonium breaks out as everyone runs for cover. The governor and his entourage duck and draw their weapons as fighting breaks out among the crowd. Men shove, punch, and hit each other as frantic onlookers try in vain to escape the chaos. Women scream and search with panicked eyes for children missing among the throng; old people cry out in a panic, sensing that disorder has broken out, or worse. People flee in with terror-stricken faces, some of them resorting to climbing over each other in their attempt to escape. Soon, mayhem erupts as everyone tries to flee the unknown assassin's bullets. When I attempt to run for cover, I realize that I am crushed from all sides, hopelessly trapped.

CHAPTER 28

A gendarme blows his whistle to stop the melee but is drowned out by the screaming and shouting. Policemen shove their way through the bedlam, searching for the gunman, but more pandemonium ensues when people catch sight of their drawn pistols and react with panic. Fighting and shouting spread as helpless policemen try in vain to separate them. All around me scuffles and brawls erupt among the outraged horde. The danger of being crushed is very real and I panic when I realize that my life is at stake.

A lieutenant draws his pistol and fires two warning shots in the air, but instead of calming down the panicked crowd, more chaos ensues as people trample each other in their mad rush to flee. People are now desperate to reach safety, but the crowd is too thick; the wails of lost children rise above the terrified screams of the mob.

Suddenly, a posse of machete-wielding native men appears out of nowhere. They offer to find the shooter and bring him to justice. My heart races as I catch the glimmer of the razor-sharp machetes in their muscular, outstretched arms. These men are after Erich and there is no way to stop them.

I push my way through the crowd, attempting to flee to the safety of the Grand Hotel. All around the square, panicked faces emerge from windows and doorways, each one trying to make sense out of the confusion and strife. I crane my neck over the commotion, hoping to catch a glimpse of the governor. Thankfully, he's still alive, although dazed with confusion. Two policemen haul him to his feet and lead him through the park to the safety of Fort Christian. There is still no sign of Erich anywhere. If Erich was indeed was the shooter, he has simply vanished.

Just then, someone screams, "There he is. Grab him!"

I look up. A dozen men, all brandishing machetes, take off in hot pursuit of a solitary individual who resembles one of the Cha Chas from Frenchtown who races through the park in horror. Making out his features is impossible as he has a scarf tied around half his face, rendering him unrecognizable. Judging by his size and height, I am pretty sure it is Erich. I yell for him to run faster, but my voice is drowned out by the deafening roar of the crowd.

Erich scales a low wall and races down the nearest alleyway with a posse of men in hot pursuit. His pursuers shake their fists with indignation, yelling out threats as they attempt to catch him. Somehow Erich is faster, remarkably agile, and adept at outrunning an angry mob, but his life is in great danger. With no thought to my own safety, I chase after the posse, hoping I can somehow help to avert disaster.

Erich races down Norre Gade as if he's on fire. He climbs up the steps of the Frederick Lutheran Church two at a time. When some of the men catch up with him, he swings around, kicking one in the chest, sending them all toppling backwards like a line of dominoes. Another one catches up with Erich, but receives a blinding punch in the face that sends him rolling down the steps like a broken wheel. Then Erich disappears inside the church, barring the door shut.

Another group of indignant men reaches the front door of the church and pounds on it with tremendous anger. They lunge at it, trying to push it open. All their force is no use; Erich has barred it from the inside with an iron rod. Amazingly, while they fumble with the front door, Erich slips out the back with the stealth of a mongoose and heads to the back of town.

I catch sight of him as he races down Kongens Gade, dodging bewildered donkey carts and flustered market women as he runs for dear life. Just then, a thought occurs to me that by going through with Langsdorff's diabolical plan, Erich has sacrificed his own life to save mine. My heart swells with love for him. Fueled by the hope that I can somehow repay the favor, I follow the trail of angry Natives intent on bringing justice down on Erich's head.

As Erich heads to the poor part of town, the part they call Back o' All, he still has a legion of furious natives hot on his tail. Suddenly, one of them grabs him by his shoulder, but Erich spins around and lands a solid punch across his jaw, followed by a forceful shove that sends the man hurtling to the ground. His pursuer collapses in pain, writhing in agony. Another man tries to tackle Erich, but a forceful blow broadside sends the poor devil reeling backwards and safely out of commission.

Erich takes shelter inside an old shack. As more men pound on the door, he leaps out the back and dashes across the sparse yard, scattering a flock of emaciated chickens. I watch as Erich scales a fence and then disappears into the bush.

The men of the posse throw up their hands in resignation and decide to return to town. As they march down the street, they are approached by a mounted gendarme who gallops towards them, demanding to know the whereabouts of the shooter. Each man points to a different direction, causing the gendarme to gallop back towards the fort, shaking his head and muttering under his breath.

Following a hunch, I head down Kanal Gade. If I know Erich, I'm sure he has a well-thought-out plan for escaping his pursuers. By shooting Langsdorff's pistol into the air, he caused a riot and may have delayed the transfer, which is what Langsdorff wanted. Nevertheless, the governor is still very much alive in keeping with Erich's vow not to cause any more innocent civilians to die. I pray this slight change in plans will keep the hot-headed Langsdorff off his back for a while. Still Erich must be careful to avoid capture; even though the governor is alive, revenge is still hot on the lips of all the islanders.

But where did he go? To figure out where Erich is hiding, I try putting myself in his shoes. With his well-honed sense of self-preservation, it makes sense that Erich would choose the safest, quietest part of town to hide, the place that's never searched and always overlooked, namely, the cemetery.

By the time I reach the Danish Cemetery, my eyes scan the road to make sure no one is following me. I unlatch the gate and push it open. Slowly, it creaks open and I take a tentative step inside, mortified by the sound of a snapped twig or the rustle of dry leaves under my feet. Thankfully, there's no one else roaming through the cemetery on this fateful day.

A stone wall lines the perimeter of the cemetery, providing some much-needed privacy. Additionally, a grove of ancient mahogany trees shield the graves from the burning sun and muffle any sounds with their rustling leaves. I crouch down and creep between the stone wall and a line of tombs along the eastern wall, careful not to make the slightest sound as I listen for any sign of Erich.

The wind rustles the leaves of the trees. Off in the distance, a donkey brays and a dog barks. These are lonely sounds, yet I get the distinct impression that I'm not alone. It feels strange communing with the dead when the whole island is erupting in turmoil, but I ignore my fears and continue searching. By the time I reach the far end of the cemetery, I put my ear to the ground and listen. A distinct scuffling noise seems to be coming from behind a large tomb. The hair on the back of my neck stands up when I realize that the sound is distinctly human. I am not the only living person here.

I inch my way forward, aware that my heart is pounding like a drum. When I get as close as possible without giving myself away, I crane my neck around a large granite monument, terrified of what I might find.

When I see Erich, I almost collapse with relief.

He's crouched on the ground between two large crypts, struggling in the oppressive heat to change his clothing. His face is red and sweat pours down his forehead as he tears off his filthy old shirt and replaces it with a smooth, white cotton one, and then proceeds to button it with military precision. Next, he extricates himself from his khaki pants and replaces them with a pair of fine linen trousers. All of these items seem to have been carefully stored behind a particular gravestone for this precise moment. Erich's efficiency amazes me. Next, he runs a comb through his blond hair, wipes his face with a handkerchief, and assumes the appearance of a fine Danish gentleman. The crazed, murderous peasant is nowhere to be found.

Realizing that Erich is armed and dangerous, I inch my way to a place of greater safety. With his finger close to the trigger, I don't want to startle him and cause a catastrophic accident. One wrong move could prove my last. Yet somehow, I must make contact.

"Pssssst…"

Erich freezes in his tracks. His body tenses and his eyes look all around, searching for the source of the sound. He lifts his Luger pistol, cocks it, and slowly aims it in my direction. I gasp and close my eyes, waiting for the burst of gunfire.

When no explosion occurs, I open my eyes to see Erich's mouth hanging open in astonishment.

"You?" he says, uncocking the gun and pointing it towards the sky. "What in the blazes are *you* doing here?"

He crawls over toward where I sit trembling, and pulls me back to his safe corner with a few forceful jerks.

"Abby, have you lost your mind?" he says, modulating his voice so the sound doesn't carry too far. "Don't you realize I might have killed you? What the devil are you doing here?"

"I came here to save you."

"Save me in the middle of a riot? Have you completely lost your senses?"

I stare at him with indignation. "Have I lost *my* senses? Who was it that fired at the governor? I should be asking *you* the same question."

Erich's face softens. "I have the situation under control, but now with you here... Don't you realize how dangerous it is for you to be seen with me? Now I have to worry about saving your neck in addition to saving my own worthless one. I warned you not to go downtown today. Now look what's happened! You're caught in the middle of an assassination attempt." Erich shoves the pistol back in his holster and shakes his head. "Your love of intrigue will get us both killed. Don't you realize that life is not an adventure novel?"

"What about you?" I say. "You claim to hate war and killing innocent people, yet you told me, 'Once a soldier, always a soldier.' And by the looks of things, you can't even shoot straight."

Erich chuckles. "Let me tell you something, Miss Maduro, if I wanted to kill the governor, he'd be dead by now. Did you think I would really shoot him? I just caused that commotion to get Langsdorff off my back. And if I manage to disappear for awhile, my plan will be a success. But none of this changes the fact that your life is in danger just by being near me. I have the entire Danish militia plus hundreds of angry natives hunting me down with machetes and now I have to worry about protecting a headstrong girl with more courage than common sense."

I'm suddenly filled with remorse. I look down, ashamed. Erich cradles my face in his hands. "And more heroism than most men I've ever known. But if they catch us together, you'll be in worse trouble than a goat on New Year's Eve. Not to mention that auntie of yours, who will probably disown you and ship you off to some orphanage. Did you consider for a minute the consequences of your actions?"

"First of all, I couldn't leave you to fend for yourself, soldier or not. And second of all, if I disobeyed you, it was because I knew I couldn't live with myself if something terrible happened to you. There's something you don't know about me. I've been through this before. When I was on the ship coming over, a German spy who resembled Lothar Langsdorff murdered a friend of mine, a very good friend. I promised to make Langsdorff pay for what he did."

Erich studies me, his eyes intent. "Who was this friend?"

"My room steward, a plucky Irishman by the name of Ian McShane who took me under his wing and taught me all I know about German spies. When Ian got a little too close to a man known as Fritz Dreyer who I believe is really Langsdorff, a fight broke out that left a puddle of blood as the only remaining trace of Ian. So now you know the whole story. I have a very personal stake in this matter."

"This story just gets deeper and deeper, my dear Abigail. But don't do anything to endanger yourself further. Leave Langsdorff and his men to me. Now run home; they mustn't catch us together."

Erich cranes his neck around the crypt, searching for any sign of angry pursuers, but the only sound we hear comes from a creaky donkey cart rattling down the dusty road alongside the cemetery. The donkey's harness bell jingles cheerfully, tapering off the further they go. A few minutes later, the donkey cart is gone and we're alone once again. All we have for comfort is the rustling of the trees and a few curious lizards. Erich lets out a deep sigh and slumps against the tombstone. He pulls out a crumpled pack of cigarettes from his pocket, lights one, and takes a deep, satisfying puff.

"Sometimes I think we were meant to be together," he says, touching my cheek. "Maybe that's why I had to come to this far-flung island, but if something ever happened to you, I would never forgive myself. That's why we must be extremely careful in dealing with Langsdorff. He wouldn't hesitate to hurt you as a way of getting even with me. But now my situation is even more dangerous. The minute I fired the pistol at the governor, I crossed the line from being a deserter to being a wanted German spy."

I lean my head against his chest. "What will you do now?"

"For the moment, I'll go into hiding," he says. "Then when all of this commotion dies down, I'll come back and finish off Langsdorff."

"Maybe you could turn the tables by proving it was Langsdorff's idea to kill the governor, and that he blackmailed you into carrying it out. It's no secret that Herr Langsdorff wants to claim these islands for Germany."

"Proving anything against Langsdorff is a long shot," he says. "For now he has diplomatic immunity. And don't forget, I'm just a common foot soldier among rich and powerful men. Who would believe that the manager of the Hamburg-America Line is behind a grisly assassination plot? Naturally they'll say it was the act of a lone, deranged gunman."

"Unless..."

"Unless what?"

"Unless we can prove that Langsdorff is a spy. We need credible evidence, something like a radio transmitter or messages written in code. Or even his code book."

"And do you have any idea how to carry out this highly ambitious plan of yours?"

"I consider that a minor detail to be worked out later," I say, giving him a mischievous wink.

"A minor detail—" he mimics, raising one eyebrow in mock seriousness. Then he stands up and brushes grass and dirt off his pants, surveying the surroundings.

"My lady, I would love to stay and chat a bit longer, but the gendarmes will be arriving any minute to invite me over for tea and cake before they stick my head in a noose. I'll return home as soon as it's safe. Meanwhile, keep out of sight and promise me no more heroics. And stay away from Langsdorff and his men."

"But—"

Erich shakes his head. "I can already see it's no use talking to you. You'll never change. Now listen to me, go back to your auntie's house and stay out of trouble. Be a good girl, do your sewing. Remember, playing with fire can get even beautiful girls burned."

I swallow hard. "Very well."

Erich gives my arm a squeeze. "Good girl."

Before I have a chance to say goodbye Erich takes off in a flash. He races through the cemetery, disappearing behind a mahogany tree and reappearing at the front gate. My heart skips a beat as I watch him unlatch the gate, nod in my direction, then hurry off in the direction of the road that climbs up the highest mountain then leads you toward the north side of the island. As Erich disappears, a huge lump forms in my throat. Deep down inside, I fear we may never see each other again.

CHAPTER 29

The near-fatal shooting in the park is the subject of gossip behind closed jalousies over the next several weeks. Everyone claims to know the shooter's name, where he lives, and why he went berserk. Theories range from an escapee from the hospital's lunatic asylum to a disgruntled sugar cane worker. Some bold eye-witnesses even claim the man is an embittered gendarme out to stop the transfer at all costs.

Nobody in his right mind believes that the shooter is a German spy. That's too far-fetched for anyone to accept. If I were to suggest to a passing stranger that the shooter is not a disgruntled sugar cane worker, but really a deserter from a German U-boat, they would erupt in house-shaking laughter and tears would start rolling down their cheeks at the absurdity of the idea. I guess that's just human nature.

According to the news cables, the mood in Washington is deteriorating. President Wilson addressed the Senate with the words, *"Only a peace between equals can last. Only a peace the very principle of which is equality and a common participation in a common benefit."* It seems even Wilson is running out of patience with the war.

By early February, Berlin announces that Germany will resume unrestricted submarine warfare. As a result, the United States breaks off relations with Germany. Soon we hear reports that Germany is already sinking up to a quarter of all ships entering the British Isles.

How much longer can America stay neutral before rushing to Britain's aid?

At the beginning of March, the situation reaches a tipping point. Something called the Zimmerman Telegram is making headlines across the United States and the entire world. The story goes that Germany's Foreign Secretary, Arthur Zimmerman, sent a coded cable to Mexico offering the Mexicans a handsome reward if they side with Germany during the war. The Germans also promise to return all the lands in the Southwest that the Americans captured from the Mexicans. According to the newspapers, the Americans became furious when they heard of this treachery; the people are demanding that Wilson stop his peaceful posture and declare war on Germany immediately.

Meanwhile, I keep my eye on the calendar, growing more despondent over Erich's disappearance with each passing day. He hasn't sent word and seems to have fallen off the face of the earth.

Soon thereafter, my prayers are answered. A stone with a note wrapped around it lands through my open window. As soon as I see it, I pounce on it and open it with boundless joy. By the time I peer off the balcony, he's gone.

In the note, Erich writes that he is safe and sound, and that I should meet him down by Market Square later today, bringing with me some of the money he has stashed under the loose floorboard in the basement. He says he desperately needs a new pair of shoes since his old ones are worn out from hiking up the mountains, but he's afraid to be spotted coming home in broad daylight. I throw on a dress and lace up my shoes, and then I scurry down to the basement to locate the money. I spend the rest of the afternoon watching the clock tick off the minutes one by one.

By the time I get to Market Square, something has gone terribly wrong. An angry mob is surrounding some unfortunate soul, yelling, screaming, shaking their fists, and stamping their feet. Half a dozen Danish gendarmes and a few policemen are arresting a frightened man. Policemaster Fischer questions the bewildered suspect while another policeman holds up a crude sketch of the gunman. I worm my way through the crowd to get a better look, but then I draw back in horror when I realize the suspect they are arresting is none other than Erich.

Beads of sweat trickle down his face. Erich trembles noticeably as he shakes his head, denying any connection to the shooting. His denial just incites the mob further who respond by snatching his straw hat off his head and trampling it beneath their angry, calloused feet. Everyone believes that Erich is guilty and now they want vengeance.

The frowning policemen shackle Erich's hands, and then shove him into a rattling motorcar. As they speed off, the mob screams, "German Spy!" and "Bocra!" at the top of their lungs. I gasp in fright. Dropping the package of food, I race home.

CHAPTER 30

For the rest of the day I keep my spyglass peeled on Fort Christian, wondering what the gendarmes are doing to Erich. When Nana Jane returns, she fills me in on all the latest news from Miss Lucy over at the Governor's Mansion. When I hear what she says, my heart sinks.

Apparently, the governor is elated that they finally managed to catch the would-be assassin; the guards are watching him like a hawk to make sure he doesn't escape. Eager to avoid any more embarrassing situations, they placed Erich in solitary confinement. It's also for his protection. Apparently, the other prisoners have threatened to kill him for his brazen act. And since the Danes are not exactly sure what to do with him, they decided to turn him over to a British cruiser that they expect to arrive any day now. *What will I do now?*

It appears that this catastrophic turn of events came about as a result of a local drunkard who recognized Erich from the day of the shooting. For the first time in the miscreant's life, the police actually listened to his version of the events and arrested Erich on the spot. But just for good measure, they hauled in the drunkard for questioning as well.

Now the drunkard is being hailed as a local hero while Erich sits in a dank cell in Fort Christian. And from what Nana Jane tells me, the drunkard is now demanding an audience with the governor! Some members of the Colonial Council can't bear that a street urchin is basking in the glory, so they track down a dozen other people who also claim to have seen the shooter. Aunt Esther predicts that by tomorrow morning, the nameless drunkard and his part in capturing the German spy will be all but forgotten.

Nothing escapes Nana Jane's watchful gaze. She sees the worry etched on my face, and the forlorn way I stand on the balcony for hours with the spy glass trained on the windows of Fort Christian, hoping for a chance to glimpse Erich's face through the bars. She puts her hand on my shoulder and murmurs, *"Rescue me from my pursuers, for they are stronger than I. Release my soul from confinement to acknowledge Your Name. The righteous will crown themselves with me when You bestow kindness upon me."* I lean over and hug Nana Jane. As always, her words are a soothing balm to my soul.

***

The next day I learn that the British cruiser is expected in two days. Time is running short and Erich is still in prison. If I don't get him out, they'll turn him over to the British for questioning, which will undoubtedly result in a court martial. I shudder when I think of what could happen to him in the Prisoner of War camp once the other German prisoners realize he deserted. I spend the entire day wandering through the streets and alleyways of Charlotte Amalie, worrying about my dear friend, trying to imagine life without him. Somehow I always end up in Market Square, the place where I last saw him. Without his presence in my life, without his strength, comfort, and support, what do I have to live for? To fight for?

And then I see her. The one person who never backs down from trouble, the one person with more gumption than an entire regiment of soldiers: Queen Coziah. As usual, she's perched under her beloved frangipani tree surrounded by her usual coterie of followers. This time, however, instead of expressing anger at the governor, the steamship companies and the terrible working conditions, Queen Coziah is raging against the Germans. She is denouncing the attack on our beloved governor with bitter, outraged words and calls for swift justice.

"De Germans sent a killer man down here to confuse us, to steal our peace," cries Queen Coziah. "We will not give in to this confusion! We have no tolerance for killers! Down with German spies!"

"Throw out de Germans!" shouts the crowd.

I advance across the plaza, weaving through the crowd of angry natives until I find myself face to face with Queen Coziah. Her blazing orbs settle on me, making her face appear even angrier and more frightening than before, but I refuse to cower.

"Well young lady?" she spits out. "What you be wanting?"

No sound emits from my throat. My knees shake like quivering stalks of sugar cane and I feel my throat tightening.

"Speak up!" she roars. "Don't waste Queen Coziah's time."

"The German man is innocent," I say. "He's not a killer. The chief *bocra* from the Hamburg-America Line is responsible. He wanted to kill the governor so he can take over the islands."

"Queen Coziah not afraid of the *bocra*," she spits out. "The *bocra* afraid of Queen Coziah!"

Then Coziah does a little bamboula dance, turning and twisting, cackling with malicious delight as she sways back and forth. Then she opens up her hollow mouth and lets out a devilish shriek, "Hahahahaha!"

The blood runs cold in my veins. The crowd roars with delight. Coziah's face contorts into a grinning mask of death. I feel the hair on the back of my neck stand up and goose bumps erupt on my arms. The crowd loves it. They join in her raucous laughter, loving every minute of her joke. I realize too late that the joke is on me.

"He's innocent!" I shout. "They've got the wrong man!"

Queen Coziah goes silent. She stares at me with those ferocious yellow orbs as she contemplates this new twist on the matter. The crowd tenses as Coziah opens her toothless mouth to speak as the beating of my heart grows louder and louder.

"To win de *bocra* man you got to fool him," she says, grinning from ear to ear. "De *bocra* man not so smart when you turn de rules of de game around. De *bocra* man thinks straight but Queen Coziah can think backwards, forwards, up, and down. De *bocra* like an old mule, only going in one direction. If you outsmart him at his own game, he has no more power than an old wash pail. When you can outthink de *bocra* man, then you will become just like Queen Coziah. You can fool de *bocra* man, but only if you want it bad enough."

At these words, I back away from the crowd. The people erupt into a noisy chatter as I realize that the secret to Queen Coziah's power is pure and simple bluff. To free Erich, I must fool the jailers, buy how? I turn and head back down Main Street, in the direction of the house of a certain judge on Government Hill who would move heaven and earth to help me.

***

When I arrive at Judge Neergaard's home, I pound on the door. His irate housekeeper bursts through the opening, her face and hands covered with flour, her turban all askew. The vexed expression on her face tells me once again I'm skating on thin ice.

"You again?" says Wilhelmina, narrowing her eyes to tiny slits. "What you be needing now?"

"I have to see the judge, it's urgent."

"What's your problem?"

"It's an emergency."

"It's always an *emergency*. Well, de judge can't see anybody today," she says, slamming the door in my face. "Come back tomorrow."

I bang on the door even harder. "Open up, please! It's a matter of life and death."

Wilhelmina opens up the door again, but this time, she's even more irate. When I see her lifting the rolling pin she's carrying, I take a step backwards.

"You again?" she screeches. "Don't you ever learn your lesson? *I just told you de Judge not seeing anyone today.* Do you want me to knock some sense into that thick head of yours?" She shakes the rolling pin with malicious intent. Clearly, this lady means business, but I didn't come this far to back down.

"Tell the judge that Abigail Maduro, Sam's granddaughter, is here," I plead in earnest. "I know he'll see me. Tell him a man's life is at stake."

"Are you making *pappyshow* of me, girl?"

"No! This time it's for real."

The irritated woman shakes her head and mutters, "Hold on a minute now…" She closes the door while I count the minutes. When she reopens it, she is suddenly sporting a smile. "You got lucky today. De judge says he will see you in his study. And *nobody* ever goes into de Judge's study. Not while he's on de bottle." She points to a door down the hall.

I make my way over to the door and give it a soft tap. When nobody answers, I turn the knob and gently open it. Inside the room is stuffy and dark; light streams in through the jalousies, but even with this minimal lighting, I can tell the room is lovely and it holds many beautiful things. Books and Danish porcelain line an entire wall. Another wall is decorated with stunning paintings and photographs in gilded frames, while at the far end sits an intricately carved mahogany writing desk and two overstuffed chairs. A sonata plays softly on a gramophone, filling the room with the exquisite sounds of a sad, but haunting melody.

Judge Neergaard sits in a comfortable chair, propped up by pillows as he listens to the music with half-closed eyes. On the table next to him is a partially consumed bottle of rum and a crystal glass.

"Judge Neergaard," I whisper, inching closer. "It's me, Abby. I have to speak to you about something urgent. I need your help."

Judge Neergaard's eyes flutter open. He looks at me and smiles.

"Abigail, is that you?" Once he's satisfied that the voice belongs to me, he closes his eyes again. "So it is you. I guess that naughty Wilhelmina was right after all. Perhaps it's time I finally gave her that raise she's been bothering me about. How would I ever manage without her?"

"What about Mrs. Neergaard?"

"Do you see that picture hanging on the wall over there?" He points to a photograph hanging above the writing desk. "Go and have a look."

The photograph is of a beautiful young woman with silky blond hair in a lace wedding gown, holding a bouquet of roses.

"Is this Mrs. Neergaard?" I say, admiring the picture.

"Yes, as I will always remember her," he says, with just the hint of a smile.

"Where is she now?"

"Down in the old Danish cemetery for over ten years now."

Judge Neergaard rests his right hand on his chest, closes his eyes, and reminisces. "She was the most beautiful woman that ever graced the island. She used to love picnicking over at Magens Bay and dancing at the governor's balls. And though she left me far too young, I don't consider her really gone. She's still very much a part of my life. Her laughter, her smile, her admonishments, her cajoling, it's all up here." He taps his forehead. "I visit her every Sunday with a bouquet of wild flowers that grow outside her bedroom window. She always loved those flowers."

"What happened to her?"

"Typhoid fever," he says, pouring himself another glass of rum. "There was nothing further they could do."

"I'm so sorry," I say. "I had no idea. Please forgive me for interrupting you, but something terrible has happened that requires your urgent assistance."

"What is it?"

I kneel down by his side and press on his arm.

"A man's life is in danger," I say, in a pleading tone. "You're the only one who can help him."

"Who is this man?" he says, eyeing me with seriousness.

"Do you remember the sick man that Dr. Christensen treated up at the Maduro house? The one he thought was a German naval officer?"

"How could I forget? Of course, I remember him. What happened to him?"

"He's been arrested. They locked him up in Fort Christian because they think he's the man who fired at the governor."

"Let me think for a minute," says Judge Neergaard, scratching his beard. "Yes, now I recall you saying this mysterious patient left some time ago on a boat headed down to South America. I also remember Dr. Christensen saying that the man appeared to be a German Naval Officer, of a U-boat no less. Makes you wonder how a German U-boat officer could suddenly appear on a little Danish island in the West Indies out of thin air. And just before the transfer. Abigail, I think it's about time you told me the whole truth. I want the whole story."

"The whole story?" I say, seeing my story crumble to dust.

"Everything," he says, taking a sip of rum. "Abigail, there are times in life when a man can fool himself with half truths and complete fabrications. After serving more than thirty years on the bench, I can assure you that when a man's life is at stake, the doctor cannot begin to cure the patient until the patient starts telling the truth. Lucky for you, you've caught the doctor on a good day. I have the company of a fine bottle of rum and Schubert's Piano Sonata No. 13 on the gramophone. Although I would have preferred to spend my day in the company of Mrs. Neergaard, as this sonata was her particular favorite."

I swallow hard. It appears I have no choice.

"Very well, I'll tell you the truth," I say. "The man Dr. Christensen treated is indeed a German Naval Officer, *Leutnant zur See* Erich Seibold to be exact, but he deserted when he refused to sink any more civilian vessels. He's not a Prussian brute as everyone seems to think, but a man of conscience. Langsdorff discovered his true identity and blackmailed him into carrying out sabotage and this crazy plan of his to take over these islands for Germany. Erich's not a killer. He deserted because he refused to sink any more passenger ships. You must help him; he's innocent. He never meant to shoot the governor."

"Abigail, this may sound absurd but I actually believe you," says Judge Neergaard. "Your story is so convoluted; it can't possibly be untrue. In fact, the more I think about it, the more I realize it sounds quite plausible. So let me repeat, according to what you're saying, Langsdorff discovered a German war deserter hiding on the island and blackmailed him into assassinating the Governor so the Americans would back out of the deal, leaving the Kaiser free to invade the islands and claim them for Germany."

"That's exactly what I'm saying."

"How fiendishly clever."

"Langsdorff threatened Erich that if he didn't shoot the Governor, he would ruin his parents' lives back in Germany. Erich had no choice in the matter. He went along with Langsdorff's plan, but only up to a certain point. Langsdorff gave Erich his Luger pistol, but Erich had no intention of shooting the governor. All of this was so Langsdorff could become the new governor."

"He always loved boasting about that," says Judge Neergaard. "Tell me more about your soldier friend. Are you saying that he's some sort of pacifist?"

"Oh, he's a trained soldier who loves the fatherland, but he's not willing to kill innocent civilians for it. And now he's locked up in Fort Christian waiting to be handed over to the British to face a military tribunal where they'll no doubt find him guilty of espionage. If I don't help him, there's no telling what they'll do to him. But he's in even more danger from the other German prisoners once the British make it known he's a deserter. The Germans always kill their deserters."

"Do the gendarmes know his full name and rank?" says Judge Neergaard.

"Not likely," I say. "Erich would never reveal his real identity. The police picked him up on the testimony of some drunkard who claims to have seen Erich pulling the trigger. I'm sure his testimony can be refuted as Erich was wearing a scarf at the time."

"I see," mutters Judge Neergaard, scratching his chin. "It seems that your friend Erich didn't run far enough away from the war. Nonetheless, with a little careful planning, it may be possible for your friend to gain his freedom. But it may require a little subterfuge. Are you up to the challenge, young lady?"

"I'll do anything for him."

"Just remember one thing," he says. "Sometimes simple deception is more effective than complex strategizing. Do you see that chest of drawers over there? Open the bottom drawer and fetch the uniform down at the bottom."

I open the heavy drawer and feel under a stack of clothes until I find the familiar blue tunic, spotless white trousers, and tall blue cap of the Danish gendarmes. The judge's plan starts to materialize in my mind.

"I've found it," I say. "But I don't understand Judge Neergaard, whose uniform is this?"

"It belonged to my son, Kaare. He died thirteen years ago in a typhus epidemic while serving in the gendarmerie corps. His dream was to go to medical school, but he never quite made it. His death was too hard for my wife to bear; she died soon after. I don't know why I kept that old uniform; I just couldn't bear to part with it. I guess I'm just a sentimental old fool."

The gramophone stops playing.

"Kaare had my wife's blue eyes and sandy-colored hair," he continues. "He also inherited her quick wit and spirited nature, the side of her I loved so much. Kaare was also a generous soul. I'm sure he would have wanted to help a man of integrity and honor like your friend Erich. Take the uniform and let your friend find his own freedom. I owe your grandfather at least that much."

I hug Judge Neergaard with all my might. And then, without another word, I race out the door to save Erich's life.

CHAPTER 31

Judge Neergaard's plan is daunting, but I can't back out now. The British cruiser will be arriving any day. When I consider the fact that no prisoner has ever escaped Fort Christian with its iron bars and impenetrable walls, I'm overwhelmed with the task I'm about to do. Nana Jane used to joke that Queen Coziah had her own private cell in the fort for whenever she needed some cooling down, but Coziah is just a troublesome old firebrand, a public nuisance. They wouldn't dare put her in shackles. Erich, on the other hand, is a dangerous would-be assassin. A wanted German spy. Surely, they will be posting guards day and night near his cell, guards with rifles and bayonets.

Sitting alone on the balcony I peer through the spy glass, studying the fort in great detail. Fort Christian was built in 1671, when buildings were meant to last forever and prisoners had no chance of escaping. Its walls are several feet thick, built from solid stone that has stood the test of time. Its entrance is through a Danish clock tower where a guard is posted night and day except for short breaks or between shifts. Family members of the prisoners show up with food at various times of the day, coming and going with relative ease. At last, I see an opportunity.

I wait until Cooky Bettie leaves the kitchen, then I sneak in and take the market basket to my room where I place the gendarme uniform all the way at the bottom, then cover it up with bread, fruit,

Johnny cake, bottles of lemonade, and a newspaper. I cover all this with a kitchen towel and then slip quietly out of the house.

I hurry down Crystal Gade, turn right on Raadets Gade, and then head down Main Street in the direction of Emancipation Gardens where I can observe the comings and goings of the fort with ease. While on the surface I look like any ordinary visitor enjoying a lovely day in the park, my insides are all a jumble.

To make matters worse, the park is crowded with tourists who have arrived on a large passenger steamer docked out in the harbor. They fill the park with their endless chatter as they stroll about, taking photographs, congregating near the bust of old King Christian IX, and laughing over funny stories. Just before noon the tourists vacate the park for their noonday meal, heading like a flock of ducks to the Grand Hotel. It's a relief to be rid of them. Their merry talk and laughter has made me jittery. I know that if I don't act now, I'll lose my nerve.

When the clock tower strikes noon, the policemen trickle off to their dinner and the gendarmes return to the Barracks. Finally, quiet descends over the hustle and bustle of Charlotte Amalie. I calculate that I have a small window of opportunity to carry out my plan. If I fail, I lose everything, but failure is out of the question where Erich's life is concerned.

Trembling, I stick my hand inside the basket, making sure the uniform is still there. Confident, if only for a brief moment, I rise to my feet despite my quivering knees, and after mustering up my remaining courage, stride with purpose over to the fort.

When I reach the entrance, I take a deep breath and rap on the wooden gate. Sitting nearby is a guard, a young West Indian, who appears to be fast asleep. His chair is leaning against the wall as his feet dangle carelessly in the air. To my relief, the guard appears to be unarmed; he's dressed in the standard policeman's uniform consisting of a black tunic with brass buttons, white trousers, and a black cap. From his mouth comes an audible snore, as if he has no plans of waking up soon. Unless I can rouse him from his slumber, I may miss my only chance to carry out my plan.

Peering past the guard, I survey the inner courtyard, trying to memorize its layout. Holding cells built into the outer walls of the prison, one prisoner per chamber. The doors are secured with iron bars through which the jailers observe the prisoners as they make their rounds. Any one of these cells could be holding Erich; I have just a few minutes to find the exact one.

At the far end of the courtyard, two grooms are hard at work polishing some leather saddles and bridles. They laugh and joke, occasionally splashing water on each other. A third groom is nearby, washing and combing a spirited brown horse. As the trio is so absorbed in each other's company, they pay no particular attention to the comings and goings of the fort; I foresee no trouble coming from their quarter. Meanwhile, something else catches my eye. About halfway down the southern wall of the courtyard sits an important-looking office which I assume belongs to the Policemaster. His door is conspicuously open.

"Excuse me, sir," I say, shaking the guard's shoulder, but I fail to rouse him. I try to catch the eye of a passing policeman, but he hurries past as though I don't exist and heads down a hallway where he disappears.

"Is anybody here?" I call out, at which point a dozen pairs of mahogany-colored arms shoot out from between the iron bars, each one waving frantically as the prisoners hiss and cat-call in shocking, frightful tones. After another dreadful minute, a senior policeman strides with great authority toward the gate.

"Yes, Miss?" he says in a deep, commanding voice. "Can I help you?"

The policeman's white hairs peek out from his cap and his muscles bulge from under his shirt. As soon as he realizes the guard is asleep, he places his hands on his hips and gives the chair such a forceful kick, the hapless guard topples to the ground.

"Have you gone *bazudi*?" says the policeman. The chided guard looks around in a daze as he rubs his backside with a painful grimace. "Now go report to the captain for extra duty or I'll tan your worthless hide. On the double!" The guard pulls his hat on with a show of indignation, picks himself up, and scurries down a nearby corridor.

"Now what do you want, Miss?" says the policeman, his voice displaying mounting impatience.

"I-I've brought food for a p-prisoner," I stammer. "The one they arrested the other day."

"Which one is that?" asks the policeman, scratching his head.

"The one they call the German."

"Oh, de Kaiser man. Just a minute, let me first check with Chief Larsen, the Assistant Policemaster." He pulls a black key from his pocket and opens the lock. The huge door creaks open, allowing me just enough room to slip through. "Come inside, but before I let you in, let me see that basket of food." He opens the lid and sticks his hand inside, feeling around for any sharp objects. Satisfied that the basket contains no weapon, he hands it back to me.

"Follow me."

The policeman leads me through the blazing hot prison courtyard. When I pass by the cells, dozens of prisoners thrust their writhing, sweaty arms through the bars, letting out horrifying, desperate wails. I draw back in fear, mindful that the only barrier between me and the prisoners is the iron bars. We make our way through the courtyard as the shrieks, groans, and hisses of the prisoners rise to a fearful climax, each tormented captive begging for food, cigarettes, or worse. I shield my eyes from the sight of them, but one grabs hold of my skirt and jerks me towards him until I find myself pulled against the bars. I scream bloody murder and push myself away to free myself from the fearsome grip of the prisoner while my whole life flashes before my eyes.

The policeman swings around and when he sees what the prisoner has done, pulls out his club and in one swift motion, pounds it against the wretched prisoner's arm with unrelenting fury.

"Get your damned black hand back inside the cage, you worthless good-for-nothing or I'll tear you limb from limb," he screams, the veins on his face pulsing with anger. The chastised prisoner withdraws his hand and slinks back inside the cage until all that remains are two sullen yellow orbs that glare in indignation from the darkness of his cell.

The office of Assistant Policemaster Peter Larsen juts out from the interior walls of Fort Christian into the courtyard, a small fortress within a fortress, and boasts an enormous wooden desk, a filing cabinet, and a rotating fan whose loud whirring drowns out the din of the prisoners. The policeman knocks on the door and waits for permission to enter.

Larsen, a middle-aged Danish police officer with a curly moustache and wearing a white, single-breasted tunic, sits upright at his desk, composing a letter in elegant Danish longhand. The only other objects that occupy his prominent desk are a large police registry book, an inkwell, and a copy of the *Tidende*. Hanging on the walls behind him are pictures of King Christian X and Queen Alexandrine, who gaze down with the proper noblesse oblige.

"Chief Larsen," says the policeman, jingling his keys. "A girl came here saying she brought food for de no-name prisoner. Says she wants to see him."

"If it is food she brings, you may show her in," says Larsen without bothering to look up. The policeman snatches a jagged key off a hook on the wall and says, "This way, Miss."

I trail the policeman through the courtyard, attempting to avert my gaze from the hissing prisoners as I search for any sign of Erich. We halt in front of a cell at the far end of the prison. With my heart pounding in my chest, I peer through the bars, hoping to catch a glimpse of Erich. When my eyes finally adjust to the darkness, I make out its sparse furnishings: a metal bed, a thin, dirty mattress, a yellowed, threadbare sheet, a porcelain receptacle in a corner, a pile of cigarette stubs on the floor. Sitting on the bed with his back to us is a silent, sulking prisoner.

"Put that basket down and run along," says the policeman. "These prisoners are a violent, rowdy bunch."

"Please sir, I have to see this man. He has no family to bring him food. I must give it to him myself. I'm the only person he trusts."

"You have five minutes, no more, and then be on your way," he commands, inserting the key in the lock and calling out, "Hey Kaiser man, you got a visitor."

When the prisoner turns around, my relief is boundless. Although his face is obscured by the shadows, there's no doubt it's Erich. As soon as he sees me, Erich bolts upright and starts toward us, but the jailer holds up a huge, powerful hand.

"Not so fast, Kaiser man," he yells. "Stop right there. Talk from over there."

The policeman turns and retraces his steps through the courtyard, leaving us alone for a few precious minutes. With the door ajar, I slip inside Erich's cell and throw my arms around him.

"Erich! I thought I'd never see you again. Are you alright?"

"I'm fine," he says, with a mixture of shock and relief. "What about you? How did you manage to get inside here?"

"I have my ways," I say. "I did what anybody would do under the circumstances. I had to see you again, no matter what. What are they going to do to you?"

"They've charged me with espionage and plan on handing me over to the British for interrogation. We might as well say goodbye now, Abby. I'm sure they're going to shoot me."

I hiss in his ear. "Listen carefully. I'm going to get you out of here. Just do as I say…we've no time to lose."

"What are you talking about?"

"I have a plan," I say, pulling out the gendarme uniform. "This is your only chance. Put it on quick. The outside gate is still unlocked and there's only one policeman on duty. Larsen's in his office daydreaming and if you hurry, you might be able to slip out through the front gate. You've got about two minutes."

Erich's eyes go wide as he assesses the uniform, then he tears off his clothing and pulls on the uniform with the desperation of a condemned man. First the trousers, then the jacket, careful to fasten each button as he mutters, "This is the craziest thing I've ever heard." Next, he smoothes back his hair, tops it off with the cap, and lowers it until it almost conceals his eyes.

By now, Erich's forehead is sweating profusely. "If they catch me, they'll shoot me. You realize that, don't you?"

"Shhh!" I caution. "He's coming back."

My knees quiver uncontrollably as I hear the policeman's footsteps approaching. I glance over at Erich. Though his knuckles are white and his face is drained of color, his disguise is perfect. He's virtually indistinguishable from the other gendarmes on the island. He presses me against the wall with his left arm while he holds his right index finger to his lips, motioning for me to be quiet. I nod and we both fall silent. The policeman's whistling reverberates off the thick walls, blending in with the banter of the grooms and the splashing of the water. When the noise reaches a crescendo, I hold my breath. Next to me, I feel Erich's muscles tensing, waiting for the moment to strike.

A dark shadow appears in the doorway. In one fell swoop, Erich draws up his knee and kicks the policeman squarely in the stomach with a powerful blow of his leg. The policeman staggers forward, clutching his stomach. Erich punches him in the jaw, then draws his fists together and smashes them down on the back of his head with one powerful thrust. The hapless policeman groans and collapses to the floor.

I look at Erich in surprise.

"Quick! Help me get him on the bed," Erich hisses. Erich lifts the policeman by the shoulders while I grab his feet. Together, we drag him onto the bed; the policeman is out cold. Erich removes his shoes and ties his legs together with his old trousers, and then we cover the lifeless man with the sheet.

"Is he dead?" I say.

"Not half as dead as he'll be once the Policemaster and the Governor find out he let a dangerous German spy walk out of Fort Christian. Now, let's get the hell out of here. We have to cross the entire courtyard undetected. Stay behind me until we get outside, and then run away as fast as you can. Make sure no one follows you." I nod, silently praying that neither of us gets caught.

Erich pokes his head through the doorway and then strides with confidence out of the prison cell. He continues marching through the courtyard with the brisk, military stride of a soldier, his eyes focused on his goal of exiting the front gate alive. The prisoners jeer us and taunt us, they stick their arms out and try to grab us. This time I've learned my lesson and keep well out of reach. Erich passes the laughing grooms, who take no notice of us. With less than thirty feet to go, I see relief etched in Erich's shoulders and feel an undeniable elation surging inside of me. With freedom only seconds away, Erich reaches out to open the gate.

"Just a minute, Private," says a booming voice behind us. Erich stops dead in his tracks and slowly turns around.

A West Indian policeman in a crisp uniform with shiny buttons is observing us with the arrogant posture of the over-confident. At his side is a gleaming pistol. I feel my throat tighten.

"Have you checked in with Chief Larsen?" he says with the slightest trace of irritation.

"Yes, indeed I have," says Erich.

"Then please deliver this message to Captain Pedersen over at the Barracks," he says, handing Erich a large, official-looking envelope.

"It would be my pleasure," says Erich, tucking the envelope securely into his jacket pocket.

"So, I guess you'll be heading back to Denmark soon, eh?" says the policeman with a wide grin. "That is, after Transfer Day."

"Most definitely, but I'll certainly miss it here."

"I don't believe we've ever met, I'm Constable Gumbs."

"Pleased to meet you, sir," says Erich, sweat now trickling down his forehead. "The name's Lund."

"Well Private Lund, you'll be relieved to know we'll be getting rid of that German prisoner any day now. A British cruiser is due to arrive shortly."

"The sooner the better."

"And another thing," says the policeman.

"Yes?"

"Watch your back crossing over. Those damned U-boats are sinking every bloody ship they can find. The old Kaiser hasn't given up trying to win this bloody war."

"I'll remember that," says Erich, swallowing hard. "Thank you and good day, Constable."

"Good day, private, and don't forget us down here in St. Thomas. We'll miss you Danes when you're gone," he says, locking the wooden gate firmly behind us.

CHAPTER 32

With Fort Christian safely behind us, my breathing returns to normal. Erich says he knows a good hiding place down in Frenchtown where he plans to spend a day or two before returning to Aunt Esther's basement after dark. I press a few Danish kroner into his hand as he urges me to get lost in the crowd, to blend in as much as possible, then go home and stay out of sight for a while. He blows me a kiss goodbye before taking off while I turn and head in the direction of the Fish Market. I weave my way through the crowd of fish women as they yell out, "No fish, no dinner!" They are surrounded by an army of cooks, errand boys, and servants who have trudged from all parts of Charlotte Amalie to procure the day's sustenance—each one oblivious to the drama that has just unfolded at the fort. If there's an extra spring in my step it's because I have just accomplished something I believed was impossible: I have secured Erich's freedom.

My elation is short-lived when I realize that I have an entirely new dilemma on my hands, one that could prove extremely dangerous: several policemen, including the Assistant Policemaster, have seen my face. It's only a question of time before they connect my sudden appearance in the fort to the German prisoner's escape. If they figure out my identity, they may arrest everyone in Aunt Esther's house until they determine which one of us is the conspirator. The thought that Nana Jane may be implicated with me leaves me reeling with guilt. Either way, my life will be ruined.

Later, as I sit in the sewing room darning the latest sock, sweat trickles down my face when I realize that the Danish gendarmes could pound on our door any minute.

News of the prison break races around the island with the speed of a mongoose. By late afternoon, Nana Jane returns from the Governor's mansion with stories about angry accusations and furious allegations that have been hurled around the highest offices in this formerly laid-back Danish colony. Governor Konow banged his fist on his desk, blaming Policemaster Fischer for this embarrassing mishap, while Assistance Policemaster Larsen is holding the unfortunate policeman on duty responsible, who is pointing his own finger at the guard on duty who claims he doesn't remember a thing. The situation is a disaster and Governor Konow is calling for resignations. And to make matters worse, the militia and the gendarmerie are distributing wanted posters all around town which bear a crude likeness of Erich. When Mr. Isaiah brings one of them home, Nana Jane snatches it from his hand and tears it to pieces.

There's only one thing that everybody can agree on. Nobody thinks the escapades of a German spy who's obviously *bazudi* will hold up the long-awaited transfer. Everyone says that once the twenty-five million dollars are safely in the hands of the Danish Ambassador, the Americans will sail into the harbor and eat that no-account German spy for breakfast.

Those words are far from comforting. I feel as though I'm trying to stop a tidal wave from crashing over our heads. And with American ships in the harbor and Marines marching up and down the streets, my problems will increase a thousand-fold. Erich and I are playing a game of cat and mouse and I don't relish the idea of being a mouse in the jaws of an enormous cat. As Transfer Day draws near, I can barely contain my anxiety. My heart pounds and my nerves are on edge.

On the last day of March, I wake up to a dreadful sight. During the night the American cruiser *Hancock* arrived in the harbor and has taken her place beside the *Valkyrien*. At almost 500 feet in length, the *Hancock* is dreadfully large, emblazoned with a gigantic American flag, six large gun mounts, and the entire Fifth Marine Regiment that recently succeeding in quelling a rebellion in Hispaniola. Today's copy of the *Tidende* relates that the Commander of the *Hancock*,

Edwin T. Pollock, will assume the title of acting American Governor once the transfer goes through. This news gives me the sudden urge to take the *Tidende* and fling it over the balcony.

Over breakfast, Aunt Esther announces grimly, "I see no need for changing governments, changing flags, or any of this disruption to our lives. We were perfectly fine as a Danish colony for over two hundred years. This transfer is no reason to celebrate."

"Now Miss Esther," soothes Nana Jane. "We are being bought by the United States of America, that wonderful country. Isn't that something to be happy about?"

"Certainly not," says Aunt Esther with venom. "I don't want to be bought by anyone. I want all of you to leave me alone in peace!"

Nana Jane frowns and shuffles out to the kitchen, her brown slippers chafing the floor like the feet of an enormous tortoise. Cooky Betty picks up the breakfast dishes and follows Nana Jane outside. They don't have the patience to deal with Aunt Esther's tirades any more than I do.

When the time for the ceremony draws near, horse carriages start to appear from all over the island. We see groups of people arriving from Frenchtown, Smith Bay, Estate Tutu, Nazareth, Sugar Estate, Long Bay, Mafolie, Anna's Retreat, Bovoni, and as far away as the East End. People arrive by the dozens, some on foot, some in horse carriages, some in the occasional motorcar, while still others hop a ride on a cavalcade of donkey carts. It seems the entire island of ten-thousand souls has come to witness the historic transfer of the Danish West Indies to America first-hand, all dressed in their best clothes and with faces both solemn and hopeful.

At half past three, Nana Jane and I put on our straw hats and make our way down to join the spectators gathered near the Barracks. We assemble by the old frangipani tree just near the fence that borders King's Wharf. From here, we should have a perfect view of the ceremony, an occasion I have both anticipated and dreaded.

The harbor fills up with dinghies, schooners, and small sloops that huddle close to shore, their occupants standing on deck, eager and excited as they await the cannon salutes, the military bands, and the great wave of patriotic fervor that permeates the air. High up on the balcony of Fort Christian, another group of anxious spectators awaits with rapt attention. Schoolteachers, merchants, bankers, reverends and other respected members of society wait with great anticipation for the historic ceremony to start.

Over at the Hamburg-America Line, the inhabitants are anything but eager. Herr Lothar Langsdorff shows a disgruntled face as he glares out of his second-story window while the German flag flutters defiantly overhead.

All over Charlotte Amalie, spectators climb onto rooftops and balconies, hoping to catch a glimpse of the ceremony with their naked eye or through spyglasses. Erich says he will be watching from the safety of Mr. Greaux's fishing sloop out in the harbor, but as I scan the dozens of rickety schooners and sloops lining up offshore, his ship is nowhere to be seen.

A hush falls over the crowd as a Guard of Honor of Danish soldiers from the *Valkyrien* marches in unison, lining up in front of the Barracks. They stand at attention facing the harbor, a symbolic gesture that marks their imminent departure. Off to the side, a delegation of Danish officials in formal suits and top hats including Judge Neergaard, Lawyer Jørgensen and other members of the Colonial Council take their seats. I can scarcely wait to see what will happen next.

A Guard of Honor of American Marines from the *Hancock* in drab khaki breeches and yellow flannel shirts arrives on the scene, marching in perfect formation as they line up facing the Danish soldiers. Two soldiers—one Danish and one American—march together over to the flagpole on the Saluting Battery to change the national flags while a Danish gun crew mans the cannons.

Just before four o'clock, Governor Konow strides over to King's Wharf to greet Commander Pollock with a fifteen-gun welcoming salute. As Pollock alights on shore, Governor Konow draws his sword and thrusts it high over his head in formal greeting. Commander Pollock tugs at his sword to return the salute, but it refuses to budge. He pulls and pulls, but the sword stays put. Finally, the sword slides out as the relieved American draws it high over his head, returning the Danish Commander's salute. They cross swords as the audience draws a collective sigh of relief, and then they march through the parting crowd towards the Barracks to sign the transfer protocol.

After what seems like an eternity, Governor Konow and Commander Pollack emerge from the Barracks to take their places in front of their respective Guards of Honor. An expectant hush falls over the crowd. The only sound comes from the rustling of the leaves in the trees and the flapping of the Dannebrog high above. Governor Konow, stiff and somber, proclaims in English for all to hear, "Conforming to the order of His Majesty, King Christian the Tenth of Denmark, I have now with the representative of the President of the United States of America, signed the protocol for the transfer of the Danish West Indian islands to the United States of America and I fulfill this act by hauling down our old flag. Lower the Dannebrog!"

Down it comes. After the Guards of Honor present arms, a lone Danish soldier is given the difficult task of lowering the Dannebrog for the last time over Denmark's beloved colony. As the flag is lowered, a band plays the Danish National Anthem and the cannon brigade fires a twenty-one-gun salute. By now the crowd is silent, watching the scene unfold as they shed many tears. Nana Jane, too, is crying. Every woman young and old is crying; all the men are crying as well. Big tears roll down their faces at the sight of the Dannebrog coming down for the last time. All the Danish officials are crying and everyone watching from the balcony of Fort Christian is crying. It seems the entire town of Charlotte Amalie is crying.

Two weeping gendarmes who make no attempt to hide their emotions remove the Dannebrog from the flagpole and present it to Judge Neergaard, who stands stoically in the middle of the delegation, just like the bust of old King Christian IX over in the park. Judge Neergaard takes the flag, salutes the gendarme, and accepts it in the name of the King.

The Guards of Honor change places and present arms while Commander Pollock proclaims he is officially taking the islands into possession of the United States in the name of the president. Three petty officers from the *Hancock*, tall, spry, and deeply tanned after spending several months quelling rebellion in the Dominican Republic, hoist the Stars and Stripes up the flagpole, where it flutters proudly in the breeze. The sight of it shocks us into a new awareness that we are now standing on American soil. The transfer of the Danish West Indies is complete. Denmark's two hundred and fifty years of colonial rule has officially come to an end.

Commander Pollock announces that he is the new Acting Governor of the Virgin Islands of the United States of America. Governor Konow passes in front of the Danish Guard of Honor and the two Commanders march off to the landing stage where Commander Pollock returns to his ship to a seventeen-gun salute in his honor. The ceremony which I have both longed for and dreaded is now complete.

The crowd slowly disperses, most of them in a state of shock and bewilderment. Nana Jane points out Mr. Lockhart, one of the richest merchants in town, as he makes his way through the crowd, sobbing audibly. Lawyer Jørgensen supports a very tearful Madame Moltke, a local Danish aristocrat, as she retreats to her waiting carriage, dabbing her eyes with a lace handkerchief and pressing her hand to her heart.

Nobody expected the huge outpouring of shock and grief at being cast aside by Mother Denmark. As I gaze through the weeping crowd, I notice that on the roof of the German Consulate, the German flag that was flying so proudly just a few moments before has suddenly been snatched off the flagpole and removed from view.

Later that evening Deborah De Castro invites me to a formal dinner her parents are hosting for some friends and dignitaries. Over a sumptuous meal, Mr. De Castro holds his glass high and toasts, "To the jewel in Denmark's crown. On paper they may call us Americans, but in our hearts, we will always be proud Danes, servants of His Majesty." Everyone returns the toast and drinks, albeit with a certain measure of sadness. A banker named Clausen remarks that the transfer ceremony reminded him of a state funeral.

"I suppose I shall have to sell my farm out on Leinster Bay," he says with profound grief. "I will always miss the dignity and warmth of the island people when I return to Denmark."

"If it weren't for this damned war, the Danes wouldn't be in the awful position of selling their colony," says another man with a scornful face. Everyone nods in agreement.

"If you ask me, it's the planters' fault for not dealing fairly and honestly with the sugar cane workers that brought this calamity upon us," wails Mrs. Clausen, the banker's wife. "Governor Helweg-Larsen fell under the spell of that David Hamilton Jackson and greatly mismanaged the situation. The last straw came when he ordered us to cancel our plans for celebrating two hundred and fifty years of Danish rule, as if a celebration of that magnitude were something to sweep under the carpet. It was one grave error after another."

"Politics, my dear, pure politics," replies Mr. De Castro. "Governor Helweg-Larsen was afraid that any show of celebration would be perceived back in Denmark as an act of rebellion against the transfer. They were afraid it would quash the negotiations. The governor held himself up under extraordinary pressure, but the situation became too much to handle. There was nothing further he could do."

"If only he had urged Copenhagen to bring about the reform measures sooner," mourned another Dane.

"It wouldn't have helped," countered Banker Clausen. "The people lost heart and began to cry out for change. Sadly, it seems that after all these years, they never thought of themselves as proud Danes, but as simple island folk. Seeing the Dannebrog lowered was like losing Schleswig and Holstein all over again. Today was a sad day indeed."

Everyone agrees and clink glasses.

Mr. De Castro then relates a curious story that as soon as Commander Pollack returned to his ship, Lothar Langsdorff delivered him a terse note announcing his immediate resignation as German Consul of the former Danish West Indies. Everyone at the table agreed that matters between Berlin and Washington are deteriorating rapidly and war seems imminent. Will Langsdorff leave the island for good or will he stay and fight? These thoughts swirl through my mind as I watch the dinner guests mourn the loss of their beloved colony.

CHAPTER 33

Under the leadership of Major Dyer, the Fifth Marine Regiment hastily assembles their headquarters, which consists of a cluster of army tents set up in front of the Barracks. For their part, the Danes pack up their belongings, sell their homes and businesses, kiss old friends and neighbors good-bye, and start trickling back to Denmark. They are visibly despondent at having to leave their elegant homes, comfortable positions, and cherished way of life. Many tears are shed as they leave a lifetime of memories behind, feeling as though their Mother Country has cast them aside like an unwanted child.

Nevertheless, trouble still looms on the horizon. New posters appear all over town bearing a crude sketch of Erich and the words, PRISONER AT LARGE. I find one hanging in front of the Custom House and tear it down. Then I run to the Grand Hotel and the Apothecary Hall and tear more down as well. Everywhere I look, I find menacing posters of Erich that I tear down. Then I run home to show them to Nana Jane. When she sees them, she lays her hand against her cheek and declares, "Abigail, your Erich is in a lot of trouble. And so will you be if you don't tell him to leave."

Later, Deborah De Castro stops by to show me one of the posters her father found lying on the Governor's desk.

"I showed this to Mrs. Robles and she swears this is the man she saw with you," she says, eyeing me like a cat eyes a bird. "Is this the poor fisherman you befriended?"

"No! It doesn't look a thing like Knud."

"I sense that you're hiding something," she says, narrowing her eyes. "Tell me the truth, Abigail Maduro. Is this the man you've been helping?"

"No, of course not! How could you say such a thing?"

"Because this is the man that tried to shoot the governor," she says, eyes blazing. "That's called attempted murder. Do you know how serious that charge is? Tell me the truth: are you mixed up with this man?"

"I already said I wasn't. Anyway, Langsdorff forced him to do it. Erich never meant to harm—"

"Oh, so now his name is Erich," she says in a voice dripping with sarcasm. "I caught you in a lie and now I see you've been lying all along. And to think that I once trusted you."

"He's not a murderer," I say, hotly. "He was blackmailed. He was pretending to cooperate with Langsdorff to protect his family."

"So the story keeps changing," she says, her face contorting with rage. "Do you really expect me to *believe* that harebrained tale? Do you think I enjoy being made a fool of? I brought you into my house and lent you my books so you could turn around and give them to a cold-blooded killer?"

"You're wrong. Langsdorff is the killer, not Erich. Erich deserted so he wouldn't have to sink any more passenger ships. He abhors killing. You've got to believe me."

"Abby, have you lost your mind? Have you befriended a German spy?" she says, her face a mask of disgust. "How could you do this to me?" She crumples up the poster and throws it on the floor, tears streaming down her face. "Shame on you, Abigail Maduro! And to think I treated you like a sister."

Her accusation leaves me speechless.

"Look how you repaid me..." Her voice trails off as she buries her face in her elegant lace handkerchief.

"Please Deborah," I whisper. "Please understand. I never meant to harm you or anyone else."

"I don't believe you anymore," she says, her face a mask of rage. "What will people say when they find out I associated with you? I never want to speak to you ever again."

My cheeks burn with shame as Deborah turns on her heels and marches off.

***

Later when I'm alone with Erich, I show him the poster and his face turns white. The likeness is so similar he can no longer hide the fact that he is the wanted man in the picture. Simple disguises are no longer enough to guarantee his freedom. And if the Americans catch him, God knows what will happen.

Erich throws the poster down, grabs his knapsack and starts collecting all of his belongings, but I know in my heart that running away is not the answer. He has to stay and fight.

I grab his arm. "What are you doing?"

Erich jerks free and faces me with eyes I have only seen once before, the day we first met. Once again, Erich has the eyes of a hunted animal.

"I'm getting out of here," he says. "Things have gone from bad to worse. The island is crawling with Marines. It's just a question of time before the Americans declare war on Germany and the next time they catch me, I'll be finished. I was a fool to stay here for so long."

"What will you do?"

"Catch a freighter, or maybe one of those tramp steamers docked down at the wharf. Frankly, I don't care anymore. I just want to get as far away from here as possible. I've had enough of this lousy war."

"Don't be so rash," I say. "Here you have a job and a safe place to stay. Out there, you don't know a soul."

"Which may be the safest option."

"Perhaps, but you'll be a sitting duck. One lone German doesn't stand a chance."

"What do you mean?"

"When I came here from Panama on a Canadian steamer, the ship and every port we docked in was crawling with German spies and saboteurs. They're literally everywhere. They'll recognize you in an instant. Now, if we can turn the tables on Langsdorff and get him arrested for espionage, your problem will be solved. Later, I can get you papers saying you're a Danish citizen. No one will be the wiser." I watch as Erich listens in thoughtful silence. "And besides, you'll never find another pair of nurses like me and Nana Jane the next time you catch dengue fever."

"Of course, how could I ever think of leaving dear old Nana Jane," he says. "But has Nana Jane ever faced a firing squad? Has Nana Jane ever been tortured to confess?"

317

"Before they torture you, they first have to catch you, and I'll make sure they don't. Our first order of business is Herr Langsdorff. We've got to find a way to stop him, and then the rest of your problems will just fade away."

Erich shakes his head. "You're still a naïve young girl. Don't forget, Langsdorff is an ambitious man who wants nothing more than to end up in the Governor's mansion while I languish in prison or worse. Nobody will believe me. It's his word against mine."

"You're forgetting I have friends in high places that can help us. Don't run away. Stay and fight for what you believe in. If you leave now, I know we'll never see each other again. Stay here and we'll fight this together. Between us and Langsdorff, he doesn't stand a chance."

Erich listens in silent contemplation, and then he lets his knapsack drop to the floor. With a loud sigh, he collapses on the bed and buries his face in his hands. I suspect that for now, I have won the argument. It seems that Erich will stay.

"I have it on good authority that a tramp steamer is leaving town in two hours," he mumbles, rubbing his forehead with the palm of his hand. "My last ticket to freedom. But you make a convincing argument. All right, Miss Abby, I have no choice but to stay and fight."

***

The next day, Erich and I plan our attack.

"Abby," he says, pointing to a map of downtown Charlotte Amalie. "The Marines have imposed a strict curfew over the entire island. No one is allowed out after sunset. Our only chance is to act in broad daylight which increases our risk of getting caught. And with my German accent and lack of papers, I can't risk being stopped and questioned. We must infiltrate the Hamburg-America Line building and search for any tangible proof that Langsdorff is spying under the noses of the Allies."

"I'm certain he has a secret radio transmitter and a code book."

"That's good," he says. "Any one of those items would buy me good will with the Americans, but not my freedom. A code book is always a golden prize during a war. And that's where I'll need you. Together we can enter into the Hamburg-America Line building under the pretext of purchasing a ticket. Somehow, we have to get to his second floor office and search it. If Langsdorff is there, I will

318

keep him busy while you search his desk, his closet, his filing cabinet. Once you find anything resembling a code book, snatch it and get out fast. Don't worry about me. Exit as if your life depended on it. The Marines would never bother to search a girl like you. Are you up to the challenge?"

"This sounds crazy."

"You're the one who wanted to fight," he says, lifting my chin. "And remember one thing, if Queen Coziah could stare down the Danish gendarmes and win, you can tackle a pussycat like Langsdorff. You are uniquely suited to crawl under Langsdorff's desk to search it. I need you."

"Erich, I don't think I can do this."

"I know you can. You have all the makings of a superb intelligence agent. You're brave, resourceful, cunning, and you've got a helluva right hook. Besides, it beats sewing for a living, doesn't it?"

"What if Langsdorff pulls a gun on you? He's liable to do something desperate."

"Don't worry about me," he states firmly. "Just find the code book and get out."

"And how will I know when I've found it? I don't speak a word of German."

"Good question," he says, taking out a pencil. "Let me give you a quick lesson. Codes are merely a simple form of substitution. They can be a combination of letters, numbers, phrases, or symbols. You don't need to know German to recognize a cipher book. Just look for a small, nondescript manual filled with meaningless words and phrases that are connected to groups of numbers. Once you see something that fits this description, grab it and get the hell out. Let me handle Langsdorff. Then go and find a safe place to hide. If you don't hear from me in a day or two, take the book to that judge friend of yours. He'll know what to do with it. Do you understand everything I've told you?"

I nod my head, but inside I'm quaking with fear.

When it's time to go, I slip Queen Coziah's secret obeah potion into my pocket, hoping and praying it will bring me luck, then we head downtown. It's amazing to see that despite all the changes that have taken place, life still goes on. Stores open their large wooden doors, donkey carriages still meander through the crowds to market, merchants and clerks lean under the shade of their awnings, watching for customers, while laborers lazily push wheelbarrows back and forth; the smell of tobacco, rum, and exotic spices waft through the air, lending an air of mystery to the surroundings.

A gang of prisoners from the fort trudges out to repair a road as foremen shout out orders. Every now and then, the prisoners cast a wary eye at the khaki-uniformed Marines with their field hats, breeches, rifles, ammunition packs, and boots as they patrol the town in platoons of twenty. As the Marines march through town with their rifles on their shoulders, they chant in loud, American-accented English while keeping their eyes forward, never wavering from their duty. Watching these American boys out here in the tropics reminds me of my days in Panama, which are quickly fading from my memory.

As we make our way down an alleyway, my heart skips a beat as we spy Marines patrolling alleyways, inspecting shops, questioning everyone's identity. As we pass the Grand Hotel, we see some officers loitering in the lobby, sending telegrams or waiting for a haircut and a shave. Keeping a low profile, we pass by, avoiding eye contact. Thankfully, the Marines disregard us, considering us no more than nondescript locals in straw hats and sandals. The relief on Erich's face is palpable.

By the time we reach the Hamburg-America Line Building on Tolbod Gade, I sense that Erich is getting tense. Sweat starts running down the sides of his face, and his muscles are taut. Out of the corner of my eye, I catch his hand brushing up against his Luger pistol, making sure it's safe and secure. At the building's entrance, Erich stops short, turns to me and says, "Remember to stay behind me and keep out of sight as much as possible. When I confront Langsdorff, go to work. Search all his drawers, and then get out as fast as you can. Don't worry about me."

I nod and brace myself for the mission we're about to undertake.

Erich swings open the door and strides in with forceful steps. He marches past a sea of desks, each one occupied by a harried clerk typing out endless bills of lading or talking to customers on telephones against a cacophony of clacking typewriters. A few of the clerks notice us as we pass, but soon return to their tasks at hand.

At the far end of the office is a nondescript staircase. Erich hurries toward it when a voice suddenly booms behind us.

"May I help you?"

We spin around to face a petulant clerk with a black moustache and eyes that radiate impudence. Erich eyes him with a good measure of caution, but doesn't flinch.

"No, thank you," says Erich, turning to leave. "I have a meeting with Herr Langsdorff."

"Don't bother thanking me," says the surly clerk. "Until I've actually done something for you."

"I'll remember that," says Erich, who mounts the staircase with aplomb while inside I can feel my stomach turning somersaults. When we reach the second floor, we head down a dimly-lit corridor as the din of the downstairs fades in the background.

About halfway down, we arrive at an office flanked by a plaque bearing an official-looking coat of arms and a prominent German flag. The sign underneath proudly proclaims this to be the office of the German Consul. We pause for an instant, our eyes locking. Though no words pass between us, we both know what the other is thinking: it's now or never. Erich touches my cheek and silently turns the knob.

Erich storms into the office and marches right up to Langsdorff's desk, catching him off guard. Langsdorff is seated behind an imposing mahogany desk, talking to someone on the telephone. As soon as he sees Erich, he fumbles with the receiver and almost drops it. When he realizes he has no other choice, he mutters something in German and slams the receiver down. Although I'm standing behind Erich, I can almost feel Langsdorff's eyes burning a hole right through him. Just to be safe, I crouch down and hide where he can't see me.

"Well, well, the great German hero," sneers Langsdorff, feigning disgust. "How do you have the nerve to show your face after the disgraceful way you conducted your mission?"

"You got your headlines," says Erich. "You wanted shooting, you got shooting. I turned the whole island into pandemonium. All you lack is a dead body, which you'll never get from me. I'm sure your ineptitude has Berlin in an uproar."

Langsdorff's face darkens. "You swine! You're a disgrace to your uniform and your heightened sense of morality has clouded your senses. You're useless to the Fatherland."

Erich doesn't flinch. "I fired the gun and caused uproar. Killing a neutral naval commander won't bring the Kaiser the quick victory he craves. Give up, Langsdorff. You're fighting a lost cause."

Langsdorff jumps to his feet, instantly catching sight of me.

"What is *she* doing here?" he says with outrage. "I happen to know she's connected to some very important Danish officials on the island. Seibold, have you crossed over to the other side?"

This time, I decide to stand up to Langsdorff.

"Erich is not a disgrace," I say. "He just refuses to take orders from men like you."

"What do you know about men like me?"

"A lot more than you think."

Langsdorff wags a finger in my face. "I know I've seen you before. Yes...now I remember. You came over on the *Guiana*. It was you who was running around with that nosy sailor."

"You mean the nosy sailor that you killed."

Erich looks at me with astonishment.

"He got what he had coming," says Langsdorff, picking up the telephone again. "As will your bumbling friend here. Seibold, not only am I *not* going to recommend you for the Iron Cross, I'm going to recommend they court-martial you for desertion and treason. I'll have my man in San Juan wire a message to Berlin—"

Before Langsdorff can finish, Erich smashes his fist into his face, sending him hurtling backwards. Blood spurts from Langsdorff's nose as he screams out in pain. And then, one of Langsdorff's henchmen, the same one who accosted us on the street, bursts through the door and pounces on Erich. He tackles him from behind and throws him against the wall. Stunned, Erich recovers and responds with some well-placed blows of his own. Not quite finished, the German launches his fist at Erich's face and sends him staggering to the floor.

I dive under Langsdorff's desk and start rifling through his drawers, looking for any evidence that will put him away for good. I search through files, boxes, memos, journals, fueled by a thirst for vengeance and justice, determined to make Langsdorff pay for what he did to Ian and what he plans to do to Erich.

Meanwhile, the German grips Erich's arms behind his back just as Langsdorff staggers to his feet. With menacing eyes, Langsdorff lands a solid punch across Erich's face, sending blood spurting everywhere. Erich braces himself for another blow, but Langsdorff holds off, sneering, "I should have shot you the day I found you hiding out on this tropical island, you worthless coward."

Erich jerks his head backwards, striking the other German in the nose. He connects with such force that the goon totters backwards in pain, rendered useless. Erich turns and finishes him off with a swift, powerful blow to the back of the head. The German stumbles and collapses. Meanwhile, Langsdorff charges at Erich. Erich blocks his fist and lands some well-placed blows to his stomach and chin. Langsdorff retaliates in a blind rage, then picks up a vase and launches it at his face, but Erich ducks in time, causing the vase to shatter against the wall, spraying the two men with blinding shards of crystal. Erich races forward and strikes Langsdorff with his fists, then lands a solid kick against his left flank.

I peer inside the last drawer. Hidden at the bottom is a wooden box smaller than a shoe box and about half as high. I pull it out and tear open the lid. What I find makes me freeze in shock. Inside is a small, nondescript tan volume containing the words *Kaiserliche Marine* embossed on the front in bold black letters. *Is this the coveted cipher book?*

As I leaf through it, I'm shocked to see it contains pages upon pages of words and simple phrases, each one linked to a random group of numbers, some three digits, some four, some up to five. This has to be it. I stuff the book inside my dress and then crawl out from under the desk. Avoiding the combating men, I make a dash for the door. Before I reach it, the other German regains his senses and realizes what I've done. He lurches forward and dives for my legs, causing me to topple forward and land on my stomach. Like a deranged lunatic, he pulls me towards him as I scream at the top of my lungs. He grabs my skirt with such ferocity that I fear he will tear me to shreds.

I pound my attacker's head with my fists, but this only causes him to tighten his grip on me. When he makes a grab for the book, I sink my nails into his face and he cries out in pain. And then, to my horror, he wraps his iron grip around my neck and starts to squeeze.

In that moment, my whole life flashes before my eyes. I see my father and my mother, both faces gripped with fear. I reach out to them, but they shake their heads. The message is clear: this is my battle and my battle alone. Mustering every last ounce of strength, I reach for a broken vase, but I can't quite grasp it. It's out of reach.

Time is running out. By some stroke of luck I grab the broken vase. With supreme effort I manage to lift it and smash it against the German's head. He screams in shock. Blood spurts from a large cut on his head. He reaches up to touch the wound, releasing his death grip from my neck. To my eternal gratitude, my attacker falls backwards in shock.

By now Langsdorff has his hands locked around Erich's throat. Erich's face is bloated and turning blue, sweat pours down the sides of his face as he gasps for air. My muscles seize with fear, but deep inside my mind's eye, I see a vision. My mother tells me that if I don't act, Erich will be gone for good. A second later, I grab Langsdorff's telephone and smash it against the back of his head. He utters a moan and loosens his grip on Erich's neck.

Recovering quickly, Erich grabs Langsdorff by his head and pounds it against the wall. Then he smashes the side of his face with his fist. At last, Langsdorff slumps to the floor, immobilized. Quick as a wink, I retrieve Queen Coziah's potion from my pocket and pull out the cork. I kneel down and pour a few drops into Langsdorff's gaping mouth. Though I have no idea what the potion contains, my only hope is that it keeps Langsdorff in his stupefied state. As Nana Jane says, there's no harm in a little obeah magic for some added insurance.

With Langsdorff safely out of commission, Erich grabs my hand and we race out of the office. We hurry down the hallway frightened out of our wits as I manage to blurt out that I pinched Langsdorff's code book right out from under his nose. Erich breaks into a grin and squeezes my hand. I don't remember the last time I saw him looking so happy.

By the time we reach the landing, Langsdorff has pulled himself to his feet and comes staggering to the doorway. We hear his blood-curdling scream reverberating down the hall, "Traitor! Disgrace! You betrayed your Fatherland!"

Erich jerks around. "I don't work for you anymore, Langsdorff."

Langsdorff drops to his knees and passes out. Wasting no time, we race down the staircase and head for the exit, running as if our lives depended on it while I clutch the code book for dear life, terrified it will slip through my fingers. When we reach the bottom,

Erich pushes aside a clerk who has wandered into our path, causing him to cry out. A few other clerks glance up from their typewriters, their faces darkening with suspicion. Just before we reach the door, another clerk, the haughty one from before, steps in front of us, blocking our path.

Erich gives the man a powerful thrust, sending him staggering backwards, spilling his coffee, and overturning a large stack of files. Some of the secretaries jump up to rescue him, but they are stopped by a shower of files, telegrams, and memos that Erich has thrown in their path. To the sounds of loud oaths and insults, we jump over the beleaguered clerk, who is splayed helplessly on the floor, as Erich calls out in as cavalier a manner as possible, "Thank you, old boy."

Once outside the building, we dive into the nearest donkey cart with Erich promising the driver two dollars if he'll take us to Judge Neergaard's house on Government Hill. The driver smiles cordially, tips his hat, and says, "Good day to you, sir." Without another word, we start off down Norre Gade as Erich pulls a threadbare blanket over our heads to the gentle clip-clop of the tired old donkey. A short while later Erich lifts up his shirt to reveal the holster and the incriminating Luger pistol that has caused so much trouble for the governor.

"This and the code book will be the final nails in Langsdorff's coffin," says Erich, beaming. "Once we get these into the hands of the Americans, he's finished."

A short while later, the carriage driver points us towards the 99 Steps, explaining it would be faster to finish the journey on foot. We tumble out of the cart and after Erich dusts himself off and pays the driver, he explains that we must deliver the code book to Judge Neergaard with the understanding that he will take it without delay to Major Dyer of the Marines. Once Langsdorff recovers from this unexpected assault, he's sure to have his men hunt us down to exact their revenge, but by that time we should be in hiding. Just thinking that Langsdorff's end is forthcoming gives Erich every reason to smile.

"Langsdorff will soon be reading about the war from the inside of a prisoner-of-war camp," he says, smiling with satisfaction. What Erich doesn't consider is that Langsdorff may slip away and evade justice for good.

CHAPTER 34

After many insistent knocks and a few shrieks for help, Wilhelmina thrusts open the door, her face a look of annoyance.

"Not you again," she says, eyeing me with displeasure, but when she sees Erich's bedraggled appearance, she does a double take. She sizes him up and shakes her head, "Look what the cat dragged in." It takes a few more minutes of begging and pleading before she finally allows us inside.

When she sees Erich's bloody nose, she retrieves a wet rag and presses it against his bruise, then she races off to fetch the judge, occasionally casting worried glances in our direction.

Thankfully, Judge Neergaard is in good spirits and comes marching down the hallway to greet us. I introduce him to Erich, and the judge shakes his hand with the warmth of an old friend. When I explain to Judge Neergaard the urgency of our visit, he ushers us into his private study. When he closes the door, I hand our war prize over to the venerable judge as my chest swells with pride. Unabashedly, I explain that the German code book came straight from Langsdorff's own desk, and will undoubtedly be a valuable prize to the Americans. Judge Neergaard leafs through the volume with awe and admiration, his blue eyes twinkling with delight.

"This is astounding," he proclaims. "You've both made a valuable contribution to the Allied war effort. I commend you both for your bravery and initiative." Judge Neergaard turns to Erich with a mischievous grin and adds, "So, at last I get to meet the mysterious stranger who's been stirring things up on this once tranquil island. I happen to know that Abby thinks the world of you, as I do of her."

"That makes two of us," says Erich. "I just hope I can pay you back for everything you've done for her, and for me."

"Not necessary," says Judge Neergaard. "I leave all score settling to the Man Above. I realize it must have taken tremendous courage to stand up to Langsdorff. You both deserve a reward for that."

"My greatest reward is Abby's happiness," says Erich. "She's the best friend I've ever had. And I'm also grateful for all you've done for her. Without the two of you, I would have given up long ago."

"Nonsense," says the Judge. "You were brought here for a reason. Sometimes we don't see the results of our efforts for many years, and that's if we're lucky."

"There's one last thing, sir," says Erich, handing the Luger pistol, minus the magazine, over to the judge. "This also belongs to Langsdorff. Please make sure it reaches the proper authorities."

"My, my, you are a resourceful character," says Judge Neergaard, his eyebrows shooting upwards as he accepts the incriminating evidence from the man who may possibly have saved Governor Konow's life. "I take it this is the pistol that caused so much commotion. Erich, despite what the police say, I believe you risked your life to save the governor's, and for that I commend you. It took me until now to comprehend why my work in the Danish West Indies has continued unabated for so many years. Indeed, I relish the chance to accomplish this final task if it means putting Langsdorff and his men out of commission for good."

Judge Neergaard calls out to Wilhelmina for his jacket and hat, then calls to his driver for his carriage. He places the code book inside his briefcase and winks at me, "Come, my dear. We shall deliver this war booty to the Allied soldiers and return to your friend later for a celebratory dinner. In the meanwhile, I suggest that Erich take a hot bath and change into a clean shirt to improve his bedraggled appearance. Wilhelmina, please draw a bath for this young hero and give him a fresh shirt. And now, dear Abby, let's head down to Marine Headquarters and have a little chat with the man in charge. We have some very important business to attend to."

During the ride to town, Judge Neergaard is silent, lost in his thoughts. "Do you realize, Judge Neergaard," I say, interrupting his reverie. "That this is the second time you've saved my friend? Are you worried that people will accuse you of aiding and abetting a German war deserter?"

"My loyalties are to my King, my family, and my beloved country. I don't fear their accusations for the simple reason that I have a distinct advantage."

"Oh? What's that?"

"I'm an old man," he says, eyes twinkling. "At my age, there's not so much at stake. This is also my way of taking care of a little unfinished business. It's the least I can do for my good friend, Sam Maduro."

We arrive in front of Marine Headquarters and pass through all the checkpoints. They take us to the officer on duty who, in turn, leads us to Major Dyer. The Corporal pulls me aside and tells me to wait in the hallway until I'm called for. He points to a wobbly chair and goes back to typing a report. Through the clackety-clack and the constant ringing of telephones, I make out the conversation between Major Dyer and Judge Neergaard. I wait for the corporal to get sidetracked by a long-winded conversation before I snatch a look through the half-open door.

Major Dyer's office used to belong to the Captain of the Gendarmes and has been stripped bare except for a makeshift desk, a rickety wooden chair, and a useless-looking filing cabinet. Every other usable object has been cleared out by the Danes and shipped back to Denmark.

Major Dyer stands up as Judge Neergaard enters. He has the same rigid bearing and muscular build as the American soldiers I used to see policing the Canal Zone on horseback; he's exceedingly tall, broad-shouldered, and possesses a firm handshake and determined eyes that communicate a strong sense of duty and purpose. Dyer wears a khaki jacket secured with a generous leather belt, breeches, and on his head he sports the wide-brimmed field hat with the rounded top. Judge Neergaard shakes hands with the tall, handsome Marine.

"Please excuse the lack of suitable accommodations, your Honor," says Major Dyer, waving his arm to show the sparse furnishings. "Once your countrymen started packing up all their furniture, they got a little carried away and shipped everything back to Denmark save a few gas lamps and one or two wash basins. I sure hope they're not in desperate need of gas lamps back in Denmark." Dyer calls out to a waiting corporal to bring in another chair, which he places next to the judge.

"Have a seat, your Honor," says Dyer, heading for a bottle of rum and two glasses. "Can I pour you a drink? What's your poison?"

"Thank you, Major, but no," says Judge Neergaard, removing his hat. "I'm turning over a new leaf. After all these years, I've decided to listen to my better half and swear off spirits."

The Major removes his hat, pours himself a drink, and takes his seat. "As you wish, now, to what do I owe this honor?"

"I'm here to clear up a rather messy matter," says Judge Neergaard. "I've come on behalf of a man who has being wrongly accused of espionage."

"Are you referring to the man they picked up for attempting to shoot the governor? The one that slipped out of the fort?"

"Precisely," says Judge Neergaard. "You see, there's been a terrible misunderstanding. It's very difficult for me to say this, but the man responsible is actually my son. He's been suffering from an acute mental condition for some time now..."

"Excuse me, your Honor," says Major Dyer, reaching for a cigarette and lighting it. "This story sounds like it's going to be a good one and I don't want to waste the opportunity to enjoy a fine Cuban cigarette."

"Please go right ahead, Major. You see, my son is suffering from a condition they call *dementia praecox*. It's quite serious. He complains of peculiar voices telling him to do strange things. Sometimes, the voices are so persuasive he gets carried away and forgets right from wrong. I believe that on the day in question, the voices told him to shoot the governor. Somehow my son managed to steal the pistol that caused that awful scare to His Excellency the former Governor, but I assure you that he had no cognizance or forethought about what he was doing. I know my son; he meant no harm. He was just trying to quiet the voices in his head. He has no history of violence and is usually kept secluded. On the day in question, he slipped out of the house and joined the crowd in front of the podium. We may never know why he fired that pistol but he can't be held accountable for his actions."

"So, the man who tried to shoot the Governor is in fact your son?" says Major Dyer, taking a long puff of his cigarette. "And according to you he's mentally deranged and you're willing to vouch for him?"

"That's precisely what I'm saying."

"Then how do you explain that the bullet came from a German Luger pistol?" says Major Dyer, eyeing the judge through a grey column of smoke rising from the burning cigarette.

"He could have acquired it from any number of places," says Judge Neergaard, taking the pistol from his briefcase. "Although I have reason to believe it belonged to Herr Lothar Langsdorff, the former German Consul. It's even possible that Herr Langsdorff tricked my son into shooting the governor for his own personal benefit. He has bragged quite openly about wanting to launch a German invasion of these islands and would do almost anything to achieve his goal. Major Dyer, everyone here, including the King's physician, Dr. Viggo Christensen, knows about my son's condition, but no one ever dreamed he would steal a gun and attempt to shoot someone. He is quite insane and we're still not sure how he escaped. Right now, he's heavily medicated and doesn't remember anything from the day in question. Tragically, this condition has no cure."

"I see," says Major Dyer, pensively. "How unfortunate, but somebody on the inside had to be helping—"

"With all due respect, Major Dyer, you don't know my son. He can imitate anyone. The only explanation I can offer is that he somehow managed to fool the jailers and talk his way out the front gate. Now there is another matter that may be of even greater interest to you." Judge Neergaard pulls the code book out from his briefcase and hands it over to the Major.

"What's this?" says Dyer, opening up the book.

"This is an SKM, or *Signalbuche der Kaiserliche Marine*. A German code book. Until today it was the property of Lothar Langsdorff. I suggest you pay him a little visit to chat about some of his recent expeditions tracking Allied ship movements and sending coded messages to the German Consul in Puerto Rico."

"Excuse me if I'm a bit speechless right now," says Dyer. "It's been a long and hot afternoon, but could you please explain to me how you acquired a German code book? I'll need it for my report, not to mention when I finally get to writing my memoirs."

"I would prefer not to divulge that information," says Judge Neergaard with a wry smile. "It's a little complicated to explain."

"Let me guess," says the Major. "Is this also connected to your son?"

"Would you believe me if I told you?"

"Probably not," said the Major, polishing off his drink. "From the look on your face, I knew this was going to be a whopper. I'm pleased to admit you have not disappointed me."

Dyer stands up and walks over to the window. He picks up a pair of field binoculars and trains them on the Hamburg-America Line building across from King's Wharf.

"I've been waiting for instructions from the War Department in Washington as to when to start rounding up the Germans on the island," he says without averting his eyes. "We've got them under constant surveillance but they're getting awfully jumpy lately. They're used to operating in broad daylight, but in the short time we've been here, we've already managed to cramp their style."

Dyer turns to face Judge Neergaard. "Right now, we have forbidden the German ships from leaving the harbor, at least the seaworthy ones, and my boys are just walking around picking ripe mangoes off the trees, waiting for the orders to impound those devils. When the day comes, we'll invite the Kaiser's boys over for some tea and crumpets." He holds up the code book with admiration. "I'm sure this code book will be of great interest to Naval Intelligence, and it could mean a promotion for somebody, although I'm not naming any names. I'll take the matter regarding your son under consideration, and I'm obliged to you for taking the time to come over here and clear up this matter." Dyer shakes the judge's hand and adds with a wink, "It was a pleasure meeting you, and I wish you and your son a pleasant trip back to Denmark."

"Oh, the pleasure is all mine, Major Dyer," says Judge Neergaard. "...all mine."

CHAPTER 35

It's happened. America has finally declared war on Germany.

Less than a week after Transfer Day a telegraph arrived from Washington and within an hour the Marines went marching through town, rounding up nearly the entire German community to the collective gasps of their neighbors.

After pounding on the Germans' doors, they order the men to get dressed before they haul them off to the *Calabria* for safekeeping. They locate the entire crew of the two German steamers plus all the German employees of the Hamburg-America Lines. All along Kongens Gade and down the entire length of Tolbod Gade, spectators gape and point as the Germans are led through town and down to the docks where they are forced to board their prized steamer as prisoners.

Soon word goes around that the Germans are protesting their arrest and demanding to be set free. They insist they are innocent civilians and have nothing to do with the war in Europe. They scream and shout, demanding to speak to the American commanding officer. To their credit, the Marines ignore their incessant demands and go about their business with equanimity and steely resolve. However, there is one important official who is noticeably absent from the procession of surly Germans. Herr Lothar Langsdorff is nowhere to be found.

Given his high-profile position as a former German consul and director of the Hamburg-America Lines, I can't imagine how

Langsdorff managed to slip past the Americans. According to the prattle around town, when the soldiers came pounding on Langsdorff's door, his wife was in hysterics, claiming that he'd been gone for days. For all we know, he could be anywhere.

For their next order of business, the Marines descend on the Hamburg-America Line building. In a massive onslaught, they raid the office and cart out boxes full of incriminating evidence while the few remaining employees look on in outrage. I can only imagine the anger on Langsdorff's face as he watches the Americans hauling away all his precious evidence as he stands in the shadows, powerless to stop them. As I walk back through the alleyways and side streets of Charlotte Amalie, I worry about how and where Langsdorff will strike next.

Since Transfer Day, Commander Pollack has left his position as governor and returned to his duties on the *Hancock*. In his first official act as the new governor, Rear Admiral James Oliver, issues an Executive Order with ominous overtones:

All citizens or subjects of the German Empire, or of those countries allied with Germany in the present war, who are now residing or sojourning in, or who may in the future come into, the Virgin Islands of the United States, are required to register with the nearest Policemaster—on or before May 1, 1917—and within twenty-four hours after landing.

Later that day, Erich informs me that he wants me to meet somebody important at the Grand Hotel. Together we head downtown, walking past dozens of Governor Oliver's placards that scream out to us from almost every door and wall that we pass. As a German soldier behind enemy lines, Erich and I are well aware that the stakes are now much higher.

The hotel's lobby is crowded with sun-tanned Marines who loiter about, getting haircuts and shaves, writing postcards, drinking bottles of soda, or buying cigarettes and souvenirs. Erich pushes his straw hat lower over his face as we wend our way through the throng and up to the second floor dining room. With Erich's dark tan, nobody would ever dream that he had once been an officer on a German U-boat. The wandering vagabond I stumbled upon six months ago has been transformed into a regular native.

We reach the second-floor restaurant and head over to a table at the far end where a bearded man sits contemplating a steaming mug of coffee. I've never seen this man before, and am quite certain he's not from the island. He's a swarthy middle-aged man with a black beard, a broad chest, and he wears a Captain's hat and a navy blue shirt. I get the strangest sensation I know him from somewhere, but I can't remember from where.

As soon as he sees us, the stranger gives us a broad smile and waves us over. Erich shakes his hand and the man claps him on the back like a brother.

"Abby," says Erich, "Allow me to present Captain Miguel of the *Cartagena*. He arrived here only yesterday and as soon as I spotted her, I ran over to greet him. I never dreamed I would see this old sea dog again. I knew it had to be a sign."

"I told you that you wouldn't be able to get rid of me that easily," says Captain Miguel. "And now that you're back on my crew, I'll make double sure you stay put for a while."

"Back on his crew?" I say, surprised to hear my voice rising. "What's he talking about? What's going on?"

Erich places his hands on my shoulders and gazes into my eyes.

"Abby, it's for the best," he says. "Look around you. The island is crawling with Marines. I'm not safe here anymore. Deep down, you knew the time would come when I would have to leave. The longer I stay here, the worse it will get. It's time I moved on."

"After everything we've been through? How could you even think of leaving?"

"There's a war going on," he says. "Don't forget who I am and what I am."

Captain Miguel polishes off his coffee and throws down a few coins.

"A sailor is what you are," states Captain Miguel. "And a damn good one at that. I'll see you at 1600 hours. Close up business and be prepared to sail at 1800 hours. I need to pick up a few supplies downtown."

"Aye aye, Captain," says Erich. Captain Miguel nods in my direction. "Goodbye, Miss," he says, and then he disappears down the staircase.

I turn my back to Erich.

"Abby, don't do that," he says, turning me back in his direction. "Don't you see it's all for the best? Do you want to see me end up in a dirty prison camp like the other Germans? Don't forget I'm still a wanted man. There's a price on my head."

"Of course, I don't want you to be arrested. But I told you Judge Neergaard can get you Danish identity papers. Don't give up so easily."

"Judge Neergaard has already done enough for me," he says. "And what if they think my papers are forged? And what about the policemen and the prisoners who could recognize me from the fort? My picture is all over town now. Don't you see? It's only a question of time before the Americans put two and two together. Staying here is too dangerous."

When Erich reaches for my hand, I pull it away. I follow him down the stairs and back through town in a black cloud of despair. We've been through too much for me to go it alone now. We stop at the house to collect his knapsack and his few belongings, and then we head back downtown to a dry goods store so he can buy a new pair of dungarees. After we make the purchase, we pass through an alleyway on our way to the dock. All of a sudden, from out of the shadows, a shadow jumps in front of us. Startled, Erich and I stop short and utter a collective gasp. Standing there is none other than Lothar Langsdorff.

Langsdorff eyes us with menacing intent. His face is crimson, his breathing heavy. He advances toward us. Fearful, Erich and I take a step backwards.

"I believe we have some unfinished business to attend, Herr Seibold," sneers Langsdorff, clenching his fists.

"I have nothing to say to you," says Erich. Next to me, I sense Erich's muscles clenching as he shifts his weight from side to side. "Step aside and let us pass."

"This time I'll make you pay for your betrayal," screams Langsdorff, his face contorting with rage. "Traitors are always tried and shot, but I'll save you the trouble of a trial."

Langsdorff brandishes a knife and raises it. Quick as a flash, he lunges at Erich's throat. Erich dodges the blade, but almost loses his balance. With the agility of a leopard, Erich pounces on Langsdorff, shoving him so hard that he stumbles backwards. Furious, Langsdorff screams and charges at Erich again, this time aiming for his heart. Erich grabs Langsdorff's arm with one hand and punches him solidly across his face with the other. Infuriated, Langsdorff smashes his fist into Erich's face and kicks him so hard, he falls backwards. I scream at the sight of Erich lying on the ground, but I'm powerless to save him. I'm too paralyzed with fright.

Erich staggers to his feet, blood oozing from his nose as his breath comes in heavy spurts. He dives at Langsdorff and with one powerful thrust of his leg, kicks the knife from Langsdorff's hand and sends it flying. The knife lands several feet away, out of reach of both men, giving Erich the opportunity to pound Langsdorff's chest with the full force of his fists, sending him flailing backwards.

With one final burst of fury, Langsdorff pounces on Erich, punching him until he's lying helpless on the ground. Then Langsdorff smashes Erich's head into the cobblestones, almost knocking him unconscious.

Wounded and weakened, Erich manages to draw his knees to his chest, and then pound his legs into Langsdorff, hurling him backwards onto the cobblestones. Enraged, Langsdorff stands up, draws his Luger pistol and aims it at Erich's head.

"Say goodbye, traitor," he says coldly. "I have every right to defend myself from a deranged lunatic."

"Go to hell, you madman," Erich hisses, blood oozing from the gash in his head.

Desperate, I look around for some way to save Erich. In a flash, I seize a wooden crate and smash it down on Langsdorff's head. The crate shatters into a hundred pieces; Langsdorff drops the gun, stumbles a little, and then falls to the ground, motionless.

Erich pulls himself to his knees, his face a bloody mess. He crawls over to where the pistol lies on the ground, picks it up, points it skyward, and removes the magazine. He staggers to his feet and looks down at Langsdorff's lifeless body, then up at me with sheer amazement.

"Good work, Abby," he says.

"Is he dead?" I say, my whole body shaking with fright.

Erich kicks Langsdorff's shoulder. A faint groan emits from Langsdorff's bloody lips as he turns his head to the side.

"Not yet, but he'll be a pussycat now, thanks to you."

He grabs my hand and leads me swiftly towards Back Street just as two Marines clamber out of a rum shop. Erich pulls me to the side and tells me to run over to the Marines and inform them that one of the Germans was caught trying to escape, the one who was in possession of the secret code book.

"Make sure they understand that Langsdorff is wanted by the Authorities, they should take him down to Major Dyer at Marine Headquarters at once. I've got to get out of here before they spot me. I'll be sailing soon, so I'll say my goodbye now. Abby, thank you for everything. I'll never forget you. You're the best friend I've ever had. I hope one day I can repay you for everything you've done."

"You're leaving?"

"I have to go. Listen to my accent. It's quite obvious I'm German, not to mention the fact that my face is on a hundred wanted posters. I have to leave the island as soon as possible. You know it's for the best. Goodbye, my precious one. And remember this…I will always love you."

My eyes fill with tears. "Erich…"

But it's too late. Erich is gone.

He disappears into the crowd. I swallow hard, trying to burn his face into my memory. His smile, the color of his hair, his boyish grin, his muscular arms, his sense of humor, the way his eyes light up whenever I tell him a joke; these are all aspects of Erich I have come to love. Without realizing it, this impromptu tropical interlude has meant more to me than I ever imagined. It has restored my very soul. It brought me a love so profound it changed my life forever.

But now it's all over.

I sigh and head toward the two Marines, intent on ridding these islands of Lothar Langsdorff, and his plot to take over the Danish West Indies, forever.

As I stand there while the Marines haul Langsdorff away, I'm filled with the greatest feeling of accomplishment and joy I've ever experienced in my life. Watching their eyebrows shoot up when I explain that the man lying crumpled on the ground is a wanted German spy is reward enough for possibly losing Erich forever. My only wish is that somewhere in heaven, Ian McShane is watching too.

***

Despite my elation at seeing Langsdorff taken away, I'm miserable by the time I get home. Without Erich, the house is empty and lacking purpose. Nana Jane and Cooky Betty are arguing over something, but as soon as they see me, they go silent.

For a minute, the three of us just stare at each other, not knowing what to say. Nana Jane seems somehow different. Her eyes have lost their usual glimmer. She looks thinner, frailer. Her beautiful, childlike eyes seem distant.

"What were you two arguing about?" I say.

Cooky Betty raises one eyebrow and then crosses her arms over her chest in indignation.

"Never you mind that Miss Abigail. You just tell me how you thought you could keep such a big secret from Cooky Betty. Yet you told *her*," She points an accusing finger at Nana Jane. "Whose *best* friend I happen to know is de biggest gossip on de whole island."

"I wasn't supposed to tell anyone. I only told Nana Jane because I needed her help."

Cooky Betty's expression changes from one of resentment to one of hurt. I realize for the first time how awful she must feel always living in Nana Jane's shadow. After all, Nana Jane was quite a beauty in her younger days, and she still draws a crowd whenever she goes down to Market Square. The thought that I might have inadvertently caused Cooky Betty anguish fills me with tremendous guilt.

"Where is your Erich now?" says Nana Jane.

"He's gone. He's leaving the island for good."

"Good for him," she says. "This island ain't big enough for a regiment of American Marines and a crazy German soldier who can't decide which side of the war he's on."

Cooky Betty shakes her head. "Abigail, you were either *very* brave or *very* foolish. You could have gotten yourself killed."

"Yet I'm still here, aren't I? And I stopped Herr Langsdorff from going through with his wretched plan to invade these islands. I guess that means the two of you are stuck with me for a little bit longer."

I grin at their surprised faces until they burst out laughing. Then they hug me and tell me to go wash up for dinner.

I retreat to the quiet of my room where my mother's photograph waits for me on top of my desk. I waste no time filling her in on all the latest details, how I saved Erich's life by knocking Langsdorff senseless, how I got rid of Langsdorff by delivering him to the Marines. But most of all, I tell Mami how Erich and I saved her beloved island of St. Thomas from a German invasion, and how it will at last fly the American flag. In her own way, Mami smiles back at me, though I know she can't see me or hear me. I hope that wherever she is, she's proud of me.

I shut my eyes for a moment, imagining what life will be like without Erich around. No jaunts down to Market Square, no pony rides, no hikes up Bluebeard's Hill, no swimming down at Mosquito Bay. Life without him will be dull, dreary, and colorless, like Aunt Esther's lifeless string of pearls.

Maybe it's still not too late.

I bolt from my chair and race to the balcony. To my eternal relief, I see the *Cartagena* floating down at the dock. Maybe there's still time.

I peek down the hallway. Nana Jane and Cooky Betty's good-natured bantering reverberates from the dining room, then grows softer as they leave for the outside kitchen. A thought enters my mind and then a wave of guilt rushes over me. I know they'll both miss me, but staying here without Erich is impossible, unthinkable. I hope they understand.

I grab my satchel and throw in some clothes, a toothbrush, some soap, a brush, my diary, and most precious of all, Erich's cameo pin. I rip a piece of paper from my diary and scrawl a quick note telling them I'll miss them, but I couldn't bear to live without Erich. I fold the note in half and leave it on my desk. Then I grab my satchel and hurry out the door.

I arrive down at the docks without incident. The *Cartagena* flies the Spanish flag, but is a wreck if I ever saw one. Rust has taken hold and spreads over her seams, hatches, superstructure, and anchor chain like a bad case of scarlet fever. Her derricks are bent out of shape, her ropes are in tatters and her one remaining lifeboat looks as if it's in danger of sinking. I wonder if Erich knows what he's doing.

Her crew looks like derelicts from Devil's Island. They're on the main deck engrossed in a rowdy game of cards, yelling and shouting and pushing each other with glee. Other sailors lounge on the wharf smoking cigarettes and eyeing me like wolves. A wave of relief washes over me when Erich appears on the deck. I shudder to think of him spending months at sea with this rowdy bunch of good-for-nothings.

Erich doesn't see me; he's hard at work arranging shipping crates on the hot deck as he checks items off a clipboard. I call out to him and he looks up, surprised to see me. He throws down the clipboard and races down the gangway to greet me.

"Abby, why did you come here?" he says. "I thought we said goodbye."

"I'm coming with you."

"You're *what*?"

"You don't expect me to stay here all alone, do you? Not after everything we've been through. Look, I've even brought my very own sea bag. This time I'm coming with you and you can't stop me."

"Now hold on a minute," he scolds. "Do you think I'd let you board this broken-down kettle drum with these no-good ruffians? A ship like this is no place for a lady. Besides, you've got dreams and goals. Didn't you always say you wanted to become a teacher? I'm not going to let you throw that away to chase a no-account scoundrel like me around."

"You're not a scoundrel. You're all that matters now. Don't you realize that I love you?"

He grabs my shoulders. "Don't talk like that. Come to your senses. I'm a German war deserter. An enemy. Don't pin your hopes on a man with no future. You've got your whole life ahead of you."

"And I want to spend it with you."

He stares into my eyes. "Do you think I'm made of stone? Don't you think I want the same? But now is not the time. I'm a wanted man. You've done all you can to help me, but now I must move on. And as for you, no more heroics. Keep a low profile. Maybe, just maybe if I manage to survive this damned war, I'll come back and we can build a life together. Promise me one thing. Don't give up your dreams. Keep them alive and work toward them. A wise man once said, *If you dream so big it fills the sky, you'll move men's hearts.*"

"Did you just make that up?"

"No," he chuckles. "That was also Goethe. But I know that when he said it, he had you in mind. You're a girl who dreams big. Don't throw it all away for me."

I press my cheek against his chest. "You're all I want, Erich. Promise me you'll come back for me one day."

He strokes my face. "You know I can't promise that. Not with the war still going on. Not with a price on my head. I can tell you this, you've changed my life. You taught me how to trust again. I'll never forget how you sacrificed everything for me."

"You can still change your mind..."

"Abby, I have to go," he says, lifting my chin. "Just keep your dreams alive. You've already come very far. Do you remember what Queen Coziah said about looking down the barrel of a gun? You've done it and you've won. Look how you tackled Langsdorff. You're the bravest girl I've ever seen. Nothing can hold you back. Promise me you'll stay put and believe in your heart that some day we'll see each other again."

I nod with hesitation and then I press a slip of paper into his hands.

"At least take this. It's a letter of introduction to my cousin in Curaçao, a safe, neutral Dutch island. Try to stay there until the end of the war. Maybe he can help you find a job and give you a place to live."

Erich glances at the paper then tucks it into his trouser pocket for safekeeping.

"Oh, I almost forgot," he says, taking a folded handkerchief out of his pocket and handing it to me. When I open it, I'm astonished to see that it contains his prized U-boat medallion. I stare at it in shock.

"Keep it, Abby," he says. "As a thank you for everything you've done. You've shown me the meaning of loyalty and friendship. But more than that, you've shown me the meaning of love."

I'm too shocked to respond. "But, Erich, this is your most precious possession. Why?"

"I came here hoping to escape the war, but instead I found something truly worth fighting for, you my dear."

A single tear slides down my cheek as Erich pins the medallion on my dress. Then he brushes the tear aside, saying, "I hope this goodbye is only temporary."

I throw my arms around Erich as he kisses my hair and clasps my face between his hands. Then he plants a kiss on my forehead with such tenderness that all my fears and worries melt away. He gives a courtly bow, then turns and heads up the gangway. When he reaches the main deck, he gazes down for the last time. He salutes me like a soldier and then disappears down the hatch.

CHAPTER 36

For the longest time, I sit in Emancipation Garden watching the usual comings and goings, the fish women bantering and teasing each other as they scale and clean the fish, children frolicking in the dirt, nannies in high-necked dresses pushing baby carriages, soldiers loitering about, writing postcards and smoking cigarettes. The clock on Fort Christian strikes the hour as the leaves rustle gently in the breeze. Life moves on with or without one's permission, with or without the ones you love.

I caress Erich's medallion, feeling its gentle curves, admiring its glistening gold surface. Then I slip it into my pocket, pick myself up, and wander back home, wondering how I'll ever be able to go back to my old life of sewing endless piles of clothing. Somehow, I have to find a way to change my life before I sink into the same despondency and bitterness that claimed Aunt Esther's soul. If that happens, it may be too late.

By the time I reach home, something strange is going on. A crowd of people stream into Aunt Esther's house as the dreadful sound of wailing pours out to the street. What happened? I quicken my pace, terrified of what I may find.

When I reach the door, I collide into Cooky Betty. She has a frantic look on her face and pulls me by the arm through the crowded hallway, telling me how worried sick she's been since my sudden disappearance. She tells me she doesn't have the strength to handle two losses.

"What do you mean by that? What's going on?"

"Oh Abigail honey, she collapsed right in front of my eyes," says Cooky Betty. "Mr. Isaiah and I dragged her to the bed, but she lost all movement in her arms and legs. She just wore out. Now she acts like a doll, not speaking, not moving. It can't get much worse. What's gonna happen, Oh Lord?"

"Who collapsed?"

Cooky Betty leads me to Nana Jane's room where I find her lying helpless on the bed, while huddled beside her are Dr. Christensen, Aunt Esther, Mr. Isaiah, Miss Lucy, and a few of our neighbors. Everyone is crying, wringing their hands, wailing in agony at Nana Jane's sudden illness.

"Abigail," says Aunt Esther, grim-faced. "Nana Jane had a stroke. She can't speak very well, but she wants to see you."

I kneel down next to Nana Jane, tears streaming down my face. Nana Jane's face has lost all expression; her warm and tender smile is all but gone. When I gaze into her fading eyes, I see the same love and kindness as before, a love I know can never be extinguished, but her body is slipping away. I fear her time with us will soon be over.

"Nana Jane..." I sob. "What happened? What's wrong?"

"The good Lord calling me home," she whispers.

"You can't leave me now," I say, burying my face in her chest. "I need you."

"I have to go," she whispers. "My job almost finished."

"But Nana Jane, I can't live without you."

"You gonna be fine," she says, closing her eyes. "You already home. You almost all grown up. Now I can go home ..."

Dr. Christensen pulls me aside. "Nana Jane's worn out, Abigail. Let her rest awhile. I've already instructed your cook and Aunt Esther on how to keep her comfortable. Later, I'll send over a trained nurse, but right now, she mostly needs your prayers."

"Yes, of course. Thank you, Doctor."

Dr. Christensen doffs the brim of his hat and leaves.

Standing behind him is Deborah De Castro, who managed to enter the house unannounced. As soon as Aunt Esther spots her, she yells, "How dare you enter my house?" Everyone gasps. Deborah's face blanches. The neighbors look visibly shaken; some of them cover their mouths and take a step backward. Deborah purses her lips and says, "Esther Maduro, I know you've held a grudge against my father for thirty years, but he didn't take your money as you've always accused him. He's innocent."

The room falls silent. All eyes turn to Aunt Esther.

"Then tell me where my money went," says Aunt Esther, her body shaking with anger.

"That question can only be answered by your fiancé, Jacob Curiel," replies Deborah. "He left for Panama with a trunk full of money, but fate intervened and took his life. Some of the money he absconded with belonged to *my* family as well. And my father has all the bank records and drafts to prove it. My father is a decent, honorable man; he would never resort to stealing. It's time somebody finally told the truth."

Deborah turns and storms out of the house. I watch as she slams the door behind her.

"I suppose I won't be seeing any more of Deborah De Castro," I mutter under my breath. Cooky Betty pushes me into a chair and urges me to drink a cup of bush tea. "That's alright," she says. "A crab never forget he hole. Your home is here with us. Let her find another friend."

***

Nana Jane's funeral is held in her beloved Moravian church after which her coffin is placed on a simple wooden carriage and driven down Main Street as a procession of mourners follows close behind. The mourners, almost all women and most of them from the old days of Charlotte Amalie, are dressed in the appropriate mourning attire of navy blue, purple, and black. They cry bitter tears into dainty handkerchiefs, heaving their shoulders and raising their hands to the heavens.

All along Main Street, the shopkeepers close their doors and awnings out of respect for the dead. Men remove their hats and stand by the side of the road as the funeral procession wends its way to the Moravian cemetery on the west side of town. Nana Jane's passing has left the town of Charlotte Amalie bereft of one of its beloved daughters.

Under the shade of a glorious mahogany tree, Nana Jane is laid to rest near the graves of her sister Adelaide and her mother as the Minister recites the Twenty-Third Psalm. Aunt Esther is so overcome with emotion she clings to Cooky Betty's arm like a helpless child as she sobs for her beloved Nana Jane. I suspect that she is finally coming to terms with the death of her long-lost fiancé who died so many years ago in the malaria-infested jungles of Panama. Perhaps these tears will at last free Aunt Esther's soul from the shackles of a doomed love.

Nana Jane's death leaves me deeply saddened. She was my last link to my parents, the last link to my family, the last link to my past. And now that she's gone, I realize that she had been more than a friend to me. While I watch Nana Jane's coffin being lowered into the earth, I recall an old expression my mother used to say, that if life is a gift, then friendship is the ribbon on that gift. For me, Nana Jane had been the ribbon of true friendship.

By the end of summer of 1917, Judge Neergaard announces over dinner at the Grand Hotel that he's well enough to return to Denmark. His final wish is to spend his remaining years with his daughter, son-in-law, and grandchildren. He promises to leave me all his English books, his phonograph, his writing desk and all the proceeds of selling his horse and carriage as a down payment for teacher's college. He says I've learned so much over the past year that he's sure I'll pass the entrance test with flying colors. "It's the very least I can do for my old friend, Samuel Elias Maduro," he says, giving me a wink. When the time comes to say goodbye to Judge Neergaard, I wave to him from the dock as his ship pulls out of the harbor. I owe so much to this courageous, kind-hearted judge. In many ways, I owe him my life.

***

Mornings are different now that the Americans have taken over the island. Instead of the gendarmes hoisting up the Dannebrog and firing the old cannon, a solitary Marine raises the Stars and Stripes to the accompaniment of a bugler. No one is quite certain what to make of all these changes, but sometimes down by the Fish Market, when the Marine band starts playing the American national anthem, I catch the old women standing with their hands placed reverently over their hearts, their eyes gazing up to the Heavens in awe.

Before she died, Nana Jane used to say that although everyone was poor under Danish rule, they were happy. Life followed an old, established pattern. Their food came from the sea, their water from the sky. The sugar cane brought the gift of rum and gladness, the chance to forget the past. The quadrille dance brought merriment and celebration. She said that one of the reasons why Transfer Day had been so solemn was because nobody knew what the future would bring. She believed with all her heart that coming under America's protective wing would be good for the people and now I believe it too. When the war finally ends, I hope the people will be imbued with a greater sense of optimism about their future. I hope I will be as well.

CHAPTER 37

While dusting out the sitting room, I catch a glimpse of the calendar and realize that more than a year has passed since Erich sailed away. When I reflect on all that's happened I can scarcely believe that I managed to navigate my way through all the turmoil and upheaval like a sturdy schooner through the eye of a hurricane. By the look of things, I would say I've even managed to thrive. I learned to make Aunt Esther respect me, and I managed to build a new life for myself on the island. Everywhere I go people wave to me and call my name. The market women down by Market Square and the fish women over at King's Wharf, even the children frolicking down in Emancipation Garden, they call me "Miss Abigail." They know I'm the granddaughter of Samuel Elias Levi Maduro. Mami and Nana Jane would be so proud of me.

But I don't have much time for reflection nowadays. Since Nana Jane passed away, I've taken on more responsibilities around the house. I do most of the housework and I've learned to cook almost as well as Cooky Betty; Aunt Esther even confessed that my sweet bread is far superior. The money I earn from sewing pays most of the bills, and sometimes there's even a bit left over for a new dress, some stockings, or a bit of face powder. After all, I am a young lady of eighteen now.

Lately I've noticed that Aunt Esther has grown quite frail, so every morning I bring her a cup of coffee and some sweet bread to her room. Sometimes I even sit beside her and read her the newspaper. She accepts my presence and on several occasions I'm pretty sure I saw her cracking a smile when I read her a cartoon.

***

One hot, listless day in June of 1918, I receive an unexpected present. Down at the post office a letter is waiting for me bearing a postmark from the Netherlands Antilles. Erich! For the longest time I stand there staring at my beloved prize, tracing his familiar handwriting with my finger, reading the words over and over, scarcely believing my good fortune. I head over to the park, clutching the precious letter to my chest, hoping this feeling will last forever. I sit basking in the presence of old King Christian as I read the letter over and over. Since Judge Neergaard left, he advised me to keep the old king company from time to time, to make sure he never feels forgotten.

In the letter, Erich tells me everything that's happened to him since he sailed away on Captain Miguel's tramp steamer. Together they traveled as far south as Dominica, Barbados, St. Lucia, and Trinidad, then they headed over to the port of Willemstad, Curaçao where Erich decided to hop off and wait out the end of the war.

Needless to say, Captain Miguel was sorry to see his old friend leave for the second time, but he guessed by then that Erich was a man in exile; as long as the war in Europe continues to rage, he will never belong to any country or have a proper home. With a twinge of regret, he watched Erich descend the gangplank for the final time, then turn to salute his dear Spanish friend. Then Erich made his way through the marketplace before disappearing into the crowd.

Captain Miguel didn't realize it, but Erich stood for several minutes behind a display of straw baskets, watching his old friend alone on the deck, wishing his dear Spanish friend Godspeed. Erich was never good at long farewells.

He also writes that he located my cousin in his fine home in Scharloo, presented him my letter of introduction, and my cousin responded by helping him find him a job and renting him a room in his house. Erich says he's saving all he can so that once the war is over, he can return to Germany to reunite with his parents. Since all the mail is censored, he can't write to them directly, so he just stuffs the letters in his knapsack and waits for the day when the fighting is finally over. He assures me that he misses me, especially when he sees a girl with long, unruly brown hair and large, inquisitive almond-shaped eyes. He ends his letter with a quote by Goethe, '*A noble person attracts noble people, and knows how to hold on to them.*' Erich ends by saying that I am that noble person, and one day he will repay me for saving his life.

A few days later, while I'm out sweeping the porch, I hear a familiar bird call followed by a strange rustling sound up in the branches of the mango tree. I peer upwards and am amazed to see my old Teddy high up in the branches, strutting back and forth, fluttering his wings like a proud peacock. I call out to him, but he just cocks his head as if to mock me. For some strange reason, I burst out laughing. My dear Teddy is alive! My heart soars with joy and my hope for the future is renewed. If Teddy can survive all by himself, then I know that somehow it will all work out.

When the days get too hot and stifling to sit in the sewing room, I steal down to Mosquito Bay to take a refreshing dip. Then I relax on the powdery white sand, watching the turquoise water that stretches all the way to the horizon, glistening like diamonds on a field of sapphire. I strip down to my petticoat and wade in the warm water, letting it envelop me. As I stretch my arms, kick my legs, and glide through the water, I imagine that across the vast stretch of ocean Erich is doing the same thing, letting the water embrace him like a dear old friend. Although miles separate us, we have the same silky sand beneath our feet, the same salty blue water hugging our bodies, the same warm sun on our faces. In this manner, the sea connects us. We are never truly apart.

***

Today I wake up with the strangest feeling that I must get out of the house. As soon as my chores are finished, I throw together a lunch and take old Clara over to Mosquito Bay. While Clara grazes on tall grass by the side of the road, I sit under the shade of a palm tree to savor a bottle of lemonade and some of Cooky Betty's Johnny cakes. Overhead, a flock of petrels soars in a circle, chiding me for not sharing my bounty. One of the bolder birds drops to the sand and runs toward me, like an admonishing schoolmarm, scolding me even as he tries to take a nip of my food. I wave him off, laughing at his childish prank. For now, my only companions are the island's creatures. They are my ever watchful, ever faithful friends.

Suddenly I hear a voice. Someone in the distance is calling out to me! Alarmed, I jump to my feet and search the long stretch of beach from side to side. Fear courses through my veins as I realize I am no longer alone. Up until now, the only sounds I have heard are the waves lapping on the shore, the palm trees rustling in the breeze, and the cries of the seagulls. Thinking that someone has been observing me while I was lost in my reverie gives me goose bumps.

About a mile down the beach, I catch sight of someone racing toward me: a man. He waves his arms and yells something I can't quite make out. My heart flutters with uncertainty and my knees quiver under my petticoat. I shield my eyes against the sun to get a better look at him, but he's still too far away.

Suddenly, he calls my name: *Abigail!* I realize all at once who it is and my heart pounds with excitement although I can't quite believe it. The man breaks into a run and when the sunlight catches his golden hair, my mouth falls open. *Is it possible?*

I race toward him, stumbling across the cascading sand dunes, and then fling myself into his arms. Hugging like old school chums we collapse on the sand in a state of utter delight, our laughter mixing with tears of joy. I cup his face in my hands and stare into those familiar blue eyes with shock and disbelief.

"You came back. You didn't forget me," I say, overcome with joy.

Erich runs his hand through my hair. "I was counting the days until I would see you again. How you've changed! You're different. You're all grown up now. My Abby is a fine young lady."

I smile with pleasure and wrap my arms around the man I have come to love, grateful that my wandering U-boat sailor has finally come home.

EPILOGUE

March 31st, 2001

By the time Claire finished reading the diary, the sun had risen, cruise ships were gliding into the harbor and all along Main Street the stores were opening for another day of frantic, duty-free shopping.

"That was incredible," said Søren, nursing a cup of lukewarm coffee. "An amazing story. A true gift, much more than I ever expected. So now I know the whole story, that your grandfather—"

"Was Erich Seibold," she said. "After the war he returned to Germany to see his parents. Naturally, they were both delighted beyond belief that their son was indeed alive, but the war had left his father's heart in a weakened state and he died soon afterwards."

"And then?"

"Grandpa stayed in Germany to take care of his mother, but the sea was calling him. He also had a little unfinished business to attend to. So, like the good sailor he was, he headed out to sea again. Erich and Abigail were married in 1919 and lived together in this old house until 1967, when he finally succumbed to a long illness. He lived just long enough to witness the fiftieth anniversary of Transfer Day. He was always proud to say that he had witnessed the first transfer and the fiftieth. And he always gave Grandma credit for risking her life to make sure it went on as scheduled."

"And Aunt Esther, what happened to her?"

"She died about fifteen years after their wedding. Her heart just gave out. But she loved Erich and Abby's children. She became their surrogate grandmother."

"And Deborah De Castro? What happened to her?"

"She married an American Naval Officer stationed on the island during the early days of naval rule. After the war, they moved to New York and I don't believe she ever returned to St. Thomas."

"Did your grandfather ever talk about how he gave the German code book to the Americans? Did he have any regrets about switching sides?"

"He never mentioned it. In that regard, he was a closed book. I was shocked to find out about it in Grandma's diary. I don't think anybody else knew about it other than Judge Neergaard. The story only came out after we read the diary. My grandfather was so secretive he never talked about the war at all. It was one of his big taboos. I think he was constantly haunted by how he had deserted his men. It was like a black mark on his soul. Of course, when his ship was sunk, he would have died alongside them, but when he married my grandmother, it was as if he was somehow making amends for his past mistakes. He knew that by marrying Abby, he not only saved her life, but his own."

"How so?" said Søren.

"He said that what they accomplished together showed that even ordinary people can do their part to change the world. Funny, but I never knew what he meant at the time."

At those words, Søren's expression changed.

"My God, now I understand..." he said. Claire looked at him, not comprehending his meaning. He walked to the balcony and stared out to sea, lost in thought.

"What happened?" she said, touching his arm. "Did I say something wrong?"

"You reminded me of something," said Søren. "My mother once showed me a letter written by my great-grandfather after he'd returned to Denmark. In it, he wrote something very peculiar that has haunted me all my life. He wrote: *'I did what I did because I never wanted to say the words 'I should have.' If I attempt to do something and fail, at least I can say I tried. And if I succeed, then I'm a far better man for having done it.'* Nobody knew what he meant by those words. It was always a mystery. Now I believe I've found the answer. I think I found what I came here seeking. I think I've finally solved the riddle."

"I'm not sure I'm following you..." said Claire.

"Then allow me to enlighten you."

***

After a quick breakfast, Søren and Claire freshened up and drove down Crystal Gade and over to the back part of town, to the section the locals called *Hospital Ground*. They pulled up alongside the quiet, fenced-in Danish Cemetery that lay under a canopy of ancient mahogany trees. Søren held the door open for Claire and together, they unlatched the gate of the cemetery and ventured inside. They strolled among the graves, enjoying the calm, peaceful setting as they read the various names and the dates on the headstones. Some of the deceased were born in Copenhagen and lived until a ripe old age; others were born in the West Indies and lived just a few short months. Søren and Claire were astonished by the sheer quantity of young men struck down in the prime of their lives, most of them the victims of some tropical disease, what they used to call *West Indies fever* in the old days. A young girl named Ingeborg, the daughter of a former Governor, was born in Copenhagen in 1880 and died in St. Thomas only three years later. Each austere tombstone represented a human drama. A life cut short. A young Lieutenant named Carl Dorph in the Danish Marines died at age twenty-eight; a young woman named Juliane Nissen died aged nineteen; a Captain of the Infantry, Ole Buntzen, born in Copenhagen, died in St. Thomas in 1820 aged just eighteen years; a baby named Oluf Eggars was born in 1874 and died in 1875, and on and on.

After several minutes of walking through the cemetery, Søren and Claire came to a stop in front of a monument that read:

Karen Neergaard
Born Bjerre, Denmark 1852
Died St. Thomas 1907
Beloved wife and mother

"There she is," said Søren, laying a bouquet of wild flowers on her grave. "My great-grandmother."

"Karen Neergaard?" said Claire, narrowing her eyes as she read the inscription. "Is she Judge Neergaard's wife? And she's your great-grandmother? That would make you—"

"Judge Neergaard's great-grandson," he said, matter-of-factly. "You see, I had more than a passing interest in Abigail's story. I came here to also discover a little about my own past. I grew up hearing stories about my great-grandfather. He was always a towering, larger-than-life figure in my family. He had been a respected judge in the colonies and was honored wherever he went.

But through Abigail's diary, I got to feel as if I knew him personally. He was a quiet hero; I'm convinced he never got over losing these islands. The day he watched them lowering the Dannebrog for the last time, a part of him died as well. But he knew that transferring the islands was the right thing to do. He passed away years before I was born, but I'm told I resemble him greatly. I'll leave that to the history books. But thanks to you and Abigail's diary, I know everything I need to know about who I am and where I came from. Now I understand everything."

Claire looked astonished. "I'm in shock. This is all so unreal, but everything's starting to make sense, especially when I got that crazy feeling that we'd met before. In a way, we have, a long, long time ago. Somehow we are connected through our ancestors, through history, through a bond of friendship that existed until today. But what did you mean when you said, 'now I understand'?"

Søren swallowed hard. "When Erich said that sometimes even ordinary people can change the world, I remembered something unusual about my great-grandfather. People used to say he would do the impossible if that's what life asked of him. I never quite knew what that meant until I read Abigail's diary. It wasn't his nature to operate strictly by the book; he did what he believed was right regardless of what society said. He lived his life for truth and justice.

"You see, ever since my wife's death, I've lived under a cloud of guilt. I've been blaming myself, thinking there was more I could have done to save her life. I worry that I'd left too many stones unturned. The guilt and the stress have come very close to pushing me over the edge. And though I'm ashamed to admit it, I'd even turned to alcohol to ease the pain. Oh, intellectually speaking, I know I did everything possible to save her life, but for a man like me, doing only the *possible* is never good enough. Like Henrik Neergaard, I should have attempted the *impossible*.

"When Henrik Neergaard risked his career and his good name to help Abby and Erich, he was doing the impossible. He knew his actions weren't right by the book, but they were morally right because he knew Erich was innocent. Believe me, if I could have done the impossible to save Lina, I would have. But only God can do that. In any case, I'm at peace now. For the first time in a year, I feel forgiven. Thank you, Claire, for sharing Abigail's story with me. By opening up your grandmother's diary, you've given me a priceless gift of all: peace. I felt my great-grandfather communicating with me through the pages of Abigail's diary; I also believe that Lina wants me to move on and find happiness again. And now, looking at my watch, I see we're almost late for an important ceremony we must attend."

Søren and Claire sped down Kanal Gade towards the waterfront. After parking in the large municipal lot adjacent to Fort Christian, they joined the hundreds of spectators heading to the annual gathering that convenes in the same spot every year to mark the anniversary of the transfer of the Danish West Indies to America.

By the time they arrived, a large crowd had already assembled in front of the bright green Legislature building that sits on a promontory in the harbor of Charlotte Amalie. This day, the 31st day of March was the 84th Anniversary of Transfer Day. Since Søren's ancestors had played such a pivotal role in the transfer, the Legislature had asked him to give a short speech about his family's recollections of the event.

The crowd, consisting of a smattering of local residents, government officials, members of the press, and the Danish Ambassador and Consul, was all abuzz with excitement. The weather was splendid; the sky was a brilliant blue and a welcoming breeze blew in from the harbor. When it was time for the ceremony to begin, a hush fell over the assembly. After a few obligatory speeches by the Governor, the Lieutenant Governor, the Danish Consul and several delegates from Washington, Søren was called to the podium.

He looked out over the assembly, trembling a bit, not only out of trepidation, but from the enormous pride and satisfaction that swelled inside of him.

"As the great-grandson of a Danish judge who presided over the first Transfer Day," he began. "It's my honor and privilege to be with you here today. My great-grandfather was not a man of many words. He was a private man, a dignified man, but he knew his responsibilities and he did what he believed was right. When the people of the Danish West Indies voted overwhelmingly in favor of the treaty to transfer their islands to the United States, he knew that stepping aside was the right thing to do. He loved the people of the Danish West Indies. This was his adopted home; the place where he raised his three children, where he hoped to see his grandchildren grow up. It's also the place where his wife and son are buried. Just a short while ago, I was in the cemetery paying my respects to them. They are at eternal rest in the land they loved so dearly that parting from it, even in death, was unthinkable. So, as you see, even though I was born thousands of miles away in Copenhagen, my connection to these islands runs deep. I know how painful it was for the Danish residents to relinquish the islands they loved so dearly. When it comes to giving up something you love, I unfortunately have very personal experience. It is often harder for the person who relinquishes.

"But today, it warms my heart to see that the ties between Denmark and the Virgin Islands continue to grow stronger with each passing year. I recently discovered that there are many stories regarding Transfer Day that have yet to be told. I have good reason to believe that, with time, these stories will be written down and more people will learn about that momentous time when a small Danish colony in the Caribbean passed from one flag to another, yet managed to keep the spirit and memory of both traditions alive and well. I have good reason to believe that Judge Henrik Neergaard would be proud of that. I also believe that if he were alive today and could see all the progress that's been made, he would be very proud of your accomplishments. May you continue to flourish and prosper in the land he called his home.

"I believe that one of the lessons of Transfer Day is that second chances in life are possible. Each new era brings its unique challenges and opportunities. Although it's painful to live for centuries under one flag only to be transferred to another nation, I believe that we can capture the best of both worlds by holding onto the values and customs we hold dear, and forging our dreams and visions for the future into a reality that we both can share."

When Søren had finished his speech, the crowd gave him a standing ovation. He shook hands with all the dignitaries as they handed him a small plaque in commemoration of the event. When he finally returned to his seat, Claire greeted him with a congratulatory hug, saying, "You were wonderful. Your speech was extraordinary, a real gift."

Søren gazed into Claire's eyes. "And meeting you has also been one of the greatest gifts of my life. Thank you for sharing Abby's diary with me. I hope we can spend many more years together, getting to know each other, and the island that brought us together."

Blinking back tears, Claire was too overwhelmed to speak. Søren squeezed her hand and gave her a gentle kiss. As their eyes connected, Claire was amazed to see that Søren's appeared to be glowing.

Author's Note

While *Transfer Day* is entirely fictional, after the first draft was completed, my research partner came across an astounding real-life event that proved that the story was entirely plausible.

The event concerned the murky fate of the U-581. The U-581 was a German U-boat operating during World War II (many years after the setting of my story) that was noted for its unusual and abnormal breakdown in the camaraderie and respect that usually existed between U-boat officers and their crews, something that was considered necessary for the proper functioning of the vessel. This deterioration caused the U-581 to be rammed and sunk, and 41 members of its 46-man crew were taken prisoner.

The U-581 was operating under the command of *Kapitänleutnant* Werner Pfeifer who, according to the testimony of the crew taken under Allied detention, fell under the influence of his Engineer Officer, Helmut Krummel, a man roundly hated by the other sailors for being an uncompromising martinet. While prowling the waters around the Azores, the U-581 was rammed by the British destroyer *Westcott* on February 2, 1942. Just prior to the ramming, the crew managed to don lifejackets and abandon ship. One of the officers, a well-liked fellow by the name of *Leutnant zur See* Walter Sitek, managed to escape the British by swimming to nearby Pico Island—neutral Portuguese Azorean territory—where he eventually found his way back to Spain and then Germany, where he ended up in command of *three* more U-boats: the U-17, the U-981 and the U-3005. Beating all odds, *Oberleutnant* Walter Sitek survived the war and lived to tell the tale.

Another true incident that provided enormous inspiration for the novel involved the April, 1917 arrest and imprisonment of German enemy aliens working as officers and crew of ships belonging to the Hamburg-America Line (*Calabria* and *Wasgenwald*) in the island of St. Thomas in the former Danish West Indies. The Director of the Hamburg-America Line office, a generally well-liked German citizen, was also found to be in possession of a code book, which he used to send wireless messages to Germany in contravention of President Wilson's proclamation. Subsequent research suggests the Director was actually a member of the secretive German organization called *Ettapendienst*, a Naval Supply System that was a division of German Naval intelligence. The *Ettapendienst* was charged with collecting intelligence and supplying German auxiliary cruisers, merchant marine ships and U-boats. As Germany had lost most of her overseas colonies and territories by the beginning of World War I, the *Ettapendienst* agents needed superb organizational skills since they acted as the primary suppliers of food and fuel for the German Navy as well as coordinators for the transportation of German agents. Most members of the *Ettapendienst* were naval officers, but in addition, many possessed qualities such as a) the ability to blend in with civilians, b) the ability to speak local languages, and c) social finesse. Many of these *Ettapendienst* agents ended up establishing their own espionage networks as well. The real life *Ettapendienst* agent portrayed in my story had a happy ending. After the Americans took over the islands, he was picked up as an undesirable alien and shipped to a military detention center in Georgia. After a bit of legal wrangling, he was reunited in 1918 in Ellis Island with his lovely Danish wife (a descendant of a Danish Gendarme who became a prominent St. Thomas businessman) and their three young children. The family was deported back to Germany (via Copenhagen on a Scandinavian steamer) where they spent the remainder of their lives.[1]

By November of 1918, the United States Government had seized property belonging to the Hamburg-America Line valued at $100 million dollars (a value equal to $1.6 billion in 2011 calculated at 3.03% inflation p.a.), according to A. Mitchell Palmer, the Alien Property Custodian of the United States Government. The terminal facilities in St. Thomas, Virgin Islands were sold to the Government as was all its property located in the United States. None of the property seized was sold to private corporations. Incidentally, Kaiser Wilhelm II was a heavy stockholder in the corporation.[2]

Queen Coziah is a popular figure in St. Thomas history and her memory is passed to the younger generations in poems, plays and books written by local authors. An account of the 1892 coal women's strike is recorded in Dr. Charles Edwin Taylor's book, *An Island of*

---

[1] Source: National Archives and Records Administration II, College Park, Maryland. State Department Records of German Detainees during WWI.
[2] "Line's Big Holdings Here," *New York Times*, 11 November 1918.

the Sea published in 1898, although it doesn't mention her by name. The story is also recounted in a book by Geraldo Guirty, who personally witnessed the transfer ceremony in 1917. Queen Coziah remains an important early symbol in the struggle for civil rights and equality, even though, to this day, no one knows her exact name, the dates of her birth and death, her final resting spot, or the names of her descendents, if any exist. Regardless of the lack of documentation, Queen Coziah's legend as a fighter for civil rights grows with each passing year.[3]

I hope you've enjoyed this book. Writing it was the culmination of a childhood dream to recreate the island of my youth during Danish times. The old red fort still dominates Charlotte Amalie, and the bust of King Christian IX still stands in Emancipation Gardens as testimonies to the island's Danish past.

Sincerely,

Sophie Schiller

---

[3] "Coal-Carrier Queen Coziah burns in V.I. history," *Virgin Islands Daily News*, 25 February 2005, Ayesha Morris.

Transfer Day
Discussion Guide Questions

1. Who was your favorite character? Why?

2. Early in the novel Abigail explains that she comes from a Sephardic Jewish merchant family that fled from Spain to Holland, and then to Curaçao and St. Thomas before settling in Panama. How much of a person's character is shaped by their family's migrations? How much of a family's heritage is lost in the process?

3. Abigail slowly learns that Aunt Esther is penniless and her own future is limited. How did a woman's dependence on men form and shape their characters?

4. Aunt Esther resents Abigail's presence and seems to equate her with her mother and father who abandoned her years before Abigail was born. Given all of Aunt Esther's losses, is she ultimately a sympathetic or an unsympathetic character?

5. Nana Jane's only diversion seems to be gossiping with the market women down by Market Square. How much of a person's character is shaped by their culture or the times they live in?

6. Judge Neergaard is wary of Lothar Langsdorff, yet he claims to be the German's only friend on the island. Can a person be both friendly with another individual yet mistrustful of them? How so?

7. Erich's strongest motivation was to escape the war, yet he allowed Langsdorff to manipulate him with blackmail. At some point did Erich's motivations change? Was he more motivated by a desire to protect his parents or a desire not to desert Abigail?

8. When Abigail visits Judge Neergaard at home, she discovers he has been harboring a secret. Have you ever known a person who was habitually living in the past or self-medicating with alcohol as a means to escape their inner pain?

9. Queen Coziah riles the people up against the Danish government, the planters, and the steamship companies. Was she justified in her mistrust of white people?

10. Jens Jørgensen sees nothing wrong with using his Danish citizenship to help Langsdorff cover up the fact that the Hamburg-America Line is a German company. Is Jørgensen a traitor or merely pragmatic?

11. Just before the hurricane strikes, Abigail takes the lead in helping to prepare the house while Aunt Esther seems to revert to a childish state of helplessness. In what way is this the turning point in the novel?

12. Why did Judge Neergaard risk his reputation to help Abigail? How much of people's motivations are based on settling old scores?

13. On Transfer Day, Abigail describes the faces of the islanders as both solemn and hopeful. She tells us the Danish gendarmes and the entire crowd is anguished and crying as the Dannebrog is lowered for the last time. What accounts for the intense sadness of the people? What were they silently hoping for?

Transfer Day: Special Centennial Edition 1917–2017

Sophie Schiller ISBN: 978-0-615653-43-3

The 1917 transfer of the Danish West Indies to the United States, which forestalled imperial Germany's hopes to control strategically valuable ports during WWI, provides the background for Schiller's engaging historical thriller. In 2001, journalist Søren Jensen, still grieving over the loss of his wife, travels from Copenhagen to the Virgin Islands to investigate a report that documents exist supporting the claim of Abigail Maduro to have "personally thwarted a German invasion" of the islands. Abigail recently died at the age of 101, and Søren meets her granddaughter, Claire Lehman, a possible new love interest (Claire's eyes have "an inner fire, a boldness that resonated deep within him"). Claire gives Søren access to her ancestor's diary, which details the teenage Abigail's growth into self-sufficiency and her role in countering German espionage before the sale of the islands. Schiller deftly blends fact and fiction in a page-turner with emotional resonance.

Bibliography

No novel of historical fiction can be written without drawing upon the contributions of writers from previous generations who painstakingly documented life as they knew it. I drew upon the following works when I attempted to recreate life in the Danish West Indies during the Great War:

Anonymous. 1917. *A German Deserter's War Experience.* New York: B.W. Heubsch.

Arbell, Mordechai. 2002. *The Jewish Nation of the Caribbean: The Spanish-Portuguese Jewish Settlements in the Caribbean and the Guianas.* Jerusalem: Gefen Publishing House.

Bisher, Jamie. 2008. *World War I Intelligence in Latin America. Chapter 2: 1914-1916-European War in the Americas.* Unpublished Manuscript.

Brock, H. G., Philip S. Smith and W. A. Tucker. 1917. *The Danish West Indies: Their Resources and Commercial Importance.* Washington: Government Printing Office.

Cohen, Judah M. 2004. *Through the Sands of Time: A History of the Jewish Community of St. Thomas,   U.S. Virgin Islands.* Hanover: Brandeis University Press.

Curtin, D. Thomas. 1917. *The Land of Deepening Shadow: Germany at War.* New York: George H. Doran Company.

Debooy, Theodoor and John T. Faris. 1918. *The Virgin Islands: Our New Possessions and the British Islands.* Philadelphia and London: J.B. Lippincott Company.

Dookhan, Isaac. 1974. *A History of the Virgin Islands of the United States.* St. Thomas, Virgin Islands: Caribbean Universities Press.

Franck, Harry Alverson. 1920. *Roaming Through the West Indies.* New York: Blue Ribbon Books.

Franck, Harry Alverson. 1913. *Zone Policeman 88: A Close Range Study of the Panama Canal and its Workers.* New York: The Century Company.

Gerard, James W. 1918. *Face to Face with Kaiserism.* New York: George H. Doran Company.

Gerard, James W. 1917. *My Four Years in Germany*. New York: George H. Doran Company.

Goldish, Josette Capriles. 2002. *The Girls They Left Behind: Curaçao's Jewish Women in the Nineteenth Century*. Unpublished Manuscript.

Hørlyk, Lucie. 1969. *In Danish Times: Stories about life in St. Croix and St. Thomas in the 19th century*. Stockholm: Tiden-Barnängen Tryckerier. First published in Denmark 1913 under the title *Under Tropesol*.

Knud-Hansen, Knud. 1947. *From Denmark to the Virgin Islands*. Philadelphia: Dorrance & Company.

Landau, Captain Henry. 1937. *The Enemy Within: The Inside Story of German Sabotage in America*. New York: G.P. Putnam's Sons.

Taylor, Dr. Charles Edwin. 1896. *An Island of the Sea. Descriptive of the Past and Present of St. Thomas, Danish West Indies*. Self-published, St. Thomas, D.W.I.

Taylor, Dr. Charles Edwin. 1888. *Leaflets from the Danish West Indies: Descriptive of the Social, Political, and Commercial Conditions of These Islands*. Self-published, St. Thomas, D.W.I.

Tomlinson, H. M. 1912. *The Sea and the Jungle*. A RIA Press Edition, 2005.

Wile, Frederic William. 1914. *Men Around the Kaiser: the Makers of Modern Germany*. Indianapolis: The Bobbs-Merrill Company.

Zabriskie, Luther K. 1918. *The Virgin Islands of the United States of America*. New York: G. P. Putnam's Sons.